THE MIL

THE MIL

ALLYSON BENNETT

To all of the emotional abuse and narcissistic abuse survivors. You all deserve peace, love and happiness.

To all of the daughters-in-law who have been tormented by their monsters-in-law.

A delicate, tiny new face that makes your heart swell out of your body. Little sounds that turn to babbles that turn to "mama." Going from barely being able to hold their head up to crawling and then to walking. The first year of being a mother and watching your baby grow is magical. All you want to do is drown in these sweet moments and gulp up every ounce of it. Some things you never would have imagined are hands around your neck, being yanked down into an abyss of sadness, self-doubt, stress, heart-gripping anxiety and loneliness. You feel even more confusion and betrayal when you are able to look into the eyes of the person whose hands are vigorously tightening around your gasping breath and see that they are familiar. Why is someone who said they are there to help, it takes a village and they love you now doing this to you?

As I sit and reflect on my first year as a mom, I look back on the most precious of moments with my baby, learning with my husband and feeling so much love. Yet there is also a dark, suffocating, complete opposition paralleled to this beauty. There is the moment that the tiniest boundaries were wildly violated. Manipulation, guilt trips, complaints, betrayal and isolation that started as a cloud has turned into a full-on hurricane. This is the story of how my monster-in-laws took over my first year postpartum.

Intro

If it was between imagining how life would go after having my first baby or winning the lottery, I would've won the lottery. Except, unfortunately, that didn't happen, either. I never would have expected what happened once I gave birth. Yeah, sure, I thought there was a chance I'd have some postpartum depression or maybe I would struggle with learning how to be a mom. I definitely didn't think that my mother-in-law would try to sabotage my marriage, turn my husband's family against me and emotionally abuse me. I had envisioned a safe, happy family. I thought I would get to soak in every wonderful, special moment with my baby. Don't get me wrong, I fought tooth and nail to do just that. It was a bit difficult in the midst of my emotional breakdown, though.

Then, more than a year later, I sat with someone who was supposed to aid me in getting back to being a normal person. It wasn't that I was a complete mess or unable to function anymore, I just had these lingering issues that were making living more difficult than necessary. I was basically living in survival mode, always bracing for impact. It was hard to distract my brain from thinking about what happened and how to protect myself from it ever happening again. During peaceful walks outside, I would suddenly be reliving one of the moments that almost broke me. I'd jump when my phone rang. Scared of everyone, I cradled my trust and my heart. Slowly, I removed myself from the outside world. But I didn't want to feel so scared anymore. I wanted to be able to play with my toddler without panic tugging me out of the current moment. I wanted to enjoy family time without fear of a phone call. I wanted to live.

"Let's go back to the beginning, you know, the first major traumatic event. I want you to tell me about it, Adison," my narcissistic abuse specialist told me, looking at me with her kind, emerald eyes.

Her buttery blonde hair was ultra straight and cut bluntly at her shoulders. She was in her forties, yet she looked twenty-five.

"Oh god, okay. It's a long story. How much time do we have?" I asked, laughing nervously. I could feel my eye beginning to twitch slightly. I twisted and twirled my long, wavy, chestnut hair with my fingers.

"As much time as you need."

I took a couple deep breaths and let my eyes wander around her cozy office for a minute. I glanced at her gold-framed PhD certificate hanging on the wall, the green potted plants of various sizes scattered around, and took in the warm beige color scheme of the room. Her large window overlooked a well-manicured yet woodsy park. It did feel comfortable and relaxing being in her office. Although, I couldn't help the electric nerves and nausea I felt while thinking about the story I had to tell. I looked back at my specialist sitting with her legs crossed in the chair across from me. I sat shaking slightly, my petite body tightly pressed together and my skin paler than usual.

I took another deep breath, rolled my jaw, and said, "Okay, here we go."

1

Chapter One

It was still inky black outside when I suddenly woke up to a stab of intense pain. I rolled out of bed holding tightly onto my aching, outstretched belly. I was nine months pregnant and two days past my baby's due date. My husband, Colt, had just begun to snore, only recently making it to bed after working all night. I stumbled into the bathroom connected to our bedroom. I had a miserable stomachache. I lowered myself down onto the toilet with my tired eyes half shut, clutching my bulging stomach in immense pain. All at once, I noticed on the floor in front of me a trail of blood. My heavy eyes shot wide open.

"Colt... Colt..." I mustered out.

My fingers searched for my phone, which I had set on the counter next to me. I quickly pulled up my timer app and started tracking the length of my pain versus the short moments of relief. Although I wasn't sure what labor felt like, I was pretty sure it was happening to me right now. My hands were shaking uncontrollably as I called the hospital.

"Hi, my name is Adison. I am nine months pregnant and I think I'm in labor. I'm bleeding and I have horrible stomach pain. I think I'm having contractions and if I am, they are about two minutes apart.

Am I able to just come in?" I quickly blurted out once a receptionist had answered.

"Yes, you should definitely come in," she quickly said back. I raced to press the end button on the screen.

"Colt! Colt, wake up!" I shouted.

I couldn't speak as another wave of immobilizing pain overtook me. Once it was over, I leapt off the toilet, raced to put my contacts into my amber eyes, brush my teeth and wash my pale face. I just couldn't leave our home without at least doing those things. It took me longer than usual as I had to pause multiple times due to the pain.

"Colt, babe, we have to go!" I yelled again, this time with panic rising in my voice.

"What?" Colt asked as he finally came to. His eyes were still mostly closed.

"I think I'm in labor, we need to go," I said, breathing heavily as another wave of agony washed over me.

Colt quickly leapt out of bed, grabbed the hospital bag and threw on shoes. I held onto his muscular arm as he helped me down the creaky, metal outdoor stairs of our apartment building and into the parking lot. We paused as I couldn't move due to another contraction. Through the pain, I noticed the light fog sweeping along the dusty terrain. Once we had made it into his truck, I leaned my head against the cool window. As we rushed the fifteen minutes across town to the nearest hospital, my labor pains escalated.

I kept losing consciousness at times as the pain overtook me. I grabbed onto the edge of the leather seat as we zipped through town, noticing just how long the red lights seemed to take. The next thing I knew, somehow, I had made it across the parking lot, into a hospital room and was sitting on a long bed.

"Do you want an epidural?" I managed to hear a nurse ask me.

"Yes," I cried out, barely able to breathe. It was as if my vision was going out with how overwhelming the pain was to my system.

Once I was given the epidural, the pain slowly started to lessen. I was still feeling absolutely miserable, but I was breathing normally now. For the next twelve hours, nurses came in about every half hour and checked on me. Every so often, they turned my body from one side onto the other. During all this, Colt sat loyally in a large, plush chair next to my bed. He had put *Impractical Jokers* on the TV in front of us. It was a welcome distraction from my current situation.

My mouth felt dry as my head began to pound harder and harder. It felt like nails were being hammered into my skull. I ignored it, until the pain became so intense that I started seeing spots when I blinked.

"Is there anything that can be done about my head? I feel like I have a migraine right now." I asked a middle-aged nurse who was looking over the monitor I was hooked up to.

"Oh, yes. Let me get you some pain relievers," she said, quickly leaving the room. Time ticked by slowly. I felt tortured as I stared at the clock. Almost forty-five minutes passed before the nurse opened the door.

"I am so sorry. Here is your medicine," she said as she handed me a small paper cup with two pills inside it.

I quickly swallowed them and then sipped on ice water, praying the pain would go away.

It was by far the longest twelve hours of my life. The pain was all-encompassing. I had no idea what I was doing. I felt miserable, terrified and tormented. At last, a young doctor walked in. She had brown hair in a long, thick braid and wore seafoam green scrubs.

"Hi Adison, I'm Dr. Beally. Your doctor isn't in today, so I will be delivering your baby. I take a very holistic approach to birth. If you have any questions, please feel free to ask me anything. We will start pushing shortly. I am going to get the room ready," she said as she sat on a swirly chair next to me. Her eyes were kind and her voice was soft.

My body had been shaking all day due to the pain, but now it shook harder from nerves. I was so scared. I wanted my baby to get here, but I couldn't get my mind past the fear of her exiting my body. Nurses paced around the room, prepping for delivery. I shut my eyes until I heard Dr. Beally speak again.

"Are you ready to meet your baby, Adison?" she asked.

"Yes. I am really scared though," I responded.

"It is scary, I know, but I am right here with you. I will be helping you every step of the way. We are going to start pushing now. You want to push with your lower belly, like the Kegels your doctor told you to practice. Make sure to take deep inhales and then exhale during your push," instructed the kind doctor.

I nodded. I noticed a nurse on both sides of my bed, near where my arms were. Dr. Beally was down by my propped-up feet and Colt was slightly off to the right side of her. I realized that he was standing now.

I listened to Dr. Beally and followed her instructions. I squeezed my lower belly, trying to push, but feeling like it was doing nothing.

"Would you like a wet towel for your forehead?" asked the nurse standing on my left side. I ignored her. She asked me again.

"No," I managed to spit out.

I was so focused on trying to somehow get my body to expel my baby. It wasn't happening easily. The nurse hurried away and then came back, slapping a wet towel on my head. The moistness of the towel made me want to vomit. I reached my arm up and threw it off.

"Keep your hand on your knee!" the same nurse yelled out.

I was in awful pain. It literally felt like my body was splitting apart, and now I felt hot with anger. The nurse slapped the wet towel back on my forehead. I once again threw it off. She grabbed my hand and forced it back on my knee.

"Can you stop?" I barked at her.

"Come on Adison, you can do it. Push your baby out," coached Dr. Beally.

After forty-five minutes, I finally heard the glorious music of my baby crying. It was a sound I wish I could have bottled up and drank for life. I saw the most perfect little pink baby in front of me and happiness flooded over my entire being. All the pain was suddenly irrelevant. All I felt was my heart overflowing with adoration at the sight of my newborn. I loved her as soon as I saw the two pink lines, but I never knew how much this love could multiply. I did it. We did it. My husband and I wished for a baby, spent nine months creating this life and together watched her take her first breath.

"Adison, you did it. She's finally here!" Colt exclaimed, his tired eyes full of love. The redness in his eyes matched his hair and auburn beard. Colt's white smile was wide and unwavering, even with his lack of sleep. The joy we experienced in this moment was immense. It was a once-in-a-lifetime experience, having our first child. She was tiny, adorable and all wrapped up in my arms. My sweet Talli. Talli Witley.

"I can't believe this is real life. I have never felt happier than I do right now," I cried, beaming at our newborn.

It was almost ten at night, but I was wide awake and extremely happy. Staring at Talli's face made time unimportant and vanished my exhaustion.

"I brought you guys some food. I'm sure you're starving!" said one of our kind nurses as she handed us two clear plastic boxes. Inside each was a turkey and cheese sandwich cut in half, a bag of chips, a fruit cup, a packet of mustard and a packet of mayonnaise. It doesn't get more "hospital food" than this, yet it tasted like dining at a Michelin star restaurant. Joy could make anything exceptional.

The next day, Monday, after very little sleep, I woke up in the small hospital room unable to move. My legs were swollen to three times their usual size and I was drowning in pain. I clicked the large red button on my remote that was kept on the side of my bed. A nurse came in minutes later.

"Is there anything we can do for this pain? I am really struggling," I pleaded.

"Yeah, let me go get you a couple pain relievers," answered the nurse, turning to leave the room.

This song and dance continued for the rest of the long day. I laid in the hospital bed, loving my baby, feeding her, nurses coming in and out for tests or to replenish supplies, and I felt so happy. I loved looking at my perfect newborn. I'd stare at her face while she was swaddled in my arms. She slept a lot, her sweet eyes closed and her rosy pink lips relaxed. It felt like living the most beautiful dream. Colt stayed faithfully by our side through everything. I could see the exhaustion on his face, but he didn't let his lack of sleep affect his immense support for us.

"My mom is on the way down from Ohio, so I'll just have her come here while I go back to get the Doona. I don't want you and Talli to be here alone," Colt said.

In our rush to get to the hospital, we had forgotten to grab the Doona, Talli's car seat, so that we could bring her home.

"That's okay, we have the nurses. Plus, it won't be that long. Talli and I will be fine. We aren't going anywhere. We don't need your mom to come here," I said, my happiness dipping with a sudden spike of anxiety. "Also, how is your mom on her way down? I thought she was flying in tomorrow."

"I really don't want to leave you guys here alone. It's fine. I'm going to have her come," Colt said, pausing before continuing. "I guess she changed things to come down early, but I don't know."

I felt strangely uncomfortable with the thought of Colt's mother, Hilda, coming to the hospital. I couldn't put my finger on it, but I didn't feel comfortable being myself around her. I had always felt like I had to shrink myself down and say as little as possible. Alarm bells were going off in my head. I wanted to try to convince Colt that his mom should not come here, but I was too tired. Maybe it would be fine. Maybe she would be kind and helpful.

A couple of hours before we were to be discharged, Colt called his mom to see where she was at so that he could have her come to the hospital while he left to get Talli's car seat. He held his cell phone close to his ear. I felt an uneasy feeling in my stomach as he spoke to her. Once he ended the call, he looked over at me. I was still laying in the bed, trying not to pass out from the pain but holding Talli close to my heart.

"Apparently my mom drove a rental car down instead of flying," he said. "That is why she is getting here earlier. Also, she brought Clayton and Mackenzi as a surprise."

"Oh, wow, what? That's crazy," I said, feeling strangely repulsed and troubled.

My head felt like it was spinning. I was shocked and nervous that she was here so early. I also was not expecting Clayton, Colt's step-dad, and Mackenzi, his seventeen-year-old sister. Originally, we had planned that Hilda would stay in a rental with my mom and my two twin younger sisters, Daisy and Calli, for a couple of days while they all visited. Everyone was supposed to arrive the next day.

I tried to get my head wrapped around the abrupt changes and the out of the blue shock. I hated last-minute changes or, "surprises" and, having just given birth, I especially hated it. All I wanted after having my baby was to relax, be comfortable and feel calm. I had been nervous enough about having all these visitors two days after Talli's birth. I had hoped that Talli would've arrived a week before any visitors came so that I could have time to settle in with her and hopefully recover a little bit.

The people pleaser in me had let everyone tell me when they wanted to come. I was just grateful they were traveling down to meet our baby. I didn't want to make things difficult for anyone. I couldn't predict how I would feel after giving birth.

The only preparation for visitation I had done was send a group text to everyone reading, "Since it's getting closer, sharing this with everyone visiting now. I'm going to be overprotective as I'm sure everyone can understand, so my biggest rule is no kissing Talli/no touching her face/make sure to wash hands. Her health and safety are my number one priority. I'm sure you all are aware of the no kissing a newborn rule and why it is so important, but wanted to reiterate since I know everyone is excited. Please keep Talli in mind as we get closer and with everyone traveling. The last thing anyone wants is for her to get sick. We'll probably make use of masks while holding her just as a precaution. Glad you'll all get to see her in person as a newborn!"

I had also sent additional information explaining boundaries when visiting a baby such as asking permission to visit, please be kind, wash hands, don't visit if feeling ill, please ask before posting any pictures and don't stay too long as we are all exhausted.

I thanked everyone for acknowledging my message and sent them a list of restaurants and things to do in our small Texas town.

Hilda had responded by saying, "Awesome, looking forward to relaxing by the pool but still be close enough to help you if you need me," followed by a heart emoji.

I felt better sending everyone my boundaries and basic expectations. Although, now with everything about to happen, I wished that they were all coming a week later. I had a deep feeling in my gut that this was going to be difficult.

"Well, that's nice that your stepdad and sister will be able to meet Talli," I said, trying to be positive.

It was fine that they were included. I just wished that I had been informed of it before laying in a hospital bed. I could understand their arrival to be a nice surprise for Colt, but I didn't want it as a surprise for me. I didn't need any surprises. I just needed to relax, recover and bond with my newborn. I shook off the strange feeling that Hilda was being manipulative by bringing extra people without having talked about it first. I wondered if my mom was aware of the extra guests that would be staying with them.

"Yeah, it is," Colt said, regarding his stepdad and sister coming. "My mom is dropping them off at the rental house and then coming here."

My stomach dropped. I wanted to scream but I swallowed it.

"Adison, it will be okay," I silently told myself, trying to calm the storm inside me. I took deep breaths in and out, attempting to soothe my nerves. I couldn't seem to kick the uneasiness that had swallowed me up. I looked at Talli sleeping peacefully in her bassinet next to my bed. I kept having to put her down due to how much pain I was in and how weak I felt.

Suddenly, there was a knock at our door. It opened up to Hilda's heavily made-up face. She had straight, brick red hair cut in a bob with bangs. She wore a plum V-neck shirt with denim shorts.

"Oh, my goodness," she gushed, instantly rushing over to my newborn.

She gave her son a quick hug before going back to looking at our baby. It was almost as if my swollen, post-birth self wasn't laying miserably in the hospital bed in the middle of the room.

"Can I hold her?" she trilled, without caring for an answer.

She lifted my swaddled, sleeping baby out of the bassinet. She rocked my baby, staring at her. Luckily, she had put on a mask, but she was lifting Talli so close to her face that I was feeling uncomfortable. She then proceeded to carry on a lengthy conversation with Colt. I had no idea what they were talking about because my focus was on Talli. I stared, nauseous, as Hilda stood, rocking Talli and talking loudly. I just wanted Colt to go get the car seat and get back already. I wanted her to leave.

"Hey, Colt, you should probably get the Doona," I said, speaking up during a break in their conversation.

"Yeah, I'll go in a minute," he said.

"Maybe go now," I urged.

My head was pounding. I wanted Hilda to set Talli down, but I also didn't want to be unkind. I hated this.

Colt looked at me, squinting his eyebrows and said, "Okay."

"Colt, before you go, take a picture of Talli and I," Hilda said, digging her phone out of her oversized purse with one hand, her other arm still cradling Talli.

The hair on my arms stood up. I didn't like her holding my baby with just one arm. God, I felt crazy. Colt took a picture and then left. Hilda stood there ignoring me, just looking at my baby in her arms. She was whispering something to Talli that I couldn't make out.

"How was your drive?" I asked, attempting to smile while shaking out my discomfort.

"Oh, fine. We just drove all last night and today. It was long, but we're here," she said, still staring at Talli.

She then set Talli down, unwrapped her from her blanket and changed her diaper. My face flooded with heat. I felt like I could throw up. Why did she have to change Talli's diaper? Why couldn't she just set her down and go sit? This felt so overbearing already. After Hilda had finished putting a clean diaper on my baby, she picked her back up and continued to rock with her. Finally, I couldn't take it anymore.

"Maybe it's time for Talli to go back to her bassinet and rest," I spoke up, my voice shaking. Hilda ignored me.

"Hey, I think it's time to set Talli down," I said, again, after about ten minutes had passed with Hilda continuing to hold her. For the second time, I was ignored.

"Hilda, please set Talli down now," I said, this time more firmly and a little louder.

"Um, okay," Hilda murmured in almost a whisper, acting taken aback.

She held Talli for another minute before lowering her back into the bassinet. She stared at her, and then turned to go to the couch at the furthest end of the room. There was a recliner near the bed that Colt had been sitting in, but I didn't mind that she ignored it. I was okay with her back there, further from Talli and I. She sat, huffy, and went on her phone, scrolling. She lifted it to her ear and began to have a conversation with someone, loudly.

"Yeah, I know," she said, nearly shouting. "Right? I know."

I sat uncomfortably and miserably, wishing Colt would walk back in the door. I grabbed my phone and pulled up his location. He was at the apartment. He had been gone for almost an hour. Why was this taking so long? Hilda started to laugh at whatever was being said on the other end of her call.

"Are you almost back?" I texted him.

"I should be back soon, yes," Colt texted back.

Eventually, Hilda's phone call ended and she began scrolling on her screen. She didn't look up from her phone until Colt came back.

When he finally walked in, I felt a rush of relief.

"Okay, now Hilda can leave," I thought. That isn't what happened though. Hilda stayed for almost another hour. She held Talli again and took pictures of Colt rocking our baby in his arms.

"Hey, would you like us to give Talli a sponge bath before you guys' head out? We can do it under a warming bulb in another room or here in the room, but she won't have the warmth," asked a kind, twenty-something nurse who had just walked in.

"Under the warming bulb is probably best for Talli, that's fine," I said back.

"Hmmm, I would've figured you would want to do it in the room," Hilda said in her scratchy voice, nose turned up.

"I'd rather Talli be comfortable and not cold," I said.

That was true, but I also didn't want Hilda crowding Talli during a bath. Hilda was a tall and wide woman whose mere presence took over the room. I could just imagine her hovering over my baby, shifting her body so that I was pushed out of the way. I also hoped this would be a good excuse for her to leave. Instead, she went back to talking to Colt. I had gone from feeling on top of the world to feeling like I was being buried underneath it. I wanted to go home and be alone with Talli.

When Talli was wheeled back into the room after her bath, Hilda took more pictures.

"Okay, well, we'll see you guys tomorrow," Colt was saying to her.

"Yeah, text us when you're up and we'll come over," Hilda said.

She didn't make any motion to leave. It was almost nine at night, and about time for us to be released.

"Okay, well, we are probably going to be leaving soon, right Colt?" I said, speaking up.

"Yeah, we are, in about ten minutes."

"Do you want any help taking your stuff to your car?" Hilda asked Colt.

"No, we are good, thank you for offering," I quickly said.

Hilda looked over her shoulder at me dismissively.

"You've got a lot of stuff. I'm sure you'll need help," she insisted.

"No, I think we'll be good," I said, standing up.

I pushed down the pain. It was more painful having her there than the physical pain I felt due to having had a baby twenty-four hours ago.

Hilda finally left, taking her sweet time to exit the room, but once she did, I exhaled out my stress. Colt and I carefully buckled Talli into her Doona and gathered our things. The discharge nurse came in to give us information before we left.

"So, I should take two Tylenol every six hours and then switch to Ibuprofen?" I was repeating back what the nurse had told me. I was purposefully trying to waste time to make sure we wouldn't run into Hilda on our way out. Colt stood impatiently by the door, holding our bags.

"Yes, and let us know if your pain gets worse instead of better. Make sure to rest. Congratulations, again," the sweet nurse beamed.

I felt so thankful for the kind nurses that had been so helpful to us. I followed behind Colt, trying to mask my pain, as I wheeled Talli out of the hospital and into the world.

2

Chapter Two

When we got home, I hurried to get into the shower. My hair was greasy and matted in a low bun, my skin was sallow and I felt grimy. I didn't want to shower in the hospital because it didn't feel as clean as our own home. Also, I was only able to stand again shortly before we left. I let the warm water wash over my aching, bleeding body. It proved to be a challenge to stand, but more so to bend over to grab my shampoo bottle.

"This is the best and worst shower of my life," I thought.

I hurried to finish my shower so that I could return to Talli. I ached being apart from her. I didn't care that my hair was half clean and my legs were still stubbly. I shut off the water and grabbed my plush towel that hung over the metal handle on the door. I dried off and looked at myself through the condensation in the mirror. My empty belly looked like a large, deflating balloon. It was still puffy, but slumped. Everything was swollen. I felt deeply insecure about my body, but simultaneously grateful as it had created a new, beautiful life.

I pulled on my gray disposable underwear with three damp witch hazel pads layered on top of a giant overnight pad and sprayed Dermoplast on my stitches for pain relief. I put on my baby blue striped pajamas and walked out of the bathroom to my husband holding our newborn.

"Should we try to put her in her crib after you feed her?" Colt asked.

"Okay, yeah," I said.

I wouldn't admit it, but I was nervous for this first night at home. I was scared of SIDS or "sudden infant death syndrome," of Talli not being able to eat well enough, of her getting hurt and basically every other fear a new mom could possibly have.

We got Talli ready for bed and then slowly lowered her sleeping body into her crib. The second her back touched the mattress, she burst out crying. I instantly scooped her back up.

"Maybe we should lay down with her," I suggested, after we tried a few more times.

We went into our bedroom and I laid down on my left side with my arms enclosed around her little body. We barely slept, but made it through the night that way.

The next morning, after fluttering open my eyes, I saw Colt sitting up in bed on his phone.

"They are coming over soon," he said, when he noticed that I was awake.

"Oh, okay. Can I at least eat a granola bar first?" I asked.

"Can you do that while they are here?"

"I guess," I said.

I heaved myself out of bed to put my contacts in, brush my teeth and wash my face. I put on a black maternity dress and brought my still sleeping Talli into the living room with me. Our apartment was pretty small. Not the smallest we've lived in, but still small. There weren't many places to sit. We had our L-shaped couch and two little barstool benches at the counter in the kitchen. Colt had made the tiny dining area into an office space so he could work from home while we settled into parenthood. We had Talli's little room, which still had boxes of random stuff overflowing in the closet. Our bed took up most of our room. Overall, it felt cramped. Only two years ago, we were homeowners in Ohio. Now, we were moving in and out of small apartments, which proved to be a bit of a struggle for us.

I grabbed a granola bar and water before sitting on one end of the couch with Talli swaddled in my arms. As I went to take a bite of my breakfast, there was a knock at the door. Colt was still in our bedroom.

"Colt, I think your family is here," I spoke up, but not loud enough for them to hear me from outside.

"Okay, you could've gotten the door," he said, pulling a shirt over his head and heading toward the door. I sensed he was feeling stressed.

"Hello," trilled Hilda as she hurried inside. Mackenzi followed close behind her, struggling to carry a large box wrapped in colorful paper.

"Here you go," Mackenzi huffed, dropping the box at my feet. She stretched her tall body, as if in pain.

"Thanks," I said, smiling at her but also unsure what the enormous gift was for. .

Clayton stumbled in last, grunting while lugging Colt's old golf clubs. Clayton was a towering man with shaven black hair. His dark eyes were always empty.

"We thought we'd bring your clubs for you, since you had asked about them once," Hilda said to Colt.

Clayton glanced around at the limited space and then leaned the clubs against the wall close to the door.

"Did you guys sleep at all?" Hilda asked, laughing.

"Not really," Colt answered.

"Ooh, can I see the baby?" Hilda cooed, peering into my arms at Talli. She went into the kitchen, quickly washed her hands and reached out for me to give her my newborn. I reluctantly complied.

"There, now you can open your gift," Hilda exclaimed as if she was doing me a favor, looking down at Talli.

"Oh, okay. Colt, do you want to help open it?" I asked, wanting to watch Talli. I didn't want to appear ungrateful, but I really didn't want a gift right now. I only wanted my newborn.

"No, you can," he said.

I struggled to undo the double wrapped and heavily taped box. Once I had the paper off, I pulled at the packing tape that held the box shut.

"Honey, scissors," Colt said, scrambling for our scissors and then cutting it open for me.

Inside the box was outfit after outfit, books, a stuffed cow, different small boxes of children's medicine and a tulle butterfly costume for a newborn.

"Thank you," I said.

All the gifts were overwhelming. This was too much. Many of the outfits were super frilly and a couple of them were even sizes up to twelve months. The stuffed cow had a large tag hanging off its ear with a cancer warning in bold, bright yellow lettering. I also didn't need the medicine. Colt and I had gotten medicine for emergencies, but made sure it was without dyes or too much artificial additives. I didn't know what we were going to do with all of this stuff.

"Here, I picked up some of this for you guys, too. I figure you will need it," Hilda smirked, handing me a large container of Dreft laundry detergent that she lifted off of the ground with her free hand.

I again thanked her, even though we had already bought a safer detergent without so many chemicals. I didn't tell her this, though.

"Oh, yeah, and here's this," Mackenzi said as she handed me a tiny box.

I opened it and saw inside a purple beaded bracelet. I thanked them all. It was a strange gift since I thought they knew I never wore bracelets, but the gesture was nice. I looked up. Hilda was still holding Talli. I really wanted my baby back.

"Here, Clayton, hold Talli for a picture," Hilda said, passing off my baby to Clayton.

She snapped picture after picture on her phone.

"Okay, Mackenzi, your turn," Hilda said. "Oh, by the way, look Mackenzi, she has that red hair you wished you had."

Clayton passed Talli to Mackenzi. I sat there, watching and trying to push down my discomfort.

"Oh, yeah, she does. Lucky," Mackenzi said, peering at Talli's head. Mackenzi touched her own shoulder-length, black hair she had gotten from her dad's side of the family.

"Take some of me and Talli," Hilda said, holding her phone out to Mackenzi.

This continued for what felt like hours. Hilda posed for picture after picture.

"I think I should feed her now," I finally said.

I had been staring at the clock, anxiously waiting for the two-hour mark so I could have an excuse to get my baby back. Hilda took her time handing Talli back to me. Once I had my baby, I quickly rushed into my bedroom, ready for a break. I sighed, leaning back against the pillows on our bed with Talli.

"Well, I guess I should go pick up Adison's mom from the airport now," I overheard Hilda saying. "You guys can stay and visit since you aren't here for that long."

I assumed Hilda was talking about Clayton and Mackenzi. Apparently, they were leaving the next afternoon so Clayton could get back to work and Mackenzi back to school. I heard the front door shut, which meant Hilda had left.

"At least my family will be here soon," I thought, feeling some relief.

It wasn't long before I heard an increase in voices as Hilda had returned with my mom and Daisy. Calli was getting in later since she was coming from Colorado instead of Ohio and was on a different flight.

"Is she still in there feeding the baby?" I heard Hilda ask in shock.

I sighed and got up with Talli. I walked out of the room. I saw my mom and Daisy, standing slightly uncomfortable amongst Colt's family. They hurried over to me. Hilda stood in the living room by our tall floor lamp while Clayton and Mackenzi sat on the couch. Colt sat on one of the barstools at the counter, with his body turned to face the living room.

"I thought they were going to leave so we could have some time together," I whispered to my mom and sister as we awkwardly stood back by Colt's office space while everyone watched us.

"Oh, I don't know. Yeah, that would be nice," my mom whispered back, touching her sandy blonde hair that was pulled up into a loose ponytail. She was wearing light jeans and a navy zip-up hoodie.

Daisy and Calli had the same color hair as our mom. Daisy's was cut shorter in a cute crop that brushed the middle of her neck. Calli's was long, flowing to her mid-back. They were all slightly taller than me, with similar athletic figures.

As we stood off to the side, I let my mom and Daisy meet Talli. Hilda continued to watch us. Everyone was awkwardly quiet.

"Calli just landed," Daisy said, breaking the silence as she stared at her iPhone.

Daisy's fingers flew across her screen and I could hear the clicking of her long, maroon painted nails as they continuously hit the surface.

"I should ride with Hilda back to the airport to get Calli," my mom said.

"Oh, we are going now?" Hilda asked.

"Yeah, she landed, she'll be waiting for us," my mom said, moving toward the door.

"Daisy, you should stay here," I whispered to her, touching her arm. She nodded.

As soon as Hilda and my mom left, I waved Daisy into my room.

"So, this sucks," I said to her. "I'm glad you guys are here now, though."

"Why? What's wrong?"

"Well, they got here last night, a day earlier than I expected, and I didn't know she was bringing Clayton and Mackenzi," I started to explain.

"Oh, yeah, that is weird that she didn't tell you guys. She didn't tell us either until we got in the car with her today. Mom and I looked at each other like, what the heck. We aren't sure where they are going to sleep. The rental is really small. It's smaller than your apartment," Daisy said.

"That's so weird that she didn't tell you guys, either. When they got here Hilda came to the hospital. It was really uncomfortable. I just feel really anxious and overwhelmed," I said, feeling nauseous again as I talked to Daisy about it.

We sat in my room until Hilda and my mom returned with Calli.

"Where are they?" Daisy and I heard Calli say from the living room.

About thirty seconds later, Calli opened the door and poked her head into the bedroom. Her tan, make-up free face glowed.

"Hey," she said in her soft, buttery voice. "Can I come in?"

I waved her in. "How was your trip here?"

"It was fine. The car ride here was a little awkward. Speaking of which, we should probably go out there so mom isn't alone," Calli said.

I readjusted Talli in my arms as I got up and followed my sisters out of my bedroom. Hilda was back at her post by our lamp. My mom was sitting on the couch, quietly. Mackenzi and Clayton were both also on the couch. Mackenzi was on her phone and Clayton was talking to Colt, who was still on the barstool across the room. My sisters and I stood outside my bedroom door, in front of Colt's office space.

"Wow, this is awkward," I thought.

I was confused why Colt's family was still lingering. I thought they were going to give my family a chance to say hi and settle in. Apparently not.

Everyone stayed for a little bit longer until they decided to go to the pool before getting dinner and bringing it back to our apartment.

I was exhausted. Unfortunately, it felt like only minutes passed before everyone was crowded back in our living space.

"Adison, I can hold Talli while you eat," Hilda said, moving toward where I sat on the couch, her arms already outstretched.

"Oh, okay. Thanks," I said, uncomfortable and not wanting to give up Talli.

I had been passing her around all day. It was only our first day back at home and her second day of life. I tried to speed up my usual slow pace of eating. My mom had brought me back sushi, which I hadn't had in a while. I had been excited to eat it, but I barely tasted it. I was so focused on getting Talli back. Hilda carried on conversations with those around her while holding my baby.

After I finished eating and once there was a break in the conversation, I spoke up.

"I can take her back now," I said, getting up to go retrieve my newborn.

"It's okay, you can take a break," Hilda said.

"No, I want her," I said, reaching out my arms.

Hilda reluctantly passed my baby back to me. She huffed under her breath and got up from the couch. She went over to stand back by the lamp. Our apartment was hot and chaotic, filled with people. There was so much noise and so many people moving around. I sat back down with Talli and tried to relax. All of a sudden, our lamp came crashing down, slamming violently against the hardwood floor.

"I don't know how that happened, whoops," Hilda said, bending down to pick it up.

She awkwardly laughed as she readjusted the holder that came out of place and said, "It's fine, it's not broken."

I tried to swallow how overwhelmed and exhausted I felt. I was in a daze until everyone finally left for the night. This was going to be a long couple of days.

3

Chapter Three

It was Wednesday, and thankfully, Clayton and Mackenzi's last day. Hopefully two fewer people would mean it would be a little quieter and less crowded. I woke up that morning to the sound of Colt's phone ringing.

"Hello?" Colt sleepily said once he answered it, sitting up. "Okay. Yeah, we did just wake up. No, it's fine. Okay."

He hung up the phone and groaned.

He laid back down and said, "That was my mom. She said she wants to come over now with Clayton and Mackenzi since they are leaving today."

I groaned. I reluctantly got out of bed and got ready for another day. I looked at my phone and saw a text from my mom asking if I wanted a smoothie. I definitely could use a smoothie. I went into the bathroom to wash my face and deal with my disposable underwear situation. Recovering from birth was more difficult than I had anticipated. Time felt like it was flying that morning. I was so exhausted. Colt, Talli and I were still in our bedroom finishing getting ready as we heard loud knocks at our front door.

"Can you get it? I still need to find a shirt," Colt asked me.

I grabbed Talli and went to get the door.

"Hello," Hilda sauntered inside past me.

Clayton came in next grumbling and Mackenzi followed. My sisters and mom looked uncomfortable as they came in last, holding smoothies. Daisy handed me one and gave me a wide-eyed look. I sat with Talli on the couch, drinking my smoothie as the noise levels quickly rose. More pictures ensued and more passing Talli around. Of course, time decided to slow down now that everyone was there. It felt like an eon until Clayton and Mackenzi had to leave.

"We need to get to the airport," Clayton finally said to Hilda.

"I know, I just don't want to leave," Hilda whined. "Okay, we can go in a minute. I need to go to Walmart again on the way back. Colt, do you want to ride with me?"

"Uh, sure," Colt said.

I felt a huge wave of relief when they left. Finally, I was alone with my sisters and mom. I had been holding in my pee for at least half an hour, though. It hit me that I needed to get to the bathroom immediately. I started to make my way, but as I took my second step, pee rushed down my legs. I started to cry as I was unable to control my bladder.

"I have had to pee for a little while but I just wanted everyone to leave so I didn't really notice how badly I had to. This is so embarrassing. Why is this happening to me?" I cried.

"Oh honey, it's okay. Just go to the bathroom, take a shower if you need to, we'll take care of it," My mom said, hugging me. She gently took Talli from my arms and passed her to Calli.

"Where are your towels?" she asked.

I went into the bathroom and finished peeing. I threw off my wet, disgusting clothes and wrapped a towel around my beat-up body. I grabbed a stack of towels to take to my bmom. I helped her clean for a minute before she motioned for me to go take care of myself.

"This has been a lot," I said to them once I had finished showering.

"I know, sweetie. This is a lot. We should have waited longer until we visited. I feel so bad. We'll keep the visits short, okay?" my mom said.

"It's not you guys. I just feel really overwhelmed with Hilda." I explained to my mom what had happened so far.

"Wow, I can't believe she didn't tell you she was bringing extra people. She definitely should have told you," my mom said. "Also, speaking of that, we need to get our own rental car. This isn't working, sharing with her."

My mom and sisters got on their phones, working on finding a rental car. Once they reserved one, Daisy and my mom got up to go get it. Calli stayed back with me.

Luckily, my mom and Daisy made it back first. We watched a movie and relaxed until Colt came back with his mom. Everyone left shortly after Hilda's return so they could go to the pool. I decided to use the quiet time to take a nap with Talli. They came back for dinner and my mom brought me take out. I again had to pass Talli around. Hilda held her for a lengthy amount of time, of course. I looked at my phone and it was eight at night. The minutes dragged on until they all finally left, almost an hour later. My mom and sisters had left first in their new rental. Hilda left about twenty minutes later.

On Thursday, we met everyone in town for breakfast. It was nice to not feel crowded around in our apartment for a change. It also felt good to get some fresh air and to be outside. Both of our moms and my sisters went back to their rental to hang out at the pool before they came back for dinner, which, as usual, came too quickly. Soon, everyone was again in our living room, passing Talli around. Not surprisingly, Hilda was holding her the longest.

"Hilda, I'm going to let Daisy and Calli hold Talli now, since they are leaving tomorrow," I said.

Hilda silently passed Talli over to Calli. She focused on the TV while my sisters took turns holding my baby.

"It's getting really late," my mom said, uncomfortably. "We should probably get going so you guys can get some sleep."

"Yeah, I'm really tired, too," Daisy said, standing up.

Calli passed Talli back to Hilda. Hilda excitedly took her. I sighed. My mom and Daisy were standing near the door while Calli went to use the bathroom. I got up to get Talli. I stood over Hilda and she stared down at Talli, ignoring me.

"Okay, I think we are ready to go. Hilda, you have the keys, right?" my mom asked. They had all rode over together for dinner.

"Yep," Hilda said.

She took another couple of minutes to stare at Talli before she handed her back to me. Hilda slowly rose off the couch, continuing to watch the TV. My mom and sisters stood as patiently as possible by the door. Daisy leaned against the wall with her hand over her face. My mom stood with her mouth in a tight line, watching Hilda watch the TV.

"Are we ready?" my mom asked again. "It's nine."

"Yep," Hilda said, finally moving toward the door.

Colt and I said goodbye to Calli since she was leaving early in the morning. As they shut the door behind them, I collapsed onto the couch.

"I am so exhausted and still in so much pain," I said to Colt. "So, my sisters leave tomorrow, my mom leaves Saturday morning and when does your mom leave?"

"Um, I think she leaves Wednesday," Colt said.

"What?" I shouted, and then lowered my voice. I quietly repeated, "What?"

"Yeah, I think she told me her flight leaves Wednesday either morning or afternoon, I don't remember the time. Maybe it was eleven in the morning," Colt said.

"That is so long. Oh my god," my stomach fell to the ground. I felt like I was going to vomit.

"It's a couple days longer than a week," Colt said.

"It's like a week and a half. You literally go back to work on Wednesday, too. We have no time together alone, just our family. This sucks," I said, feeling defeated.

"It'll be okay. I will be working from home for the next two weeks," Colt said.

"Yeah, but it's not like you have weekends off. You work, you're usually busy all day every day until your week off. Also, won't you be gone during your next week off to go up to Ohio for Paul's wedding?" I asked.

"Yeah. It will be okay, Adison."

"It just sucks. We just had a baby. I wish we had time alone together and had a chance to settle in," I complained.

My back suddenly felt like it got hit with a hammer. I moaned. I needed to lay down. My body ached horribly, I was exhausted and my stress was making me feel dizzy. I got up with Talli and went into our bedroom, laying down in bed for the night. I struggled to get my brain to settle down. I kept trying to figure out how I was going to get through this without going insane. My body and mind begged me for time alone with my newborn, for some quiet and rest. I couldn't seem to convince myself it was going to be okay.

Friday, my mom took Calli to the airport early in the morning and dropped off her rental car. Hilda picked up my mom and Daisy and they all came over to visit.

"I need to call my dad. He's having surgery today," Hilda said without looking at any of us. She put her phone to her ear.

"Hi Dad, how are you feeling?" she asked once he answered. "Oh, okay, please be positive. It will be okay. Listen to the nurses."

Soon she hung up. She sat staring off into space.

"Are you alright?" my mom asked Hilda.

"Yeah, it's just my dad. He gets so hopeless and negative whenever he has to have surgery or go to the doctor. I should be there with him right now," Hilda said as she began to tear up.

My mom rubbed Hilda's shoulder.

"Is it a very serious surgery?" she asked her.

"Every surgery is serious, but no, he should be fine. It's his negative attitude. You can't go into surgery thinking it is going to go badly," Hilda said as she wiped her tears away. "I need a minute, please."

We all sat, quietly. I wasn't sure what to do or say. I clutched onto Talli in my arms.

"I hope everything goes well and he will be okay," I said softly.

"Yeah, me too," Daisy said.

"Have someone keep you updated. I'm glad it isn't a serious surgery, but I know how scary that can feel. It sounds like you are really close with your dad, Hilda. That is so nice," my mom said.

"Yeah," Hilda said. "I wish I was there to take care of him. His girlfriend is so dumb. She never does a good job. It really sucks that I'm not there."

I wondered why she wasn't there. She definitely could have gone home earlier. I felt guilty that she was here, like it was somehow my fault she wasn't with her dad. I tried to shake off that feeling. It wasn't my fault. She is an adult who makes her own choices.

They all hung out at our apartment until they had to take Daisy to the airport around one in the afternoon. We had a short break between that and when they came back for dinner, so I was able to catch up on some chores. My mom and Hilda brought chicken that they had already cooked with a can of green beans and a can of corn. They heated the two veggies up on our stove. As soon as they were done, Hilda took Talli from me and sat on the couch.

"It's best for you to eat bland foods to avoid upsetting the baby's stomach with your milk," Hilda said, smirking at me.

That seemed very eighteenth century, but I didn't say anything. I politely ate the dinner they had made and thanked them for it.

"How is your dad doing?" I asked Hilda.

"Oh, he's fine. He is home and resting now," Hilda said, looking at the TV while she bounced my newborn in her arms.

"I'm glad I am leaving tomorrow," my mom said. "I think you guys need space and time together to settle in. I feel bad that I came so soon. I should've waited to come visit."

"It's okay," I said, even though I agreed with her that it would've been best for them to have waited to visit.

I didn't blame anyone. No one knew when Talli was going to arrive and I had never had a baby before so I didn't know how I was going to feel. I did feel a bit annoyed that Hilda had decided to stay so long. She should have planned to leave when my mom did.

"No, it was too soon. You guys really need time and space. This was a lot too soon," my mom said.

Hilda ignored her and stared at the TV. Colt had put *Friends* on, so she was completely entranced in what Rachel and Ross were doing. She was still holding Talli. I got up and reached for Talli. I could tell Hilda was annoyed, but she handed her back to me.

"Since you leave tomorrow, do you want to hold her?" I asked my mom.

I was so tired of sharing Talli, but I felt as though I had to.

"Okay, thank you. I won't hold her for too long," my mom said, gratefully.

My mom held Talli, talking to her through the mask she was wearing to protect her. She held her for about twenty minutes before passing her back to me.

"Thank you," I said, grateful I didn't have to ask for her back.

I held Talli close and moved further back into the couch. I didn't want Hilda taking her from me again.

"We should probably get going soon. It's getting late. If you don't mind, can we stop by in the morning before I go to the airport? Maybe around eleven? I have to be at the airport by one. Is that alright?" my mom asked.

"Yeah, that's fine," I said.

My mom started to get up and get ready to go. She put her shoes on and stood near the door. Hilda stayed put on the couch, oblivious to my mom getting ready to leave.

My mom waited a few more minutes before saying with a twinge of annoyance in her voice, "Hilda, are you almost ready to leave?"

"Oh, I hadn't even noticed you get up," Hilda chuckled. "Yeah, in a couple minutes. I want to finish this episode."

My mom looked at me with wide eyes and then sat down on one of the barstools, resting her elbow on the counter with her hand cradling her head. I gave her a knowing look and then cuddled Talli closer to my face.

Once the episode was finally over, Hilda slowly got ready to leave. My mom once again stood by the door, waiting for her.

"Okay, well, we'll see you guys tomorrow," Hilda said, lingering.

"Okay, goodnight," Colt said as he guided them out and shut the door.

"How in the world was I going to survive the next couple days with Hilda," I again thought. Dread flooded me, seemingly spilling out of my ears. My skin burned. I clutched onto my sweet Talli, who was asleep in my arms, and stared off into space.

4

Chapter Four

Hilda and my mom came over in the morning before my mom had to leave for the airport. I said goodbye to my mom and thanked her for visiting.

"You guys should FaceTime with Grandma while I'm gone," Hilda said, looking at us sternly before walking out of the door.

"Well, let's just get it over with," Colt said while searching for his grandma's contact.

"Let me see that baby!" Cynthia, Hilda's mom, shouted when she answered the video call.

Cynthia cooed at Talli. She talked to Colt and asked us questions about what we were doing as parents so far.

"I'm glad your mom is there to help you guys. That was really nice of her to come. She is so excited to get to be with Talli," Colt's grandma said, eyeing us.

"Yeah, it was nice of her to come," Colt said.

Colt moved his phone camera so Cynthia could see Talli better.

"Take those things off her hands," Cynthia scolded, referring to the mitts we had on Talli's hands to protect her from scratching herself.

Earlier, I had tried to cut her nails, but they were so small and I was scared to accidentally hurt her. I had ordered a battery-operated nail file that wouldn't hurt her. Shipping said it would arrive within the next couple days.

"She's wearing those so that she doesn't scratch her face," I said.

"Cut her nails! Take those off her. She shouldn't be wearing those," Cynthia scoffed in disgust. "She won't know where her hands are."

I sat back against the couch, my face red, and kept myself out of view of the camera until we said goodbye.

After taking my mom to the airport, Hilda went to the pool before she came back over. During Talli's nap, I caught up on things around the house like laundry and dishes. It was nice to get things done and have some quiet time. At about four in the afternoon, Hilda came over by herself. She and Colt decided to go pick up Chinese takeout.

"Adison, are you sure you're okay to stay here alone?" Colt asked. "You can bring Talli with us or my mom could stay here with you."

"No, no. Talli and I are fine here by ourselves," I said as I smiled at Colt.

I did not want to be alone with Hilda again. Throughout the past couple days, my anxiety was growing. It was becoming something that felt out of my control. It scared me. Colt and Hilda left, and I sighed out relief. I rested contently with Talli until they came back.

"Adison, I'll take Talli so that you can eat," Hilda said, moving toward where I sat on the couch.

"It's okay, I can eat while holding her," I said, reluctant to give her up.

"That would be hard. You don't want to spill something on her. I actually like to eat Chinese food when it's cold. I don't like it hot. I will take Talli, it's not a problem."

Hilda reached out for Talli. My insides felt hot as I handed my baby over to her. I scarfed down a handful of bites of sweet and sour chicken. It felt like rocks going down my throat and piling up heavily in my stomach. I decided I would rather starve than be without Talli for one more minute. I got up, quickly put my food in the fridge and walked over to where Hilda sat with Talli.

"Thanks, I'll take her back now," I said.

"Oh, but I just got her," Hilda said as she looked up at me, feigning innocence.

I stood over her, feeling exhausted and frustrated. I shook slightly. I wasn't good at being assertive. Since grade school I had been taught to put everyone, especially elders, before myself.

"You can hold her later. I'd like to hold my baby now," I said, not giving up.

Hilda quickly rolled her eyes and then slowly passed Talli back to me. I took Talli and went to the other end of the couch, away from Hilda. I scrunched all the way to the back, putting pillows and blankets around us in a makeshift fort. I sat, drained, but happy to be holding my newborn. I didn't notice what Colt had put on the TV, I just stared at Talli's sleeping face. I caught Hilda staring at us a few times. She looked annoyed, but once she saw me noticing her, she immediately went back to staring at the TV.

The clock showed it was nine at night. I yawned, exhausted. I kept checking the time, wondering when Hilda was going to leave. I wished my mom was here to get her moving.

"I am super tired. I am going to go to bed," I said, yawning again almost an hour later.

"Goodnight, Talli," Hilda trilled, making baby faces at Talli as I stood up to go into my bedroom.

"Goodnight, Adison," Hilda deadpanned, then turned back to the TV.

Before I closed the door to my bedroom, I looked back to see what Colt was doing. He was still sitting there on the couch with his mom, watching TV. I sighed and closed the door. I got ready for bed and laid down to go to sleep with Talli. I couldn't get my brain to shut off. It was hard to relax when I could hear the noise of the TV along with the muffled conversation between Colt and Hilda. The longer I struggled to fall asleep, the more frustrated I grew. I checked my phone for the time. It was past midnight.

"Are you kidding me?" I thought.

I groaned silently. Why was Hilda still here? I focused on taking long breaths, in and out. Finally, I fell asleep. About half an hour later, I woke up to Colt coming into the bedroom.

"Your mom finally left?" I asked.

"Yeah. I didn't realize how late it had gotten. I kept trying to get her to leave, but she wasn't taking the hint," Colt said. "I'm really tired."

I struggled to fall back asleep.

"Three more full days," I thought to myself.

Three more days.

The next morning, I felt like I had been hit by a bus. The circles under my eyes were extra dark and puffy. I got up with Talli at seven in the morning. I wanted to enjoy a quiet, calm sunrise with her. It was my first Mother's Day. Colt had left to go run an errand. I laid with Talli on the couch and started watching *Walk the Line*. Colt came back inside with a stunning bouquet of colorful flowers and an iced honey latte for me.

"Oh my gosh, Colt, they are beautiful!" I exclaimed, excitedly. "Thank you so much!"

I inhaled their sweet, floral scent. I was super excited for the latte, too. Fancy coffee was a weakness of mine and always got me excited. Colt knew me so well. He was so in tune to the small things that were actually the big things to me.

"Happy Mother's Day, honey," Colt said, giving me a kiss.

He handed me two envelopes. I opened them. There was a card signed from Colt and another he had signed from Talli. He set a third envelope for his mom on the counter.

"Do you want to watch this with me?" I asked him.

"What is it?"

"It's a movie about Johnny Cash. It started maybe fifteen minutes ago. His little brother just passed away. It was really sad," I said.

About halfway through the movie, I noticed out of the corner of my eye that Colt was looking at his phone.

"When should I tell my mom to come over?" Colt asked me.

"I don't know. Can we at least finish watching this first?" I sighed.

"Yeah, that's fine. I'll tell her to come in the afternoon."

I felt anxiety bubbling in my stomach. I tried to ignore it. I wanted to enjoy this peaceful morning.

Hilda came over around two in the afternoon carrying a full grocery bag. She pulled out of the bag two brown, shriveled bananas and three little black plastic containers that she put in our fridge.

"I made meatloaf into balls with mixed veggies for dinner. They are in the fridge. We can heat it up later when we get hungry. I also brought these ripe bananas for you, Adison. I don't like them when they get brown, but you like to make smoothies so they should be good for that," Hilda said, coming over to sit on the couch.

"Oh, thanks," I said.

I didn't like mushy, half-rotten bananas either, even in a smoothie. Colt handed Hilda the card he had gotten for her.

"Oh, for me? Thank you," she said, opening it. "Cute."

I sat on the couch quietly holding Talli. I didn't want to share her anymore, at all. I also felt annoyed that I had to share my first Mother's Day with Hilda. I scolded myself. I shouldn't be annoyed. She came all this way to visit. I felt guilty for all the sour feelings for Hilda welling up in me. They just kept getting stronger and stronger, no matter how hard I tried to dissolve them. It didn't help that Hilda was over so much or that she was always expecting to hold Talli. If she could chill, maybe I could kick these negative feelings I had growing toward her.

Around six in the evening, Hilda got out the meals she had made. Every time she asked if I was hungry, I kept responding with, "Not yet." This had been going on for almost an hour. I was not ready to give up Talli and I knew she was going to offer to hold her while I ate.

"I'm just going to heat these up now, you should probably eat, Adison," Hilda said.

She brought over the meal in the plastic container once it was warm and set it on the side table next to the couch where I sat. She stood over me.

"I'll take Talli so you can eat," she told me, staring down at me.

I sighed, handing her my tiny, sleepy baby. I officially hated dinner. I took a couple bites of the plain meal. It was hard to swallow. I was consumed by frustration, exhaustion and stress. All I wanted was my baby and to cry out these feelings. I struggled to finish the mushy, plain vegetables. Once I did, I put the meatloaf balls back in the fridge.

"Done already? I brought an extra meal if you want more," Hilda said.

"No, I'm good. Thank you," I said, trying not to grit my teeth.

I knew I should feel grateful that she made dinner, but I didn't. I had wanted something special for my first Mother's Day. I wanted it to be just Colt, Talli and me. I especially wanted to hold my week-old baby. I sat with my butt barely on the couch, back upright, itching to grab Talli. I looked at the clock.

"Okay," I thought. "I'll give her twenty more minutes and then I'll take her back." The twenty minutes drug on. Finally, the clock turned to seven. I stood up and walked over across the couch to where Hilda sat with Talli. She ignored me as I stood over top of her.

"I have to feed Talli now," I said.

Hilda slowly handed her up to me. I spun on my heels and went into our bedroom. I laid down with Talli, feeding her and silently crying. I stayed in my room thirty minutes after Talli finished eating. I didn't want to go back out there. My phone pinged. I looked at the message I received from Colt.

It said, "When are you coming back out?"

I sighed, mustered up all my strength and walked back out.

"Can I hold Talli again?" Hilda asked me in a soft, begging voice.

"I just want to hold her," I said, half smiling from discomfort.

I couldn't even look at Hilda. I felt disgusted that she kept asking me to hold my baby and that she was still here. I hugged Talli closer against my chest. I went from looking at Talli to looking at the clock. Back and forth for another hour. At nine, I got up to go to bed.

"Yeah, I'm really tired, too," Colt said, getting up. "I need to get to bed."

"Oh, okay. I guess I'll go then," Hilda said.

She took her time leaving, but once she was gone, I exhaled.

"I'm sorry," Colt said.

He knew I was tired of sharing Talli and that his mom was staying too long.

"It's fine. Thanks for getting her to leave," I said. "Hey, maybe to-morrow can I have a day without her coming over? I don't want to be mean, but I can feel myself about to freak out. I need a break. Like bad."

"Uh, I don't know how to do that," Colt said.

"Just go hang out with her or something. Not here. I feel bad, I know she came here to see us, but this has been a lot for me. I am feeling really anxious and overwhelmed. I honestly feel like I can't even get through these next couple days," I said. "Just go spend the day with her and let me have a break, please."

"Okay, I can try," Colt said.

5

Chapter Five

Monday morning, Colt reluctantly left to go spend the day with his mom. I spent most of the day napping with Talli. My body was still all messed up. Everything hurt. Tired didn't even begin to explain the feeling of sleep deprivation I felt. If I could simply survive the next couple days, everything would be okay. I just wasn't sure how I was going to survive. I really needed this day alone.

Around four in the afternoon, Colt came home.

"Hey, how has your day been?" Colt asked.

"It's fine, we've been napping. How was yours?"

"It was fine. I'm tired. We walked around the mall and then we sat at her rental watching TV," Colt said. "So, um, she wants to come over for dinner."

"What? Are you serious? I said I needed a break from all of this," I grunted, angrily.

"I know, but what am I supposed to do? What am I supposed to say?" Colt asked, exasperated.

"Just tell her I need a break. Tell her she can come over tomorrow. I just had a baby a week ago and it's been chaotic ever since. You can go back over to her rental and hang out with her tonight if you have to," I said.

"I don't want to go back over there. I want to be at home. Plus, she just wants to see Talli," Colt said.

"I know and it is so exhausting. I'm tired of sharing Talli with her," I complained.

"Okay, well it is almost over. Only a couple more days. Can we please just let her come over for dinner so I don't have to deal with it?" Colt asked.

"Fine. Just know that I am feeling like a crazy person. I will try my very best to get through this, but I may need to go to our room," I said, sighing. "Can I eat before she gets here so she doesn't use that as an excuse to hold Talli?"

"Sure, that's fine," Colt said. "I told her I was going to make tacos."

Colt went into the kitchen and started browning the beef. When it was done, he let me eat and then he texted his mom that she could come over. I sat wedged into the edge of the couch holding Talli protectively when she walked in.

"Hello, Adison. Did you get the rest you needed?" Hilda asked condescendingly.

"I got some rest," I answered, not looking at her.

I felt too many emotions and they were all bubbling, threatening to explode.

"I can hold Talli while you eat," she said.

"I already ate," I said emotionlessly, this time meeting her gaze.

She raised her eyebrows at me, as if in warning. I looked away. I was too angry to feel threatened by her. She wasn't supposed to be here right now. I couldn't believe that she couldn't seem to empathize with what I was going through. I sat silently, staring at Talli while her and Colt ate. I felt anxiety pulsing through my veins. I was bracing for the next time she asked to hold Talli. I had a bad feeling I was going to explode.

Finally, it happened. Hilda asked in her most saccharine voice, "Do you mind if I hold Talli?"

I sighed loudly. I exaggeratedly got up and passed over my baby to the greedy woman. Why was I such a people pleaser that I couldn't say no? I did not want to do this. I wanted my baby. I stood over top of her with my arms crossed as she held Talli. I sighed again. She ignored me, cooing at Talli.

"Can you take a generational picture of all of us?" Hilda asked, with faux innocence.

She handed me her phone and then sat close to Colt. I quickly snapped two pictures. She continued to sit there smiling, as if waiting for more. I handed her phone back to her with an attitude. I held out my arms to take Talli back. She ignored me.

"I'll take Talli back now," I said, coldly.

Hilda didn't look at me. She stared at Talli, slowly handing her up to me. I snatched my baby back. Hilda suddenly looked at me as if I had slapped her. I wheeled around on my heels and marched into my room.

I laid on my bed, wrapping my body around Talli's tiny self. I tried not to shake as tears rushed down my face, spilling onto the comforter. I knew that I only had a couple more days until she left, but knowing that didn't matter. I needed Hilda to leave now. She clearly couldn't simply leave me and Talli alone. I stayed in my room with Talli for the rest of the night until Hilda left around eight. Once she was gone, Colt came into the bedroom.

"She left, you can come out now," Colt said.

"I'm sorry, Colt, I can't do this anymore. This has been probably one of the hardest things I've ever been through. I'd rather give birth again than have your mom over anymore," I said.

"I get it. I was annoyed when she asked you to hold Talli again. I tried to tell her that you are dealing with postpartum stuff and just want to hold her," Colt said. "I mean, I do understand from her perspective that she doesn't get a lot of time here and wants to see Talli, too."

"Yeah, I understand that, but I just had my first baby. She has had a baby before, maybe she should've considered visiting a couple weeks after. I also have been very considerate of everyone else's feelings, but I just can't anymore. I have nothing left in me," I said. "Also, no one has helped with anything other than the two dinners they made. Not like I am asking, but your mom just sits on the couch for hours. It's annoying."

I didn't mention my mom helping me clean up the mess I had made a couple days ago. I didn't really want Colt to know about that.

"I know, babe," Colt said.

On Tuesday morning, I gathered all the supplies I'd need for Talli and hoarded them in my room. I didn't come out while Hilda visited. I couldn't face her. I couldn't have her ask to hold Talli again. I couldn't listen to any more of her stories or watch any more of her shows. Hilda was again in our home for hours that day. I could hear her muffled voice through the door as she hung out on our couch watching TV. Colt had told her that I wasn't feeling well and needed to rest, which is why I was staying in my room with Talli. I felt empty inside. My heart was heavy with dread. I felt guilty for feeling these awful ways when I had the most incredible gift of a baby in front of me. I loved her more than anything. I hated that I felt anything other than bliss.

Hilda left earlier than usual Tuesday night, which was relieving. Colt came into the room and laid on the bed once she had gone.

"I'm exhausted," he said.

"Me too," I agreed.

I was truly drained. Each night I had to wake up every two to three hours to feed Talli. Colt and I had the same amount of usual work to do around our home, plus taking care of our newborn, plus hosting.

"My mom brought you over cookies she made," Colt said.

"That was nice of her," I said, although I was annoyed.

I had been mentioning all week that I was trying to avoid sugar because I felt disgusting in my body. It was nice of her to do something thoughtful, but it seemed thoughtless at the same time. Again, the guilt arose in me for feeling ungrateful. This was the worst.

"Oh, also, my mom said she's going to stop by in the morning before she leaves for the airport," Colt said, cringing.

"Are you kidding me? Ugh!" I groaned, covering my face with my hands. "I'm sorry for my reaction, but Jesus, is this woman oblivious? I feel like an asshole, but I just want her to leave already. She's killing me."

"You can just stay in the room again, it's okay," Colt said, slowly rubbing my back.

"Thank you. I appreciate it," I said.

I was glad that she was finally leaving soon, but at the same time I couldn't even really appreciate it. I felt so dark inside and full of anxiety. I felt overprotective of Talli, like I wanted to run away with her so no one could take her from my arms anymore. I wasn't sure whether I was traumatized from the past nine days or if all of these feelings were due to postpartum hormones. It was maddening.

At last, it was the long-awaited Wednesday. I stayed in bed with Talli while Hilda came over in the morning. I could hear muffled talking and what sounded like bags rustling from outside my door. I cuddled up closer to Talli, squeezed my eyes shut and covered my head with a blanket. I didn't want to even hear Hilda. When she finally left around ten in the morning, I came out. I did not like what I saw. Our kitchen looked like Walmart had exploded in it. Our island was covered in overfilled gray plastic bags. There was a large red cooler up against the island across from the fridge, making it so I was unable to open the fridge door more than halfway. More bags covered our counters.

"Colt, what is all this?" I asked in horror.

"My mom brought over everything from her rental. I don't know. I wasn't expecting this much stuff," Colt said from his desk.

His short paternity leave was over and he was back to work.

"This is too much. We don't have space for all of this."

I felt completely overwhelmed. This was the cherry on top. Of course she had to leave with this last punch. I looked into some of the bags. I saw a large, barely used bag of flour, sugar, three bags of tortilla chips, parchment paper, aluminum foil, single ply toilet paper, a large baking pan, partially used grape jelly, ketchup, mustard, on and on. It was as though someone had cleared out their kitchen into ours. The worst part about all this stuff wasn't just that we didn't have any room for it, but that we didn't even use most of it. We already had full containers of condiments. There was no way I was using single ply toilet paper with having just given birth and I knew Colt wouldn't use it, either. We simply had everything we needed. Plus, our lease was ending in the next couple months and we were planning on moving before then. I would have to figure out what to do with all of this.

"I need to walk away from this," I said with a sick feeling in my stomach. I despised mess and clutter. I went back into the bedroom with Talli.

After taking a moment to gather myself and my strength, I went back out into the kitchen. I put Talli in her swing and turned on classical music. I started going back through the bags, asking Colt what he would use. Anything he said no to, which was most of the stuff, I put together in a section of free counter space I had managed to clear. More than half of it we threw away. Stuff that was unopened, I was able to give away to a mom I got in contact with through a Facebook group. Sure, Hilda probably had pure intentions and thought that she was being generous. She must not have realized we eat differently than her or thought about the limited space in our small apartment kitchen. She didn't seem to think about much, other than her own wants and needs. I opened the cooler. My nostrils were assaulted by a rotten meat stench.

"Oh my freaking god Colt! There is meat in here!" I shouted.

"Can you put it in the freezer?" Colt asked.

"Well, for one, we don't have room for an extra ice cube in the freezer. It's packed full. Two, this doesn't smell good," I said.

Colt walked over and scrunched up his nose.

"Throw it away," he said, disgusted.

"This is a ton of meat to throw away. There are steaks, beef, sausage, chicken nuggets, some garlic bread and other chunks of meat that I don't know what they are. This is so wasteful," I said. I also hated wasting and throwing things away.

"Can you do it? I can't. This is too much. I'm going to freak out." My mental health was at an all-time low.

"Yeah, close the cooler and leave it all there. I'll take care of it later," Colt said. I sighed. Thank God Hilda lived in another state. I was going to need some serious time away from her to recover from this. In subtle ways, she treated me like I was nothing more than an incubator for her grandbaby. I didn't feel seen or cared about by her. I had to accommodate her the entire time, to make sure she was enjoying her stay, give her time with my baby and not be in the way.

"Maybe she didn't mean to make me feel like that," I thought. "Maybe I was being a jerk. Maybe I needed to get myself together."

6

Chapter Six

"I guess I should also clarify that while telling you this now, there is more anger than there was when it actually happened. When it happened, I felt more sadness, stress and exhaustion. Looking back, it angers me that I wasn't given the time I needed to settle in, bond with my baby and heal," I said, hugging my knees tightly against my chest.

"That's understandable. It would be difficult to have just had a baby, no less your first, and be thinking about other people. That sounds like it was really tough," my specialist said.

"It was. After it was over, I truly tried to get over it and move past it. I didn't want to have issues with my in-laws. Looking back, maybe I should have tried to discuss my feelings with my mother-in-law while she was visiting or after she left. Although, I can't necessarily blame myself since I wasn't exactly in a normal headspace. I was dealing with a lot of emotions, learning how to be a mom, trying to recover from childbirth and having other people around," I said. "Hilda didn't try to talk to me about how she felt, either. So, I thought that time was going to have to pass for me to feel normal around her."

"It sounds like you did the best you could do in the experience you were having. You're right, she could have talked to you. She hadn't just given birth for the first time," my specialist said with a nod. "Was this the first time that she had been difficult?"

"No," I said, shaking my head.

"That was just when I stopped being able to handle it. It started years ago. When I first met her, she didn't seem very interested in getting to know me. Eventually, I ended up feeling close to Colt's family, mostly Mackenzi. I really enjoyed being around her. She was fun. Colt and I didn't start dating until around six months after I had already met his family. Shortly after we were official, in May, his mom invited me to go with her and Mackenzi on a weekend trip. It was really fun, but I remember how crushed I felt as we packed up to leave at the end. Hilda had turned to me, telling me she wasn't going to post any pictures that included me on Facebook because Colt's most recent ex, Gina, would see them. She told me she didn't want to upset her and said that Gina was usually the first person to like her posts."

I took a breath.

"From there, more things happened sporadically. Weird things, like, when we got engaged, she bugged Colt to go to her church for us to take a marriage questionnaire with her priest. She wanted to see if he and I were a good match."

I sat up straight, my eyebrows raised in remembrance.

"Oh, I almost forgot about this one time soon after we started dating. It was in July, about two months after that weekend trip. Hilda invited me to go to a pool with her and Mackenzi on my birthday. I remember laying on a plastic lounge chair with Hilda sitting in the one beside me. She randomly started telling me about a friend of hers whose daughter-in-law was keeping her friend from her son and grandchild. Hilda kept looking at me quizzically and asking, 'Isn't that awful?' as she told me about how horrible her friend's daughter-in-law is. I remember how unsettled I felt at the time. I wasn't sure why she was getting so upset talking about it and why she was staring into my soul. It felt like a warning, but it didn't make sense to me why I needed one. The other unusual thing was that there was no story or explanation why the daughter-in-law suddenly pulled away from the mother-in-law. Hilda just kept saying that the young woman was horrible without any back story. At that time, I had no idea what it was like to be in such a situation so it didn't make sense to me. Now, it feels like that moment was foreshadowing the future between Hilda and me."

"That is really strange," my specialist said, frowning.

"Yeah. So, I guess her overbearing visit wasn't the start, just the catalyst," I said. "I feel like she became so jealous and fearful of her son's love for me that she started trying to break me apart as soon as she realized how serious our relationship was."

"It sounds like it. It sounds like Hilda has been bullying you since you and Colt started dating. It doesn't seem like she ever truly gave you a chance or attempted to establish a genuine relationship with you. Her relationship with you was entirely control-based. So, what happened after her visit to Texas? Did time help at all?" she asked me.

"Time didn't help. Well, I thought it was, but actually things got worse," I said, clutching tighter to my legs. "I'll continue."

7

Chapter Seven

After Colt's two weeks of working from home, I felt like I had more or less gotten into a routine with Talli. On Colt's first day during his week off, he left to fly up to Ohio to attend Paul's wedding. My mom flew back down to help me while he was away. I felt slightly bitter that Colt left Talli and I so soon. I understood his friend will hopefully only get married once and he wanted to be there for him, but it still sucked. On Friday morning, the day before the wedding, I received a Snapchat message from Paul's soon-to-be wife, Jan.

Her message read, "Hey, what does Colt like for breakfast? We are going to get everyone food and he's still sleeping."

"Weird," I thought.

I messaged back, "He likes eggs, sausage, potatoes and breakfast sandwiches."

Jan responded, "He's up now, but thanks anyways."

It left a sour feeling in my stomach. It felt like she was throwing the fact that he was there in my face. Like, you just had a baby but your husband is hanging out with us. I put my phone away.

A few hours later, Jan Snapchatted me a picture of Colt lounging on their couch with their dog in his lap. I didn't respond to her. I didn't know how I would. It felt weird of her to snap me a picture of my husband. We weren't friends and we didn't talk. I had talked to her when she first started dating Paul a couple years ago, but she complained about him a lot. Not long after we met her, the couple had gotten into a bad fight when she was planning to meet up with her ex, who had recently gotten out of jail. Paul had stayed at our house that whole weekend. She had been calling and texting him, fighting with him the whole time he was with us. We ended up taking his phone and putting it away when she started threatening to come to our house to talk to him. Paul had gotten drunk, so nothing good was going to come from him answering her nonstop calls. So now, it was weird for her to Snapchat me, especially because she was subtly throwing my husband's absence in my face.

The weekend felt like it took forever. Not as long as Hilda's visit, but still too long. I did have to admit, it was nice to have my mom there. She got me food and helped distract me from Colt being away. She left the same day that Colt returned. I tried not to be angry with him, but I was. Hilda had posted pictures of Colt on Facebook and their family all together at Paul's wedding. Hilda, Clayton and Mackenzi had been invited and attended, also. In one of the pictures, it was dark outside and Colt looked drunk with Clayton. I shouldn't have cared, but I was annoyed. In my postpartum, crazy haze, I felt abandoned and as if I wasn't as important as I should be to my husband.

It didn't help that in the days following his return, Colt went out to dinner with work friends and spent hours at the golf course. My resentment and bitter feelings grew. One night, after Colt got back late from a work party held at a bar, I couldn't take it anymore.

"I just feel like we aren't that important to you. You're always going somewhere or doing something if you aren't at work. I've just been here trying to heal and be a mom. It's frustrating seeing you doing all these things when I can't," I yelled.

"Okay, I guess I won't do anything then," Colt yelled back.

"It's not that you can't do anything, but you could've waited a couple weeks before doing all of this stuff. Everyone visited and it was really hard, then the day your mom left you went back to work, and then when you finally have time off again you leave to go to Ohio for a wedding. Then you come back to go golf, to dinners, and are out doing stuff. It's just terrible timing, Colt."

"Well, I can't control when people get married or when I have to go places for work," Colt said.

"I know, I'm sorry. I feel crazy and angry. I don't know how to feel normal." I put my hands in my face.

"I'm tired, let's just go to bed," Colt said, frustrated and annoyed with me. "Well, are you coming or what?"

I followed him into the bedroom and laid there, silently crying until I fell asleep.

As time passed, I was still feeling really anxious, overprotective of Talli, stressed and sad. My recovery process was long and without much reward. By my six-week postpartum appointment in June, I was still in a lot of pain. I lied on my checklist for my mental health so that I wouldn't have to deal with whatever would come with having postpartum anxiety or depression. I felt okay enough to be a mom, my days just felt harder and less enjoyable. It felt really tied up with Hilda's visit. I kept having nightmares about her being there and not giving Talli back to me. I felt anxious whenever I saw her name pop up on Colt's phone. She called him a couple times every week. This was all stuff I didn't want to tell the doctor about because I felt crazy for it.

"Well, your stitches did come out," the doctor said as he wrapped up the visit.

"Oh, wow, that's awesome. I thought they were still there," I said, relieved.

"No, you're good. Well, congratulations on your baby. Take care."

When we got back in the car, I started to cry.

"What's wrong?" Colt asked me.

"I don't know. I don't feel good. I feel really overwhelmed," I said, wiping away tears.

"Okay. Well, we are done with the doctors, so that's good."

"Yeah, it is," I said.

We had started packing up our apartment. We were working on buying a house. Colt ended up spotting a cute, newer home with land in northern Ohio. We had been looking at houses in Texas without much luck. Texas made more sense with Colt's job, but we thought it would be nice to live closer to family for Talli. When Colt and I sent my mom the listing for the house in Ohio, she got to work. She was helping us buy it since she was a realtor and it was in her area. I luckily hadn't heard from Hilda, or from anyone else in Colt's family, for that matter. It was a little strange to not hear from anyone, since randomly during my pregnancy his grandma had started calling me and his aunts would text me from time to time. Now, it was radio silent. I was okay with it because it was kind of a relief to have a break from trying to make conversation, so I didn't think too much of it.

The moving process was long. It took a while to finish packing since I had to do it around Talli's sleep schedule. During the first week of July, when it was finally time to move, we loaded what we could into Colt's truck and my car. We hooked my car onto a trailer that we hitched onto the back of Colt's truck. Once we made it up north, Colt was going to fly back down to West Texas and make the drive up again with the moving truck. Colt hadn't told anyone in his family, besides his mother, that we were moving. He had asked Hilda to keep it to herself until he was ready to tell others. He had told me he wanted to wait until we were settled in so as to avoid the comments he was sure he would get while we were busy with the strenuous process.

After moving from Dallas to Miami for an incredible job opportunity for me, we received a slew of "moving again?" comments. It happened again when we moved from Miami to West Texas. It isn't tough to decipher the judgment dripping from the comments. It got exhausting trying to explain to everyone what we were doing, why we were doing it, and then having to hear about their thoughts on what we so carefully decided to do with our lives. It didn't really seem like anyone else's business. So, when Colt wanted to wait until we were more settled in to go through that process, I didn't argue.

We left on Colt's birthday. I sat in the back of the truck with Talli. I looked at the dusty, sandy dirt outside of the window as we drove out of West Texas and a bittersweet feeling gripped my heart. I was excited for the new adventure, but I was going to miss the south. A couple of hours into our drive, Hilda called Colt. Talli was sleeping, and I focused on the small western town views outside while he talked to his mom. At the end of their conversation, it got quiet before Hilda spoke again.

"Goodbye, Adison," Hilda sneered with tar and hatred in her voice.

I shook my head, coming out of my daze.

"What the heck," I thought as my jaw dropped.

I personally hadn't heard from this woman since she was in our home a month and a half ago. I looked at Colt, confused. He looked back at me.

"Okay, bye," he said to his mom, hanging up the phone.

"That was weird," I said.

"Yeah, it was," he agreed.

He got a couple other phone calls during that first stretch of our drive. Cynthia called him and then his Aunt Nancy. He avoided telling them about our move. I sat silently in the back.

The move was long. The first night we stopped in Texarkana, Texas and the next in Bowling Green, Kentucky. As we neared Ohio on the third day, I cleared my throat.

"Hey, Colt? Is there any way we can wait two weeks before we have any visitors? I've been thinking about it a lot. I want to be able to unpack, settle in and feel more comfortable before people start coming over. After the way the visits went after having Talli, I'm afraid to have another big moment feel taken from me," I nervously said.

"I don't know how that's going to go over with everyone. We can try. Why can't people just come check out the house?" Colt asked, unsure.

"They can come see the house, just once we are more settled. I mean, we are going to be living there. We aren't going anywhere. They can visit whenever. I really feel like I need two weeks to settle in. I'm worried about your mom coming over immediately, making it about her and leaving me with more resentment. I want things to get better, not worse."

"That makes sense to me. I get it. I just know that they are going to have a problem with it," Colt said.

"But that's ridiculous. We will be living there. There is no reason that your mom needs to be there immediately. I think it's okay for me to have some space. You are more than welcome to go visit them, that's fine. I just need this chance to settle in and try to relax before they come," I insisted.

"Okay," Colt said. "It would be nice if you and my mom didn't hate each other."

"What? I don't hate your mom? I just want two weeks to settle in. We plan on living there for a while so there is plenty of time for family to visit," I said, confused.

"Okay. I just keep hearing things on both ends and wish it would stop," Colt sighed.

"I'm sorry, what have I said? The last time I talked about her besides right now was after she left Texas and I said that she made me feel super anxious with how her visits went. What are you hearing?" I asked, confused.

"Nothing, it's fine," Colt said before turning up the radio.

The conversation left an uneasy feeling in my gut. I had a bad feeling that Hilda had been talking negatively about me to Colt.

We finally made it to Ohio. Talli and I stayed with my mom for a couple days while Colt flew back to Texas to drive up with the moving truck. My mind had started to wander as my uneasiness grew. I began to ponder whether Hilda had been talking about me not just to Colt, but to other family members. It would explain why they all had suddenly stopped talking to me. What could she have been saying? Was she telling people about how I went into my bedroom with Talli during the last couple days she was in town?

I tried to empathize and figure out exactly what she could have been thinking, but each time I would try to travel down the rabbit hole my brain would stop me. My inner self would remind me that however wronged she felt, I had just given birth. She has been in the world for fifty-four years; she should have more emotional intelligence. She could have communicated and she could have tried to talk to me about her feelings. She could have tried to empathize with me and been understanding that I needed space to bond with my baby. But instead of doing anything that would have been positive or cohesive, she decided to pour acid into the fissure.

8

Chapter Eight

Colt made it back to Ohio with the moving truck and we met up at our new house. It was beautiful. It was custom built for the previous owners and sat on a couple of green, open acres. Moving in was easier than moving out. My mom had thoughtfully hired us movers to help us unload the truck. Colt had agreed upon the two weeks to settle in, so I was relieved about that. The first week, we were busy with cleaning and unpacking. The work felt never-ending. Boxes were spread throughout our new house. We also had to wait to unpack half our clothes since we were going to have to install a closet in our bedroom. There was currently a measly two-foot bar and two baskets screwed into the wall.

During that first week, Colt received a call from his mom. He was sweating, leaning back on the couch, exhausted. I was holding Talli, standing and looking out the window. We were taking a break from unloading boxes. He answered his phone and put it on speaker.

"Hello?" he said.

"Hey there, just seeing how everything is going," Hilda's voice blared over the speaker.

"It's good. We just have a lot of work to do," he said.

"Mmhmm, I'm sure. We could've helped," Hilda said with a hint of attitude.

"It's fine. It's easier for us to just do it so we know where everything is," Colt said, trying to laugh. "The house is really nice though. We are happy with it."

"Would be nice to be able to see it," Hilda said.

"Yeah, but we aren't invited," Clayton shouted aggressively in the background.

"Honey, shh," Hilda purred.

I felt my heart pick up speed and my skin begin to prickle. My body slightly shook.

"It's just two weeks. We are going to be living here now," Colt said.

"Yep. Well, let us know when we can come," Hilda said.

"Literally in a week. You can let us know what day," Colt said.

"Alright. Well, we will let you guys have your time to settle in. Talk to you later." Hilda's voice was an octave higher and saturated in disgust.

"I didn't think two weeks to settle in was going to be the end of the world," I said, still staring out the window, shaking.

"I told you they weren't going to like it."

"Why does everything always have to be about them?" I asked.

"I don't know. That's just how it is," Colt shrugged.

A couple days later was my twenty-sixth birthday. Colt was working from home on the night shift so I spent the morning with Talli while he slept. We walked around outside, exercised and listened to music. Sometimes I felt sad on my birthdays, I wasn't sure why. Today, I felt kind of sad and time passed slowly before Colt woke up. Throughout the day, I received some happy birthday messages from people in Colt's family. It was hard not to notice that a lot of them were much more bland than usual. Hilda had texted me a simple happy birthday in the afternoon. Cynthia wrote it on my Facebook wall instead of her usual call. I would also typically get a birthday card from Nancy, Hilda and/or Cynthia. I didn't receive any cards, but maybe they had been sent to our previous address. Maybe they had to get forwarded.

Mackenzi FaceTime called me in the afternoon. I felt relieved that she was being normal. When I answered, she was sitting on a towel at the beach.

"Happy birthday!" Mackenzi said.

Waves crashed loudly in the background and the bright sun cast shadows over her face.

"Thank you! How are you? The beach looks nice. That's fun," I said.

"Yeah, it is. We decided to go to Ocean City since you guys needed time to settle in," Mackenzi said, turning the camera to face her mom. Hilda barely waved.

"Yeah, the move was just a lot. We need some time to get stuff done and catch up on sleep," I said, feeling a hot, sick feeling well in my stomach. "I'm glad you guys were able to go to the beach, though. That's good."

"I'm going to run back to the hotel for a minute," I overheard Hilda say to Mackenzi before she got up and left.

"Okay," Mackenzi yelled after her. "So, what are you up to?"

"Just hanging out with Talli. Waiting for Colt to wake up," I said.

"Aw, that's nice. Why is he still sleeping?" Mackenzi asked.

"He's working the night shift."

"Oh, makes sense. Okay, well I'm going to go, but just wanted to say happy birthday," Mackenzi said.

"Okay, have fun! Thank you for calling. It means a lot," I said, waving goodbye through the camera.

When Colt woke up, we attempted to go out for dinner. We had only gotten our salads when Talli started to cry. I took her out to the car to feed her and wait for Colt. He asked our waitress to have our food boxed up to go and stayed at the table, waiting for it to arrive. I tried not to feel like my day had sucked. I stared at my sweet baby and felt grateful for her. She was the best and only gift I needed.

After my birthday, my brain started to churn more and more with thoughts regarding the difference in how Colt's family was acting toward me. What had Hilda said to everyone to make them regard me as if I had committed a crime? There was no way she hadn't said something, anything, to them about me. It was a night and day difference. Subtle, yes, but still very intentionally different. I could sense it in my bones. I wondered why no one had reached out to me, though. If she was talking about me, why hadn't someone reached out to see if what she was saying was true? I felt crazy thinking about all these things. There was a chance she wasn't saying anything about me and people were all just doing their own thing. I could be overthinking it all. I didn't think I was, though.

Colt still worked in West Texas part of the time, so we barely made progress in our feat of unpacking and setting up our furniture before he had to leave. His family hadn't made any plans with us yet, which I wasn't exactly upset about. I kind of just wanted them to visit already to get it over with. Maybe things would go back to normal after they visited. I wasn't sure, but I was definitely feeling anxious about it. I was also still trying to recover from giving birth. I was a rock when it came to bouncing back. I was still excruciatingly exhausted. My body was still puffy and I was still in some pain. I felt nowhere close to what I had felt like throughout my life. I was trying to navigate all that on top of establishing a new routine with my baby while unpacking the house.

While Colt was away for work, I received a phone call from Hilda. When I saw her name flash across my phone, I instantly was hit with nausea. I was laying on the couch with Talli and didn't feel like answering. It was August, and I hadn't heard from her besides the generic happy birthday text. A voicemail popped up on my screen less than a minute after the phone stopped ringing.

"Hello, this is Hilda, give me a call back, thanks," she spit in the fifteen-second message. Her tone was icy.

I felt anxiety coursing through my veins. I told myself I'd give it a few hours before returning her call. I had a bad feeling she wanted to come over. I was about ninety-nine percent sure that is why she called, because two days ago Mackenzi had FaceTime called me asking a ton of questions. It was a rather uncomfortable conversation. She asked me about my labor length, declaring it wasn't that long when I answered. She had heard of someone being in labor for twenty-four hours. There were a few more questions with judgmental undertones before she asked what I was doing on Monday. She said her mom and her were thinking about coming over. I told her I had plans. I did not want my in-laws over without my husband there. Hilda would never leave, would walk all over me and it would be the same old thing.

I thought back on other times, even years ago, when she treated me much differently when my husband was not in the room. One of those times was a couple weeks before our wedding, when she came to my house with her daughter to visit. Colt had been away for work. She stayed most of the day and prodded me about my knowledge of my husband's life before me. She discussed his past with his best friend growing up and how Colt was the one that pressured his friends into going to strip clubs with him, how he liked to do that kind of thing and how he was a partier. She talked about his old porn magazines or whatever that he hid in his ceiling. She and her daughter laughed through the conversation while she feigned innocence regarding what she was saying. I remember how I felt after they left, how exhausted and emotionally drained I was. I also remember how she made me start to question if I was the right woman for Colt, that maybe he shouldn't be marrying someone who isn't okay with her husband going to strip clubs.

So now, after all that had happened to this point, I did not want to be alone with her so she could then test me with my baby. I drove Talli and me twenty minutes down the road to my mom's house to camp out just in case Hilda decided to randomly show up at my house. Once I arrived at my mom's empty condo, I decided to be nice and give Hilda a call back. I paced around holding my dear baby while the phone rang.

"Hello," Hilda droned in her scratchy voice. She paused a hair before continuing. "What are you doing?"

"I was out and decided to stop over at my mom's today," I said, still pacing.

"Okay, well, we are up in the area dress shopping for Mackenzi so we figured we would come over. When will you be home?" Hilda demanded.

"Oh, I don't know. I just got to my mom's and I have some stuff to do after," I stammered.

"Okay, well what stuff do you have to do? How long is it going to take?" Hilda prodded further, her tone growing more aggressive.

"I don't know. I don't think today is a good day to come over. I already told Mackenzi I was busy today. Colt will be back home from Texas in a couple days, why don't you guys come over then?" I asked, trying not to sound too desperate for some relief from this awkward one-sided conversation.

"We really thought today would be good since we are already up in the area. I was not aware that you spoke to Mackenzi. Well, if you get home soon, you can let me know," she sliced back at me, not giving up.

"Okay. Are you dress shopping for homecoming?" I asked, trying to change the subject.

"Yes. She has one in two weeks and another in October. Mackenzi, that one is great. Oh, try this one. This one will really bring out your eyes," Hilda started having a conversation with Mackenzi while leaving me on the line.

"Hey, I really should go. My mom is waiting for me," I lied, still pacing.

"Oh my gosh, Mackenzi, no. Are you kidding me? Wow. I told you to do something about that earlier. That is ridiculous," she yelled into the phone. "Sorry, what did you say? Hold on."

I started to feel impatient as the conversation between her and her daughter continued. I really wanted to hang up, but I didn't want to be as rude as she was by leaving me hanging on this call. I clutched onto Talli in my arms. Hilda then proceeded to tell me about football games her daughter was cheering at that she expected us to attend. After that, she got into an argument with Mackenzi as I continued to pace with sweat beading on my forehead.

"Hilda, I really should get off the phone now," I breathed.

"Yeah, I need to get off here. Bye," she said before the line went dead.

I exhaled relief but still felt jittery with anxiousness.

"At least I got that over with," I thought.

Chapter Nine

My anxiety had been slowly growing every day since the tension had begun. Hilda called Colt on Saturday and made plans to come over the following day. I felt so sick to my stomach, so shaky and so weird leading up to their visit. On Sunday, I woke up uneasy at six in the morning. I spent the day trying to distract myself as much as possible. The in-laws were supposed to come over at two in the afternoon. The day dragged on. Eventually, two rolled around and I waited to breastfeed Talli since they were expected to arrive at any minute. I paced around as the minutes ticked on.

"Have you heard from your parents?" I asked Colt as two-thirty came and went.

"I haven't. I'll text my mom and see if they are close," he said as he typed a message.

Within a couple minutes, he showed me his phone with a message received from his mom.

It read, "Just getting ready to leave."

I sighed. Now I had to endure another two hours of dread, since that is how long it would take for them to drive to our house from theirs. I decided to go lay down with Talli and feed her since I had plenty of time now. Time felt like it was dragging on as my dread grew.

It was now four-thirty in the afternoon and I felt like I could vomit. I was exhausted from a day of worrying and wanted to be free of these feelings. I decided to get up and pace around. I thought walking might help ease my anxiety. I checked my phone after what felt like a little bit, and the time showed five-fifteen.

"Honey, what is going on?" I asked my husband as I walked into his home office.

"I have no idea. This is weird. I'll call them," he said back to me.

I walked out of the room and back through the kitchen into our bedroom. As I made my rounds back into the main area, he called out to me from his office to come in.

"They said they are thirty minutes away," he said.

"They said they would be here at two and it is now almost five-thirty. This is crazy. I am really tired now and I hope they don't stay too late. I have to get Talli to bed in a couple hours," I sighed, exasperated.

"I know, I agree. It is annoying," Colt said.

They finally arrived at six-fifteen in the evening. I was sitting on the couch with Talli, who really needed to be fed again since she was only three months old and ate often. They came inside loudly, arguing with each other over nothing. Hilda, Mackenzi and Clayton rushed over to Talli in my arms. They said hello in baby voices while ignoring me. They all sat down on our couch, on the long end furthest from me, which I was glad about. Colt was still on the phone in his office so we sat in silence and awkwardness. Talli started to cry.

"I should really go feed her. I am sure Colt will be out in a minute. I'm sorry, I know you guys didn't come all this way to sit around with yourselves," I said, attempting to lighten the mood. I didn't know what else to say. Their presence had suddenly made our home feel dark and uncomfortable.

They glared back at me as I turned and went into my bedroom with Talli.

When I came back out, Colt had just finished up his phone conversation and walked into the living room. Hilda went into the bathroom, Clayton slapped Colt on the back and Mackenzi laid back on the couch clutching her phone, typing vigorously. I felt better that the countdown to when they would leave had begun, but still very uneasy. So much was going on around me, so I just looked down at my wonderful little baby girl and sighed a breath of love.

As soon as Hilda came out of the bathroom, she started carrying on loudly, telling some story about herself. Colt offered to show his parents and sister around the house. I stayed on the couch with Talli. After they were done looking around and talking about all the things Hilda thought we should do with our new house, they came back into the living room. Except Colt, who stopped in front of the door to the garage. He opened it and Clayton followed him out. Oh, no. Panic filled me as they left and the door shut. Hilda and Mackenzi sat on the couch. I was scared of Hilda asking to hold Talli so I figured I should just take control and let it happen on my terms.

"Would you like to hold her?" I reluctantly asked Hilda.

"Sure," Hilda said in a bored voice as she held out her arms.

I set my baby down in her arms and sat back on the couch, uncomfortable. Hilda started making all kinds of strange faces and voices. She propped her right foot on her left knee and had Talli laying in the crevice of her leg. I didn't like how close my three-month-old was to this woman's bare foot and how close Hilda was getting her bare face to Talli's. I was extremely terrified of anything happening to my baby or her getting any kind of illness. I was always super careful with her. This was the riskiest position she had ever been in. Mackenzi was talking to me about people from her school that she followed on Instagram, but I was only half listening, yearning to get my baby back. Colt was still outside looking at the ditch at the end of the yard with his stepdad. I could see them out the window. I held myself together for at least a half-hour before I asked for Talli back. Hilda ignored me.

I asked again and received no response for a second time. I stood up, walked over and waited above her.

"I'll take her back now," I said, reaching out my arms.

Hilda disregarded me completely, as if I didn't exist. I contemplated what to do for a minute, before slowly scooping Talli out of the crevice of Hilda's leg. Hilda sat back as if I gut punched her, but quickly straightened up, tightening her face. She instantly pulled out her phone, acting as if something insanely important was going on in her virtual world.

Colt and Clayton came back inside. Clayton was stammering loudly about the options of filling in the ditch and how it would be expensive. Clayton always looked and sounded like he had downed a twelve-pack. I guess most likely he had. He was loud, aggressive, a drunk and intolerant of anyone who had differing thoughts. After Colt and I got married, Clayton called me once while Colt was at work. I thought it was odd, but had answered. He proceeded to ramble on about his horrific views and opinions. I remember the outrage I felt when he acted oppressed by other races and how he believed they were taking what was his. How he feels angry, convinced he is paying for their livelihoods through his taxes. How all his black co-workers use drugs. I could not listen to it. I argued he shouldn't say something like that and that, quite frankly, saying that is racist. He got angry. I argued back and forth with him for an hour. I felt as though there was no helping him. His ignorance was too deeply rooted and he did not want to change his thoughts for the better. That was the last time he ever called me, or really talked to me to my face. After that, there was small talk whenever we had to be around each other, but no effort to establish any further connection.

"Are we going to eat or what?" Clayton grumbled.

Hilda slowly ambled into the kitchen and pulled out a glass pan of lasagna. As Colt and his family each got themselves a plate and then microwaved the cold meal, I stayed on the couch grasping my baby. My stomach was too tied up with anxiety to eat, plus I had questions about lasagna that had traveled in a car for two hours and then sat out here on the counter for over an hour. I really didn't care to eat anything this woman made or have her use this as another excuse to hold Talli, like she did when she came to Texas.

"Aren't you eating, Adison?" Hilda asked in more of a statement than a question.

"Oh, no, I'm not hungry. I ate earlier," I said as politely as possible.

I sat with them at our dining table as they ate the reheated, crusty lasagna. They talked amongst each other and I nodded along, trying to fake normalcy. The conversation mostly consisted of high school football and cheerleading. Mackenzi is a cheerleader and dancer for her high school, so Hilda lives vicariously through her. After they were done, they wanted to go into Talli's room and watch her lay on her belly. Like circus animals, we followed their instructions. I felt completely overwhelmed, like I wanted to scream "No!" but my brain just made me go along with what they said. After they felt satisfied, we went back into the living room.

"Mackenzi, take a picture of me with Talli," Hilda said, shoving her phone into Mackenzi's hand.

"Would you please wash your hands before holding her again?" I asked Hilda, who was seated on the couch, arms outstretched.

She squinted her eyes at me. Mackenzi quickly set Hilda's phone on the couch and darted for the bathroom.

"Excuse me? I did when I got here," Hilda said matter of fact with a venomous glare.

"I know, but since then you've been on your phone, eaten and stuff. I am not trying to be annoying. I am just so nervous about Talli getting RSV or another illness. I heard RSV is getting really bad this year. Someone I know who lives in Barnesville has it. I saw she posted about it on Facebook just yesterday," I rambled, trying to be nice while expressing my concern. Barnesville, Hilda's hometown, was small, a place where everyone knew each other.

Hilda lifted herself up and went into the kitchen since Mackenzi was in the bathroom.

"Do you have soap?" she heaved with a sigh, annoyed.

"Yeah, we use the Dawn dish soap in the sink," I said, not bothering to explain the fact that we hadn't finished unpacking since there were boxes all around the room.

"You don't have hand soap? Really? This is going to ruin my hand oils," Hilda complained while squirting about two tablespoons of Dawn into her palm. "There go my hand oils."

She dried her hands and rubbed them together, looking at them in disgust. She took Talli from me and in a mocking voice while staring into Talli's eyes said, "RSV has been around forever. Everyone has survived it. It's ridiculous to be scared of it."

I stood in shock and felt my brain turn to mush. Mackenzi returned from the bathroom and proceeded to take picture after picture of Hilda smiling a large, rehearsed grin with my baby in her arms. After the montage of pictures was finished, she continued to talk to Talli in a quiet, unintelligible baby voice. I gave her a couple more minutes and then asked for Talli back. She again ignored me. This time I marched over and swiftly took back my baby. Hilda held on for an extra second, but my grab was empowered. She ignored me for the rest of her stay.

"Clayton, don't you want a picture with the baby?" Hilda asked before they got up to leave.

Clayton grumbled something I couldn't make out.

"Oh, sure you do. Sit down," she said.

I reluctantly handed Talli to Clayton, who held her with his palms clenched around her head and butt. After a few pictures, I took her back. They left shortly after. I felt completely drained. I was glad they were gone, but their negative energy hung in the room like stinky old lady perfume. I was shaky from the anxiety high I was coming off. My stomach was twisted and nauseous. That night, I hardly slept.

The next day, I felt a little better. I was relieved I had survived their visit and that it meant I would probably get a little break from having to endure that again. It was Monday, so Colt, Talli and I spent the day running errands we needed to get done before Colt went back to work on Wednesday. We finished grocery shopping and were on our way home after dark that night. As usual, I sat in the back seat next to Talli in her car seat. All of a sudden, Colt's phone rang over his car's speakers. The name that flashed on the screen read, "Mom."

"Hey, what are you guys doing?" she said in a sing-song voice.

"Just driving home from the grocery store," Colt said as he slowed at a stop sign before taking a left turn.

"Oh, wow, it's late. What time is it? Almost eight. Shouldn't Talli be in bed?" she critiqued.

"Yeah, we just had a lot to get done today, but we will be home soon," Colt replied.

"Hmmm, okay. You probably could've done it earlier. Anyways, I was calling to see if we can come over early tomorrow morning with your grandma," she said in more of a telling rather than asking kind of way.

"What time were you thinking?" he asked.

"How early is too early? We could be at your place by eight in the morning," she said.

Colt paused a minute before saying, "Uh, I'll have to talk to Adison and let you know."

"Isn't she sitting right there," Hilda pressed.

"I'll call you back," Colt said before getting off the phone.

He turned to me. "What do you want to do?"

"Babe, they were just over yesterday. I hate that she always calls at the last minute. It feels really overwhelming. Also, eight is way too early. This sucks," I said, my heart racing.

"I know, but my grandma should meet Talli," Colt said honestly.

"Yeah, I know. I just wish it wasn't such a last-minute thing and I wish it wasn't so close to their last visit, especially with how uncomfortable it was for me. But I do agree your grandma should meet Talli. Okay, well, please say more like ten or eleven in the morning because eight is way too early. I have to brush my teeth, wash my face, change Talli, feed her, etcetera," I sighed.

"I agree, eight is way too early. I'd like to sleep in on my last day before going back to work. Okay, I am going to call her back," Colt said before pressing the redial button on his car screen.

"Hey, you guys can come over at ten," Colt said when his mother answered.

There was a pause before a sharp inhale. "Why can't we come earlier?" Hilda breathed out.

"We want to sleep a little bit and we have some stuff to do in the morning. You guys can come at ten," Colt said firmly.

"Alright, well, we will be at your house at ten. Great, we can't wait to see you then," she said before they both hung up the phone.

I felt like a little piece of me died inside. I could not believe she was coming over again in less than twenty-four hours. I felt like I was suffocating, like she kept tightening her grip on my throat. Every time I tried to take a breath of air her fists clenched harder. I felt like everywhere I turned, I had to see or hear or deal with something related to her. I sat in my anxiety and stress for the rest of the drive home. When we got home, I handed a sleepy Talli to Colt.

"I need to take a shower," I mumbled.

I slid out of my clothes and into the shower. I turned the heat up and let the steamy water run down my still puffy belly. I still had a visible brown line that ran from my belly button straight down. I felt tears building up in my head behind my eyes. I screamed silently and then let them fall. As the tears fell, I felt all my energy leave me. I dropped down and sat curled over my knees, letting the water hit my head before going down the drain. I stayed like this until I realized I needed to finish my shower and get to bed. I heaved myself up, finished shampooing and conditioning my hair and turned off the water.

I stared with dead eyes in the mirror as I dried off and put on an over-sized T-shirt.

"Hey, are you okay?" Colt asked me.

"Not really. I feel so overwhelmed. Your mom is really stressing me out," I said to him.

"Honey, it's just one day. It will be okay," he said as he rubbed my shoulder.

"It doesn't feel like that. It feels like it is always something," I said.

"Let's get to bed," he said before turning back to the bedroom where Talli was asleep.

The next morning, I went through my routine as usual with Talli. I changed her diaper, put a new onesie on her, put my contacts in, washed my face, brushed my teeth, got dressed, had something for breakfast and fed her. Once we were done, I sat with Talli in her room and read her books while she laid on the floor. Hilda, Cynthia and Mackenzi all came through our door at ten. Cynthia came straight to the entrance of Talli's room and stared at us. I enthusiastically said hi to her. She meekly said hi back, her eyes wild and the rest of her face covered by a blue mask. I instantly felt uneasy and unsafe. Cynthia called me on the phone occasionally, we had all gotten together many times before we had moved out of state and, although I never neces-sarily felt loved, I at least felt accepted. Or like I was getting closer to being accepted. That is pretty much how I felt with everyone in my husband's family. I now saw in the subtle things they all did, whether in person or online, that I was the black sheep. Mackenzi was the only exception. She and I got along great. We were genuinely friends and sisters, although, things felt so complicated now. Mackenzi was older, a senior in high school, going through her own life, yet not quite old enough to understand the mess I found myself in. I understood she had no idea what was going on with me or this whole situation that was building up. Mackenzi now sat on our couch again with her phone close to her face and thumbs flying across the screen. Her mother and grandmother sat in the room as well, talking to Colt. I held Talli close to me the entire visit. I felt uncomfortable and stayed quiet. The only thing holding me together was Talli's sweet, small body against my heart.

"Sit down, Adison. You're making my back hurt seeing you stand there holding the baby," Cynthia said.

"Oh, it's okay. I sit most of the day. I don't mind standing," I said, smiling nervously.

"Seriously, sit down," Cynthia repeated.

I reluctantly sat on a plastic box behind me. It was uncomfortable. I had preferred to stand, but I wanted Cynthia to stop squinting at me.

Everyone acted civil for the entire visit. Hilda was putting on a good show in front of her mom. The only subtle disrespect I picked up on was when Talli fell asleep in my arms and Hilda started shouting instead of talking.

"Cut, Grandma, cut!" Hilda yelled, laughing as she recounted for the hundredth time her story of when she gave birth to Colt and the umbilical cord was wrapped around his neck.

Apparently, Hilda's doctor had been yelling at her mom to hurry up and cut the umbilical cord so the baby could breathe.

"Shh, the baby is sleeping," Cynthia laughed along.

As the visit came to a close after four hours of standing and sitting around, Hilda turned to Mackenzi.

"Do you want to skip your practice today? We could stay longer," Hilda pleaded to her daughter.

"Ugh, no, I want to go to practice," Mackenzi groaned.

"Yeah, it's okay, we really should get going," Cynthia pitched in.

Hilda puffed out air before dragging out every last minute she could until Mackenzi, as well as Cynthia, were itching to leave. They left and a weight instantly lifted off my chest. It was okay, almost normal. Maybe things would be okay. There was definitely weirdness, but maybe it was just some giant misunderstanding. Maybe things would get better. I thought about how maybe in just a couple months we could all get together for coffee and laugh about it.

10

Chapter Ten

It was now September. Colt went down to his hometown for a high school football game to see his sister cheer during it. He left around four in the afternoon to make sure he was there for dinner first. He saw his whole family. His grandparents, aunts, uncles, cousins, sister and parents. He came home around eleven at night afterwards. When he came home, he was acting a little strange. He was quiet and distant.

"How was the game honey?" I asked him in the dark, having been woken up from the noise of him returning home.

"It was fine. Everyone asked where the baby was," he said to me as he got in bed.

"Well, I hope you told them she was home in bed. She wouldn't be sitting out in the cold for hours at night past her bedtime with a two-hour drive waiting after," I said, kind of annoyed anyone thought that was to be expected.

"Yeah, I get it," Colt said, and left it at that.

Based on his strange, distant demeanor, I felt strongly more had been said regarding Talli and me. With how things had been going, I was certain in my gut there had been some gossip about me. I shivered and tried not to feel nauseous as I attempted to fall back to sleep.

A few days later, I learned that apparently sons and daughters each have a special day in the year. On National Son's Day, Hilda shared a group of pictures of Colt on Facebook. There was one with Clayton, another with herself, one with Mackenzi, one of all four of them, and there was even a picture I had shared on my own profile weeks ago of him with Talli. It appeared she had subtly made sure to not use any pictures with me included. It was something stupid that I did my best to ignore, but my gut told me this was an intentional slight. I was even more certain about her intentions with trying to hurt my feelings when she also excluded me from any pictures she shared on National Daughter's Day. Hilda's mother-in-law, Didi, posted about her two daughters and included Hilda as well. I did not know much about their relationship, except for the random unflattering comments Hilda has made throughout the years about Didi. Again, it was a really stupid thing to notice. I felt dumb for even thinking twice about it, but it was something that I felt I had to store in my brain. I kept trying to piece together what exactly was going on. I was pretty sure this entire situation started because I went into my bedroom with my newborn while Hilda was visiting. Colt had told me his mother was upset about it. She had never said anything to me, so I didn't feel like it was my job to go to her to discuss it. I was also incredibly nervous to do anything like that and unsure what to even say. So, I knew where it had originated, I just wasn't sure what all was being said about it. Or why it was being blown out of proportion. I kept trying to figure out what Hilda might be thinking. Maybe she was thinking I was ungrateful, unkind and disrespectful for going into my room with my baby. Every time I tried to think about what she could be thinking, my brain would stop me.

"I literally just had a baby," my brain would echo throughout my being.

That first week of Talli's life was supposed to be my week. It was supposed to be about what I needed, wanted and was best for me. Of course, for Talli as well, but I was the one taking care of all that for her. I needed support. I needed love. I needed to do whatever my exhausted, bleeding, agonizing body told me to do. I should not be shamed for needing alone time with my newborn. I should not be shamed for needing rest. I should not be shamed for not being a perfect host and for not wanting to share my first baby, which I had spent nine months creating. I spent months sick on the couch, my body hurting in ways I had never before experienced, and dealing with emotions that I felt little control over. It was all worth it for Talli. I just wished that my pregnancy, birth and postpartum experience could have been seen and accepted.

I also started to feel a creeping anger for the way I had been treated and was being treated. It was frustrating that my mother-in-law did not show me any empathy or respect in my experience. It was wrong that she was going around complaining about me to others. While I still had a bump on my belly and dark circles under my eyes, and while I was doing everything for my baby. I couldn't understand how she could be so careless. I kept trying to see things from her perspective, but quite frankly, her perspective seemed insane. It seemed to me that any normal person would be patient with a new mom who was trying her best. It seemed to me that a normal person would have kind words, love and grace for a daughter-in-law who just gave birth. It angered me because someone who I gave a great deal of thought to treated me like I was a stranger on the street. Actually, a stranger probably would've received much better treatment from her.

I wasn't feeling well due to the anxiety that wouldn't go away and the constant overthinking I couldn't seem to silence. I was laying in Talli's room with her and Colt when I decided I would try to talk to him about my feelings.

"I want to talk to you about something, but I feel nervous to bring it up. I don't want to upset you. I feel like your mom has been treating me unkindly and it is making me feel uncomfortable being around her. Things have been really weird since Texas," I let the words pour out.

Colt sighed and put his hands over his face.

"I don't understand why everyone can't just get along and play nice. You and my mom hate each other and it is getting really annoying."

"I don't hate her. I just feel really overwhelmed by her lately and a lot of anxiety from how things have been," I said softly.

"All I ever hear about is this. I am so tired of hearing about it," Colt said, annoyed.

"I haven't really talked about it with you before. I don't understand where that is coming from. I tried to talk about it once before, but like I said, I feel really nervous talking to you about it. What do you mean all you hear about is this?" I asked, genuinely confused.

"From my mom and Clayton. Every time they call me, they bring this up. When I went to Ohio in May for Paul's wedding, this is all I heard about. They think you have been treating them rudely. My mom is angry with how you kept going in the room with Talli. You guys need to figure this out," he said in frustration without looking at me.

"Oh, wow. That is really upsetting to hear that they are talking about me this much. Why wouldn't they try to talk to me? I can't believe this is happening. I needed to go in the room. Your mom was over way too much. It made things really hard for me. I felt really happy when Talli was born. Then as the week went on, I felt like I was drowning in anxiety due to how I couldn't catch a break with your mom wanting to hold her so much." I started to get upset too.

"God damn. I don't care anymore. Just fix it," Colt yelled back at me.

"It hurts me that you say you don't care. It hurts me that you're yelling at me. I wish you would listen to how I feel. I feel like I am drowning," I said as I started to cry.

"Really? You're crying?" Colt scoffed.

"I can't do this. I need some air," I pushed myself up and started to get Talli's diaper bag together.

"Where are you going? You are not leaving!" Colt shouted, jumping up too.

"I need to get out of here for a minute. I feel so overwhelmed. Please just let me leave," I cried.

"Whatever, I don't care," Colt yelled, stomping off into his office.

Tears slid down my cheeks as I got Talli into the car and left to go to the library down the street. As I sat in the parking lot staring at the mist-covered pine trees in front of me, I thought about what had just happened between Colt and I.

"How was he not seeing what was happening? Why wasn't he sticking up for me?" I thought.

I tried to put myself in his shoes. He wanted a happy family. He wanted his mom and wife to get along. He wanted to ignore what his mom was saying and doing, he didn't want it to be reality. I could understand that. It had to feel stressful and despairing having two of the most important people in your life not get along. He probably felt backed into a corner, as if his worlds were crashing and caving in on him.

Talli and I went into the library and aimlessly looked at kids' books. I felt so sick with anxiety and sadness. We grabbed a handful of books, checked out and left. I wanted to go home and lay down.

After letting things cool down for a couple hours, I went into Colt's office.

"I am really sorry I upset you. I understand this must be a hard position for you to be in. I understand that these are your parents. I will never make you choose. I will try my best to fix things. I love you and I always will," I said honestly to Colt. "The only thing I really want to ask you for is to try to understand how I feel in this, too. This sucks. I don't know why things are like this. I hate it, too."

We hugged and I felt slightly better. I still felt pretty sick about the fact that I was being talked about so much by his parents. Also, that I didn't feel like he was standing up for me.

11

Chapter Eleven

I woke up on the first day of October feeling excited and ready to celebrate fall. Crisp colorful leaves, warm pumpkin spice lattes and the smell of the cool, fresh air filled my mind. I love fall. Today was also Talli's five-month birthday, so I was excited to celebrate that milestone with her. After being so busy for the past couple months, Colt and I were finally going to spend some quality time together. We had decided to call it a "family date day" since neither of us wanted to leave Talli with anyone. We were happier with her being with us constantly. We found our time to bond together intertwined with our time with her and that is how we felt most comfortable. Our plan for the day was to go to a pumpkin patch and then relax together afterward. I got up, went through my morning routine and then took some pictures of Talli. She was wearing a cute outfit and laying on her milestone blanket with a piece of thick paper that said "Five Months" on it. I usually took some pictures for a couple days leading up to her monthly milestone day, that way if I wanted to do three different outfits, we weren't doing all those changes in one day. There is no way she would be up for that. I selected some pictures from the previous days and some from this morning to share on Facebook while we all laid back in bed. Shortly after I uploaded the adorable pictures, Colt's phone rang loudly. He got up and went into the kitchen to answer it.

It was on speaker so I heard Hilda's voice blare, "Hey there, I just saw Adison's post and saw that you guys are up. What are you doing today? We figured we would come on up to spend the day with you guys."

"Uh, I will talk to Adison and call you back," Colt said, turning the corner to look at me on the bed. He hung up the phone.

"Are you kidding me? We have plans today," I said to his unsure face.

"I know. Could they come over after?" he asked.

"I would rather they come over on a different day. This is so last minute. I would really like one full day to be together, just us," I said, standing my ground.

Colt threw himself onto the bed and groaned.

"Can they come over tomorrow then?" he asked me.

"I guess so," I said. I was still bothered by how sudden these plans were. Why couldn't his mom make plans ahead of time instead of calling the same day she wanted to get together?

Colt texted his mom saying, "We have plans today. Can you come over tomorrow?"

He looked at his phone once it dinged and then tossed it to the side before covering his face with his hands. I looked over to where his phone rested and at the text back from his mom.

It read, "What are your plans? Can't we just come over after?"

"Can they just come over after?" he groaned again.

"Honey, please. We need a day just for us. We haven't done that. It's important for our relationship. This is so last minute. I agreed to them coming over tomorrow. Why isn't that good enough?" I started to get annoyed.

He texted his mom back saying, "We are having a date day at the pumpkin patch today. You guys can come over tomorrow any time."

His mom quickly replied, "We can meet you at the pumpkin patch and then come over after. That sounds like fun. Which pumpkin patch are we going to?"

"No. No. This can't keep happening. This is so overwhelming. Please tell her no," I said, feeling stressed.

"Why can't you make things easy and just let it happen?" Colt said, frustrated.

"I am not trying to make things hard. I just think it is really important that we stick to our plans. They can come over any other day," I said with panic in my voice.

Just then, his phone dinged again with another text from his mom which to that read, "Hello? What pumpkin patch? We are ready to leave any time."

"This is so annoying. You are so difficult. I feel like I always have to walk on eggshells around you," Colt yelled.

"How do I make you feel like you have to walk on eggshells around me? I can't believe you just said that. This is insane. I just want to get out of here. Why don't you have your family over and Talli and I will leave? I don't care anymore!" I yelled, feeling my stomach twist and my face hot.

"You're not leaving. I feel like everything always has to be your way," Colt yelled.

"Why do you feel like that? I think that I am flexible and I do what your family wants most of the time. After having Talli, I think we need to be more mindful of what is important for her and our little family. If you really want to have them over today, fine, but I need to get some fresh air first," I sighed, feeling drained.

Colt looked down at his phone and started typing.

"I just texted my mom and told her to come another day. This is so stupid," Colt said.

Colt's phone dinged. He looked down at it and then grunted, throwing his phone onto the bed.

"What is it?" I asked.

"Just look at it," he said.

I glanced over at his still lit screen.

The recent text from his mom read, "I want to join in on your plans, I'm not asking you to change plans."

"What do I say back to that?" Colt groaned.

"I don't know anymore, Colt. You do what you want. I am so overwhelmed and exhausted. Please just let me leave for an hour with Talli. I need time to think," I sighed.

"No, I said you're not leaving. You don't need to do that. God damn," Colt said angrily.

We fought back and forth for two hours.

I cried, we both yelled and we were getting nowhere until I finally said, "Okay, do you want me to call your mom and try to get this all figured out? Maybe there is a misunderstanding here."

"Okay, yeah," Colt said.

"Do you want to be in the room?" I asked him as I grabbed my phone.

He winced back at me and I said, "Okay, fine, I will go to Talli's room."

I walked to the other side of the house and sat in Talli's rocking chair, staring at my phone. My hands shook forcefully and I felt my throat tightening up. I tried to clear my throat a couple times. I breathed deeply, in and out. After a few long minutes, I clicked on her contact and pressed the call button.

"Hello?" her scratchy voice came through the line.

"Hey. I think we have been having some misunderstandings and I want to clear things up. So, Colt and I did have a date day planned for today. That is important for us and our relationship, as we haven't had any special time together with how busy life has been. Can you guys come over tomorrow?" I said while focusing on my breathing.

She paused before responding, "Well, we are busy tomorrow and this is the only day we can come up. So, I just figured we would join in on your plans. I haven't been to the pumpkin patch in ages."

"Okay, well, we can go to the pumpkin patch again with you guys any other day this month. You called a little last minute and we do already have plans today. What other day can we make plans?" I said respectfully.

"We are busy every day this month," Hilda spit back coldly.

"Okay," I paused, caught off guard. "How about next month?"

"Busy every day," she said flatly.

"Okay," I paused again, even more caught off guard. "Look, I am trying to work with you. This is one day. Colt and I need this special time for our relationship. If you are free any other day, please let us know and we will make it work."

"Today is the one day we are free and I just don't understand why you won't let us join you? I have a job, I work. Mackenzi is in school and has practices. We are busy. We have this free day and thought it would be great to see you guys. We never see you guys anymore. You guys are always together. Also, I would like to go to the pumpkin patch, too," she shot back at me.

"I already said it is important for Colt and I to have a fun day together, as we haven't in a long time. We are usually too busy running errands or doing chores. Colt also works out of state. We don't get much quality time together. I'm sorry today doesn't work, but it was last minute that you called and today we are busy. Please, can you accept that answer? I love and care about you guys so much. I'm not trying to be difficult. I just need you to work with me. I would love to go to a pumpkin patch again with you guys," I said calmly back to her.

It was quiet for a minute besides music playing in the background on her end of the line.

"You guys don't make an effort to come see anyone. You guys don't come down here. Everyone in the family feels like you're keeping them away. No one really knows what is going on with you. Everyone feels uncomfortable around you," she said aggressively.

"What? No one has even talked to me. Anyone is welcome to come over here. If they reach out to me, I will work with them to find a day they can visit us," I said. My body was shaking and I felt sick.

"Oh, so everyone is expected to drive two hours to see you guys? No one wants to drive up there. It is too far. They are waiting for you guys to come here. Didi is hosting a fall party at the end of the month and everyone would really like to meet the baby. You guys should make an effort to do that. It is really annoying that you guys won't drive the two hours down here. You know, I used to drive eight hours from where I lived back to my hometown every month when Colt was a baby. He's fine. You just have to keep the baby entertained," she said.

"Okay, that was your choice. I wouldn't do that. I have a different parenting style than you. I am not having Talli in the car for over four hours when it isn't recommended for her to be in the car seat for over two hours in one day. Also, everyone besides Talli is an adult and can handle the drive much better. We no longer live out of state, I think that a drive is better than a flight. If they want to meet Talli, they are welcome to come here," I said straightforwardly.

"It won't hurt her. You just have to keep her distracted from crying. It's not hard," Hilda sneered.

"We are waiting until she is the recommended age to be in the car seat for over two hours. Again, we have different parenting choices and styles. It isn't up for discussion and I do not want to argue with you about it any further," I said sternly, holding onto my belief.

"Fucking bitch," she half-whispered.

I stopped, unsure of what I had just heard, but also so sure. "Pocketful of Sunshine" played in the background and that was all the sound that was heard for a moment. I shook it off.

"Colt and I are allowed to parent differently than you did. If you guys want to come over on a different day, let us know. It would help if you gave a couple days' notice so that we could be sure to make it work," I said in a soft, calm voice, as if I was talking to a child.

"Okay," she said emotionlessly.

There was a heavy, uncomfortable pause.

"I've only ever had fifteen minutes with the baby," Hilda whined.

"I'm sure it feels short, but you've had multiple days of hours with her," I said, rubbing my temples.

"I have not. I have had fifteen minutes. I would like to have a relationship with her," Hilda sneered.

"I would like you to, too," I said.

"Well, I am never allowed to see you guys."

"That isn't true at all. This is the first time I have said no to you. Maybe the second time. The first time I wasn't home and it was also last minute. You have to realize that if you call at the last minute there is a fifty-fifty chance that we may be busy. Please, just let me know another day that you can visit. I just need a couple days' notice and we will make it work," I sighed.

She blew out a puff of air.

"Alright. Well, I am getting off of here. Bye," she said.

"Bye," I said.

I hung up the phone. I stayed in the chair for a moment, shaking. I called my mom and told her what had happened. I started to get heated about it so I got up and went outside. I paced back and forth in the green, rich grass in our backyard as my mom and I talked about the conversation I had with Hilda.

"That sounds ridiculous. Go try and have a fun day with Colt and Talli. It'll be okay. Try not to let it bother you," my mom said calmly before we got off of the phone.

I saw Colt standing in the window of the back door. I focused on breathing in deeply and exhaling as I walked back to the house.

"I'm sorry if you heard any of what I was saying out there," I said breathlessly to him as I walked in the door.

"Yeah, I heard some of it. What happened?" he asked quietly.

"I tried my best to be kind and respectful. Your mom was being very argumentative and not working with me," I said. "Also, I don't know if you want to know or if I should tell you, but I am pretty positive she called me a fucking bitch."

Colt laughed before he said, "No way. I'm sure you heard wrong. I doubt she said that."

I felt my body tense up and my heart shrink into itself a little.

I took a deep breath and said, "Colt, I wouldn't just make that up or hear it out of nowhere. Everything else was quiet when I heard those words. Except for the song playing on low in the background."

"Maybe she was driving and said it about someone on the road," Colt shrugged.

"Maybe, but I don't think she was driving. She may have been sitting in the car, but I didn't hear the typical sounds of someone driving. No turn signals, no muffled voices, no tires or other vehicle sounds. Everything was very quiet besides her voice when she talked and for the soft sound of that song in the background," I said. I was sure of what I had heard.

I liked to think of myself as a rather observant and thoughtful person. I took in what I was experiencing. I also thought about what hundreds of thoughts others could be thinking, how they could be feeling, exactly how I should try to talk so as to make sure I am not coming off wrong, how to show others that I am thinking about them. My brain feels like it is constantly working on many different angles, as if I was a soccer player on both teams, sprinting across the field with the ball, kicking it toward the goal and then lurching in front of it so as not to score. It was exhausting to live like this. I yearned for and loved extra hard the people I didn't have to do this song and dance for. The people where things come naturally and I know that they see me for me. The people that if I say something that doesn't come out quite right, they carry on, hearing it the way I meant it or asking gently so that I can clear it up.

"Are you ready to go?" Colt asked, shaking me from my thoughts.

I didn't even want to go to the pumpkin patch anymore. So much time had been spent fighting, worrying, trying to talk to Hilda and feeling very unsettled. I got dressed anyway and shoved my feelings way deep down to my boots. As I walked, I could feel them down there beneath my feet, hot, heavy and bubbling.

We drove to another town close by with a pumpkin patch that had food and lots of pumpkins. The parking lot was an enormous mass of cars. There were a few men standing around the parking lot with flags waving where to park. Colt parked his truck by a giant wheel of hay with an orange Jack O'Lantern spray painted on the side of it. We got out into the brisk, chilly air and walked toward the entrance.

"Wow, this place is huge," I said as I looked around, trying to make sense of what was going on.

"Yeah, and really busy. Let's not stay for too long," Colt said as he motioned for me to go in the door to the large wooden barn.

"That's fine. It is probably best for Talli if we make it quick anyway," I agreed as I looked around at all of the picnic tables filled with people eating, and the other half of the barn full of merchandise.

We walked out the other end of the barn and into the area with food trucks, giant play areas and pumpkins. We waited in line at a food truck serving chicken tenders, fries and cider. We got our lunch and carried it over to a picnic table outside near the fire pits. I bit into the steaming hot chicken tender that I had dipped in barbeque sauce and sighed. It felt good to eat. I had forgotten I hadn't really eaten anything yet today.

After we ate, we got cider doughnuts to go, snapped a couple pictures and picked a pumpkin. I was glad we went. I usually would stay home and be in a slump after a morning like the one I had. Even if we were only there for less than an hour, it was still nice to get out. It wasn't exactly the happy date day I had imagined, but we still were together doing something out of the ordinary.

When we got home, I looked at Colt.

"I've been trying to think about how to fix things, or at least try to get rid of all the miscommunication. Your mom said everyone feels uncomfortable around me. I feel like I should try to explain myself to everyone so they don't believe whatever your mom is telling them. I typed something up in my notes while we drove. There are so many people I feel like I'd have to say something to so it would make the most sense to do a giant group text. It basically would say everyone is welcome to our house, but as new parents we have made the decision to wait until Talli is at least six months old before we drive over two hours in one day. It would say that we love and care about all of them, that we are trying to clear up any miscommunication."

Colt sighed before saying, "I don't think we need to do that. They won't care about it anyway. It will just make us look stupid."

"Okay, but I feel really exasperated trying to fix this mess. I don't know how to clear this up," I said as I closed my eyes and rolled my neck. "Maybe I'll just reach out to the people that post kind comments on Talli's pictures I share on Facebook."

"You can do what you want, but I don't think it is going to change anything," Colt said, grabbing the TV remote and sitting on the couch.

I looked at the family members who had been commenting on Talli's pictures. I decided to send a Facebook message to Didi. I thought she would be a good place to start because she commented a lot, hadn't met Talli yet and could relay the information to her two daughters. I also remembered that Hilda had mentioned Didi was hosting a fall party, so that could be a good way to start the conversation. I started typing and deleting and typing again.

Finally, my message read, "Hi Didi, how are you? I was wondering when your fall party is. Talli does not do well in car rides lasting longer than thirty minutes, but I'd like to at least talk it over with Colt and see if we can figure out a way to make it work. Otherwise, everyone is welcome to visit us at our house! I'd love to get something arranged (smiley face emoji). I don't have your number, here is mine so you have it."

I reread the message over and over then sent it along with my number. As the hours passed after I sent it, my nerves started to settle.

"At least I tried," I thought.

12

Chapter Twelve

On Sunday, the very next day, Clayton called Colt while we were busy building our new closet. They talked about work and small talk, such as the weather. After some time, Colt walked into the bedroom where I was with Talli and put his phone on speaker.

"I came home to my wife upset last night. You know, something has got to be done. I don't like to see her upset. She said you guys might as well still live in Texas," Clayton roared in his slurred, thunderous voice.

"We told her she could come over another day. It was only one day that we said we were busy," Colt said, laying back on the bed.

"You could've let her come over. You could've changed your plans or included her in them. You know, she is not an overbearing grandma. She is not. I think you need to grow some balls, have a talk with that wife of yours and put her in her place," Clayton said, pausing before continuing. "You only get one mom. And she's a good one. You should do what you can to keep her around. It looks like you have a choice to make here."

My jaw dropped when I heard that. Put her in her place? You have a choice to make? What is he implying? Why does my husband have to choose between his wife and mom? This felt so crazy. I turned and left the room. I went into the living room and put Talli in her swing.

I could feel myself getting really shaky. My blood ran cold and I felt my stomach wring itself up. I kissed my sweet, smiley baby and made sure she was secure in her swing before I turned to go back into the bedroom.

"Your wife needs to remember that you have family, too," Clayton was saying when I walked back in.

"Adison does things equally between you all. Mom did call at the last minute," Colt said.

"So what? Life can be spur of the moment," Clayton scoffed. "You guys never come down here. It's crazy, actually. You guys should be coming down here."

"Talli cries when she is in the car. The longest we've driven with her since our long-distance move has been thirty minutes. She can barely last that long and usually in the last ten minutes she will scream," Colt said.

"Let her cry," Clayton stated matter of fact.

Without thinking, I held up both of my middle fingers toward the phone and angrily mouthed, "Fuck you."

I felt a hot tear slide down my cheek as I wheeled around, stomping silently out of the bedroom for the last time while Colt was on that awful phone call. I went straight for Talli, who was perfectly content in her swing and undid her straps to scoop her up anyways. I held her close to my heart, rocking back and forth.

"I will never force you to suffer. I will never just sit there and let you cry if I can do something to fix it. I will do everything I can to keep you healthy, safe and happy for as long as I can," I whispered to her as tears leaked out of my eyes.

Once Colt was off the phone, I walked back into the bedroom with Talli in my arms. Colt sat on the bed, scrolling on his phone.

"That phone call was pretty messed up," I said, sighing before calmly continuing. "I am not going to give you an ultimatum. I do not believe this needs to be your mom versus me. There's no reason you can't have both. I do believe you need to talk to your mom about respecting us as adults, our boundaries, and treating me a little kinder."

"Yeah, I agree about all of that. I will talk to her," Colt said.

I secretly felt like a complete mess. I was so confused over what was going on. I couldn't make sense of how saying no to one day led to an explosion. The difficult conversation I had with Hilda, now followed by a difficult conversation between Colt and Clayton. I couldn't fathom why it had to be like this. Why couldn't they accept or at least respect the choices we were making as new parents? It didn't seem like the rules we had established were too much. We wanted to wait until Talli was six months old before driving four hours in one day, we weren't going to have her out after dark past her bedtime, we weren't going to have her sit in the cold for an extended time. We asked that if anyone wanted to visit, they would come to us and we asked that they not be sick. We asked for them to wash their hands before holding her.

I wondered how it would work if we did drive down to visit them. I have a whole slew of things I need to bring wherever we go. I still breastfeed. There is nothing wrong with how each person chooses to live, but I choose to keep Talli in clean places. Hilda and Clayton have two large dogs and a couple cats that go outside frequently. Every time we went over there, I'd get covered in pet hair and slobber. Their home is an older cabin style filled with objects of various sorts. Based off the clutter and excess items, it seemed like Hilda was somewhat of a hoarder. There were always papers piled high on the kitchen table, things flooding the living room floor and Mackenzi's baby room was like walking into a time machine, but with everything covered in a thick coat of dust. Due to her room being uninhabitable, Mackenzi migrated to Colt's room when he moved out. She had her stuff intermingled with all his stuff from growing up. Whenever we went over there in the past, we usually sat on what was now Mackenzi's bed or squeezed in on the couch. They also had a cow barn out back that they had been working on trying to make into a place to hang out for a decade, so sometimes we would go stand or sit on a metal barstool there.

My dilemma was I couldn't think of any good place where I could perform a diaper change or breastfeed Talli. I remember how uncomfortable I was during both times we had visited them overnight while I was pregnant. Once was in November and another was in February. In November, Hilda made us stay up past midnight so Colt could set up some arcade-style basketball game in the barn and we could then play it. I remember I was completely exhausted and wanted to go to bed. My bag was still in the locked rental car and Colt had the keys so I wasn't able to get my stuff to take my contacts out, change or brush my teeth. I remember saying I was tired and Hilda making a comment about how we never saw them. When I finally did get to lay down on Mackenzi's bed, I couldn't get to sleep because I struggled to breathe from the dust. They also only have one bathroom, so I remember feeling like I was going to pee my pants while waiting for Clayton and then Mackenzi to get out of the shower in the morning. Speaking of the bathroom, it was the only room in the home with a door.

Both times that we did this, I struggled to sleep and breathe. Then we were so busy visiting everyone and hearing all about their parenting opinions. I barely got through it while I was pregnant, so I couldn't imagine all that with a baby. Well, actually, I could imagine it. I imagine it would be a nightmare where I probably would feel trapped and overwhelmed. I would be guilt-tripped into doing things I didn't feel comfortable doing, pleasing everyone in the whole family and uncomfortably trying to breastfeed my baby in the car or in Mackenzi's little room you could see into from the living room. I shook it out of my head.

It was a few minutes before nine at night and I was lying in bed with a sleeping Talli. My phone buzzed. I looked down and read the Facebook message reply from Didi.

It read, "Sorry I haven't gotten back to you sooner. Hope things are going well. Talli's pictures that you share are so adorable! Tentative date for fall party is Sunday, October twenty-third around one. Having to work around homecomings and fall baseball. Fall baseball ended this past weekend. Now the next two weekends are homecomings. Hopefully I'll have a definite answer in a day or two. Hope you guys can come. Take care."

I set my phone back down and focused on my breathing so I could try to fall asleep.

On Monday, two days after our date at the pumpkin patch and the day after Clayton's phone call, Colt drove two hours to his hometown for the funeral of an old high school friend's grandma. He was going to see his family as well. After everything that happened over the weekend, Colt decided he was going to try to talk to his mom to see if he could resolve the issues. I tried to go about my day as normally as I could, but I felt incredibly anxious. I had a strong gut feeling Colt would come home with more upsetting information and we'd most likely fight again. The crazy thing was that being a new mom and taking care of a baby, mostly on my own, was a walk in the park compared to this issue with Colt's family. I was thrust into motherhood with no real chance to embrace it because I was so completely consumed with anxiety over Hilda's behavior. It wasn't just that she was unkind, talking about me behind my back and arguing about everything. It was also the widespread effects of all that. The fighting with Colt because of it, the other family members treating me differently, it felt so enormous, like I was ten feet under water with rocks tied to my ankles.

I remembered I needed to message Didi back.

I typed, "Thank you so much! I hope so, too. Any time you guys would like to come up and see us, we'd love to have you all (smiley face emoji). Take care as well!"

Less than an hour later, I received a reply on Messenger saying, "Date is set. Sunday, October twenty-third at one. Hope you can come. Excited to see little Miss Talli. (smiley face with heart emoji)." I simply double clicked the message to "love" it. There wasn't anything inherently wrong with the conversation. I just felt a smidge annoyed that she kept ignoring my offer for them to come visit us. It was nice of her to invite us to her family party, but it wasn't going to be easy to go down there. I felt determined to try to figure out some way to do it, but also disheartened that it was going to take a lot out of me. I ached for someone to understand I was a new mom and what that might feel like for me. I wanted others to make an effort to meet Talli instead of putting all the responsibility on me.

I called Daisy to try to get out of my head while Colt was still away. I told her about what had been going on and the recent conversation between Clayton and Colt.

"Okay, so do you remember when we came to visit when Talli was born and we wanted to get our own rental car?" Daisy asked.

"Yeah."

"Well, we didn't want to say anything at the time because you just had a baby. We wanted to get our own rental car because of Clayton. He kept complaining and we couldn't take it anymore. The morning when we brought you a smoothie, he bitched the entire time about us getting it. It was maybe five minutes down the road, right, but he kept complaining we were wasting his time. He was saying he didn't think we needed to bring you anything and it was stupid," Daisy admitted.

"Oh my god. That's insane. I had literally just given birth. He is such a piece of crap," I said, shocked.

"Yeah. We all were really angry about it and couldn't even believe it. It's crazy what he said to Colt, though. To let Talli cry? To put you in your place? He's disgusting," Daisy said.

"He really is. I don't think I will be able to look him in the eye ever again. Thank you for listening and talking to me. Thank you for telling me about what he said in Texas, too," I said before hanging up the phone.

Colt called me late that night while he was driving back from the funeral. Talli had been asleep for a couple hours already. I was laying on my stomach in bed with the TV on for background noise.

After about forty minutes of small talk and after he asked me to explain the exact location of a random box in the garage, I said, "So how did talking to your mom go? I'm guessing not well since you have avoided bringing it up."

He got quiet. My anxiety had been bubbling to the surface more and more throughout the day before now exploding out all over me. It covered my body and I felt every cell tingling from the electricity of it.

"I talked to her before the funeral and then again after for a while. She is really upset. She said you are keeping Talli from her, have been rude to her and you never let her visit. She said she's tried to come visit multiple times and you keep saying no. She cried while talking about it," Colt said over the phone.

I felt like my head and the room were spinning against each other. I felt like I couldn't do anything right or even keep up with this woman.

"I tried so hard to be kind and respectful during my call with her. I told her she could come visit any other day. Why is she doing this?" I quietly responded.

"I know. I think she's just really upset. I told her you are trying. I told her she needed to work with you a little," he said.

"Okay, but it doesn't sound to me like that did anything."

"Well, I don't really know what else to do. I told her to work with you and she can come up. It's not that hard. Did she try to come up other days and you said no?" Colt questioned.

"The only other time she called me, again the day of, was in August while you were in Texas for work. I said no because I didn't feel comfortable with her coming over without you there. I told you about that. Then she came over the next week and then again with her mom. So that time in August was the only other time besides the other day that I have said no. Also, I really wish she would give me a few days' notice rather than call on the day of. It makes it so difficult to make it work and it feels really overwhelming," I said, exasperated.

"Okay, that's what I thought. She made it seem like she's called over and over and over again and that you are making things very difficult. I think she was exaggerating a bit," Colt said. He paused before continuing, "There's more. She also said everyone in the family is scared of you. No one knows how to act around you because they think that you're going to freak out. She said you're making things hard for everyone. She argued we should be driving down to them, that she drove far with me when I was a baby. I think she said a lot of the same stuff that she said to you the other day. She said that you act like she's never been around a baby before. She said you were disrespectful to her when she came to Texas and she hasn't gotten over it. She said you treat her horribly."

My breathing stopped entirely for a moment.

"Yeah, I just don't know what to do. That is a lot. I feel like she's making me out to be a villain and it makes me nervous. Should I try to talk to other members of your family to clear the air? I don't want them all to think I am being difficult. I don't want them to think that stuff about me. It isn't true. I don't know why they think I am going to freak out. I really am able to work with anyone. This feels like such a nightmare," I said, gasping for air. "I need to get off the phone. I am feeling really overwhelmed."

I was struggling to breathe. I felt like I couldn't get any air. My head was dizzy and I was sure I was going to pass out. I quickly pressed the end button on Colt's call and then called my mom. She didn't answer so I called my dad. When he answered, I explained to him what had gone on this past weekend.

"Hey, that does sound very weird. It sounds like you tried to schedule another day to visit with Hil and she wasn't working with you. I don't think you are doing anything wrong here. Clayton is an asshole. Don't listen to anything that guy says," my dad said. "I think you need to breathe. It will all be okay. Colt is smart. He'll handle it."

"I wish I could just be done with them and be done with this. It's causing me so much stress. I feel sick every day because of this. I don't feel normal anymore. I can't stop worrying or thinking about this," I cried to my dad.

"Well, you can't do that. She may be difficult, but she's Colt's mom and Talli's grandma, too. I am sorry you don't feel good, but you have to just focus on breathing. Focus on Talli. Try to get some rest," my dad said before we got off the phone.

I felt so alone. I felt like no one could help me and no one understood what I was experiencing. Colt called me back.

"Hey, don't hang up on me," he said.

"I just feel crazy and so overwhelmed. I don't know what to do," I cried.

"You need to calm down. I talked to her and it's handled," he replied sternly.

"It doesn't feel like anything is better. It feels worse. She lied about me, cried about me to you and is still arguing everything! I can't do this. I need to get off the phone. Please just let me go," I sobbed.

"I can't do this, either. Fine. I'll be home soon anyways and we can talk about this then," Colt said before hanging up.

I felt my gut rip open and my heart bleed. My brain sounded millions of alarm bells. It felt like I was self-destructing due to all the misinformation. I leaned back against the headboard. I took a giant deep breath and started typing in my Safari app. I was determined to find some kind of explanation on why this all was happening. After doing some research on difficult in-laws, I clicked on Facebook. I typed in the search bar, "monster-in-law." I came across a slew of support groups. I requested to join the top two. I quickly got accepted by one of them. I opened it and scrolled through some posts. A flash of fear shot through me as I realized I should check who was in the group. After I clicked on the "members" tab, I saw one mutual friend pop up, Jan. I blinked, startled, but shook it off. I wasn't worried about Jan.

"Heck, maybe her and I could even bond over this," I thought.

When Colt got home, we didn't look at each other. He laid down in bed, turned away from me.

"I think I need to go to a therapist. I do not feel normal. I feel so anxious and sick," I said to his back.

"Okay," he said.

"Can we talk for a minute?" I asked, sitting up in bed.

"Yeah," Colt turned toward me.

"It sounds like your mom doesn't want to change or be nicer," I said.

"No, not really," Colt admitted. "She definitely believes you are the problem and she is the victim."

"Okay, well I'm not sure how much I want to be around them until I can figure out how to handle this or they can be kinder," I said.

"Okay," Colt said. "I really need to get to sleep. I have to leave tomorrow to go back to work, remember?"

"Yeah, I'm sorry. Good night," I said.

He turned back around and went to sleep. I stared at the wall until my eyes eventually closed with exhaustion.

13

Chapter Thirteen

I started therapy the week that Colt got back home from Texas. I did some research and decided to try BetterHelp since it wouldn't require me to leave the house. It is an app that would connect me with a licensed therapist and facilitate all our communication. I would have one virtual meeting per week and I could text with my therapist through it as well. It sounded like the best situation for me. I didn't want to drive anywhere far or leave Talli. It also was quicker to start and I needed help now.

On Thursday at eight-thirty in the evening, two days before my first therapy session, Hilda called Colt to ask him if we would drive to their hometown for the high school football game at seven the next night. After he got off the phone with her, Colt turned to me.

"I am sure you don't want to, but my mom wants us to go to the game tomorrow night," he said.

"It's not that I don't want to, it's that it's a bad idea with a five-month-old baby. It's a long drive, it's cold and it's late at night. Plus, she isn't listening to what we said about wanting to wait until Talli is six months old to be driving over two hours in a day with her," I said, sighing.

"Yeah, I agree," Colt said.

"You can go, though."

"I'd rather not go by myself again," he said.

"Why not? Your family will be there. You won't be by yourself."

"I don't know. I'd go if Paul went with me, but I doubt he would. If he went, it would make the drive better and I wouldn't have to deal with my family as much," Colt thought out loud.

"Why don't you ask him then?"

"Yeah, I can. I don't think he will go, though. His wife probably won't let him," Colt said as he got off the couch to go into the bedroom and call Paul.

When he returned, he told me Paul said he wasn't able to go.

"So, I'm not going," Colt said with a laugh.

"Okay, that is your choice. Whatever you want to do," I said, with an uneasy feeling in my gut that told me this would come back as my fault.

My first therapy session was an introduction, discussing how therapy goes and getting started by answering a bunch of questions. Over the video chat with my new therapist, Faye, I explained what I had been experiencing with my in-laws and how it was making me feel.

"Would you consider yourself someone who tends to prioritize the feelings of others over your own?" Faye asked me softly.

"Yeah, I think I am a people pleaser," I responded, thinking about the hundreds of times I've put others first when it ended up hurting me in some way.

"We can work on that. I also want to talk to you about boundaries. They are not a way of keeping others out, but keeping them in while protecting ourselves. I think it is important for you and your husband to discuss what exactly your boundaries are. It sounds like you are already doing this in a way with the boundary of waiting until your baby is six months old to go for longer drives. Once you know what your boundaries are, then you both can work on establishing them with Hilda," she explained. "I am going to send you an article and worksheet about boundaries that also goes over how to respectfully implement them."

I agreed, feeling good that I was doing something to help myself and the situation I was faced with.

Hilda called Colt again the next week, asking for us to come visit for a long weekend. Talli and I were reading books in her room while Colt talked to his mom on the other side of the house. Once his conversation ended, he stood in the doorway looking down at us. Colt relayed to me that she offered for us to stay in their barn for three days so that we could attend various events for that long weekend. She again wanted us to attend a Friday night football game. On Saturday, she said we should go to a surprise birthday party at a campground for Colt's old best friend from high school. Lastly, we were expected to finish the weekend on Sunday with the fall family party at Didi's house.

"Colt, you can go do all that, but that is way too much for Talli. Talli is not sleeping on the floor of a barn. Talli is not going to be out late at night in thirty-degree weather at a football game. Our baby is not going to a party at night at a campground where people will be drinking. I'm not leaving her to be watched by anyone, either. I wanted to try to make that family party work, but I just really want to hold onto my boundary that Talli is not to be in the car for longer than two hours in one day until she is older than six months. Also, I tried reaching out to Didi to talk to her about her party and ask if she and Gerald would come to our home to visit us. I thought I would do that since she has been commenting on my Facebook updates about meeting Talli. I asked twice and she ignored both. I really feel if anyone wants to see us or Talli, they can come here. We drove halfway across the country to move back, the least they can do is drive the four hours total for their own wishes to be granted," I said.

"I don't disagree with you. I agree they should come here. I've said the same thing. But, when it comes to the barn, it is insulated now. We would sleep on an air mattress," Colt offered, moving over to us and sitting down.

"I don't want to sleep on an air mattress in a barn in late October. With a baby. I think everyone is forgetting we have a baby. This would all be fine and dandy if it was just us. We have suffered through similar things to appease others, but I am not doing it to Talli. She can sleep at home in our own bed where everything is the right temperature and comfortable for her," I stated firmly.

"Yeah, you're right. I'm trying to make things work, but everyone is making it really hard," Colt sighed.

"I am not trying to make anything hard. I am sorry for making you feel that way. I am trying to work with you as much as possible, but I am also a new mom putting her baby first. Also, I don't feel very comfortable with your mom or family after everything that was said."

"I get that. I'm not saying you're making things hard. I feel like my mom is really pushing us to do things that we have explained we are not going to do with Talli being so little. Everyone in the family keeps pushing us and won't listen," Colt said, shaking his head. "It's frustrating."

He pushed himself back up to stand.

"I guess I should call her back and get this over with," Colt said, groaning and rolling his eyes. He turned to leave, closing the door behind him.

When he came back in the room he breathed out as he sat down.

"Well, that went great," he said sarcastically.

"What happened?" I asked.

"She just kept arguing. She said Mackenzi wants us to watch her cheer at the game. That she could watch Talli so we could go to the party on Saturday night. That the barn has a heater and we would have it to ourselves. She insisted everyone will be upset if we don't attend the party and that they want to see us. How everyone wants to meet Talli. On and on," he said, rolling his eyes.

My heart was racing more than usual. My heart had never really gotten a chance to settle since this drama with Colt's family began. I put my hand over it to try to calm it.

"Colt, you should go. I don't want your mom upset and things getting worse. I am not budging on my boundaries with Talli, but you can go. They will be happy to see you and you can do all those things."

"I don't want to go without you guys. It wouldn't be fun. I don't even want to do any of that stuff anyway. I'd rather sleep in our nice bed in our nice home that I pay for," he sighed.

It had gotten late while we were discussing what we were to do about this request from his mom. We both were exhausted and decided to go to bed.

I couldn't sleep. I pulled out my phone. I had been doing an extensive amount of Google research. Tonight, I searched, "How to deal with a difficult mother-in-law," which took me down different paths. I read about how I can work on myself so that I can better handle situations. I also read articles about toxic in-laws. It didn't take long for the word narcissist to appear. I wasn't really sure what a narcissist was by definition. I knew it was someone self-absorbed, but that was really all I knew. As I read a story about a narcissistic grandmother, things began clicking and making sense.

I learned that a narcissist is someone with an excessive need for validation from others. They are sensitive to criticism, arrogant and feel entitled. When narcissists become upset, they usually react, are defensive and may even become abusive to others. As I read, I felt like SpongeBob when he and Patrick finally feasted their eyes on Mr. Krabs's treasure map, the moment their eyes shot back into their heads and turned black as they stood silent in realization. My mouth hung open as I continued to read more about narcissists.

This was totally my mother-in-law. The various articles talked about the signs of a narcissist, most of which I saw in Hilda. She definitely thought she was important; you could see it when she spoke as if she were a celebrity. She certainly felt entitled to be treated special and she acted as if she were superior to others. It wasn't just me. I could tell by how she treated waitresses and other people out in the world. I read about how a sign can be exploiting others for personal gain or selfish reasons and thought about how she was treating me. I surely felt exploited. All she wanted was to feel important and special. She never seemed to be interested in my baby because of my baby, I thought. It appeared as if my child made her feel more accomplished or important. It made me feel sick. Another huge sign that resonated with me was lacking empathy and being unwilling to understand other people's needs. She never seemed to care about other people's feelings, not just mine. She was unwilling to understand my perspective when it came to needing some space and basic boundaries.

Playing the victim, yes. Passive aggressive, yes. Guilt trips? Ever since I've known her. Everything kept pointing to Hilda either having narcissistic personality disorder or at least having narcissistic tendencies. I read on. I learned that they try to find ways to make themselves the center of attention. This added up. She very rarely asked me questions about myself unless she was trying to pry.

Even when I first met her, she didn't seem interested in getting to know me. I remember the way I started to connect with her was by asking her questions about herself. We were sitting in the gym at one of Colt's cousins' high school basketball games. Her voice was extra scratchy and hard to hear. She said she had been cheering too loudly at a high school game the night before. She was focused intently on the game. I can't remember everything I asked her, but something I asked led to her telling me a story about a trip she took in high school. She told me how she went to Mexico for a school trip and went off to hang out with local boys for the majority of the time. It was basically the plotline of the Lizzie McGuire movie. She had a wistful, dreamy look on her face while she spoke, still just staring straight ahead at the game. She smirked with pride when she told me she wrote her teacher a letter in perfect Spanish to get out of trouble when they had gotten caught sneaking out. Even though her story was long and elaborate, she never once felt uncomfortable taking up so much time speaking. It was the first time I saw her actually open up. Before that moment, she had been very quiet and cold around me. I thought back on this memory and wished I knew then what I know now.

I had minored in psychology in college, so I had a very basic understanding of psychological terms and how to use them. There was so much I didn't know, but I did know you aren't supposed to self-diagnose people when you're not licensed. The troubling thing about narcissists is that such a small percentage of them have actually been professionally diagnosed. They usually go undetected, causing chaos in the lives of others and carrying on with their own lives undisturbed. I wasn't sure if I should say something to Colt about my suspicions. I wanted to talk to him about it because he grew up with her and he may have better insight.

A few nights later, while we were playing with Talli, Hilda called Colt. As usual, he went into another room to talk to her. A half-hour later, he came back into Talli's room, stressed.

"Are you okay?" I asked Colt, who laid on the floor, knees bent toward the sky and his hands covering his face.

"Yeah. It's just every time my mom calls, it is always something. We aren't doing something right or enough. She's always complaining. I'm getting tired of hearing her complain about you and saying you're keeping our baby from them," Colt said, sighing.

I felt electric bolts attack my heart. It made me feel like a caged animal being poked at whenever I heard Hilda was complaining to my husband about me behind my back.

"Colt, can I ask you something? I have been doing a lot of reading lately."

"What do you want to ask?"

"Do you think your mom is a narcissist?" I asked.

Colt removed his hands from his face and looked over at me. "What makes someone a narcissist?"

I pulled up the last article I had read and handed him my phone. He scrolled and read.

"That does sound like my mom."

14

Chapter Fourteen

"I have to say, I was really starting to get confused around this point. I was searching for answers on why this was happening. It didn't make any sense to me. I wondered what my mother-in-law was gaining or trying to gain. Doing research on Google was helpful for me. The Facebook groups were helpful. Her being a narcissist made sense. I just feel like normal people don't do this, right? Normal people don't try to cause issues, argue and make things difficult for someone else, right? Who would do that to a new, young mom?" I looked at my specialist across from me.

She was listening intently and compassionately. Her office was calming. I sat in a giant cushy armchair wrapped in a throw blanket I had brought with me.

"Healthy people don't do those things. Your mother-in-law doesn't sound as though she is healthy. Based on everything you've told me so far it sounds like she has many characteristics of a narcissist. I also wouldn't say anything you've told me you've experienced has been normal. It's not how a family member with an infant should expect to be treated. It sounds like these issues with your in-laws had an effect on the relationship between you and Colt as well, right?" my specialist asked me.

"Yes. I was starting to feel like I couldn't trust him. I was starting to feel resentful. I should have communicated with him more about what I was experiencing, although what I was experiencing felt hard to put into words. Like I said, it didn't make sense. I do think when I communicated with him more about what I was going through, it did help us. He wasn't trying to hurt me. He was just stuck feeling unsure what to do. I mean, his mom is incredibly manipulative. He grew up with that. I told him I wouldn't make him choose, but I felt by him not putting his foot down for me, he was choosing them," I sighed. It was still tough to talk about.

"I am sure he was really struggling, too. That is not an easy position to be in. Although, I will say, as your husband he should have stood up for you immediately. I can understand your budding resentment and lack of trust," my specialist said, pausing to clear her throat. "Adison, you also said you tried reaching out to other family members of Colt's. That was never your weight or responsibility to carry. I think it was brave and thoughtful of you, but you didn't need to hold that burden. They could have communicated with you. Colt could have communicated with them. At the end of the day, you were still recovering from having a baby and now taking care of that baby. Anyone who put you down or treated you poorly for not reaching out to them is not healthy. Communication goes both ways. If anyone had an issue, wanted to meet your child or wanted to hear about your life, they should have called or texted you. It is never your responsibility to read others' minds."

"Thank you for saying that. I did feel very guilty at the time. I felt like I wasn't doing enough. Yet it never felt like I was doing enough," I pulled my blanket up higher, cuddling it in front of my chest.

"It is a losing battle trying to please a narcissist," my specialist said, giving me a soft smile.

"No kidding. Also, it made me feel uncomfortable that Hilda kept mentioning everyone in the family was scared of me. I wasn't sure what she was telling them that made them afraid of me," I sucked in a breath of air. "I should explain a little more. So, Colt has a large family of grandparents, aunts, uncles, cousins and a sister. He has his dad's side, his mom's side and his step dad's side. I think I've mentioned it, but they all started treating me differently after his mom came to Texas when Talli was born. I used to get a couple birthday cards, I got none, and half of them didn't even say happy birthday at all. A lot of them stopped liking stuff I shared on Facebook. I don't post much. It is always just occasional pictures of Talli or our family. Colt's grandma, Cynthia, was super odd toward me when she came over and again when we FaceTime called her on her birthday in September. I think I forgot to mention that. She was criticizing my parenting and then talking about how Colt is such a great dad. Both times, she kept giving me looks out of the corner of her eyes. Colt's sister, Mackenzi, and I used to talk a lot. We were Snapchatting every day. We don't at all anymore, but at the time, she had started sending me pictures of the ceiling to keep the Snapchat streak. There was no conversation. Hilda was posting old pictures of their family on Facebook and used specific ones that I was not included in. At the time, she had done that for Colt's birthday, his grandma's birthday, son's day and daughter's day. It seemed very intentional. I know it's all really stupid stuff and stupid to even notice. I've typically been good about picking up on vibes and sly, hidden messages. Do I sound crazy?" I finally breathed out.

"You don't sound crazy. That sounds like they were subtly trying to hurt you," my specialist said.

"Yeah. At the time, after being treated so weird for the past five months, I had started to check out of caring about their opinions. I was really hurt after my birthday. I felt like I was cast out. At the end of October, I just wanted to stay distanced as much as possible. My head was jumbled since it was Colt's family, but I strongly felt like I needed to protect myself from them," I sighed. "Sometimes I feel crazier now than I did back then."

15

Chapter Fifteen

It was November. The air outside had turned even brisker, the clouds hardening into their winter gray. The trees towered high, leafless, like menacing skeletons. The moody scenery matched how I felt inside. I had been in therapy for a month and was about to cancel the renewal. It was expensive and I felt guilty. We had more important debts to pay off. Therapy was helping me greatly though. It was like having someone next to me while I drowned, someone else who was trying to help me untie the weights around my ankles that were pulling me down. Faye was helping me break free of pleasing people and building my confidence. She was teaching me to establish boundaries and how to handle difficult people. Half of me didn't want to cancel, but the other half felt like I'd gotten what I needed out of it. Also, I secretly hated always complaining to someone and felt kind of strange paying someone to listen to me and care about my life. I was starting to feel like I was getting more control over my feelings and thoughts. I felt like I could handle the situation better. So, when my month was up, I said thank you and goodbye to Faye. Of course, I also hadn't put into perspective the fact that during my therapy, I hadn't had to endure any in-person visits.

I had been struggling to sleep more than usual, which was really bad because I hadn't been sleeping well since Talli was born. At night,

I would often get on my phone to read information on the usual topics like narcissists and difficult in-laws. One night, I felt especially uneasy and anxious. I felt like I was going to explode, like I needed to get out what I had been through. I opened up my Notes app and furiously started typing a bullet-point list of everything that had happened since Hilda had come to the hospital in Texas. Deep in my bones, I felt it was important to keep track of what she had been doing and what she would do next. I was feeling dazed and confused. I didn't want to forget. I was growing increasingly concerned that something really bad was going to happen. I felt like I needed to take every step necessary to protect myself from whatever it might be.

I occasionally checked on the members in the two monster-in-law support groups I had joined on Facebook. I wanted to make sure no one I knew was in there. When I checked one day, I noticed Jan was no longer in the group. I furrowed my brow, but then released it from my mind. It seemed odd, but I had bigger issues to worry about.

Colt had recently gone to a football game to watch his sister cheer. We didn't talk much about it. He had simply told me that various family members had asked where our baby was.

"In our warm house in bed," I thought, irritated when he had told me.

Half of me felt glad he'd gone so his family could calm down a little bit, but the other half of me felt annoyed. I didn't feel like he should be breaking his back for people who were making our lives so much more complicated than they needed to be.

Hilda was calling Colt almost every day while he was home. He would go into another room to talk to her. One warmer afternoon, I was walking around with Talli in our yard when Colt opened the back door and yelled out to me.

"Adison, please come inside. My mom wants to FaceTime with Talli," he shouted.

I took large inhales and exhales as I slowly made my way back to the house with my baby in my arms.

"Come on, please hurry," Colt called out.

I picked up my pace ever so slightly. Colt took Talli out of my arms when we reached the back door. I went into the kitchen to wash the dishes that had piled up in the sink. Colt and Talli sat on the couch in front of me while he FaceTimed with his mom. I could hear Hilda saying hi in a baby voice and making strange noises at Talli. I vigorously scrubbed the soapy brush against a metal pan.

"Okay, I'm done. She doesn't know me," Hilda scoffed, putting an end to her baby voice.

I looked up at where Colt sat and raised my eyebrows in warning. He glanced at me then quickly looked back at the phone he was holding out in front of our baby. Talli was six months old. She didn't know anyone besides me and Colt.

"What is Talli doing now?" Hilda asked Colt.

As Colt began to tell her, I dropped the brush in the sink and went into the bathroom off our bedroom at the far end of the house. I turned on the faucet and splashed cold water over my face. I couldn't stomach listening to Hilda's voice. Hearing it made me want to vomit. Even hearing her name or simply seeing it flash across the phone screen made me feel sick. It felt like some kind of a trauma response. It didn't feel normal, but I didn't quite know how to explain it.

In the middle of November, Hilda called Colt to schedule a visit in two days. I had just gotten out of the shower when Colt came into the bathroom holding Talli.

"Hey, at least she listened and gave you a couple days' notice," Colt said to me after first telling me they were coming over on Friday.

"Yeah, I guess so," I said. I felt like it wasn't that big of an achievement. "It just sucks that it is on a day that we had plans."

I had met a kind woman online who I planned to meet at a coffee shop. At the time, I enjoyed meeting new people, hearing their stories and simply getting out. Colt wasn't super excited, but he didn't want me to go alone with Talli.

"So, they are coming over after we get home, I assume?" I asked Colt as I brushed my wet hair.

"Well, they thought they could come over early in the morning and play with Talli while you got ready. While we are gone, they would go to lunch and come back when we get back," Colt said.

I instantly stopped brushing and turned around to look at him.

"Are you serious," I said, defeated. "Why is it always something? Why can't they just come for a couple hours and leave? Why does it always have to be some elaborate thing?"

I shrunk down to my knees with my towel wrapped around me. God, this felt overwhelming. My heart was beating fast and I couldn't stop the tears that started to fall from my eyes. I couldn't catch a damn break, or at least not one that lasted long enough to fix anything. I hated saying no. I didn't want to be an asshole, but that request was too much for me. I didn't feel like I could do it without it breaking down my sanity even more. I needed Hilda to be normal and visit for a few hours only. I needed a couple visits to go well before we did anything more elaborate or long or complicated.

"Colt, I can't do it. I am trying so hard. Things are not normal for me and they are not normal between your mom and me. After everything that has happened to this point, I can't do it. I have not had enough time to get over all of it and there hasn't been any real change. She hasn't apologized or said anything nice. The last time I talked to her was that phone call I had and she wasn't kind to me. Then she talked about me to you and to everyone else in your family, I'm sure. I need her to come for a couple hours after we get home. I need things to slowly progress so we can get to a better place," I explained to Colt, exasperated and overwhelmed with anxiety.

"It won't be that bad. They will play with Talli while you get ready so you won't really have to see them during that, then they will get lunch, we'll do our thing and then visit again when we get back. It'll be okay," Colt explained calmly.

"It will take me five minutes to get ready. I am not doing anything special. I'm probably just going to wear a sweater and put my hair in a loose, low bun. Maybe put on mascara. Plus, they can't play with Talli because she just lays there. I am also nervous because they don't care about illnesses. Mackenzi is in high school around a bunch of other kids. She has her cheer and dance practices, plus they all go out to do whatever else. I have been so careful. I don't go anywhere. I am trying to keep Talli from getting RSV, COVID-19 and the flu, all of which are really bad this year. The pediatrician just said you can't be overly cautious. Hilda complained about washing her hands and also wouldn't give Talli back to me the last time she was here. She doesn't listen to or respect my boundaries. Also, I'd like to be able to relax in the morning. No, they can come over when we get home," I said, shaking my head in an attempt to lessen my anxiety.

I needed to remain calm and firm. I wondered whether I was being ridiculous, but I also felt so much more at ease staying true to what my heart felt was right. I felt strongly that I was making the right decision by holding onto my boundaries and needing to slowly work on building back trust with Hilda. I didn't want to give in to her and have that result in me being more resentful and uncomfortable with her. I didn't want her to continue overreaching and making more demands. I wanted to draw a clear line in the sand so she would start being more reasonable.

"Okay. What time should I tell them to come then?" Colt asked me, annoyed.

"Just tell them two. We will make sure we are back by then," I said, trying to work with him. "That gives them plenty of time to visit. I'm sure they will stay late anyway."

"Okay. This isn't going to go well, I already know," Colt groaned.

"That is honestly annoying and frustrating. It should not be this difficult. It isn't like we aren't letting them visit. I am trying to work with them, but it is not easy. The requests are always more than I feel comfortable with. In the past, I have let it happen, but for my own sanity I just can't do it anymore. They need to meet me where I'm at and we can go from there," I said, frustrated.

I finally gathered back the energy to get dressed and continue my day.

"I get it," Colt said, sighing and rolling his eyes.

On the day of Hilda's scheduled visit, I woke up with intense anxiety. I tried to push it down. I had been having very vivid, intense nightmares for the past couple months so I always woke up feeling pretty negative. I'd always immediately look over at Talli and breathe. I'd let the warm feeling of love and gratefulness for her existence wash over me. We got through the quiet morning, drove a half-hour north to meet the young lady for coffee and then drove home.

I was lying in bed feeding Talli when Hilda pulled up our driveway shortly after two. I stayed in bed as I heard them come inside and go into the living room. Once Talli was done eating, which was only a couple minutes after they arrived, I quickly grabbed a peppermint to hopefully aid in easing my anxiety and walked out. I felt electrified with nerves. I felt like an alien in my own home. I felt unwelcome and uneasy. I saw them sitting on the couch and headed toward them.

"Hi," I was able to spit out.

They ignored me, looking past me at Talli in my arms.

"Hi Talli!" Hilda and Mackenzi waved and cooed at her.

I sat down on the couch next to Colt. I stared straight ahead at the television, which was playing *King of the Hill*. I had tuned out the conversation they were having amongst themselves, trying to gather myself, when Hilda turned toward me.

"So, Adison," she sneered. "What are you doing next Friday? I know Colt will be in Texas, but we figured we would stop by on our way back from visiting Bowling Green to see Talli."

"Oh, well, I think I am busy. Yeah, next Friday is the Candlelight Walk," I stuttered, my brain not keeping up with what was going on.

"What is that? We would come at like six or seven in the evening so we could come around that," Hilda said, glaring at me.

"It's a tradition in Medina where there are candles all around the square and they have other stuff going on. Yeah, I just think I will probably be at my mom's place. I don't think that day will work out," I said, trying to stay assertive and not let her push me into submission.

"Sounds fun. We could go to that," Hilda said, staring at me coldly.

"Yeah, maybe," I said, wanting this conversation to be over.

I was most likely not going to the Candlelight Walk due to it being in the evening and so cold outside, but it was the first excuse I could come up with and it was something I had wanted to do. I would meet them there, but I also didn't want that experience to be tainted for me. If I went, I wanted to go with my family and actually enjoy my time. Just based on how this visit was already going, I didn't think being with Hilda without Colt present would be a good time.

Hilda started coughing deeply and violently. She sat there hacking up a lung until she said, "Excuse me," and went into the bathroom. I heard her loudly blowing her nose and then her cough resumed.

"Can I get a glass of water?" she asked with an attitude as she stepped out of the bathroom.

"Sorry that I don't feel like being a considerate host today," I thought.

She's Colt's mother, he can host her. He can get her water. After her behavior toward me already, I didn't feel like going out of my way for her. I let her attitude and disgust wash off me as I released myself of the need to cater to her. I also felt uncomfortable with the deepness and violent manner in which she was coughing. It sounded congested and like she was sick. Colt got up off the couch and grabbed one of his plastic Dallas Cowboys cups, filling it with water before handing it to her.

"Oh my gosh, these cups. That was such a fun time! Remember how we were all grabbing all these cups. We were running around like, 'There's one,' and 'Grab that one.' That was such a fun trip. I miss that," Hilda said, laughing obnoxiously, her eyes gleaming as she loudly spoke about it.

She looked over at me out of the corner of her eye with a smug look. The trip she was speaking of was before Colt and I met. Hilda, Mackenzi and Colt went to a Cowboys game with Colt's ex-girlfriend from college. It was the same ex that would not leave us alone for months, Gina. She had gone to our college also, which was where I met Colt. They had been dating when we first met. I was also in an unhappy relationship at that time. Colt and I felt the craziest connection when we met and agreed to respectfully get out of the unhappy, dead relationships we had felt stuck in. That is a story for another time, but once Colt and I were finally dating each other, Gina went nuts. She still hadn't let go a half-year later when Colt asked me to marry him.

Gina's brother commented on Colt's picture of our engagement by saying, "Is this the homewrecker that you cheated on my sister with? Congrats bro."

She then took a screenshot of the picture of Colt and I with her brother's comment below and posted it on Twitter. Her and her friends laughed, called me a whore, said they might come ruin our wedding and talked about how they bet Colt would soon cheat on me. They did this all very publicly, where anyone could see it. Daisy stood up for me as did a couple other random people. The fact Hilda was bringing up this girl in my kitchen while I sat there holding Colt and I's baby was insane. Hilda brought her up often enough throughout the years, even after Colt asked her to stop. While I was pregnant, she brought up both his exes a couple times and Colt told her *again* that it made me uncomfortable. It was obvious now that she was doing it specifically to do just that.

I ignored her and acted as if she had not spoken. Colt uncomfortably stared at the floor, trying not to make eye contact with anyone.

"Seriously, that was a great time. Good memories," she said, looking directly at me. "I am surprised you still have these cups. That's sweet."

Everyone had moved to the kitchen, where Hilda was opening a box of Crumbl Cookies. I took the opportunity to grab the remote and change the channel. I was so uncomfortable and needed a distraction. *King of the Hill* was making this worse because it was garbage in my opinion, just like this experience. I turned on *The Office*, because I needed a subtle, lighthearted distraction.

"Ugh, *The Office*. I never thought this show was funny," Hilda groaned, rolling her eyes.

She had been opening our kitchen drawers to locate a knife that she finally found and was now using it to cut the sugar-filled cookies into halves.

"Adison, do you want to try one of these?" she asked, waving the knife in the air.

"No, thank you," I said, smiling politely but not warmly.

"Are you sure? They are great. It's a new cookie shop. I cut them in halves. Which one would you like to try? We got all the flavors of the day. You can pick from sugar cookie, chocolate chip, Oreo, butter pecan, Animal Cracker, mint and strawberry flavor," she pushed.

"I've tried them before. They are a little too sugary for me, but I appreciate the offer," I said firmly as I held Talli and rocked her side to side.

I had stood up, positioned awkwardly between the kitchen and the living room. I had my back to the wall so that I was able to see everyone in the kitchen and also the TV on the wall. I was trying really hard to be as polite as possible. I was trying to be present and for them to be able to see Talli in my arms.

Her mouth set into a straight line. She sat down on one of our black wooden barstools at the island in the kitchen so that her back was facing me.

"Ugh. This chair is so uncomfortable," Hilda complained, her face sour as she twisted around.

She got up and went into the dining room area off the kitchen. She sat in one of the chairs at our kitchen table. The dining room was off to the side, so I wasn't able to see her anymore. I was fine with it, but I figured I'd later be called rude behind my back for staying where I was. I moved behind the couch so I was visible, but far enough away. Colt and Mackenzi followed Hilda and sat at the kitchen table with her. They all sat in silence for a couple minutes.

"Colt, you don't see your friends enough. You should be prioritizing seeing your friends more," Hilda said firmly as she turned to Colt.

"I try to. They are busy, I am busy. I do want to see them more," Colt said back to her.

"Yeah, well, friends are important. You need to spend time with them. You need to make an effort and go out of your way to see them. You should be doing that more. You don't want to lose your friends," she said again while glaring at me discreetly.

I turned away, focusing on Michael Scott and Dwight on the television.

My brain sucked back into reality when Colt was telling his mom we had Talli's six-month pediatrician visit yesterday.

"Yeah, so her leg is a little sore from the vaccine and that's why she is tired today," Colt explained to his mom.

"Well, if someone would've given her some Tylenol before you went, maybe she wouldn't be feeling bad today," Hilda criticized.

I ignored the slight. It made me a little mad because of how dumb it was. Why would I give my six-month-old baby medicine if I didn't have to? I shook off the stupidity of the comment.

"We want to see her try to crawl," Hilda said to Colt.

"Today isn't the day for that. Her leg is sore and she cries if she accidentally rolls onto it," Colt said again, protecting me from having to respond. I appreciated that.

"Well, you know, you should be forcing her on her stomach and that leg. You need to toughen her up," Hilda chided.

I had to turn my face out of sight so I could roll my jaw to stop myself from responding. That was crazy. I counted my inhales and exhales. I focused on *The Office* for the next half-hour so I could try to make time pass a little quicker. I hadn't spoken much at all during their visit. I really hadn't had a chance to even if I had wanted to. Everything was so uncomfortable and aggressive. After Hilda brought up Colt's ex and the comments about what we should be doing with Talli, I was done. I was over this. I didn't care to talk or acknowledge her any longer.

"Mackenzi, you should be friends with those girls, even if you don't like them," Hilda said, raising her voice so much that it broke into my headspace.

"Why? They are annoying," Mackenzi said with her iPhone in front of her face.

"Well, if you are friends with them, they will invite you to their parties. You can go to the parties and then meet more boys that way. The best way to get to the boys is by having a lot of girlfriends," Hilda said smirking and raising her eyebrow as if she had spilled a secret from the Holy Grail.

I had a hard time not showing the disgust and disbelief on my face. Hilda had said a lot of things that have paused me in my tracks, but to recommend to her daughter that she fake friendships to get to boys?

"So strange," I thought.

Talli had fallen asleep on my shoulder and I was really uncomfortable standing there while Mackenzi and Hilda argued. I pulled out my phone and texted my dad.

"Mackenzi and Hilda are yelling so loud at each other about something dumb and Talli is sleeping. I'm trying so hard not to go into our room," my text to my dad read.

My dad texted back, "It's okay to go to your room."

"You think so? I'm just worried she'll have more ammo against me if I go lay down," I replied, my thumbs racing across the screen.

Hilda's coughing interrupted my thoughts and I looked up from my phone at the TV for a minute.

"Say Talli needs a nap," his text came quickly through.

"Up to you," came another.

"Talli is already asleep on me. I mean I guess I really don't care what any of them think of me anymore, but just trying to be nice and sit out here," I texted.

My dad responded, "Okay. Whatever feels right."

I put my phone back into my pocket.

"I think I am going to head out soon," Colt said, repeating himself for the second time. "So, I'll just be following you guys down."

"Oh, you're coming to our house?" Hilda trilled, giddy. "Good, I'm glad."

"Yeah, Paul and Jackson are meeting me there and we are going to hunt this weekend," Colt said. "I'm ready to go anytime. Like I said, I'll be following you guys down."

It took another half-hour for Colt to finally get his mom and sister out of the door.

"Bye, Adison," Hilda said, dead and point blank, not bothering to look at me.

"Bye, Hilda," I said back as normally as I could muster.

Colt walked them out to their car. When he came back in, he was throwing clothes into a duffle bag. I was so glad they were gone, but I again felt like I was coming off a huge adrenaline rush. I was shaky, exhausted, overwhelmed, emotional and unsettled in my stomach.

"Are you sure it's okay that I leave for the weekend?" Colt asked as he finished packing.

"Yeah, you should go and have fun with your friends," I said, internally wishing he would stay.

I did want him to go have fun and see his friends, but I felt alone so often. He was out of the state for a full week every third week already. One of the other two weeks was spent busy working in his home office. With travel days, we had five days to really spend time together. Usually we were busy running errands, getting something done with the house or trying to arrange visits with people. I also felt very nervous with him going down to his parents for the weekend because

I was sure there would be more talk about me. Every time he was around them or got off the phone with them, we usually ended up in a fight. Colt gathered his stuff into his truck, gave Talli and me each a kiss and then answered his ringing phone.

"Yeah, I am leaving now. I am on the way," Colt laughed into the phone.

"Paul," Colt mouthed to me.

"Okay. Yes," Colt laughed into the phone, turning to wave goodbye before quickly leaving.

Talli and I were alone. It was quiet and dark, so I slowly started working on cleaning. I had to wipe everything down after how much Hilda had been coughing. It was four-thirty in the afternoon when I texted my dad, "Everyone just left."

I typed more, saying, "I have to clean because Hilda was hacking up a lung the entire time she was here."

My dad texted back, "Okay. Deep breaths."

Two hours later, after I had cried my stress out, my dad texted me, "How are you now?"

"I'm a lot better now. Had to come off the adrenaline or whatever. Took a little bit but I ate something and I'm laying with Talli watching a movie. Thanks for asking." I typed and sent.

"Good job. I knew you could do it. I'm very proud of you," my dad's reply read.

I replied, "Thank you, I love you!"

For the rest of the weekend, I tried to keep myself busy. I went to lunch in town with my dad, had my grandparents over to visit and visited my mom. Colt didn't text or call me much, which I wasn't surprised about. Colt arrived back home Sunday afternoon. He was quiet as he unpacked, showered and went into the living room to relax.

"How was it?" I asked, sitting next to him on the couch with Talli in my arms, as usual.

"Good. We didn't see anything," he said, referring to not seeing any deer. "You guys could've come."

"Sleep in the barn and sit in the cold with a baby? No," I said, annoyed. I was so tired of repeating myself about this kind of thing.

"Yeah, I didn't really sleep much. It was uncomfortable and hurt my back," Colt said.

"Was there talk about me again?" I asked, just wanting to know already.

Colt sighed. He paused and then said, "Yeah."

"Okay. What was said?" I asked.

"Clayton kept complaining about you to us. I couldn't get him to shut up. My mom just sat there. Paul and Jackson asked some questions. They thought it was weird. My parents kept talking about how you have been rude to them and you don't trust them. They said you are difficult, don't share Talli and you don't listen to anyone," Colt said. "My mom chimed in a couple times, but also would tell Clayton to be quiet. Every time he was around, he was talking about you. He kept telling me to put you in your place."

"Why didn't you defend me?" I asked, hurt.

"I tried. I said at least you aren't on drugs. I tried to explain that it could be worse," Colt argued.

"That doesn't make me feel good. You had to say at least I'm not on drugs? That's what you think? I'm a new mom. I'm trying to do my best for Talli, still struggling with not feeling normal, my body still isn't normal from giving birth, and that is what is being said?" I said, my voice shaky and getting louder.

I was so frustrated, hurt and disgusted. I got up from the couch and turned to go into the bedroom with Talli.

"Where are you going?" Colt yelled after me.

"To lay down," I said as I walked away.

"Get back in here. We weren't done talking. I am so tired of you getting up and leaving in the middle of a conversation. You need to stop doing that," Colt shouted, angry.

"You're my husband. You are supposed to protect me and stand up for me. I get that these people are your parents, but what they are saying is not okay. The way they are acting is not okay. I am tired of feeling so alone in this. I am honestly disgusted that you said at least I am not on drugs," I shouted back.

I looked at Talli asleep in my arms and felt a strong pang of guilt. I took a breath and lowered my voice.

"I don't want to fight with you. I am just really hurt that you said that."

"What do you want me to say? What do you want me to do in that situation? I just want to get through it so I can hang out with my friends," Colt said loudly, still angry.

"I want you to figure it out. I don't want to have to tell you what you should do. It is your choice. What would be nice is if you would tell them to stop saying unkind things about me and stop talking about me behind my back," I said calmly.

"Well, they don't stop. Then what?" Colt pressed.

"Then you should tell them if they don't stop you are leaving then follow through with that. You shouldn't be sitting in a room where people are talking poorly about your wife," I said to Colt.

"I just wanted to hang out with my friends. I never get to do that anymore," Colt complained.

"And I do?" I asked, getting annoyed again. "I haven't seen any of my friends since we came up here for our baby shower. I am not upset about it because I am busy, they are busy. It is just how it goes when you grow up and live further away."

I felt like whenever he was around his family for too long, he always adopted whatever beliefs they held. It was like they would hammer their opinions into his porous head and he would come back a zombie spewing their words.

"I guess. Well, I'm sorry. I didn't know what to do. Next time, I will just leave," Colt said, motioning for me to come over to him for a hug.

I sat down next to him and leaned into his arms. I didn't feel like there was a great resolution because I still felt disgusted that he had sat there throughout a weekend of his parents badmouthing me. I hugged him back, trying to push down my feelings of resentment.

16

Chapter Sixteen

The next time Colt was home from work was the week of Thanksgiving. We went over to my grandparents' house for dinner where my dad, mom and sister Daisy were. Colt's family was planning on having a Thanksgiving gathering the following week as they were all split up going to dinners for their respective partners' families. We were planning on attending that. I was less than thrilled, but knew I had to suck it up. Talli was six months old now and Colt was ready to follow through with traveling with her. I wanted to go down and visit other family members of Colt's, but I was nervous about how they might treat me. My days were filled with anxiety leading up to the day before we were to go down. I was cuddling with Talli on the couch, Colt was laying on the other side and we were watching a Christmas movie.

"What time is the Thanksgiving gathering tomorrow?" I asked Colt.

"I don't know. I haven't heard anything about it. I'll text my mom," Colt said as he typed a message. "There, I asked her what time we should be there tomorrow."

It was almost time for bed when his phone rang. He showed me the screen, which showed the caller ID "mom," and then walked into the bedroom, closing the door behind him. I stayed on the couch with Talli and focused on my breathing as my heart pounded. I hated how anxious I felt almost constantly now, and how triggered I felt whenever someone in Colt's family called him or was simply brought up in conversation. I silently wished that we wouldn't have to go down there tomorrow. I wanted to stay home so badly. I wanted to feel safe, at ease and not have to face this tremendous anxiety. Colt came back into the room and laid down on the couch.

"We aren't going," he stated plainly.

I felt like it was Christmas morning and I got everything I wanted. I felt relief wash over me and calm flood my system.

"What? Why?" I asked, trying to hide my elation at the news.

"My mom never put anything together like she had been talking about. There are no plans. I am annoyed because she's been reminding me about this constantly for days. She said she is going to have a gathering in two weeks for Mackenzi's birthday instead. Also, she said some other stuff that annoyed me. Then she tried to ask for us to come down for a couple hours tomorrow, anyway," Colt told me.

"Oh, what did you say?" I asked, nervous energy splashing back into my system.

"I said we had other stuff we needed to get done and we were going to stay home since the plans had changed. I am not driving all the way down there to sit at their house when I can do that here," Colt scoffed.

I felt like I had won the lottery. I was so relieved to be able to stay home and not have to deal with them, but it sucked it was pushed back two weeks because I now had to deal with the anxiety leading up to it again. I shook that thought out of my head and tried to remain in the feeling of relief. I needed to focus on the present and not get ahead of myself. I had wasted so much time feeling uncomfortable, anxious and nervous for this gathering that now, at the last minute, was no longer a concern.

I had been talking to Colt off and on for a month about taking a little trip. I had explained to him how badly I needed a getaway to try to feel normal and to enjoy life for a little bit without any worries. I had been aching harder and fiercer to get out of the state as the days went on. Colt went back to work the day after the canceled Thanksgiving gathering with his family. When he got home a week later, I brought up the trip idea again.

"I am really thinking I will be healthier and better able to handle everything that has been going on if I can just do something fun. I need to get out of this state and get a refresh. I can go with Talli or we can all go, but I need to do it," I said to Colt as we sat on the floor of Talli's room while she crawled around us.

"I need to use my vacation days before the first of the year so, okay. I'd like to go to Florida to visit my friend Nate," Colt said as he scrolled on his phone.

"I am good with Florida. I kind of wanted to go somewhere new, but I would like to go back to Florida, too. I would love to see Hadley and all of our friends there," I said, thinking how nice it would be to get out of the cold and enjoy some warmth.

I really wanted to be around people that made me happy and I would have fun with. We started planning a trip to Florida. We were going to drive there the week before Christmas. As we planned, time went on. Colt had to go back to Texas for work for an extra week, which we weren't expecting. That extra week happened to be when Mackenzi's birthday gathering was planned. Since Colt wasn't here, I did not go. Colt didn't want me driving in the now falling snow and I didn't want to face his entire family without him there for protection. I wasn't as relieved to get out of this gathering as I had been two weeks ago. I started to become more worried about how it would go when we finally did go down. I just wanted to get it over with now. I knew it was inevitable. I didn't want to avoid his entire family, but I was just feeling so many things that made being a normal person difficult. I felt genuine fear when I thought about having to see them all and for any potential comments to be made that I would have to confront. In my head, I saw Hilda doing what she always did, acting heaven sent and subtly forcing those around her into doing what she wanted. She would ask for Talli, making herself appear so innocent and pure while acting as if she was grandma of the year. Then she probably would keep Talli for herself or do the honors of passing Talli around to Colt's entire family. I really didn't even feel comfortable with anyone holding Talli besides Colt and me due to how bad this winter was becoming with illnesses. Our pediatrician even recommended we keep her sheltered and avoid others touching her. She had said to blame it on doctor's orders. She explained how badly the kids were doing who had gotten one of the many illnesses going around. She said it wasn't worth it. I agreed wholeheartedly, although I was still very green at setting and holding boundaries. I was still very much a people pleaser and felt like Ella Enchanted when commanded to do something. It was like a switch would go off in me and I'd mindlessly do what I was told. I was so scared of that happening and getting myself into a situation that made me unbearably uncomfortable. Not only was I worried about all that, but there was still this huge elephant in the room that I sensed from a hundred miles away. The fact there had been so much talk about me behind my back was concerning, especially since I did not know exactly what was being said. I didn't know what Hilda's perception was or how exaggerated it was when she talked about it. I wasn't sure what everyone in that family was thinking of me. No one had reached out to me, no one was talking to me, and I just had this overwhelming sense there were a lot of negative feelings harbored toward me. I wasn't sure how to act around anyone anymore. It felt like as time went on, things were only getting worse on every front.

A couple days before we were supposed to take our trip to Florida, Colt came up to me while I was playing with Talli in her room.

"Hey, I don't think we should go to Florida. I think it's too far to drive with Talli," he said.

"Oh. I was really looking forward to it. I already told Hadley about it," I said, feeling caught off guard. "I understand and agree it is far to drive with Talli. Can we at least do a weekend trip somewhere close? Like, say, Michigan? It's only three hours away and I've never been before. We could go to little Christmas towns."

"Maybe we can do that," Colt said.

"I really need to go on a trip. We can always stop and turn around if it doesn't work with Talli. I just need to try. I need a break from feeling like I have been," I pleaded.

Two days later, after I had done some research on locations, we were headed up to Frankenmuth, Michigan. As we drove, I could feel myself becoming lighter. Once we passed through the state line into Michigan, I felt like I was floating. For the first time since the visits started in West Texas, I felt almost normal and happy. It sucked to have to tell our friends in Florida we weren't coming, but I tried to shrug that off quickly so as to not spoil my one chance at a getaway. Snow swirled in the air and it was like we had driven all the way to the North Pole. The first night we went to Bronner's, the largest Christmas store in the United States. We walked around looking at the endless sparkling decorations and ornaments. We drove through the town of Frankenmuth and saw all the beautiful light displays. I was buzzing with excitement to wake up the next morning to get out and explore.

"Babe, come on, let's go! I want to go before it gets too busy," I whined, dressed in a white knit sweater, jeans and fluffy winter boots. I had Talli all bundled up.

"Okay, I'm coming. Where are we getting breakfast?" Colt asked me as he slid on his jeans.

"I found this cool coffee shop called The Coffee Haus I want to try. It looks cute," I said, clapping my hands in excitement.

We went to The Coffee Haus, where we ordered hot coffees and breakfast sandwiches. I sipped my steamy white chocolate gingerbread mocha slowly, really soaking in the flavor and warmth. We blissfully ate, walked around the quaint town in the swirling snow and had a wonderful day. We struggled to find somewhere to eat for dinner that wasn't over an hour wait, so we ended up at an Outback Steakhouse. The next day we went to Midland, Michigan, where we stayed in a comfy, high-end Christmas decorated hotel. We walked around that little town as well, ate barbeque and got desserts to go at the little bakery attached to the hotel. As we laid in the luxurious hotel bed with the TV on, we dug into our rich, chocolate mousse cake. It was one of the best desserts I'd ever tasted. I melted into the flavor of the ganache.

"You seem happy. You seem normal. I haven't seen you like this in a long time," Colt quietly said, truly looking at me.

"I feel happier and more normal than I have in a long time," I agreed.

"I like it. I hope you stay like this," he said and rubbed my arm.

"Me too," I sighed.

Our weekend trip flew by. The next thing I knew, I was grappling onto time and trying to squeeze out every last minute I could in Michigan. I begged Colt to stop at a coffee shop outside of town before we got on the road. I could feel the creeping sense of anxiety hovering at the state line, ready to welcome me back into Ohio. It got heavier as we drove closer. About an hour and a half into our drive, Colt's phone rang over his car speakers and the caller ID lit up "mom." My stomach clenched hard. He answered and I sank down into my seat in the back next to Talli.

"Hello, just calling to see what you guys are doing," Hilda's scratchy voice blared over the speakers.

"We are driving back from Michigan now," Colt answered.

"Oh. Wow. You went all the way up to Michigan. So how is the baby doing in the car?" she questioned with an attitude.

"She is doing alright. We have had to stop a lot," Colt replied.

"Well, you can do that when you come down on Christmas Eve then. Just a couple days away! We are all excited to see you and the baby," Hilda trilled.

I quickly reached for the AirPods in the blue JanSport bookbag by my feet. I slipped them into my ears and turned on Morgan Wallen radio on Pandora. I felt like I was going to throw up from anxiety and couldn't stand to hear another second of Hilda's voice. I stared out the window and tried to hold on to the few remaining feelings of ease in my body.

17

Chapter Seventeen

On the eve of Christmas Eve, I was granted a Christmas miracle. A giant snowstorm was forecasted to blow through the Midwest on Christmas Eve and Christmas Day. It was unfortunate due to the dangers of it and it also stopped Calli from driving from Colorado to Ohio for Christmas. As the snow and temperature fell with vigor, my hopes to be able to stay home grew.

"If the storm doesn't stop, we won't be able to go down to my family's Christmas Eve," Colt said to me while looking out the window at the endless white landscape.

"Oh, okay," I said, masking my excitement.

"I mean, we could drive slowly, I guess. I don't think it would be safe, though. If we got stuck somewhere it would be bad," he said.

I could see him thinking more and more about how to make it work.

"Yeah, my weather app says the wind chill is negative thirty right now. You could go, but maybe Talli and I should stay home. It would be horrible if we got stuck with her in the car in this cold," I said.

"I'm not going by myself," Colt said, turning his head quickly to look at me.

"I'm just saying, it's getting to the point where Talli shouldn't be going outside in this."

I was genuinely concerned over the weather now and did not want to risk Talli being out in it.

"Let's just see what tomorrow is like," Colt said, leaving his post at the window.

On Christmas Eve, the wind whipped viciously, the temperature was below zero and ice painted the town. After waking up, Talli and I went into the kitchen to make gingerbread and chocolate chip cookies. I turned on Christmas music to sing along with while we worked.

"I texted my Aunt Nancy since she lives near Columbus to see if she is still going to Christmas Eve," Colt said as he walked into the kitchen in his red pajama pants.

"Okay," I said, nonchalantly.

I focused on getting out all the ingredients needed for both sets of cookies. I covered the counter with containers. I pushed the molasses and ginger spice over to the side and out of the way.

"Nancy said they are still going," he said while looking down at his phone. "She said the weather is bad, but they are going to drive really slow."

I sighed while pouring a cup of flour into the large bowl I had designated for the dry ingredients for the chocolate chip cookie dough.

"She isn't driving with a seven-month-old baby. I still don't want Talli in this storm for a two-hour drive. Also, I am not staying there overnight, so it would be another two hours back in the dark. I don't think it's a good idea," I said.

"Yeah. I agree," Colt said.

After I had baked all my cookies and the house smelled like Christmas heaven, we all laid on the couch with *Elf* on the TV.

"Nancy just texted me that she's about an hour away from my aunt's house. She said she has had to drive twenty-five miles per hour and that it has taken her over two hours so far," Colt said, typing on his phone.

"That sounds horrible," I said, trying to focus on Will Ferrell's shenanigans to keep my anxiety at bay.

"Yeah, she said we should try to go and drive slowly."

"You can. I don't want to do that. I don't want to get stuck down there. Not for Talli's first Christmas," I replied.

I held my hand over my racing heart to try to calm it.

"I told her we didn't think it was safe or a good idea with Talli. She said to do what we think is best. She said everyone would love to see us, though," Colt sighed.

"Offer them to all come up here after this storm has passed," I said, sighing as well.

My brain swirled. I was glad that this storm made it near impossible to go down there, but I still felt the overwhelming anxiety. It would not go away. Even with more time to be physically away from the stress and drama, I still sensed the inevitable accumulation of it on the horizon. It felt heavy and unbearable. I silently wished I wouldn't have to face them, ever. I felt guilty for wishing that and for feeling that way. I ached inside because I knew things would be different if I felt safe, welcome and loved. I didn't, though. I felt scared, on edge, uncomfortable, like I was a sitting duck at a shooting range. As time had passed, these feelings had intensified. I had grappled with ideas on ways to reach out to each and all of these family members. I could never come up with an acceptable and safe way to do it. I also had a strong inner gut feeling that it would hurt rather than help.

As night fell and all of Colt's family members on his mom's side celebrated together, Colt called me over to him. I had been in the kitchen cooking dinner.

"We should FaceTime with my family since we aren't there," he said.

"Okay," I said as my heart plummeted to my stomach.

He FaceTime called his mom.

"Hi!" Hilda screeched ear piercingly.

"Everyone, it's Colt and Talli!" she exclaimed before continuing blandly. "Oh, and Adison."

I sat next to Colt as he had instructed, with Talli in the middle of both of our laps. Colt held his phone so they could see all of Talli and half of each of us. Hilda shoved her phone toward family members as she went around the room. We saw three aunts, two uncles, four cousins, Mackenzi and Clayton, then she turned the camera back to herself. Everyone who looked at the phone had made a face. They would awkwardly scrunch up their face, choke out a hi, their eyes darting around, then they'd turn away. Every last one of them looked uncomfortable. I didn't know what Hilda was telling them, but it surely was something. Something not good. My stomach burned like I had food poisoning. I sat stonelike, unable to move. It took a lot of effort to breathe.

"Does Talli have an ear infection?" Hilda said, stopping and staring at us with a look of disapproval.

"No?" Colt answered, confused.

"She keeps touching her ear. Watch her for an ear infection," Hilda said sternly.

I tried not to roll my eyes. Talli did touch her ears occasionally. It didn't mean she had an ear infection. I tried to swallow how annoyed I felt.

As Colt continued to talk to Hilda, I sat there awkwardly, trying to keep myself out of view of the camera. I slowly and quietly started to get up.

"Where are you going?" Colt quietly hissed.

"I have to check on the ham," I whispered.

I made myself busy in the kitchen, checking on all the things Colt wanted for dinner: ham, green bean casserole, mashed potatoes and rolls. I began hand-washing dishes after I finished inspecting everything.

"Hey, get back in here," Colt hissed over the edge of the couch.

I rolled my head and walked back in. Hilda and Colt said their goodbyes after Hilda made sure with Colt that we'd FaceTime again for a while tomorrow on Christmas Day.

"We have to FaceTime my grandma now. I don't know if you heard, but my mom said she's sick. She's alone at her house," Colt said as he started to pull up Cynthia's contact.

Cynthia answered with a mask on and darkness surrounding her. I tried to be a little bit more social this time since it was just her. I felt weird and uncomfortable, but it wasn't too unbearable with her, yet. Cynthia said Nancy was staying overnight with her so she wasn't going to be alone on Christmas. She talked to Colt for a while, occasionally giving me a side eye.

"What time is it? Almost nine at night. You need to get that baby to bed," Cynthia instructed, with a judgmental look.

"Yeah, I should," I said, glad for a chance to get away.

"Good night, Merry Christmas!" I said to Cynthia as I took Talli from Colt.

She didn't respond, so I took Talli into our dark room and laid down with her. My stomach growled from hunger. I hadn't eaten anything since a few cookies around lunchtime. I tried to get Talli to sleep, but she was as wide awake as any child on Christmas Eve. Talli kept rolling over and crawling, trying to get out of bed. I finally gave up, holding her on my shoulder, and went back to the kitchen to try to eat. Colt was still on FaceTime with Cynthia. I quietly pulled out a plate and filled it with the food. I had to microwave it because it was lukewarm from sitting.

As soon as I sat down at the counter to eat with Talli in my arms, Cynthia exclaimed, "That baby is still up? Get that baby to bed! She needs to be asleep!"

I fake laughed, "Yeah, she must be excited and knows tomorrow is Christmas. She isn't tired yet."

I got a bite of ham in my mouth before Cynthia replied scornfully, "That baby should be in bed. It is way too late for her to be up."

I ignored her as I tried to power chew my late dinner.

"Seriously, it is past nine. Get that baby to bed!" Cynthia screeched.

"God damn," I whispered under my breath. "Okay, Cynthia. I am taking her to bed." I said with an irritated twinge in my voice.

I let my fork fall from my hand and it clanged against my plate. I swiveled around on my toes and marched back into the bedroom. I looked at my wide-awake Talli.

"Let's just try to lay down, honey. I am sorry I am upset. It is not your fault. I am so annoyed with Cynthia. I am so hungry. She shouldn't be dictating to me or making me feel guilty. It just isn't fair that anytime they are around or involved, they are making me feel bad about something," I said to myself more than Talli, who didn't understand English yet.

I laid down with Talli until Colt walked into the bedroom.

"Thank god you're finally off the phone," I said, irritated and rolling my eyes as I got up.

Talli was still far from asleep. I took her in my arms and went out to the kitchen. My food was cold so I had to heat it up again. I took a couple bites, but didn't feel like I could eat anymore. I was still hungry, but anxiety had taken over my body so every bite lumped up in my throat.

"That was annoying, I'm sorry," Colt said.

"Yeah, it was annoying," I agreed.

We watched a little bit of *The Christmas Story* until we all were ready for bed. I laid in the dark and searched my head for some tiny ounce of Christmas spirit. I wanted to feel happy and excited about Talli's first Christmas. I had tried. I baked cookies, played music, watched movies and decorated the house. Nothing could break me from the endless anxiety. The closest I felt to Christmas spirit was during our little weekend trip to Michigan. Now I couldn't even remember how that felt.

18

Chapter Eighteen

On Christmas morning, Colt and I gave Talli her presents and helped her open them. After opening gifts, Colt went to the bathroom to shower and I worked on cooking. We scrambled to get ready to go to my family's Christmas gathering. I grabbed cookies, green bean casserole and Colt's mini corn dogs as we packed his truck to go five minutes down the street to my grandparents' house. The storm had eased considerably. It was still freezing, but it wasn't as bad as it had been the day before.

I tried to be as present as possible. I tried my hardest to enjoy the day. I tried to soak in every minute of being at my grandparents' house, and not just because I wasn't looking forward to another Face-Time call. I also felt melancholy because I didn't know how many more Christmases would be like this. I hadn't been to my grandparents' house for Christmas in years. We had been living in other states for three Christmases and then I had spent every Christmas Day with Colt's family since we started dating. The day went by too quickly and soon enough we were back home. Colt pulled out his phone and called me over to the couch.

"Can I not be a part of this?" I moaned.

"Stop it, you have to. Just do it," Colt said, glaring at me.

Time felt as though it had betrayed me as he called his mom.

"Merry Christmas!" she trilled.

She went around the room at Clayton's family's Christmas party they were having at Didi's house. The facial expressions were worse than yesterday. Clayton's sister, Brittany, looked at Mackenzi and I saw them both scrunch up their faces before looking back at the phone. Everyone's eyes darted around, everyone barely looked at us on the phone and no one really spoke. Hilda was like an actress on Broadway putting on a show of being so perfect and loving. She spoke with excitement and acted proud to show everyone her son and granddaughter. I felt even more uncomfortable than I had before. I sat there, silently suffering. Luckily, Colt had the phone showing Talli instead of our faces, so I didn't have to pretend to smile anymore. I eventually let myself get up and escape sitting on the sideline for the conversation between Colt and Hilda. I busied myself in the kitchen again as Colt and Hilda discussed plans for them to come visit tomorrow.

Tomorrow came too quickly. I kept myself busy until Hilda, Clayton and Mackenzi arrived in the early afternoon. Colt had separated our L-shaped couch so that the wide piece was by itself, spaced out from the rest. He said it was so I could sit there with Talli and not worry about anyone being too close to us. I appreciated his thoughtfulness. I had perched myself and Talli at my station on the separated couch piece when they arrived. Mackenzi clomped inside first carrying a giant fifty-five-gallon black trash bag filled with gifts.

"Oh, wow, that is a lot," I sighed, feeling overwhelmed.

"There's more!" Mackenzi laughed before running back outside.

Hilda came in carrying a box of gifts, followed by Clayton, who carried a box of gifts as Mackenzi heaved in another giant black trash bag. Our living room was filled with gifts. This was too much. I didn't want anything from any of them to begin with. All I wanted was to be treated with respect. I breathed, focusing my thoughts on this being for Colt and Talli. Hilda, Clayton and Mackenzi awkwardly sat on the leftover long piece of the couch. I tried to focus on breathing as Mackenzi opened her gifts from us. Hilda grabbed a giant gift bag and thrust it toward me and Talli. I slowly assisted Talli in opening it. Hilda hovered directly over us. I helped Talli pull out a bear in a prayer position.

"It talks," Hilda said as she grabbed it from me, pushing on its paws.

The bear recited a bedtime prayer. I cringed. We are not a religious family so this was not an appropriate gift. She knew we weren't religious, but again decided to push her own beliefs on us. Hilda took the bear into our kitchen.

"Where are the scissors?" she asked.

"Hey, it's okay, we don't need to cut the tags off right now," I said, cringing.

I would've donated it so that a family that is religious could enjoy it. Colt went into the kitchen and handed his mom our scissors. She quickly cut the tags off the praying bear and brought it back to Talli.

"There you go," she stated matter-of-factly.

I ignored it and continued to aid Talli in opening her endless gifts. We pulled out pink purses, a toy picnic basket, a toy fishbowl, a strange lump of a doll, an old telephone toy, a toy cell phone and lots of clothes.

"There, Talli can actually look like a girl now," Hilda smirked, raising one eyebrow as I pulled out some frilly pink dress. "She looks best in pink."

I froze for a second, red hot anger filling me, then promptly leaving as I blew the comment out of my head.

"Talli looks adorable in every color and anything she wears," I thought.

Hilda continued to rip apart plastic packaging while opening up the toys, leaving the trash scattered around the kitchen. Hilda would then bring the open gift and slap it down in our already covered laps. Talli and I sat completely buried in gifts. I had no idea where I was going to put all these things. Talli already had so many toys. Her toy basket was overfilled and things were always all over the floor. I looked at the mess of wrapping paper, red glitter, bags, tissue paper, tags, plastic and cardboard littered throughout the main area of our house. My head pounded and I felt like I was going to throw up. I hated mess. This was going to be a nightmare to clean. The red sparkles were all over our piece of the couch and on our skin. I officially hated sparkles. I sat with Talli in my lap, helpless and miserable. I tried to steady my shaking hands and focus on my breathing as Colt opened his gifts.

"Here, Adison, this is for you," Hilda stated, with her mouth in a tight line as she tossed a couple wrapped gifts to me.

"Thank you," I said uncomfortably.

I opened the gifts quickly and awkwardly. I really did not feel good about accepting a gift from someone who had been treating me so unkindly. I did not want anything from someone who was taking up my time and energy in such a negative way. It seemed so wrong.

"Thank you so much," I said as appreciatively as I could as I held up two packages of mascara, some Victoria Secret body spray, a zip-up Ohio State jacket and camouflage gloves.

"You're welcome. The gloves we got you a couple years ago, but they must have gotten lost. I found them in the barn," Hilda said.

"Oh, okay, that's funny," I said as I shook slightly of discomfort.

When we were finally done with opening gifts, everyone sat around the room.

"Colt, you should show me what you are talking about with your basement," Clayton coughed.

"Okay, let's go," Colt said, getting up and starting downstairs.

My eyes got big and I quickly got up, too. I clutched Talli and followed him downstairs, not wanting to be alone with his mom. Hilda and Mackenzi reluctantly followed us. We all stood in our unfinished basement as Colt pointed to the top edges of the wall, where the insulation was, and explained what was wrong with it. I started to pace around about twenty feet from where they stood. Mackenzi came over to where I was and stared blankly at me while I held Talli against my heart.

"How has your winter break been?" I asked her, rocking Talli back and forth.

"Good," she said, still staring.

"Do you have practice and basketball games to cheer at during break?" I asked, trying to start a conversation.

"Yeah," Mackenzi replied.

"That's cool. Are you excited for college?" I asked.

"Yeah, I am."

We both stood there, awkwardly looking at each other. I didn't know what else to say so I started to slowly move closer to where Colt was. Hilda was standing near Clayton and Colt, looking bored. I concentrated on breathing and the feeling of Talli's tiny body resting on my chest. Her head was over my shoulder and I could feel her starting to fall asleep.

"I want to go back upstairs," Mackenzi said, looking at me.

I smiled and nodded, not saying anything.

"It's cold. We should go upstairs," Mackenzi said again.

"You are welcome to go back upstairs," I said quietly.

She looked at me, annoyed, then made her way over to the staircase. She stood at the bottom, as if waiting for someone to follow. Hilda moved over to where she stood. I stayed near Colt religiously, gripping onto the feeling of safety that hovered around him.

"When are we going back upstairs? This is so boring," Mackenzi said, interrupting Colt and Clayton's conversation.

"Okay, fine, we can go back upstairs," Colt said.

I waited, letting myself and Talli be the last to get back up on the main floor. I shut off the light and closed the basement door behind me. I walked into the kitchen, noticing Colt standing near the stove. Clayton was sitting on one of our barstools at the island counter, Hilda was on the couch in the living room with her back facing everyone, and Mackenzi was standing near the fridge. Cynthia had sent

Colt a box full of his baby pictures. Hilda had acted so shocked, but honored, when she saw that Cynthia had given the precious memories to Colt. I noticed Hilda was now flipping through the pictures.

I stood in the kitchen next to Colt. Talli was asleep on my shoulder. Everyone was really quiet, so I cleared my throat and decided to offer up some kindness.

"I made cookies, would anyone like one?" I asked.

"Sure," Clayton said.

"Yes!" Mackenzi rushed over.

I opened a box of chocolate chip cookies and offered one to Clayton. He took two. I grabbed another box that I had prepared specifically for Mackenzi.

"Here, you can have one of these, but I also put a box together for you," I said, offering her a cookie from the large box and handing her the smaller box stuffed full.

"Thank you!" she said.

"Hilda, would you like a cookie?" I asked. I had to swallow down a frog in my throat.

"Sure," she said, half turning her body toward the kitchen. "Mackenzi, will you bring me half of one? I don't want a full cookie."

Mackenzi rushed over a cookie to her mom.

"I also have gingerbread," I said, opening a box full of gingerbread men and setting it on the island countertop.

"Are they made from a box?" Clayton scoffed.

"No, I made them from scratch," I said.

"Huh," he huffed before grabbing a large gingerbread man.

He took a couple bites and then said, "Wow, these are actually pretty good."

I felt a little bit of my guard slip away and let myself accept the sort of compliment.

"Thank you," I said.

"No one made gingerbread at my family's Christmas. We had every single kind of cookie imaginable except gingerbread," Clayton said. "Hilda, you should try one."

"I don't want one," she said.

"You should try one, they are actually pretty good," Clayton repeated.

"Fine, just break me off a small piece of yours," Hilda sighed.

Clayton handed her a quarter-sized piece and she slowly put it to her mouth. She ate it as if she was keeping a secret. She didn't say anything and resumed looking at the pictures in her lap. A minute passed and she started coughing.

"I could use some water," Hilda said, annoyed. "Mackenzi, get me some water."

"You get yourself some water," Mackenzi said, not looking up from her phone. She had almost eaten the entire box of cookies I had given her.

"Are you kidding me?" Hilda sneered.

Colt got a glass of water for Hilda and she came into the kitchen to get it. Colt and Clayton had started talking about Clayton's cows and the beef he gets from them.

"Well, we don't have anywhere to put meat right now because you still have our deep freezer," Colt said to Clayton.

"Come get it then. I just have to know when so I can take everything I have out of it," Clayton said, as he had been saying for months.

"Honey, I said we should just get them a new one," Hilda softly said, perking up.

"We don't need to get them a new one. We can get a new one after they take back theirs," Clayton grumbled.

Hilda shot him a look.

"We will get them a new one," she said, staring at Clayton with a look that said he should stop talking.

"I saw one that is very similar at Home Depot. It's on sale for a thousand dollars less than the one we had bought," Colt said.

"I don't like Home Depot. I will never buy anything from there," Clayton said.

"Why?" Colt asked him.

"Because they messed up my order…" Clayton started before Hilda interrupted him.

"Honey, you always hold grudges," she sighed.

"No, I don't. I just won't give my business to someone who does me wrong," Clayton said, raising his voice.

"Well, if you can get me this one, that would work. I'll send you the link now. The sale ends in February," Colt said, sending Hilda a text with the link to the deep freezer.

"Back to what we were talking about, Colt. Part of your Christmas present is the meat. We will bring it up here when we get it in a couple weeks," Clayton said.

"Okay, but we have to have the deep freezer first. We don't have enough space in our freezer in the kitchen," Colt said.

"You can't make room for it?" Clayton said, rolling his eyes.

"There is no room. It isn't very big, so we need the deep freezer before you bring meat," Colt repeated.

My shoulder and arm were starting to go numb with the weight of Talli's sleeping body. I pulled my phone out of my back pocket with my free hand and looked at the time. They had been here for a couple hours and it was now almost six. I stood, slightly swaying back and forth, trying to not let myself get antsy. I was hungry and wanted them to leave so we could eat dinner.

"I want to go home. I need to do my two-mile jog," Mackenzi said, interrupting the conversation currently going on between Colt, Clayton and Hilda.

"Doesn't Adison have a treadmill you can use?" Hilda asked.

"No, I texted her when we were on the way up and she said they don't," Mackenzi said.

"I thought Adison had a bunch of workout equipment from when she tried to start her personal training business," Hilda said.

"No, I used to have an elliptical, but we sold it before we moved to Texas," I said. "I wish I had a treadmill."

Hilda smirked. "Okay, Mackenzi, we will leave soon," she said.

The conversation started again, something about the government and China. I always tried to tune out these conversations.

"Oh my god, you sound as crazy as Grandma," Mackenzi groaned as Clayton talked about China spying on America through the TikTok app.

I tried to stifle a laugh.

"Seriously, the Chinese government created that app to spy on us. They created COVID and are going to try to take over," Clayton said.

"Oh yeah, by dancing videos?" Mackenzi said, rolling her eyes.

"Okay, time to go," Clayton growled, getting up and putting on his shoes.

Mackenzi followed suit and then came up to me with the box I had given her that had been full of cookies.

"Here you go. I ate them all," she said, handing the box to me.

"Okay, I'm glad you liked them," I said. I smiled at her. She smiled back at me.

At last, everyone said their goodbyes. When the door finally shut behind them, I blew out a giant gust of air. It was like I had been holding my breath for hours, even as I consciously had been focusing on breathing. I felt like a weight had been lifted from my chest. Even Talli seemed lighter on my aching shoulder.

"I'm hungry, what should we eat for dinner?" Colt asked, looking inside the pantry cabinet and then moving to look inside the fridge.

"Chinese food and a milkshake?" I asked, hopefully. "It's late, I don't feel like cooking."

"Sure," Colt agreed.

We got our coats on and climbed into his truck that was parked inside the garage. We drove the back roads to Handel's. When we got there, Colt went out into the cold to get two chocoholic peanut butter ripple milkshakes. I waited in the warm, running truck with Talli. He got back in and handed me one of the two cups in his hands.

"This is so good. Just Pavlov me with milkshakes. Every time your family comes over, after they leave, we go to Handel's. Then one day maybe I'll enjoy your family visiting, no matter how miserable it may be," I said, taking another satisfying sip of rich chocolate, peanut butter, milky goodness.

"Call Hop Hing," Colt said, rolling his eyes.

I called and placed our carryout order. Colt started to drive down the road toward the restaurant. It was dark and there were large piles of snow lining the road. As I gazed out the window, I sipped on my milkshake, letting it make me feel safe.

We picked up our take out and drove home. The air in the truck was warm and smelled like hot Chinese food. It made my body relax. If only my mind could follow suit. I felt better that they were gone, but their presence always lingered. When we got home, we put Talli to sleep and then unloaded the brown bag of food. I sat down with my steaming bourbon chicken and white rice. I took a big bite. It was delicious as always, but it felt like a lump of concrete when it hit my stomach. I felt like my insides were as frozen and dead as the ground outside. I sat for a minute, staring at the food I craved, before putting the lid back on. I got up and put the dinner I had yearned for into the fridge.

"What are you doing?" Colt asked.

"I don't feel hungry anymore," I said.

"You only took one bite. You need to eat," Colt said.

"I really can't," I said, feeling defeated.

I walked through the dark bedroom into the bathroom. I took my time washing my face. I sighed as the cold, refreshing water splashed all over my fiery skin. Tomorrow was the last day with Colt before he returned to Texas for work. I was almost relieved he was going to be gone because it meant I would have a week without worrying about any in-laws visiting. I hated that I felt like that. Colt walked into the bathroom. I saw him staring at me through the mirror over the sink.

"Tomorrow, we have to call everyone that got us or Talli gifts. We have to thank them before you leave for work," I said, patting my face dry with a soft towel.

"Okay," Colt said.

Suddenly, we heard Talli cry from her portable crib. Colt quickly scooped her up as I hurried to pat on my nighttime face lotion. As soon as I was ready for bed, he handed me our baby and I laid down with her. Colt went back out into the living room to relax and watch TV while we went to sleep.

19

Chapter Nineteen

The next day we were busy with laundry, cleaning and preparing for Colt to leave for work. After spending most of the day doing chores, the sun set what felt like abruptly.

"Colt, we have got to call your family," I said, stressed.

I held Talli in my lap while sitting on the bed, watching Colt fold another pile of his clothes.

"We can always do it when I get back," Colt said, folding up a red sweatshirt.

"Babe, that is too long. We need to do it now. I don't want anyone having another reason to talk badly about me. We need to thank them. I wish they hadn't gotten us anything because I am so nervous to do this. I mean, it was really nice of them to get us gifts, but it feels weird since no one has talked to us much at all this year. What a mess," I said, putting my face in my hands.

Talli sat in my lap making cooing sounds. I kissed her head and hugged her.

"Okay. You call them then," Colt said.

"No way, that is so awkward for me," I quickly said back.

"Fine. We can take turns. I'll call one, then you call one," Colt said.

"Okay. You can start."

Colt grabbed his phone, called his Aunt Nancy and hit the button to put it on speaker.

"Hello?" Nancy's voice echoed out of the phone.

"Hey, thank you for the gifts!" Colt said.

"Hi Nancy, thank you so much! Merry Christmas!" I added.

"Oh, yeah, you're welcome. Merry Christmas," Nancy said. "So, your mom was finally able to come visit then?"

My face scrunched up and I looked over at Colt.

"Yeah. They came over yesterday," Colt said, shrugging at me.

"That's good. I'm glad they got to. I was wondering if they would be able to," Nancy said. "How is Talli?"

Again, I looked at Colt confused.

"She's fine, why do you ask?" Colt asked his aunt.

"Hilda said she had an ear infection. She's feeling better?" Nancy questioned.

"She doesn't have an ear infection," Colt said with a confused look on his face.

"Oh, okay. Your mom said she was tugging on her ear a lot," she replied.

"No, she is fine. How was your Christmas?" Colt asked.

As they continued their conversation, I tried to stay conscious of it, but I felt uncomfortable. I felt like I didn't belong. Even sitting there quietly, I felt as if I was a fly on the edge of a dining table, an annoyance and gross. Finally, when Colt hung up his phone, I let out a giant breath. One down. I hated that I felt so obligated to do this. It would be different if things weren't the way they were, I again thought. I felt like an outcast. I wished no one had sent us gifts. At least not to me or Talli. I didn't want anything from anyone who didn't like me or didn't treat me respectfully. When it came to Talli, I felt obligated to say thank you on her behalf. I don't know, it just seemed wrong to receive a gift from anyone who gave off bad vibes toward me, Talli's mother.

"If you don't like the mother, leave the baby alone," I thought.

"Okay, your turn," Colt said.

I called his grandma and hit the speaker button quickly.

"Hello," Cynthia answered meekly.

"Merry Christmas, thank you for the gifts you sent Talli!" I said warmly.

"Thank you for the gifts!" Colt chimed in.

"You're welcome," Cynthia said. "Your mom got to come visit it sounds like?"

"Yeah..." Colt said.

Colt and I looked at one another with thoughtful faces. It was really strange that this was the second person who asked if his mom got to visit, as if implying she typically wasn't permitted to.

"Good. I know she really wanted to see you and Talli. You got the pictures I had sent up?" Cynthia asked.

"Yes, I did, thank you," Colt said.

"Good. How is Talli? Is she feeling any better?" Cynthia asked.

"Talli is fine," Colt said, looking at me.

We both raised our eyebrows at each other.

"Oh, good. Your mom said she had an ear infection," Cynthia said.

"I don't know why my mother said that. Talli does not have an ear infection," Colt said, annoyed.

"Oh, that's strange. She was all concerned about Talli. Your mom said she kept seeing Talli rubbing her ears while on FaceTime. I wonder why she said that," Cynthia said.

"I don't know, but it's not true," Colt said, solidly.

"Anyway, you had a good Christmas?" Cynthia asked Colt.

"Yeah, we did," Colt said.

Colt grabbed my phone from me, carried it into the other room and continued his conversation. I laid down on the bed with Talli and closed my eyes. He walked back into the room a couple minutes later as he was wrapping up the conversation. He motioned for me to say goodbye to his grandma. I did, and didn't get a response back. I sighed.

"Colt, it is really weird that both your aunt and grandma asked if your mom was able to visit. Also, why did she tell everyone that Talli has an ear infection? That is not okay," I said, sighing.

"It is weird. I agree, I am not happy she told people that. I don't know why she did that," Colt said with a sigh.

Colt called his Aunt Mary to thank her. She asked the same questions. Colt and I rolled our eyes. I called his Aunt Darla, who didn't answer.

"Should I leave a voicemail?" I asked Colt.

"No, don't do that, it's fine," Colt said. "We should take a break. I'm tired."

"We still have to call Didi and her daughters, though," I said.

"I really don't feel like it right now. I'm not that worried about it," Colt said. "I have to leave in the morning to go back to work. We can do it when I get back unless you want to while I'm gone."

"I really don't, but I don't want to wait too long," I said.

We got settled in bed. I fell asleep and when I woke up, Colt had already left for the airport.

I had woken groggy and somber. It was Wednesday, which meant I had a full week until I saw Colt again. I got out of bed and went about my day as usual. I kept thinking about how we still had people to reach out to and thank. I decided I would send a text to his Aunt Darla since she hadn't called back yet.

I typed, "Good morning, Aunt Darla! We just called the other day to say thank you guys so much for the sweet Christmas gifts for Talli. Hope you all have a happy new year!" I added a heart emoji and hit send.

Next, I opened up my Facebook messenger and typed a message to Charlotte, Clayton's sister. I didn't have her phone number. I had noticed earlier that it was Charlotte's daughter's birthday today.

I typed, "I hope Holly has a wonderful birthday and you're all doing well! Colt, Talli and I wanted to say thank you for the sweet gifts! Talli loves her fish bowl. Thank you and Merry Christmas!"

I sent it and thought about who was left to thank. I remembered that Clayton's other sister, Brittany, hadn't sent any gifts. I was relieved about that. I realized the only person left to reach out to was Didi. I figured I had to give her a call so I decided to wait on that.

I continued with my day. Talli and I were playing in her room when my phone binged. I received a message from Darla.

It said, "You're welcome. Hope she enjoys them. Did you find a gift card to Longhorn in the gifts? It was for you and Colt. I thought I put it in the bag with Talli's stuff. I think I lost my mind this Christmas."

I replied, "We did not see a gift card, but I'll go back and look in the bags again. Definitely want to find that! We love Longhorn. Thank you for that and for letting me know about it! And I can relate."

Darla replied, "I will search my house, too. We are heading to Cleveland this Sunday! Would you mind if we stopped to see you guys for a few minutes. Not long and it would be in the morning. Let me know if that works."

I felt little prickles pop up all over my skin and my stomach got heavy. My heart picked up pace as I tried to think about what to do. The conversation with her seemed normal. This was the first time she had made any effort to come visit. I felt like I had to say yes. At the same time, I so badly wanted to say no since I needed the week to decompress. I didn't want to have to do this without Colt there. Yet it would be a good opportunity for growth, to step out of my comfort zone and also just be normal. Maybe they would see that whatever was being said about me was not true. At least Hilda wouldn't be there. I sighed and gathered up all of my courage.

I replied, "Yes please stop by! Colt is in Texas this week, but Talli and I would love to see you guys." I followed that text with our address and added, "just in case you don't already have it."

I didn't get a response so I set my phone down. As soon as I had set it down, I received a message back from Charlotte.

It said, "She's having a great day! Glad Talli likes her toys... can't wait to officially meet her. Hope she had a good first Christmas."

I replied, "I'm glad! Can't wait for you all to meet her, also! She did, thank you!"

Charlotte read the message and did not reply. That was fine.

Later that day, when Colt called me to talk after work, I begged him to call Didi with me to get it over with.

"Please babe, we need to just do it," I pleaded.

"Tomorrow," Colt said.

"Okay, that's fine."

Thursday afternoon, Colt called me while he was driving to a work site.

"Okay, we have to call Didi. Should we just add her to our call?" I asked.

"Yeah, that's fine. You can call her," Colt said.

I pressed the add call button and scrolled to find Didi's contact information. I pressed on her number and it started to ring.

"Hello?" Didi chirped through the speaker.

"Hi Didi, I have Colt on the other line, let me add him in," I said, before I started to press what was needed to merge the calls.

"Oh, okay," Didi said.

"Colt, are you there?" I asked.

"Yeah," he said.

"Didi, are you there?" I asked.

"Yep," Didi said.

"Okay, cool. We wanted to call you to say thank you for the gifts for Talli and Merry Christmas," I said.

"Thank you!" Colt quickly added.

"Oh, you're welcome. I hope Talli had a good Christmas," Didi said.

"Thank you, she did. I hope you all had a good Christmas as well," I said.

There was an awkward silence for a moment.

"Okay, well I am out in Columbus with Brittany, we are about to get lunch and get our nails done. I should get off here, but thanks for calling. I hope everything is going well for you. We are anxious to see Talli soon and hope you will come down to visit."

I sighed silently to myself before responding, "Yes, sounds good. Enjoy your day, that sounds like fun!"

"Okay, goodbye now," Didi said.

"Goodbye," I said and quickly hung up the phone.

I called Colt back.

"That was awkward," I said as he answered the phone.

"I know. It always is," Colt said.

"Well, I feel so much better now that we've finished thanking everyone. What a relief," I said, letting out a big breath.

"I don't know why you care so much," Colt said.

"I don't know. I just do," I said, feeling my heart ache a little.

I missed feeling more comfortable around his family. I have always struggled with feeling comfortable around adults. I always felt like I had to put on a mask showing only my most professional self. I felt like I couldn't relax into who I am around adults, even though who I am isn't someone that needs to be hidden or adjusted. I grew up around many adults looking down on me, judging me and questioning me. It morphed into me feeling instantly uneasy, uncomfortable and on alert whenever I was around anyone with twenty years or more on me. There are exceptions to this, of course. Some people have naturally safe auras and the mask never goes on, but it is rarer for me to come across that.

"Are you still there?" Colt asked.

"Oh, yeah, I'm sorry," I said, shaking myself out of my thoughts. "I think I am going to try to put Talli down for a nap."

"Okay, babe. I hope she goes to sleep easily for you."

"Thank you, honey. I hope you have a good rest of your day at work. I miss you and I love you," I said.

"I miss you and I love you more. Bye, babe," Colt said.

"Bye," I said as I hung up the phone.

I had been pacing in the kitchen with Talli in one arm, her head resting on my shoulder. I walked us over to the couch and laid her down. I rested beside her and we both closed our eyes. I tried to calm my racing heart. I had felt a moment of relief in finishing the thank you calls, but my thoughts instantly turned to the fact I was going to have his aunt, uncle and cousins over on Sunday. I wasn't getting a safe week. I also felt dismayed at the fact Sunday was the first day of the year. This was not how I wanted to start it. How I would prefer to start the year would be just Talli and me, relaxing and ready for a reset. Having Colt's family over without him was stressful and a continuation of the previous year. It was like my nightmare with his family would never end. I shut my eyes forcefully. I needed to think of it differently. It could be good to have these family members over. Maybe they would be normal and would see that I was normal. Well, somewhat normal. I would have to try really hard to be normal since I felt so much discomfort and knew there was a negative narrative about me out there.

20

Chapter Twenty

The days dragged on, and each day that got closer to Sunday my anxiety grew. On Sunday morning, my skin prickled and I couldn't stop the cold sweats. I felt drunk with anxiety. I got dressed three different times. Throwing on and off jeans, a sherpa pullover, track shorts, until finally settling on a blue Nike quarter zip sweatshirt and cropped black Nike leggings. I put on mascara and a spray of perfume to try to boost my confidence. I took a few pictures of Talli to share on Facebook since not only was it New Year's Day, it was also the day Talli was officially eight months old. I wondered when Colt's aunt and uncle would be coming. I hadn't heard from Darla since Wednesday when she initially asked to come visit. I was slightly annoyed at that fact, but at least I knew it would be sometime in the morning. I had set alarms to wake up at six thirty so that I could be ready for whatever time they may arrive.

At almost nine in the morning, I received a text from Darla that read, "We are leaving!"

Now I knew that I had approximately two hours until their arrival.

I texted back, "Happy New Year! Thanks for the heads up, see you guys soon."

The two hours dragged as I tried to eat and keep my anxiety from overtaking me. I jogged in place, drank water and peed probably twenty times. My armpits felt hot and sweaty. I kept trying to air them out. I felt nauseous. I paced around the kitchen and tried to count my breathing. My phone pinged that our cameras had detected a vehicle outside. I power walked into Talli's room and sat with her to try to act normal before I had to answer the door. A couple minutes passed before the doorbell rang, followed by a knock at the door. I buzzed with nervousness as I hoisted Talli up in my arms and went toward the door. I saw Darla's face peering through the window at the front door. She waved when she saw me. I waved back, unlocked the door and opened it wide.

"Hi," I said, taking in what I saw. Darla stood in front with her arms crossed in her fuzzy, cream sweater. Her shoulder-length, mocha-colored hair was curly and her brown eyes were large. Behind her stood her son Shawn with a girl I had never met. Shawn was a tall athlete with kind, brown eyes and brown buzzed hair. The girl who stood next to him wore an oversized sweater tucked into a short skirt. Her dark hair was pulled tightly into a high ponytail that showed off the diamonds in her ears. I was shocked to not see Darla's husband, Hilda's brother, William, with her. Her other three sons were also not present.

"Hey!" Darla trilled. "Can we come in?"

"Yeah, of course," I said, blushing and stepping back from the door.

The three of them stepped inside and stopped, standing right in front of the open door. The cold air poured in and I awkwardly tried to move to close the door. Shawn looked back at it and slowly pushed it closed. He didn't push it hard enough and it stuck out slightly from the latch. As they took a couple more steps inside, I quickly pushed it shut.

"Oh, I'm sorry, I thought I shut it," Shawn said softly.

"It's okay, it popped open a little bit," I said, blushing. "I can show you around."

"Yes, please!" Darla said. "Oh, by the way, this is Sarah." She motioned to the girl with them. Sarah waved and smiled with her lips pressed tightly together.

"Hi, nice to meet you," I said and smiled at her.

"I told the others they could just go on up to my mom's and they didn't need to stop. I didn't want you to be overwhelmed with so many people," Darla said, looking at me carefully, as if I was a patient in a psychiatric hospital.

"Oh, they could've come. I had thought that they were," I said, feeling weird.

I walked them over to Talli's room. They looked inside, then looked into Colt's office, and came out into the kitchen.

"Very nice," Darla said. "How was Talli's first Christmas?"

"It was good! I think Talli enjoyed it a lot. How was your Christmas?" I asked.

Shawn and Sarah had gone into the living room and sat on the couch.

"Oh, it was good. Busy as always. We are headed up to Cleveland today to have Christmas with my parents. We missed seeing you guys at our house last weekend." Darla said as she moved to the living room to sit on the couch.

I followed and sat down with Talli in my lap.

"Yeah, we missed you, too. That snowstorm was crazy. My sister Calli was trying to drive back from Denver and had to turn around due to how dangerous it was," I said.

"Oh, wow. Yeah, it was crazy. It wasn't too bad at our house, though. A couple trees were down in the road, but we've had that before," Darla said.

"How long do you have off work?" I asked, looking over at Shawn to change the subject.

I didn't want to argue about the winter storm and our decision not to drive in it.

"I took a week off," Shawn replied.

"That's nice! Did you go to Ohio University, too?" I asked Sarah.

"Yeah, I still go there. I am a junior," she said.

"Oh, okay, cool. Is that where you guys met?" I asked.

"Yeah," she said.

"How are you liking your job?" I asked Shawn.

He had graduated the previous year and started working at a reality company in Columbus.

"It is okay. There are some things that are frustrating, but I think it will get better," he said.

"Yeah, first jobs can be tough. It always gets better. Your first job doesn't have to be the forever one," I said, trying to keep the conversation going.

"Yeah, I don't think this is my forever job. It isn't a bad start, though," Shawn said.

"That's good. I'm glad it isn't too bad. Probably better than a smoothie shop," I mustered a laugh, trying to make a joke at my own expense. I had worked as a manager at a smoothie shop after I graduated from college while I studied to get my personal training license.

"I saw that you guys went up to Michigan. How was that?" Darla asked me.

"It was really nice. I am so glad we were able to do it. We really needed a trip. Frankenmuth was a cool Christmas town. I had never done a trip like that before. It was my first time traveling during the winter," I said.

My heart was still racing, but I was less anxious. I was focused on getting through the visit. I felt proud of myself for being as normal as I was, given how messed up my head felt.

"Yeah, it looked pretty in the pictures you posted on Facebook. How far was that drive?" Darla asked.

I breathed. It felt like she was asking these questions to try to make an unsaid point.

"It was about three hours," I answered honestly.

"Okay. That isn't too bad," she said back.

"Yeah. We stopped a lot to give Talli breaks," I said. "Do you guys have any trips planned?" I wanted to change the subject.

"Actually, yes. The seniors are going on a senior trip during spring break in March to the Bahamas. I am going with them as a supervisor. Hilda is going, too," Darla said, looking intently into my eyes.

I looked down from her intense gaze.

"That's cool! That sounds like fun," I said. I was glad to hear Hilda would be out of town for some time in March. That was time I wouldn't have to worry about her bothering us.

"Yeah, it will be. It is a cruise. I haven't been on a cruise in a while so I am excited," Darla said. "Hilda is excited, too."

"I bet. I would be, too," I said, feeling strange that she was bringing up Hilda again.

Darla studied me. Shawn and Sarah sat, looking uncomfortable. The room was heavy with a thick silence. I tried to find relief in the fact I was in my own home and I didn't need to feel uneasy in my living room. Darla coughed a couple times.

"Excuse me. We are all getting over being sick. We are finally starting to feel better. Last week was rough. That time of the year," Darla said between coughs.

I shuddered. I felt a spark of anger that they came over to our home with any trace of sickness, but more so the anger was that we almost drove down there without any mention of this. I was so terrified of Talli getting sick during this tripledemic of COVID, RSV and the flu. I had shared a bunch of articles on Facebook about protecting babies from illness since it was the only way I felt truly comfortable communicating about my desire to keep Talli safe. It was also the only way I knew his whole family would see or hear it. Months ago, I had talked with Colt about sending a massive group text regarding parenting choices we had made, which others seemed to have questions or concerns about. I had wanted to clear the air and address the elephant in the room. I wanted everyone to know they were welcome to visit us, but that we were waiting to drive far with her and taking precautions to keep her from contracting any sicknesses. I felt that I needed to say something since no one was reaching out to us and since Hilda was more than likely in their ears with exaggerations or even lies. I had something typed up in my notepad on my phone, but I wanted Colt's approval before sending it. He had thought his family would make fun of it and we would look stupid. I was so wrapped up in my thoughts that I hadn't said anything back to Darla. Not that I would've known how to respond, anyway.

"Okay, well, we should probably get going soon. We don't want to overstay. Thank you for allowing us to come over," Darla said.

"Yeah, of course," I said, trying to ignore the weirdness behind what Darla said. "I am glad you guys were able to stop by. Thank you for reaching out."

"Yeah. I had been talking to Hilda and asked her if she thought we would be able to stop by on our way up to my mom's. She said I should ask you. Thank you for letting us. We had been wanting to meet Talli," Darla said, standing up.

My body shook slightly from how uncomfortable I suddenly felt. I was ready for them to leave. I stood up, too, with Talli in my arms.

"Yeah, no problem," I said, trying to keep my composure.

"Do you mind if I get a picture of Talli really quick? You can keep holding her," Darla asked, pulling out her iPhone.

"Yeah, that's fine," I said, holding Talli in front of my body.

Darla took a couple pictures.

"Thank you," she said.

Shawn and Sarah were already standing by the front door.

"You guys should come home to visit soon," Darla said, staring at me.

I cringed at the fact she said the word home, as if the house I was standing in wasn't our home. As if we hadn't started our own family and instead were bound tightly to Colt's family as faithful servants to Queen Hilda. Normally, the word home being used like that wouldn't have made me bat an eye. It may have even made me feel warm with inclusion. Although, after everything that had happened, their family no longer felt to me the way I believed family should feel. It felt more like a prison sentence.

"Yeah, we would like to visit. We have been trying to. Every time we have plans to visit, something happens. Like the storm," I choked out a little awkward laugh.

"Mmhmm. Well, everyone would really like to see Talli, so you guys should visit soon," Darla said, looking intently at me before turning toward the door.

"Okay, have a safe drive up to your mom's. Thanks for coming over," I said, following her.

"Come home soon," Darla repeated.

Shawn had opened the door and was standing outside with Sarah. I waved to them as they turned to leave and shut the door with shaking hands. I walked with Talli to my bedroom. I was so relieved the visit was over, but I was left with a lingering sickly feeling. It hadn't gone poorly, but so many of the things said didn't sit quite right. I pulled out my phone and opened up the app for the cameras to check to make sure they had left before I set Talli in her Exersaucer so I could pee. I clicked on the garage door camera and a loop swirled as it loaded. I waited. I opened up Facebook while I let it load. The first thing that popped up was Hilda's new post. Hilda had taken one of the pictures of Talli that I posted on my private Facebook and reposted it on her profile.

She wrote, "Happy New Year and happy eight months to my granddaughter," above the picture of Talli and a black image with Happy New Year written in gold. That was annoying. I did not feel comfortable with her sharing pictures of Talli on her Facebook since she remained friends with Colt's exes. I didn't want them seeing my baby. My breathing was shallow and my stomach clenched tight. I closed Facebook and went back to the cameras. An image of Darla's car popped up. Darla was opening her car door. Shawn was walking around to the other side.

"Thanks for doing that with me," I heard Darla say blandly through the speaker of my phone.

"Yeah," Shawn muttered before climbing in the car.

The car sat for a minute before they backed up and drove down the gravel to the main road. They turned right and drove out of view of the camera. I closed the app and went to the bathroom. Sadness grabbed me as I was yet again confronted with the reminder that no one really cared about me. They wanted to see Talli, which I understood, but Talli was my baby. Why couldn't they care about me, too? It just didn't make sense in my head to cast a mother off to the side so viciously and then grapple for her baby. To me, treating the mother well was treating the baby well. I was so consumed by this undefined issue building up with Colt's family that being a mother, let alone a human being, was becoming more difficult.

21

Chapter Twenty-One

"Ithink I need to go to the doctor," I said to Colt while we sat on the couch a couple weeks after his aunt had visited.

"Okay. Why?"

"I feel crazy. I feel anxious all the time, I have nightmares every night. I barely sleep and I am exhausted. I feel like I don't want to eat, I've lost so much weight. I feel so depressed," I said to my husband, my head hanging low.

I hugged my knobby knees to my chest. Talli was in her Exersaucer playing with blue monkeys that moved across a little metal arch.

"Why?" Colt asked.

"Because of everything that has happened, plus I am so scared for the next interaction with your family. It's all I think about. I don't want to post anything on Facebook anymore because I don't want the comments. I am scared of getting a text or a call. I can't stop thinking about it all. I overthink everything." I attempted to explain.

"No one is doing anything, no one is talking to you. What do you want the doctor to do? It is just going to cost money for no reason," Colt said.

"Yeah, I know. I don't want to have to pay for it, either, but I don't know. Maybe there is medication for anxiety that I can take when something happens or when your family visits," I said.

My dad had mentioned to me a couple times over the past few months that I should look into medication to help me with the anxiety I was experiencing. I was finally thinking about doing it even though I did not want to go on medication.

"I get that no one is talking to me and nothing is happening right now, although so much has happened. I feel so sick about everything that has happened and no one is treating me normal. It's only a matter of time until the next thing happens," I added.

"I thought you didn't want to take medication?" Colt asked, raising his eyebrow.

"I don't. I just need something to help me with this. Maybe I just need a break from the visits," I said, exhausted.

"Okay. How long do you need?" Colt asked.

"I don't know. A couple weeks at least. I need some time that I can feel safe that nothing will happen, where I won't be on edge every time the phone makes a noise. I need time to feel normal. I feel like the more that happens, the crazier I feel, and closer to breaking," I spit out.

"Okay. We can take a break from visits," Colt said.

"Thank you, honey. You don't have to take a break. You can go visit your family whenever you want. I just need a break and that includes Talli. I don't want her going anywhere without me. Especially not hours away and around people who treat me so weirdly," I said, breathing out.

"Talli can't go anywhere without you, anyways. She needs you to eat," Colt said.

"Yeah, that's true," I agreed.

I hoped that I would have enough time to get to a more stable headspace. I felt like my brain was hazy, filled with smoke from fires that had been set throughout my mind. I had lost probably fifteen pounds, which I wasn't necessarily upset about. I did want to lose the baby weight I had put on during pregnancy. Yet my weight was under one-hundred pounds and it hadn't been that low since I was in middle school. I knew it wasn't healthy. Anxiety was a normal state for me now. I woke up buzzing and sick with dread, spending the day exhaustingly trying to push it down until I struggled to turn my thoughts off at night. Then, nightmares would take hold of me until I woke up and started the whole process over. It was a terrible way to live.

I also felt sick about feeling sick. I despised how I felt. I hated that I could have the most precious, sweet baby in my arms and I felt this badly. I hated that this time was supposed to be the happiest and yet, it was far from it. I felt so much love and happiness when I would soak in Talli and all the adorable new things she was learning to do. Yet it was like I was surrounded by the darkest cloud I had ever experienced. That killed me. I wanted to enjoy her and for her to know how much I enjoyed her. I didn't want her growing up with a mother struggling with depression and anxiety. My thoughts fought each other constantly on many different fronts.

Besides my own struggle with my mental health, I was always facing the dilemma with the in-laws. How would I live like this? How would this affect Talli? Would this ever end? I was starting to feel like I needed to live my life without Hilda being in it. It was a deep to my core feeling that I couldn't fight off or think my way out of. I felt within me that I needed to completely release my care for her and cut her out of mine as well as Talli's lives. She was causing so much chaos and destruction. I was starting to question if our marriage could last through this. It was getting close to being a full year of dealing with the drama she was causing. Instead of attempting to repair her damage or make amends, she was carrying on as usual, as if she was basking in the success of what she was doing. She drank in my discomfort in her presence, I could feel it, yet I couldn't stop it. She sat back enjoying the tension growing between Colt and me. Her pride swelled as her family took her side, casting me out further and further from the family.

She was like a witch. She had a hold on others. She played everyone in her life like marionettes. She was skilled in mind games and deceit. She knew how to get people to do what she wanted, think how she wanted them to think and then carry out her wishes. If they were clear-headed enough to see through her, she cast them to the side so aggressively and abruptly that they were unconscious until they awoke to find themselves imprisoned. I should know.

I struggled with how I could successfully cut her out of my life without having it impact Colt. I was starting to feel uneasy with Colt talking to his mother about me or about Talli. I didn't want her to have any more ammo against me. She used everything she possibly could. I secretly wanted Colt to tell his mother what she was doing was not okay, that she wasn't permitted to treat me as she had been, that I had just given birth, that I was a new postpartum mother and that what she was doing was wrong. I wanted him to stick up for me. I had been feeling resentment bubbling up in me from the lack of him putting his foot down. I didn't like that feeling.

As I fought through the endless waves of thoughts, time ticked by. I was trapped in my head. My fears overtook me. I was terrified of Hilda taking control of my life. I was so petrified she would demand to come over, demand to do what she wanted with Talli, and she would get her way. I was doing all I could to kill off the people pleaser in me, especially the part Hilda had worked hard to build within me specifically for her.

My virtual world became just as unsafe as my physical one. I had stopped posting anything besides my obligatory monthly pictures of Talli. I was determined to make it to her first birthday with her monthly update pictures, but it was becoming a chore. I no longer wanted to or felt good sharing her pictures. Hilda was taking the pictures I shared and using them as her own. Cynthia had been doing the same thing and she was also friends with Colt's exes online. I started sharing the pictures late at night so it would discourage others from resharing them. The other downside to posting was the comments I received.

Brittany, Charlotte and Didi were persistently writing things like "anxious to meet her" and "I hope we get to meet her soon." These comments were posted to appear good natured, although they felt dark to me. These people were not reaching out to me. Brittany, Charlotte and Didi made no effort to visit us. They were close with Hilda. They certainly made no attempt to be close with me. These comments felt more like guilt trips. They appeared to me as attempts to make me look bad, as if an outsider reading them would question why apparent family members had yet to meet a baby after eight months. Sure, they could have been harmless and maybe even were attempts to start up a conversation. Yet anyone with enough common sense would know to privately message a person or call them to start a conversation, rather than a public comment on a picture posted to Facebook. The comments felt wrong in my gut, and although my gut was getting more jumbled up, I still chose to trust it.

I had also begun to notice Gina was becoming more present in the online world of Cynthia and Hilda. I noticed Gina was the only one to like a post Cynthia shared on Facebook. I started to notice it more frequently without meaning to. It rubbed me the wrong way so I dug into it. I saw that Cynthia was commenting compliments and hearts on Gina's pictures. Cynthia and Hilda were both liking her pictures. I didn't have anything against being kind or cheering for someone as they moved through their life. It was just strange that my in-laws were still in any sort of contact with Colt's ex from at least five years ago. I believe they dated for maybe four years. Colt and I had now been together longer than that, married and had a baby together. I wasn't quite sure what the purpose was of continuing any semblance of a relationship with someone who wasn't relevant in any of our lives. It seemed that continuing contact with Gina was a card Hilda wanted to keep in her hand. There was nothing pure about it. After the way

Hilda was easily casting me out and smearing my name, I didn't see her keeping in contact with Gina in the spirit of kindness.

My break from visits was helpful, but I got lightning bolt shocks of panic whenever Hilda called Colt. He would get up from the couch or out of bed, leave the room, go into another and shut the door. It was as if Hilda was "the other woman." It had gotten so weird. I ached for Colt and the dilemma he also faced. He wanted to have it all, and why shouldn't he get to? It wasn't right that he felt pressured to choose between his wife and his mom. It wasn't fair to him that every time his mom spoke to him, she talked ill of the woman he chose to share his life with. It wasn't fair to him that when he entrusted his wife with what his mother was saying, his wife spoke ill of the woman who gave him life. I knew that. I tried hard to not let my emotions overtake me and make me say things Colt didn't deserve to hear. I felt like I was failing him when I cried out how I hated his mom. But every time I heard what Hilda was saying about me to Colt or to someone else, thick, molten hatred boiled inside of me. It felt like she was trying to destroy me and my fight response was armored up, sword drawn.

All these draining, conflicting thoughts were building up to my demise. It was a cold, icy day in February. Colt was in Texas. I had just shared Talli's nine-month update the night before. The typical comments came in from the usual suspects.

"Really hoping to meet Talli soon!" commented Brittany, who added a smiley face to her seemingly innocuous message.

My phone pinged. Then it pinged again. I looked down at the screen. Hilda had started a group message with Colt and me. She was sending information about Mackenzi's dance recital.

"She's on at two-thirty and again at four-thirty," the text from Hilda read, followed by a picture of a dance itinerary.

"Here's the link," another text from Hilda popped through along with a link to watch the recital online.

My head swirled. My muscles twitched and I felt toxic energy overtaking me. I took Talli to her room and carefully set her in her crib. That caused her to start screaming. She hated being in her crib. I felt my heart ache, but I needed a minute to get myself together. I didn't want her to witness me trying to break out of my overwhelming negative feelings. It all felt like too much. Too much had happened, for too long, and my head was too messed up from it all. I didn't want Brittany's comments or Hilda's group texts. I wanted peace, I wanted love, I wanted safety. These people were incapable of providing me with any of that. I ran into my bedroom and screamed into a pillow. I jumped up and down, forcefully trying to expel the negative emotions and thoughts of wanting to be free of this torture. All these little, stupid things built up into a mountain of hell in my mind. I broke. I couldn't escape it. The jumping and the screaming weren't working. Before I knew what I was doing, I ran into the bathroom and pulled out a tiny pair of scissors. I opened the scissors wide and instantly slid them across my ankle twice. As soon as the two marks turned white, before they bubbled red blood, the darkness disappeared from me. I was instantly wiped clean back to my senses. My dread was replaced with guilt and regret. I couldn't believe what I had just done. I sprinted to Talli, who was sitting in her crib crying. I hoisted her out and held her close to my heart.

Tears streamed down my cheeks as I repeated, "I'm so sorry."

I brought her into the bathroom and set her in her Exersaucer while I cleaned my cuts. I put a large Band-Aid over them and covered it all with a long sock. I was so ashamed. I hadn't done that in years, since I had been depressed in high school. I felt like I had failed as a mother. I blew my nose and wiped away my tears. I carried Talli into the living room and I sat with her and her toys.

"I will never let myself get to that point again. Talli, I am so sorry."

I spoke out loud to my innocent baby, who had no clue what had just happened.

"I have failed you. It will not happen again. I won't allow it to. I love you so much. My love for you is stronger than my pain. It is stronger than my anxiety. You do not deserve this. You deserve a happy and healthy life. You deserve a mom who is healthy and happy. I will get rid of the darkness inside of me because I will not let this affect you. I am terrified it may already have in some way. I cannot continue living like this. I have been struggling with this for far too long. It must end."

My crazed mind was just clear enough to carve out a path to freedom, not only for my sake, but for Talli's. I wasn't able to see the light at the end of the tunnel quite yet, but I believed wholeheartedly that it was there.

22

Chapter Twenty-Two

It was the night after Colt returned back home from Texas. Talli was sleeping peacefully in bed while Colt and I sat on our living room couch.

"I need to tell you something," I said, hugging my knees into my chest.

"What is it?" Colt replied, whipping around to look at me intently.

"I did something I regret," I said quietly and looked down at my toes.

Colt's eyes were smoldering when I looked up at him and he looked at me gravely.

"Not that," I chuckled sadly. "I didn't do anything stupid like cheat on you. I wouldn't do that. No, I did something I regret to myself. I was feeling really bad, the worst I've felt throughout this whole issue."

I looked down again. It was hard for me to say it. "I hurt myself."

"What? How? Where? Where was Talli?" Colt fired off questions, fury in his voice.

"She was in her room in her crib. I put her there because I could feel my anger and pain building up. I needed to release it somehow. I did it quickly and ran right back to her. I know, I really messed up. I promise to you that it won't happen again. I am really sorry," I said, looking into Colt's angry eyes.

He looked away.

"Let me see," he said.

I took off the sock on my left foot. I peeled back the Band-Aid to reveal the two inch-long, paper-cut looking lines of red.

"I can't believe you did that," Colt said.

"I know. I can't believe I did, either. I am aware I really messed up. I cannot ever do that again, which is why I need to go to the doctor. This is getting too much for me on my own. I need something. Whether that be better counseling, medication or whatever they may suggest, I know that I need help," I said.

"Okay. Call tomorrow and make an appointment," Colt said.

"Well, the thing is, I already called. I called the day after I hurt myself. My appointment is in two days, this Thursday. I made it in the morning. You can go with me or not, it's up to you," I said.

"What doctor did you find?" Colt asked.

"I just called my old gynecologist's office. I wasn't sure where to go. It made sense to go to someone who specializes in postpartum anxiety or depression, since part of why I am struggling to cope with all this has to be that I am not yet back to my normal self. I feel so weak," I explained.

"Okay. Well, I am glad you are doing something to fix it," Colt said.

"Do you still love me?" I asked quietly.

"Yes, of course I love you," Colt said.

He pulled me into his arms and I let myself relax into him. I leaned into the feeling of being warm and safe.

"I love you so much. Thank you for being here for me. I am really trying to get better," I said, hugging his arm that was around me.

On Thursday morning, we buckled Talli into her car seat. I sat beside her while Colt drove us the half-hour to the doctor's office.

"Do you want to come inside or sit in the car?" I asked Colt.

"I don't know. How long will this be?"

"I have no idea. Maybe a half-hour, but I'm not sure," I said, un-buckling my seat belt.

"We'll just come in with you," Colt said as he turned his truck off and got out.

We walked inside the empty building, went up the elevator and checked in at the front desk. There was a pregnant woman with a small child sitting across from us in the small waiting room. I hugged Talli close and kissed her on her head.

"Adison?" A nurse called out from the doorway.

We got up and followed her into the hallway. She took my weight and then led us into a room.

"What brings you in today?" The nurse asked as she sat down at the desk.

"I think I have postpartum anxiety. I have been dealing with a lot of issues with my in-laws..." I stopped.

My throat closed up and my mind swirled. I didn't know how to explain all this.

"Okay, can you tell me more about it?" The nurse asked while typ-ing on a laptop.

"I feel really weird talking about this with you here," I said, turning to Colt.

"Okay, do you want me to go into the waiting room?" he asked.

"Maybe, I just feel bad. I hate talking about it around you," I shook my head and put my hands over my face.

Colt got up with Talli and went into the waiting room.

"Well, a lot has happened. It all began when my mother-in-law vis-ited after I gave birth."

I attempted to explain what had been going on as quickly as I could. I felt embarrassed heat throughout my body. Tears were hot be-hind my eyes.

"Okay, that does sound like a lot. Have you tried talking to your mother-in-law?" asked the nurse.

"Yes, I did. I also did therapy from October to November. It all just keeps getting worse, I feel like," I said.

"Okay, the doctor will be in shortly."

The nurse closed her laptop and left the room. About five minutes later, the doctor entered. She looked to be in her forties. She had me re-explain everything I had just said to the nurse. I felt exasperated as I tried to sum up my experiences and feelings in a couple minutes. It was disappointing to me not to be able to tell the full story. I felt like each piece was so vital to explaining the reasoning behind why I felt so crazy.

"Okay. I think you show some signs of a little bit of postpartum anxiety and depression, but you have had zero issues adjusting to motherhood. So, I don't think it is much on the postpartum side. I am not exactly sure what you want us to do. I can give you our recommendations for therapists if you would like to go that route. I can also give you a prescription for a low dose of anxiety medication if you would like to try that," said the doctor, who then explained the medication option in more detail.

It would be a low dose of some generic drug that attempts to shut down anxiety. I tried to understand the talk of SSRI's and inhibitors, but I got lost. I had learned about them before, but the information never seemed to stick.

"I would like to try the medication, I suppose, and I will take the information for the counselors. I want medication that I don't have to take every day, just as needed. I would like to not have to take it one day, when I feel better. I also want to do counseling at home so I can have Talli with me," I said.

The doctor wrote a prescription that she sent to the Giant Eagle pharmacy on the other side of town and then handed me a piece of paper with the counseling services listed. She circled her top two recommendations out of the seven. We left and I felt dismayed, like the doctor didn't understand.

"I hope this medication helps you," Colt said as we waited in the pharmacy drive-thru line.

"Yeah, me too," I said. "I don't want to have to take it that much. I am nervous to try it."

When the pharmacist handed Colt the medication, he tossed it into the back seat to me. I grabbed it and quickly put it in Talli's diaper bag. It was like a hot coal in my hand. As we drove back to our house, I looked out the window morosely. I felt like a complete mess.

When we got home, I rolled the little orange container with pills back and forth in my hands. I read the white labels taped on the sides of it and then read over the papers that were stuffed into the bag it came in. I didn't want to have to take a drug to feel better. I put the container and the papers back into the clear plastic bag they came in and pushed them to the back of my bedside drawer. I hoped I wouldn't have to use it. I was unaware that in a couple weeks I'd be ripping the bottle out of the drawer and throwing back a small white pill out of desperation.

23

Chapter Twenty-Three

It was the last Wednesday of February. The air was cold, the sky was gray and there were mushy, brown snow patches scattered outside. Colt and I were sitting in the Home Depot parking lot when both of our phones pinged. We both looked down at our respective phones and read the same text from the same person.

"Hey guys. We would like to see you this Sunday. Your place or ours, doesn't matter. Let me know," the text from Hilda read.

She had even added a red heart emoji at the end. What the hell. My body sent off alarm bells and I started to shake.

Teeth chattering, I said to Colt, "Honey, you can respond to that. I don't even know what to think. Maybe she is trying to be better? It just feels really weird after all this time. I don't know. All I know is now I don't feel good. This sucks."

"What do you want me to say?" Colt asked.

"Whatever you want, I don't know. I really am not ready to see her, but I feel like I have to. Just tell them to come over to our house, I guess," I said before moaning. "This sucks."

"Okay, I'll reply later," Colt said, putting his phone in his coat pocket and getting out of the car.

As we walked around Home Depot, I couldn't stop my body from shaking. My blood felt icy under my skin and I felt like I needed to run into the bathroom to throw up my lunch.

"We need to reply and get this over with. I am so anxious," I finally said as we stood in the rug aisle.

I hugged Talli close while Colt sighed and typed back a message to his mom.

"Okay. You guys can come to our house," Colt sent the text in the same group thread his mom started.

"Great. What time?" popped back the reply from Hilda.

Colt looked at me and then back at his phone.

He typed, "How does two work?"

"Great. See you then," Hilda texted back, again adding a red heart emoji at the end.

My anxiety grew instead of dissipating. What did I think would happen by having him reply? There was nothing that was going to fix this other than to not have this meeting happen. I felt trapped, yet again.

I quickly typed up a message to my mom.

It read, "Hilda is visiting this Sunday at two in the afternoon. Do you think it would be a good idea if you were there? To try to be a calming presence or at least someone she won't treat me badly in front of?"

I got a quick reply back from my mom that read, "Absolutely. I think that is a great idea. I'll try to be there about a half-hour before she arrives."

I breathed out. Okay, maybe this could work. Maybe Hilda would put on her show for my mom and be so focused on trying to look good that she wouldn't make me so uncomfortable. My heart thudded and I spent the rest of the day unsuccessfully trying to calm it.

Every day, every hour, every minute that stood between me and two on Sunday felt like another step closer to my impending doom.

It was torture. I could only stomach enough food to survive, my sleep was atrocious and I felt electrified. I kept trying to focus on breathing in and out, counting my breaths, and even tried thinking of all of the possible positive scenarios. Maybe they would come over and it would be fine. Maybe Hilda would be kind and start working on repairing things. Maybe I could feel okay around her again. Although, every time I forced these positive thoughts into my mind, my gut dove into depths I had never fathomed. I'd feel a dark pit of emptiness inside me and feelings of utter dread. My gut was warning me this was not how things were going to go. I could feel that things were not good between Hilda and me. I had been feeling it for a long time. The feeling only kept getting stronger and more intense. I was truly starting to feel as if she was a demonic presence in my life. That sounds absolutely insane and overdramatic, I know. I just couldn't change that feeling no matter how much I tried to talk myself out of it, yoga my way out of it or breathe my way out of it.

At one-thirty on Sunday, my mom arrived. I felt the same way I had felt for nine months: heart racing, cold sweats, vomit in my throat, dizzy and like I wanted to jump on the next flight to another country. My mom tried to converse with me, but I just couldn't. My brain wasn't working and I was too focused on not passing out. Colt had put golf on the TV. Time ticked on. My mom rested her head on the top of the couch behind her and closed her eyes. I sat on the floor with Talli. Colt sat in the kitchen on his phone. When my mom raised her head and looked over at her phone to see what time it was, her eyes opened wide.

"It is two thirty. Has anyone heard anything?" she asked.

"No. This always happens," I said.

"This is so annoying. I will text them," Colt said, rolling his eyes.

A couple minutes later, Colt's phone pinged.

"They said they are in our town," Colt said.

My uncomfortable, miserable feelings heightened. I braced for their imminent arrival. I kept bracing and bracing until another twenty minutes passed.

"Jesus Christ. I just want to get this over with," I moaned after looking at my phone and seeing it was now past three.

Ten minutes later, the doorbell rang and my heart plummeted. I sat on my portion of the couch by the window, removed still from the rest, which was on the other side of the living room. Talli was in my lap with a couple of her toys. Hilda, Clayton and Mackenzi stomped in. Mackenzi and Clayton were arguing loudly about something as they walked into the space between the living room and kitchen. Hilda walked in, nose in the air, shoulders slumped forward and quietly said hello to Colt.

"Hi, Hilda," my mom said while standing up and waving.

"Oh, hi Cara!" Hilda trilled, suddenly full of energy.

Her body posture immediately changed as she threw her shoulders back. Hilda drifted over to my mom and gave her a hug.

"It is so great to see you!" Hilda gushed.

I looked down at Talli and sighed. Hilda's acting was so cringy. All of a sudden, she liked my mom? She was civil and even nice to her when they both came to visit in West Texas when Talli was born. Before that, though, my mom used to become so overwhelmed and frustrated when dealing with Hilda. They didn't interact too often, but during our wedding planning Hilda was very difficult. Everything had to be her way and she was very argumentative.

Our wedding was originally going to be at Bolongo Bay in St. Thomas, United States Virgin Islands. It was going to be an all-inclusive wedding with a planner. I had to pick some stuff and then I was simply expected to show up. It sounded dreamy. Instead of that, the world experienced a pandemic, COVID-19, that ended up canceling our wedding a month before the scheduled date. I scrambled to plan a new wedding for the same date because I didn't want to wait any longer. We had already been engaged for a year and a half. I worked hard and with determination. I found a local venue that said it would host a small group of people so we could have a wedding. I figured out each piece and planned myself a wedding in a month. My mom helped me a ton. We also asked Hilda if she wanted to help us. She would be in charge of the flowers. Hilda became fairly difficult. She kept having her own ideas and then would ask me questions to ask my mom, so I ended up having to be their interpreter. Then one day, my mom and I were sitting at the counter in my kitchen working on planning. Hilda sent me a text asking me to ask my mom something about utensils and for me to give her a call when I was able.

"Should I call her?" I asked my mom.

"Sure," my mom answered, unenthused.

"Hey Hilda, I am sitting with my mom," I said before the two moms attempted to converse.

I remember feeling so awkward and uncomfortable as they argued with each other.

"What are the measurements for the tablecloths that you ordered?" Hilda asked, her voice full of attitude.

"I don't know the measurements. I got tablecloths. They will be fine. They aren't that important," my mom answered.

"Well, you don't want to see people's feet! You should check on the measurements of whatever you got. I have tablecloths in our barn. I can bring them. I don't know the measurements of the tables at the venue, so it would be helpful to know that, also, if you could find that out," Hilda sneered.

"Hilda, you can also call the venue and find that out if it is that important to you. I don't think Adison is worried about tablecloths, though. I think she is just grateful to be able to have a small wedding at this point. Right, Adison?" my mom snapped.

"Uh, yeah. I am mostly just worried about having the venue, my dress getting altered in time and finding someone to do my makeup," I said, trying to laugh. "So don't worry about anything else much. I appreciate all of your guys' help."

"Adison, trust me, you do not want the tablecloths to be too short. It will not look good. Call the venue and find out the length of the tables and give me a call back," Hilda instructed. "Oh, while you're here on the phone Cara, don't forget to get serving spoons. And napkins. And utensils. You should make sure that is on your to do list. It would be really unfortunate to have food but no way to serve or eat it."

"Fuck, Hilda!" my mom shouted. "I will get it handled. Thanks!"

My mom hung up the phone.

"Jesus Christ. She is difficult," said my mom, putting her face in her hands.

That difficult attitude of hers was something I had learned to live with. She didn't listen to me about how I wanted the tables arranged for our wedding reception, she just did it her way the day of. I asked her weeks in advance if she or any of the bridesmaids wanted their hair or makeup done by the two ladies I hired. She said no to the makeup and yes to the hair. On the day of my wedding, as my hairstylist was about halfway done with my braid, Hilda came up to me, asking to use my makeup artist before me. She had already asked my makeup artist. I felt so put on the spot and like I wasn't really given a choice. I ended up having to wait for her makeup to be done and then the artist had to clean all of the brushes before doing mine. This made me late for my own wedding ceremony. I wasn't able to get bridal pictures, I was basically rushed into my dress and pushed out the door. Her one job was to take care of the flowers. She did not have them cut or tied. They were all in vases. So, while I was being pushed to get dressed, my bridesmaids and my mom were cutting and tying up flowers. Her cell phone rang loudly during our ceremony and, after it, while Colt and I were getting our wedding pictures taken, she burst in demanding a picture.

"I just want a picture with my son!" Hilda cried out, pushing me aside.

I will never forget it. My photographer looked around uncomfortably before snapping pictures of the groom and his mother. I stood off to the side, watching my new husband and new mother-in-law take pictures together almost immediately after my wedding ceremony. Hilda had her hand on Colt's stomach and pressed her face against his. She posed kissing his cheek. I turned away.

As time went on, everything was more and more about Hilda, to the point where I no longer felt as if I was allowed to be my own person while in her presence. Whenever she called me, she argued with me, trying to pound her beliefs and thoughts into me like nails in a wall. I stopped telling her anything of value, but she would find out things from Colt. She also did the same thing to him where she would push her view of how our life should be on him. She thought Colt and I should be more social. She thought we should basically live as if we were in the TV show, *Friends*. Literally. She constantly asked if we were becoming friends with our neighbors across from us in our apartment complexes we lived in and scolded us for not taking advantage of apartment living in that way. There was nothing wrong with the man in his fifties whose door was across from ours, but I didn't feel inclined to become BFFs. She thought I should continue friendships that clearly were no longer working. She thought I should work without breaks, fold clothes a specific way, buy certain products and on and on. It was exhausting.

So now, watching Hilda fawn over my mom made me cringe. She wasn't being nice to be nice. She was being nice to my mom to try to make me feel uncomfortable and left out. Hilda and Mackenzi sat on the couch near my mom. Clayton sat on one of our barstools and talked to Colt, who was still standing in the kitchen. Mackenzi had her phone in her face while Hilda conversed dramatically with my mom. I sat with Talli and played with her. Things continued like this for an hour. At one point, silence overcame Hilda and Cara, so they looked over at Talli. Talli tugged on my tank top.

"Are you still breastfeeding?" Hilda asked me, point blank.

"Uh, yeah," I said uncomfortably.

Hilda slightly raised her head up and then back down. She turned back to my mom. I hoisted Talli up on my shoulder and got up to pace around for a little bit to try to burn off nervous energy. We were almost on the third hour of their visit.

"I don't agree with putting cameras on the outside of your house," Hilda was saying. "We are all being tracked and watched. Anyone can hack into them and see everything. The government watches them. You know, those cards we all carry in our wallets or purses? Our credit cards? The government is tracking us with them. They are watching what we do. Our phones are tracking us, too, always. I wish I didn't have to have a phone. It is so creepy that they are listening to everything we say."

Hilda's eyes darted wildly.

"Oh... yeah," My mom uttered, trying to hide a smirk.

I knew my mom thought this was insane.

"Yeah. You have to be so careful. They are going to use it to control us. It is really scary what the government is doing," Hilda continued.

I smiled behind her back, thankful for the comic relief. I knew Hilda had some crazy opinions and views. I had heard them before and knew she believed in Donald Trump. She believed in many conspiracy theories.

"Are you guys planning any trips?" my mom said, quickly changing the topic.

I could tell she was becoming uncomfortable with the conspiracy talk.

"Yeah. We are going on a cruise to the Bahamas in March for Mackenzi's senior trip," Hilda said, straightening her back.

"Aw, that will be fun," my mom said.

I focused on Talli. I was playing with her on the floor behind the couch between the kitchen and the dining area. I had tuned myself out of the conversations for an unknown amount of time. When my attention returned to the conversation in the living room, the women were talking about firesticks.

"Do we have your firestick?" Hilda turned to ask me.

"Oh, I don't know. I know we had one at some point. I'm not sure what happened to it," I said.

"Well, we might have yours. We have like three of them, somewhere. I think there are two in the storage unit, and one in the barn," she said.

"Oh, okay. That's fine. We don't need it," I said.

"Yeah, we don't need them, either. I don't know why they were so popular. Or how we ended up with so many," Hilda giggled.

Hilda stared at me as if she was trying to suck out my soul with her eyes, then turned back to Cara.

"Oh, as I was telling you earlier, we went dress shopping for Mackenzi's senior prom the other weekend. You would be shocked at how expensive the dresses are now," Hilda said.

"Oh, yeah, they are always expensive," Cara said.

"But of course we had to get it. It is truly gorgeous on Mackenzi. I still can't believe how much we paid, though," Hilda said.

"Was it like a hundred bucks?" my mom asked.

Hilda smiled with her lips pressed tight together and shook her head side to side as if she was trying to hold in a secret.

"A couple hundred?"

"More," Hilda said.

"A thousand?" my mom said in disbelief.

"Mmhmm," Hilda hummed. "Mackenzi, you have a picture on your phone. Show Cara the dress."

Mackenzi scrolled on her phone and then held her screen out in front of my mom.

"Wow, that is pretty. I love that color!" said my mom.

"So do I," Hilda grinned proudly.

"Aw, Talli is so cute!" my mom exclaimed as Talli crawled after her little orange ball.

I had been rolling it to Talli and she would roll it back to me. Hilda turned to look at us. Mackenzi came around to the back of the couch, sitting down across from where Talli and I sat. She grabbed the ball as it rolled by her.

"Talli, over here," Mackenzi said, waving the ball in the air.

Talli crawled halfway over to her before stopping to look back at me. Mackenzi rolled her the ball. Talli grabbed it and crawled back into my lap before rolling it again. Clayton involved himself by stepping on the ball as it rolled near him. He still had his beat-up work boots on. I made a mental note of that so I could wash off the ball after they left. Talli put everything in her mouth. I hoped I could avoid Talli putting the ball in her mouth until I was able to clean it. Everyone's eyes were on Talli and I felt uncomfortable. I pasted a forced smile on my face to try to get through it until everyone went back to their respective conversations. Once they finally did, I released the breath I hadn't realized I had been holding in. Hilda was back to laughing and carrying on her act with my mom. Mackenzi sat by her phone plugged into the wall in the living room. Clayton loudly talked to Colt about what Colt should be doing financially.

Alarm bells suddenly sounded in my head. My mind started to spiral. I felt like I was losing it, like if I sat quietly, uncomfortable in my own home for one moment longer, I'd scream. I wanted to get up and run away. The chaos got louder in my brain, making my body feel electrified. I slowly stood up with Talli and carried her into my bedroom. I closed the door behind us silently. I gently lowered Talli into her Exersaucer and then hungrily pulled out the container with the anxiety medication. I opened it and let a tiny white pill land in my palm. I looked at it for a quick second before tossing it back. I felt my heart sink and lift all at once. I hated that I felt so chaotic that I had to take that pill, but I also felt a sense of security that I had the pill to take. I felt ease wash over me as my emotions began to settle into indifference. I lifted Talli out of her Exersaucer and slowly walked back out into the kitchen. I pulled out a bubbled glass and got myself water. I took a couple sips and set it down on the counter next to the oven. I went back to my separated couch piece and sat there with Talli. I had no clue what anyone around me was saying. I sat numbly, look-ing at Talli, who played with her little toys. She dangled her plastic keys, shaking them so they hit each other as they moved side to side. No amount of numbness could keep my heart from swelling at the amount of love I had for her. I softly smiled while I watched her.

I looked at the clock. They had been at our house for four hours. I needed them to leave. I was surviving by sitting in my numbness, but I was so tired. My stomach was also beginning to rumble.

"Well, I think we are going to go to the grocery store soon," Colt spoke up.

Everyone ignored him. The conversations went on, muffled to me as my ears worked to close them out of my brain.

"Thanks for coming over. Have a good drive back. We have things to do tonight. I have to leave again for work tomorrow," Colt said, louder this time.

My heart lifted. I felt so thankful for Colt and for him saying some-thing. I hoped that his family would get up and make their way toward the door, but everyone still acted as if he hadn't spoken at all.

"Okay. Time for you guys to get the fuck out," Colt said loudly.

He said it in a straightforward way with a twinge of playfulness. He didn't say it with any lack of kindness. He said it to get everyone's attention and it worked.

"Okay, Colt," Hilda said, rolling her eyes.

She slowly stood up. Mackenzi had been in the bathroom.

"Can we leave?" Mackenzi said as she walked out into the room.

"Yeah, we are leaving," Hilda said.

Hilda rolled her eyes again as she pushed herself up from the couch.

"It was nice to see you, Cara," Hilda said.

"It was nice to see you, too," said my mom.

"Bye," Hilda said, glancing around the room.

She grimaced at Colt and then swiftly shot me a glare before walk-ing out the door. Mackenzi gave Colt, Talli and I a small smile before following her mom out the door. Clayton said bye to Colt, shook his head and followed his daughter. Once the door was shut, my mom, Colt and I stood in the kitchen in silence for a second. I suddenly noticed it had become dark outside. The room glowed yellow from the kitchen lights.

I held up my middle finger toward the door and yelled, "Fuck you," before sinking to the floor, sobbing. I was dizzy, exhausted and felt as if all the happiness had been sucked out of me.

"Oh, honey," my mom said as she rushed over to my side. "I thought you did so well. You got through it. It's over and they are gone."

"I know. I just feel so crazy. I feel so frustrated. I always feel so unwelcome in my own home," I cried.

"Yeah, I know, but you did it. Also, I hope you know I wasn't trying to make you feel bad by being friendly with Hilda. I was just trying to get us through it. I'm going to leave so you can relax. Is there anything I can do before I go?" my mom asked.

"No, thank you for being here for that. I appreciate it. It didn't make me feel bad, it helped a lot," I said, sniffling.

My mom gave me a hug before leaving.

"Let's go get food," Colt said before pulling me into his arms for a loving hug.

2 4

Chapter Twenty-Four

We brought home takeout from Hop Hing. I ordered my usual, bourbon chicken with white rice. I ate two bites before putting it in the fridge.

"Honey, what is going on? You're so quiet," Colt said.

"I'm fine," I said.

After my explosion, I felt like a robot that someone had hit the off switch on. In a strange way, I didn't really feel emotion, but I felt relief. It felt good to feel nothing.

"No, something is up. You're being really different. It's like you are dead," Colt said, concerned.

"Honestly, I feel nothing and it is wonderful," I said.

"I don't like this medicine. I don't like what it is doing to you," Colt said with his eyes narrowed.

"It's okay. I'm going to go to bed," I said.

"You barely ate."

"I'm not hungry," I said, getting up to go brush my teeth.

I got ready for bed and then laid down. It was the quickest I had fallen asleep in months.

When I woke up, it felt like I had been out the whole night before drinking. I had a pounding headache and my mouth was dry. I felt nauseous and the room spun. It took a while for that feeling to wear off. I struggled throughout the day, which followed into struggling throughout the week. I felt like I had peaked in my depression. I was completely miserable. I kept thinking that maybe everything would be easier if I was dead. Then I'd feel awful guilt for thinking like that when I had Talli to take care of and love. Luckily, on Saturday, I had my first scheduled appointment with my new therapist. The day after I had gone to see the doctor, I called the top recommended counseling service they had given me information for. They were pretty full, so my first appointment had been set for four weeks following my call. I was desperate to have a professional to talk to.

On Saturday morning, I woke up ready to go.

"Colt, I have my first therapy session today. I will go in our room to do it. Please stay out here with Talli. The instructions for virtual therapy say that I have to be alone and stationary," I said.

"Okay," Colt said.

I went into my bedroom with a steamy mug of chai tea and a chocolate peanut butter Luna bar. I sat on the bed with the therapy app open on my phone. I didn't want to be late. A few minutes later, my new therapist appeared on the screen.

"Hi Adison, I'm Nollie," she said. "How are you? Today is going to be more of an assessment so that I can learn more about you. We will also discuss how therapy will be structured and how we will work to achieve your goals."

"Hi Nollie, I'm okay. How are you? That sounds good to me."

"I'm good, thanks for asking. Now, let's start off with what brings you to therapy," Nollie asked.

"So, it is a long story. Basically, I have been having issues with my mother-in-law since my baby was born. I've felt very anxious, depressed, stressed, suffocated and miserable due to that. I also think that I am not able to handle it all as well because I am still in postpartum. I feel like I am more sensitive than I normally would be and I feel like I am unable to cope with it all. I just want to be happy and enjoy my precious time with my little baby," I said, sighing.

"I am sorry you've been feeling that way. We can definitely work on those feelings and help you to feel better. Can you tell me a little bit more about the issues with your mother-in-law?" she asked.

I told her about how it started in West Texas, how things began to get stranger, some of the comments made and where things were at currently.

"That is a lot. That sounds like it would be really hard to deal with," Nollie said.

She asked some more background questions to get to understand me and my past better. The session ended quicker than I was ready for. We scheduled to meet virtually again in two weeks. I wanted to do it every week, but the price for this counseling service was much higher than the previous one. I knew it was important and it would help me, although I still felt like I was throwing our money down the toilet. I wished I could be stronger and didn't need to do this.

***

Every day seemed to morph together. I woke up every morning, cared for Talli, pushed myself to do something positive and tried not to fall apart in the evening. Some days, I felt like I was making good progress. Other days, it was like I would never climb out of this pit. This repetitive pattern of trying to survive was draining and defeating. I couldn't understand why I couldn't just be normal and enjoy my time with my quickly growing baby.

***

It was Wednesday, the twenty-second of March. Colt left at ten in the morning to go to the airport and head out of state for work. I cleaned the house and did the laundry. That night, I was lying in bed with *Ridiculousness* playing quietly on the TV in our room. Talli was asleep beside me.

A notification lit up my phone. "Hilda CorrigonWitleyVoor invited you to her event, Mackenzi's Grad Party," the notification read.

My stomach dropped and my blood rushed ice cold. Electric bolts ran up and down my body. I had a gut feeling she did something crazy. After all of her subtle emotional abuse for the past year, I was sure she was going to amp it up by inviting Colt's exes. Hilda had been getting away with ignoring me, treating me poorly, talking about me behind my back and saying strange things in front of me in an attempt to get some kind of reaction. I clicked on the notification and was brought to the event page. I clicked on where it showed who was invited. I scrolled through the list. Even though I had a gut feeling they would be there, I still felt shock when I saw Gina and Angela's names included. No freaking way. It was kind of like I just predicted the next president or the winning lottery number. It felt surreal that my gut feeling had been so spot on. My hands shook as I called Colt.

"Hey. You're not going to believe this. Did you get that invite on Facebook from your mom?" I asked when he answered.

"What invite? Oh, yeah, I see it now," he said.

"She invited your exes," I spit out quickly.

"What? No. No way. That is insane. She wouldn't," Colt said.

"Just look," I said.

It was quiet for a moment as Colt scrolled through the list. Then I heard him breathe out.

"Oh, wow. I'm honestly shocked. I can't believe she did that," Colt finally said.

"Yeah. I had a weird feeling she did so I looked and my feeling was right. I can't believe it, either. What is she thinking? The only thing that makes sense is that she did it to upset me. She knows I don't want anything to do with your exes. She knows it makes me uncomfortable when she brings them up. There is no other reason," I said.

"I can't think of any good reason, either," Colt said.

"There isn't one. They have not been involved in anything for over five years. It is really strange that your mom seems to want to cling onto them. It's strange because she puts so much effort into bringing them up or keeping them relevant. I am certain she does it to make me uncomfortable. It doesn't add up that they were really just that impor-tant to her. If she put that effort into a relationship with me and us, we wouldn't be in this mess. It's just insane," I said, my voice shaking.

"Calm down. I agree. She didn't like them that much when I was dating them. She complained about them, too," Colt said. "I am really pissed about this. I want to call her and yell at her. Now I don't even want to go to my sister's graduation party."

"I am definitely not going. I am not risking running into your exes. Talli does not need to be involved in any of this. Talli doesn't need to know your exes. Her inviting them is so disrespectful to our fam-ily and a slap in the face. You can go if you want, although I feel un-comfortable with that because what if you run into them? Then you're there and your mom is going to act so innocent, pulling you into a conversation with them, which is so unnecessary. I hate that she put us into this spot," I said, putting my face in my hands.

"I am not going. I don't want to see them. She probably would do something stupid like that. I have to get back to work. We can talk about this more later. I love you," Colt said before getting off of the phone.

I was still shaking. I needed to talk to someone. I called my mom. The phone rang until it went to her voicemail. I called my dad.

"Hey, are you busy?" I asked when he answered.

"No, what's up?" my dad said.

"Hilda made a Facebook event for Mackenzi's graduation party and invited Colt's exes," I blurted out.

My dad slowly chuckled and then said, "What? You're kidding."

"No, I'm serious," I said.

"She's fucking insane," he laughed.

"I know."

"I'm sure you and Colt already talked about it. What does he think?" he asked.

"He said he was pissed about it and he wanted to yell at her."

"Well, I wouldn't do that. That's good he's mad about it, too. Hopefully that will get her to stop doing shit like that," my dad said.

"Yeah. I don't want to invite her to Talli's birthday."

"You have to invite her," he said.

"I really don't," I said, annoyed.

"Yes, you really do. She's still Colt's mom and Talli's grandma," he said.

"I'm really at the point where I don't think that matters anymore. She has caused so much stress and has made this year really difficult. It should've been a happy year. It never should've been like this," I said.

"I completely agree with you, but you still have to invite her," my dad said.

I hurried to get off of the phone because I suddenly felt even worse. I did not want to feel like I had to do something that I didn't agree with. I didn't want her to ruin yet another important moment in Talli's life for me. I felt as though Hilda inviting Colt's exes to a family event was a perfectly good reason to not invite her to Talli's upcoming birthday party.

25

⧉

Chapter Twenty-Five

"Wow," my specialist said, her eyes wide. She blinked a couple times. "I'm aghast that your mother-in-law invited her son's exes to a family party. You said the exes hadn't been involved for over five years?"

"Yeah. It didn't and doesn't make sense. Well, it makes sense if she wanted to cause issues and try to hurt me. Those exes are like ten years older than Mackenzi. I also don't get how their short-lived involvement in her life granted them an invite to her graduation party. I don't know. I've tried to think about it in hundreds of ways and perspectives. At the end of the day, exes are in the past and I don't believe there is any justified enough reason to continue to include them. Especially if things didn't end well." I crossed my arms, frowning. It still made a fire flicker inside me.

"I am truly sorry you had to deal with that. Are you still angry about it?"

"Thinking about it too much, yeah. I mean, it is just so messed up. It is so disrespectful. It was the one thing Hilda knew would cause a reaction from me. Colt had asked her time after time to stop bringing up his exes. He had told her it made me uncomfortable. I think it was eye-opening to how much she really wanted to cause me pain and make me feel uncomfortable," I said, shaking my head.

"Why do you think it makes you upset to talk about his exes?" my specialist asked me. "Not that it isn't justified, it is. I'm just wondering if this is something we can explore so you can feel more empowered if they are brought up in the future."

"Hm. Honestly, I think it goes deeper than the past. Yes, it does make me feel upset because of Colt and I's past where his ex continued to involve herself. More than that, though, I want to feel so fiercely loved. I don't want to think about Colt having loved anyone else. I want that fairy tale. I want to wipe clean the past and feel like we are first loves. I think as a child, I was so enamored by Disney movies and that one true love. So, I feel like by bringing up other people, I am not special. I'm not that one true fairy tale love," I said, unable to meet her eyes.

"That does make sense. I do think those things can coexist, though. Try to think about it like this: Aren't you that one true love? He didn't marry those other women. He didn't want to spend the rest of his life with them. They were steppingstones to get to you, if you think about it," she said, calmly. "Rest with that for a little bit. It sounds like that is a deep-rooted belief or feeling you carry. You can change it. It will take time. Don't get on yourself for that." my specialist said before pausing. "Your mother-in-law found your triggers, your weaknesses, and used them against you. You shouldn't feel negatively toward yourself because you were baited."

"You're right," I said, letting her words soak in. "I also want to say that separating this all out, breaking it down, opens me up to deeper thoughts and feelings. Like, I do not harbor negative feelings toward those women. I simply want them to stay on their own path and not intertwine into mine. From my personal experience, Gina is not the nicest person I've come across. I think she has, um, things she could work on." I paused for a second. "Actually, yeah, I really just don't care about Colt's exes at all. It feels like a waste of my energy and breath to even talk about them."

"That's understandable," my specialist nodded. "I want to ask about the medication and the self-harm. How do you feel looking back on those things?"

"I am embarrassed and disgusted with myself for self-harming. It did quickly get me out of feeling so chaotic and unstable, yet it wasn't okay. I feel much more clear-headed now. I really believe in my soul that I will never do it again. For myself, but especially Talli. It isn't fair to her," I said, feeling sad. "I also do not think I will ever rely on medication again. I'm hoping in the future I will have more emotional strength and better tools to get through hard times rather than using medication. I know it can be really helpful for some people, but it isn't for me."

"Yes, medication can be vital and truly life-changing in a good way for some. You are right that it isn't like that for everyone. Sometimes you just need a different medication. Everyone has different things that work for them," she said while taking a breath. "If you ever feel like self-harming again, call me. It doesn't matter if you're still working with me or not. Just call me."

My eyes watered as I said, "Thank you."

26

Chapter Twenty-Six

Colt came home a week later. Hilda had posted a bunch of old pictures on Facebook to say happy birthday online to Clayton. She made sure to purposefully leave me out, again. She included pictures of Talli and Colt, making it appear as if I wasn't part of the family, as if Colt and I were separated. Colt still hadn't said anything to his mom about her inviting his exes. A couple days after Colt returned home, he received an odd text from his aunt.

"Look at this text I just got," Colt said, holding up his phone so I could see the screen.

Nancy's name was at the top followed by a message thread. I looked at the newest one on the bottom.

"I hope everything is ok. Your family misses you. Wondering if something is keeping you away..." the text from Nancy read.

"That is really weird. It's almost as if she is implying that I might be keeping you away. I can't imagine she would be wondering if it was because of your mom, her sister. Also, Nancy hasn't spoken to me in almost a year now," I said, staring at the message.

"Yeah, I think it is really weird, too," Colt said.

He started typing.

"Yeah, we are good. Why do you ask?" Colt's message back to his aunt read.

215

His phone quickly pinged.

Nancy had replied, "We haven't seen much of you or the little one."

"I'm not even responding to that," Colt said, putting his phone down.

"I love how she left me out," I said, rolling my eyes.

"You could tell her what your mom has been doing. Your mom has clearly been saying something to her."

"I know. That annoyed me. Yeah, you're probably right, my mom probably is talking about us to her. I'm sure Nancy wouldn't believe me even if she listened. There's no point," Colt said. "This is all really stupid and I'm starting to not care anymore."

A couple weeks later, Colt and I were cooking dinner on a Friday night. It was Easter weekend. The air was starting to get warmer, birds were chirping and the grass was green once again. Colt had been receiving texts every day for the past week from his family members in their group message. I used to be included in it, but they must have made a new group without including me. I didn't mind. I actually was relieved I wasn't getting the texts, but it still felt like a gut punch. They were all discussing Easter plans. Colt wasn't responding to them or telling me much about what the texts said. He simply said they were texting about Easter. I didn't care to ask for any further information. We already had plans to enjoy the morning at home and then go over to my grandparents' house for lunch.

I was in the kitchen with Talli. We were playing on the floor while I was heating up baked beans on the stove. I had sweet potatoes baking in the oven. Colt was in the garage cooking steaks on the new grill he bought for himself. Suddenly, he opened the door to the house and popped his head inside.

"Get me that piece of paper, please," he said, raising his eyebrows.

He held up his phone so I could see the screen. It lit up with an incoming call from his mom. I ran into his office and grabbed the list of bullet points I wrote down for him. He had asked me to write down basic points to keep in mind when he finally talked to his mom about her inviting his exes. I told him he should just talk to her, but he said he always felt like she confused him. He felt like he could never remember what to say and it was always being twisted around on him. I sympathized with him. I knew how he felt, to a certain degree.

After he had asked, I quickly jotted down some clear points.

It read:

- Why did you invite my old exes?
- They have not been involved in more than five years, they were unkind, there is no reason and it is very weird.
- This makes me feel uncomfortable, angry and annoyed.
- I feel like you did this to attempt to upset my wife, which makes me angry.
- Why are you trying to upset Adison and creating further distance from our family?
- Doing things like inviting these people makes us not want to be around you.
- Because you decided to invite exes, we will not be going to the party. (Not arguing, standing firm, no guilt trip will change our mind.)
- Also, if you felt so strongly that these exes were an important part of Mackenzi's life and should be included in her graduation party, why did you not ask me first?

There was an inch of space and then at the bottom of the page I added two points for him to keep in mind during his conversation.

They were:

- If she cries or acts like a victim, call it out. Why are you crying? Why are you upset? You did this. You are fifty-something years old; you should be able to think, make better choices and be kind.

- If she yells or blows up, say you will not be spoken to like that. Immediately get off the phone. We are adults with our own family and this behavior will not be tolerated.

It didn't take me long to write. It all spilled out of the pen and onto the paper. I had left it in Colt's office for him. After he had read it, I asked him what he thought.

"You can say whatever you want, I just wrote what we talked about and what I felt was important," I said when I was finished.

"I agree with it. It's good, thank you for doing that," Colt said.

"When are you going to have that talk with her?" I asked him.

"I don't know. I'm not looking forward to it," Colt said.

"I don't blame you. I love you," I said.

That was the last time we had talked about it. Now, three days later, I was hurrying to his office to fetch him the paper.

I handed Colt the paper and he closed the door. All the organs in my chest and stomach began to quake. I felt nervous for him. I hoped he was able to have the conversation and it went all right. I tried to stay focused on playing with Talli. It felt like an hour had passed, when in reality maybe only ten minutes had gone by. I overheard Colt yelling something. I got up to try to listen by the door, but it was too muffled. I opened up the app for the cameras on my phone and clicked on the one above the garage. I could clearly hear birds chirping and the neighbor mowing his lawn. I was sort of able to make out some of what Colt was saying over the noise.

"There is absolutely no reason for it. No. Stop pretending like Adison is doing something to you. She isn't. You're the one making everything difficult," I overheard Colt say.

My heart swelled. I finally felt like I was being stood up for. The lawn mower in the background roared. I tried to make out things he was saying after, but I couldn't piece anything together.

"Freaking lawn mower and birds," I thought. I could only hear the frustration and anger in Colt's voice. I gave up on trying to listen in and continued to stir the baked beans between playing with Talli. We sat on the floor near the kitchen playing with her little green alligator piano she loved. Eventually, Colt burst through the door.

"Well, that went as I expected it to go," Colt groaned, upset. "The steaks are done."

"I'm so sorry, honey," I said, feeling bad for him. "Okay, the food in here is done, too."

Colt grabbed a plate and then went back outside. I pulled the cut-up sweet potatoes out of the oven. They were burnt black on the bottom. Colt brought the steaks in and we made up our plates. I got Talli strapped into her high chair and we sat on the barstools at the counter.

"So, I said some of the things that you wrote down, but in my own words. It did help. All she did was argue. When I asked her why she invited those people, she got really quiet. She stuttered before she said she thought we were past everything with Gina and Angela. She said she thought we could all get along. She said we were in our thirties now, all have our own families and should be over whatever has happened in the past," Colt said between bites.

"In our thirties?" I asked, confused since we were in our twenties.

"Yeah, I don't know, she's stupid," he said.

"Also, that is the dumbest excuse I have ever heard. I thought she'd make up something a little better than that," I said, giving Talli some more sweet potatoes.

I had been scooping out the fluffy, bright orange middle of the potatoes to share with her. She was loving them. She was clapping and smiling while chewing.

"I know, right. Anyway, it gets worse," Colt continued. "She of course switched things around and started complaining that you've been rude to her since she came to visit in Texas. She said she deserves an apology from you."

"Oh my god. That is crazy. How have I been rude to her?" I asked.

"I don't know. I asked that, too. She just kept saying you've been rude. She doesn't say how," Colt said. "She kept playing the victim like always. Also, super weird, she mentioned you posted about her in a monster-in-laws group on Facebook."

"What?" I asked, my heart stopping. "How could she know about that?"

"I don't know. Did you check to see who else is in the group?" Colt asked.

"Yeah, I also only posted anonymously. Except for some comments here and there. Nothing I said was mean, it was just about how I was feeling and what she was doing. It was a way for me to cope and talk to people who understood," I said, trying to think.

"Okay, well somehow, she saw something. I ignored her when she brought that up. She said it in a manner of trying to make me upset with you. As if I should be angry you said something about her and that you're in a group called monster-in-laws on Facebook," Colt said.

"That's crazy," I said, quietly.

My head was spinning. I felt so invaded that she was aware of that group. I felt a twinge of guilt that she'd seen it, but I shook it off. Maybe it was for the best. I never said anything mean about her personally, only how she was acting and how those actions were making me feel.

"Anyway, she kept complaining about you and how you are keeping them out. I told her if they were nicer to you, it wouldn't be a problem. The whole reason we have been distant is because of them. I told my mom it's not that difficult, either be nice to my wife or don't come around," Colt said.

"Wow, honey, thank you for saying that," I said, feeling warmth in my heart. It made me feel good that Colt saw what his mom was doing and was telling her it wasn't okay.

"Yeah. Anyway, she kept arguing and saying stupid things so I hung up on her. I won't be surprised if she tries to call back later," Colt said.

"Okay. I'm sorry you're dealing with that," I said.

I felt bad for Colt even though I knew it was time for him to start standing up to his mom. I was aware it wasn't easy for him. I appreciated that he was standing up for me and trying to talk to his mom about what she was doing. We finished our dinner and went about our night. I was on edge, waiting for Hilda to call Colt back. Colt must have felt the same way, because we both jumped anytime one of our phones made a noise.

As we got ready for bed close to ten that evening, Colt said, "I'm really surprised she didn't try to call back. It did not end well. I was sure she would call again and keep arguing."

"Well, that's good she didn't then," I said.

"Yeah," Colt said, although he didn't sound sure.

We got through the next day without any contact from Hilda. Colt was still surprised he hadn't heard back from his mom. I felt relieved she wasn't calling. I hated the stress and anxiety I felt whenever she contacted us or even when her name was brought up. I kept trying to focus on myself and Talli. I was really trying to work on my anxiety and trying to feel normal so I could focus on being a mom. I had been taking long breaks from social media. I noticed the days I logged into Facebook were days where I struggled more with negative feelings and thoughts.

It was Easter Sunday. We enjoyed our bright, sunny morning in our house with Talli. Talli opened the gifts we had put in her giant white bunny basket. I had scattered plastic-colored eggs all around the living room. Talli was enjoying finding them and throwing them. Lately, she had been pulling herself up to stand. She was practicing standing on her own more and more. I couldn't believe how fast she was growing.

We went over to my grandparents' house for lunch. Once we finished eating, I went to the bathroom. I pulled my phone out of my back pocket, sat down on the toilet and noticed a new text on my screen. It was from Hilda. She had sent it in that group text she made with Colt and me. It was long. I shook as I started to read.

"Just wanted to reach out to you both again today to wish you a happy Easter and to let you know we would love for you to reconsider coming to dinner today at four-thirty at Aunt Mary's. Everyone will be there and we would really like to see you. We love you guys and miss you. You're always invited every day, any time and for any reason. Your family loves you and always will no matter what. I don't believe there is anyone who is mad at either of you, except maybe me a little after the other day, but really more hurt and confused as I have been all year. All I really want to be is a mom and a grandma. I have felt really left out all year and I just want you both to want to share your life and your love for your baby. I enjoy watching you both enjoy your baby and I can't understand how I became the enemy. I'm sorry if I have made either of you upset or made you feel disrespected. It was never my intention as far as the grad party goes. I truly thought all parties had moved on and were happy with their new families. I guess I don't know the real history and I don't need to. Just know that I am sorry. And in the spirit of Easter, I would really like it if we could just forgive each other and start fresh. I would like to go back to being a loving family that trusts and supports each other, always having each other's best interest in mind. We miss you and just want to be a part of your lives," Hilda's text read.

My throat closed tight. I felt everything I had just eaten make its way back up. I was so confused and taken aback. This text felt like it was coming out of nowhere. After everything she'd done, after all this time, now she wanted to attempt to fix things? It didn't add up. I felt a twinge of hopefulness, maybe she is being genuine and we can work to move forward. My gut bubbled. No, this truly didn't feel genuine. This felt like manipulation. This was to confuse us, to suck us back in, to make us forgive her because we are forgiving people. This was because she was finally caught red-handed in front of Colt. She knew he was finally catching on to her subtle emotional abuse toward me. This text was her trying to bring us back into her grasp so she could continue to control us. This text was mainly for Colt. It was to play on his emotions and to put on an appearance that she was trying to fix things with me. If she wanted to fix things with me, not only could she have done so months ago, she should have reached out to me personally. This also wasn't something one measly text would fix. This would take time and multiple conversations to work to rebuild trust, or some semblance of it. It would take setting and honoring boundaries. There was no magic snap of a finger to make things "normal" again.

I sat in the bathroom reading the text over a couple more times. My mind went wild. It looked so innocent and good-natured. I kept having to break it down. First of all, I was never invited to an Easter dinner so I wasn't sure what was being reconsidered. That must have been part of the conversation she had with Colt on the phone the other night. She says she is mad at us? For Colt's conversation with her where he tried to talk to her about how he felt about her inviting his exes to his sister's graduation party? I didn't see how it was her place to be the one that was mad. She said she was hurt and confused. Yet, she never once tried to reach out to me to clear things up or make things better. When I tried to do that in October, she only argued with me and further escalated things. She had been trying to isolate me. She had clearly been talking badly about me behind my back to other family members and who knows who else. She had tried to drive a wedge into my marriage with Colt. After we just had our first baby. Each time she had come over, she had ignored me, made uncomfortable comments and had not once acted in a manner of trying to change the path she had been leading us down. She may be hurt that Colt was sticking up for me and she may be confused he hadn't left me. She certainly was not hurt and confused by our actions. We had tried over and over again with her. A fire started within me. I felt anger sparking and flickering. I was so sick of being a marionette in her play. I wanted out. I wanted to cut the strings and run far away, never letting her find me. I was done sitting back and being emotionally abused.

"Adison?" I heard Colt call out.

"I'm coming," I said.

I put my phone in my back pocket and left the bathroom. I went back into the living room where everyone was seated, watching a baseball game on TV.

"Do you want to take the dogs outside to play?" Colt asked me.

He was sitting on the couch holding Talli.

"Yeah," I said, taking Talli and giving her a big hug.

We walked outside with our black Labrador and Shichon that my grandparents were taking care of while we settled in. My grandma's yellow Lab had passed away right before she offered to watch our dogs nearing the end of my pregnancy. We were grateful she wanted to take care of them while I gave birth and we learned how to be parents. When we moved back, she continued to watch them since it just made sense. She was happy and we were more than busy with our little human who liked to put everything in her mouth. We were relieved not to have dog toys laying around and for the dogs to not be chewing up Talli's toys. My grandparents taking care of our dogs was something we found ourselves being judged for and questioned about by others. Yet, it was hurting no one.

Colt threw two balls for the dogs. I held Talli and breathed in the sweet, cool air. It felt nice outside in a sweater and jeans.

"Why are you being so quiet?" Colt asked.

"I don't feel good," I said.

"Why?" Colt asked.

"Didn't you see the text?" I asked, confused.

"What text?" Colt threw the ball, wiped his hand on his jeans and pulled out his phone.

"Oh," he said as he started to read.

His brow furrowed.

"What do you think about this?" he asked me.

"Well, I thought about it a lot. At first, I thought maybe it was an honest attempt at an apology. Then I read it again and started to see things that were strange. I think it is her trying to manipulate us. I think if she was being genuine, she would've tried reaching out yesterday instead of today, on a holiday. She uses Easter as an excuse for us to just forget everything that's happened. She also says she just wants to be a mom and a grandma, yet she hasn't been either of those things all year. If she wanted to be those things, she could have been. Instead, she made things really hard. She didn't care about you when she tried to push us apart and complained about me to you. She didn't think about Talli when she did that, either. She didn't think about Talli when she was difficult, argued or caused us stress. So, to me, she is attempting to guilt trip us and that is just plain wrong. She said she can't understand how she became the enemy. I think that line really sums up the entire text. She feels she got caught by you. She's been trying to make me out to be an enemy this whole year and now that you said something to her, she's aghast. That wasn't part of her plan, so she's acting as if she's been caught off guard. She apologizes only for inviting your exes to the grad party, for the thing she was caught doing and there is evidence to prove it. Then, she makes that stupid excuse again about everyone being happy with their own families. Okay, so then why do we need to all get together and Kumbaya? Out of the billions of people on this earth, the two people I do not need to be friends with are your exes. She also lies and says she doesn't know the history. She is aware there is some bad history with Gina. When I rode with her and Mackenzi to pick you up from the airport years ago, the night we got back together, she told me while we waited in the cell phone lot that she wouldn't blame me if I kicked you in the balls. She was obviously aware you were talking to your ex and that is why I broke up with you the first time. She was also aware of Gina's post on Twitter about us," I spewed.

I sighed and then continued, "Lastly, I have to ask, when has she ever had our best interests in mind? It certainly wasn't when she came to visit after we just had our baby and only wanted to hold our newborn. It wasn't when she talked badly about me to everyone. It wasn't when she tried to cause stress in our marriage. All she wants is for us to go back to having her best interests in mind. Okay, I'm done, I'm sorry for the rant. I am so frustrated."

Colt had been standing across from me, looking at me and occasionally kicking the ground.

"Yeah, that was a lot," Colt laughed quietly. "I get it. I feel the same way. I am annoyed by the text, too. I don't think it was meaningful or genuine. I also see what you see. I have been asking her for months to apologize to you and make things better. She always argues and blames everything on you. Now, with this text, she still didn't apologize to you. She ignores everything she has done. Not only that, but I don't feel like I needed to be in that text. If she was apologizing to you and meant it, it should only be to you. So yeah, I agree, the text is bullshit," he said, sighing.

"I'm also really bothered that she did this on a holiday," I said. "I feel like she keeps trying to take away from our first holidays and special moments with Talli to give herself attention. Why couldn't she send this text yesterday or tomorrow or any other day?"

"Yeah, I agree. Don't send me a text like this on a holiday," Colt said, throwing the ball and watching our dog enthusiastically chase it across the yard.

"I am not going to respond to the text. I want to talk to my therapist about it before I do anything," I said.

"Yeah, that's a good idea. You should tell me what your therapist says," Colt said.

My grandma walked outside and we stopped talking about the text. We wrapped up our visit and then went home.

27

Chapter Twenty-Seven

Six days after receiving the text, I had my therapy session. I caught Nollie up on everything that had happened.

"Wow, yeah, that is really strange that she invited those exes. That doesn't make any sense," Nollie said. "I agree with you that the text sounds manipulative. It seems there could be a better way to work toward making amends and a text on a holiday just isn't it. What do you think you will do about it?"

"I've been thinking about it a lot. I think it is best to not respond to it. I think I may need to have a phone conversation with her to discuss it soon. That way I can see if she genuinely is apologetic and wants to make amends," I said.

"That sounds like a good idea. A phone call is a good place to start, or maybe a neutral location if you were to meet in person," Nollie said.

"I don't think I would be comfortable meeting her, yet. I am still really struggling with anxiety and I don't feel safe around her."

"That's okay, too. Whatever makes you feel safe," Nollie said, nodding. "Are you going to reestablish boundaries on how to move forward?"

"That's a good idea. Yeah, I should probably do that," I said. "Thank you."

I also talked to Nollie about Talli's first birthday party and how I felt really bummed about having to invite Colt's family, who made this year so tough for us. She told me I could do whatever I felt was best. I felt like it was "the right thing to do" to invite them, although it felt like the wrong thing for my mental health. It felt like another instance where it was more about them than Talli or our little family. I decided on inviting them all, but making the party the day before Talli's birthday. I would have it at a neutral location for a set time of two hours. That way it wasn't at our house where people could over-stay or make us uncomfortable in our home. I wasn't excited about it. I was dreading it. That made me feel really sad. Colt and I were tossing around the idea of going to Florida for a vacation so I scheduled the next therapy session for the Saturday before Talli's birthday.

I had already sent out Talli's birthday invitations the past week and I had already created a Facebook event for it way before Hilda's Face-book event for her daughter's graduation party was posted. I had included information such as directions, a gift registry if anyone wanted to bring a gift, and asked for an RSVP back so we knew how much food to get. For weeks, I hadn't sent out the Facebook invite to anyone other than Colt. I quickly sent it to everyone else to get it over with. An hour later, I got a notification that Hilda had already RSVP'd yes. My stomach sank. I knew it would happen, but I wasn't happy about it.

Two days later, on a Monday night at nine, my phone lit up with an incoming call. Hilda. My body started to shake. My teeth clenched and I had to hold back the vomit. I watched the phone until the call went away. A minute later, a voicemail notification popped up. I sat up in bed in the dark room, bringing my knees to my chest. Talli lay asleep next to me. I clicked on the voicemail.

"Hello, it's Hilda. I was calling to see if you needed any help with Talli's party. I was looking at the calendar and noticed it was coming up. Anyway, give me a call back," Hilda's voice rang over the speaker.

She sounded as if she had been transported back in time and was calling me two years ago. Her voice sounded normal, as if nothing that had happened this past year had happened. What was going on? I pulled out my phone and started googling.

I looked up, "Why is my narcissistic mother-in-law suddenly acting normal?" I started to read and learned about "Hoovering," which is when a narcissist attempts to suck, like a vacuum, their victims back into their lives. Okay, that made sense. I knew it was time to have the dreaded phone call with Hilda. I needed to address everything that had happened. I wasn't going to play into this nothing ever happened act. I knew if I did, it would only be a matter of time until something else happened. I wasn't going to give her back any power over me. We were going to discuss things and establish boundaries if we were going to move forward.

The next day, at six forty-five in the morning, I received a text from Nancy. I hadn't heard from Nancy all year besides when Colt and I called her together after Christmas. She just recently had sent those odd texts to Colt, so I was really weirded out by her texting me. I looked at the message.

"I have a co-worker whose stylist will be in Cleveland this weekend and needs a hair model for a class she's giving. Are you interested?" Nancy's text read.

"That is so weird," I thought. First of all, why is she randomly asking me about being a hair model after those odd texts she sent to Colt? Secondly, why does she think I want to go to Cleveland and waste time that could be spent with Talli? Not like she knows how important my time with Talli is to me, since she never talks to me. I decided not to respond right away. I was working on not being a people pleaser and not feeling an obligation to respond as soon as I received a message. Less than an hour later, another text from Nancy popped up on my phone screen.

"Sunday or Monday nine forty-five in the morning until one in the afternoon. You can choose," her text read.

I sighed, feeling overwhelmed. I set my phone down. I had read about this last night. When a narcissist is trying to Hoover a victim back in, another tactic they employ is to send out their flying monkeys. A flying monkey is basically a person close to the narcissist who also tries to bring you back into the fold. Nancy was definitely a flying monkey. I gave myself some time to regain my composure and breathe. Then, I got to work. I searched through old boxes in the basement until I found my iPod touch from high school. Next, I searched for a charger for the iPod since it was dead. It had to be an old, compatible one. I started to get nervous that I wouldn't find one as I shuffled past my college graduation cap, old plastic wristbands and a couple pairs of crazy socks.

"Bingo," I thought as I pulled on a black cord. I ran back upstairs, gathered papers, printed out the Easter text from Hilda and grabbed a pen and highlighter. I plugged the iPod in to charge and sat down to write. I had Talli in her playpen with her toys so she was occupied. I fiercely scribbled my notes. I was going to be ready for this conversation, unlike the one last fall.

I felt determined and strong as I looked at my final work. I had my talking points laid out and my iPod was on the voice memo app ready to record. This way there would be no he said, she said. I would have evidence and facts. I felt especially inspired by the book I was nearly finished reading called, *I'm Glad My Mom Died* by Jennette McCurdy. It had been pulling me out of the darkness. It made me feel less alone. I was inspired by Jennette and how she was working on bettering her life after the abuse she endured from her mom. I had the yellow and pink hardback copy sitting close by my supplies, just for a little moral support.

I was ready to text Nancy back.

I typed up a simple, "No thank you," and hit send.

I no longer felt the need to explain myself or cater to feelings over my own. Nancy had not been a positive part of the past year. I didn't owe her anything, especially not after her ominous texts to my husband.

Next, I had to text Hilda. I wanted to send a text before calling. I wanted to limit her from creating an excuse to get off the phone, from her being busy, and I didn't want to leave a voicemail or wait for a random call back. No, I had to do this carefully so I wouldn't chicken out or lose my train of thought. It was hard to keep my thoughts straight. They would swirl and go off down hundreds of rabbit holes. I would question my own reality at times. Thankfully, I had been writing and documenting everything. So even though I felt crazy, I knew I wasn't.

I shook my head and typed, "Are you available to talk?"

As soon as I hit send, my body was overcome with cold sweats. I started to tremble and the sick feeling hit me like a wave.

"No," I thought. "I will not live my life like this. I am stronger than this." I rolled my shoulders back and waited. After twenty minutes had passed, I went back to my day with Talli. Exactly one hour from when my text was sent, I received a reply from Hilda.

"Sorry, I just saw this, still at work, Tuesdays are super busy, I can text you when I leave," Hilda's text read.

I set down my phone. I would wait for her to text me when she left work. I wondered what she could have possibly thought I wanted to talk about. Did she think I was going to grovel for her attention and love? Did she think she was going to hear me say how stupid I had been with my quiet behavior toward her? Did she expect to stand high above me and put me in what she believed to be "my place?" Or was she conscious and aware enough to have a feeling I wanted to actually discuss what had been happening for the past year. In my gut, I felt as though she thought I was reaching out to wave a white flag. I didn't believe she thought of me as a strong woman. That was fine by me. She could think whatever she pleased. It did not mean it was the truth. I breathed in and out. I was strong. I was going to stand up to someone who always towered over me and I was going to be brave while doing it.

Just over two hours later, I received a new message from Hilda.

It said, "Just leaving work. I'm on my way. I have to sign my taxes. Let me text you when I leave his house or you can call me right now but I gotta be there in like ten minutes. Thanks."

I thought about calling her to get it over with, but then shook my head. No, I didn't want this to be cut short and have to resume it later. I wanted it to be one phone call that either went toward repair or cutting her off. My anxiety and mental health couldn't handle it if this got strung out. I didn't text back. I waited for her to text me when she was ready.

Another hour passed by slowly.

Finally, I received a new text from Hilda that read, "I am home for the night and off tomorrow and Thursday so whenever you're available, call me."

My anxiety overtook me. I was sweating, shaking, close to throwing up, but I got Talli all set up in our bedroom. I sat Talli in her playpen and put on the show she liked to watch whenever it was absolutely necessary for her to watch something. As Ms. Rachel squeaked hello, I kissed Talli on her forehead.

"I love you so much, Talli. I am going to go take care of something really quick," I said, caressing her cheek.

I gathered my strength, left the door open and went around the corner into the kitchen. I really didn't want Talli to hear this. I wasn't sure how it would go and it wasn't appropriate for her. I hated that our little, new family was dealing with this dumb drama when we should have been focusing on enjoying our love. It made me angry. My courage and determination rushed back as I sat down, preparing to press the call button on Hilda's contact.

28

Chapter Twenty-Eight

The phone rang.

"Hello," Hilda said when the call connected.

"Hey, so bear with me for a second while I get through this," I started.

"Okay."

"I am not going to pretend like everything is fine, because it's not. The last time Colt talked to you; you told him I have been rude to you since you came to Texas. However, what actually happened was that I had just given birth and needed time and space with my newborn and husband. When you showed up at the hospital, you ignored or were simply oblivious to that fact," I said. I paused for a split second and then continued. "You made it about you in the way that you were constantly either holding my baby or asking to. I gave in to you and wanted to respect you as a new grandma. You didn't seem to appreciate that and got upset when I needed space and went into my bedroom after days of you being over for hours. I felt like my first week and a half was stolen from me. You left the same day Colt went back to work. I imagine you had good intentions with dropping off all your leftover food and items, but we had no space for it and all it did was cause me extra work. Instead of giving me the benefit of the doubt like I gave you, you apparently started talking about me behind my back.

233

So instead of me being able to move past what happened in Texas, I felt even more tension and anxiety. Then the comments and passive aggressive behavior started. You wouldn't give Talli back to me when you visited, I had to take her, and you made a comment that 'RSV has been around forever' when I was worried about her getting sick. And then the day you wanted to join in on our date day, you wouldn't take no for an answer. I tried to talk to you to get on the same page and clear the air because maybe there was just miscommunication. You argued with me, were unkind, even calling me an f'ing bitch at one point."

I took a breath and then kept going, "Then Clayton called Colt and said Colt had a choice to make and to let Talli cry in the car. You had a conversation with Colt where you felt like I had done something wrong to you, but you never specified besides saying I had been rude. To sum it up, you've talked about me behind my back, made strange comments while visiting, ignored me while visiting, haven't been respectful and have made things stressful for a year. And then you invited Colt's exes to Mackenzi's grad party. Your excuse as to why you did that doesn't make sense. So, I am going to ask you, because you said here that it was never your intention, what was your intention with inviting them?"

"I was just inviting people to the grad party. I just literally went down my Facebook page and was inviting people. I really didn't know there was any issue with Angela with you because you didn't even know her. She's here in our hometown, Mackenzi knows her. I wasn't even considering you guys, which I'm very sorry about. I really wasn't planning on that at all, but..." She took a sharp inhale. "I mean, everybody's married with kids and I guess it's a different generation than I grew up in. I talk to all my exes. Clayton talks to all my exes. I mean, I was civil to somebody who my husband cheated on and had a baby with so I don't think the same way you guys do, I guess. I'm sorry I didn't consider that at all, I wasn't planning on that. But a lot of things that you said just now are completely wrong. I never called you an f'ing bitch. I never did that," Hilda said in a tight voice.

"You did. You did that on October first when I called you to try to have a conversation with you. But..." I started to say before Hilda cut me off.

"I did not call you an f'ing bitch," Hilda demanded, with a slight scoff.

"Okay, I heard it so... I also want to say..." I said, trying to stay firm, before I was again cut off.

"I did not call you..." Hilda started to repeat, raising her voice.

This time I cut her off.

"Okay, okay. I'm not going to argue with you. I'm going to have this conversation with you to try to repair things. That's the whole point of this, but I need to address with you what's happened."

"Uh-huh," Hilda murmured.

"So..." I started, before Hilda began to speak again.

"Well, I hate that you have a completely different story than I have. Because I didn't call you an f'ing bitch. Mackenzi was pissed off. She said something and I kept giving her a hand. So, I did not and I apologize that you heard that. Because I covered the phone and told her to stop. I didn't call you that. So, I'm very sorry. She was upset. I did not call you that, ever," Hilda said, emphasizing the last "I."

Hilda continued quickly, "And I thought I was very respectful in Texas. I wasn't trying to interfere at all with you. I only held the baby twice."

"You did not only hold Talli twice," I said, firmly. "You held her every day you came over. I'm not here to argue about what happened, I know what happened..."

Hilda interrupted me, speaking up loudly, "Just, fine. We obviously see different things, because I didn't. I let everybody else hold her. The only time, I mean, you tried to give her to me when I was crying and I didn't want her."

Hilda spewed a sharp breath out of her nose.

"I don't remember that happening, but that's fine," I blinked. "Hilda, I'm not going to argue with you, I'm having this conversation with you to try to repair things. I'm not going to sit here and argue. I know what happened. I'm not going to let you gaslight me by saying we have two different stories."

"We definitely do and I apologize that it's gotten this far, because that is not the case at all. Your story and my story do not jive," Hilda said, sounding like she was about to say more, but I spoke up. I refused to let her get into my head and make me question my memory.

"Whatever. How have I been rude to you then?" I asked.

"Um, pardon me?" Hilda puffed out.

"You keep saying I've been rude to you. How have I been rude to you?" I repeated.

"Every time I ask you something you just cut me off. I've tried to be nice. I've tried to respect your privacy. I don't post things without your..." Hilda sounded like a whiny child, explaining why she was right.

"What?" I gasped.

I did cut her off that time, whoops. I was so shocked. She hadn't once asked me before posting anything.

"I don't do any of that stuff and I don't understand why every time I'm there, there's such tension. I don't even want to be there," Hilda said.

I waited for a second before responding.

"Okay, I've been quiet and I've been distant because of the way you have been acting. But I've never cut you off. Also, you've never asked me before posting anything. You may have the first time you came to Texas," I said.

"I don't even post anything," Hilda argued.

"Okay," I drew the word out long.

Hilda tried to cut me off, but I spoke over her.

"You posted a picture of Talli with Clayton so... you could've asked me about that. You posted something on the first of the year or whatever, you posted something of Talli. So, you saying that you've asked me when you post things, you haven't. You've never asked me. But that's not even a conversation I was going to have with you," I said, shaking off my shock.

Hilda shot another breath out of her nose.

"Okay," she said shortly.

I paused in uncomfortable silence for a moment and then spoke back up.

"Okay, well, if you feel this conversation is ridiculous or stupid or if you mock this, then we're going to be going in different directions. If you cannot have respect, empathy and don't genuinely want to fix things, then I just don't want you contacting me going forward," I said, unsure of what else to say.

"I do want to fix things. Why do you think that I'm doing that? I'm not even doing anything," Hilda questioned.

"Because you're arguing," I said.

"I'm not mocking you. I'm sitting here listening," Hilda coughed. "It's just been very stressful and very tense and I don't understand why."

"Then why haven't you come to me and tried to have a conversation about that?" I asked.

Hilda shot a breath out of her nose.

"I was hoping everything would just pass. I was blaming it on you being a new mother. You are, you know, not conscious about everything and I was letting it happen. I was being polite every time I saw you, from my perspective. I feel like I was, but I do want to mention, with Texas I did not go there with any intention to interfere at all with you guys. I told you I was going to take my vacation. I got a place with a pool. I said I would be there if you needed me," Hilda said, emphasizing the words "needed me."

"I said if you didn't need me, that was fine. I was perfectly fine by myself. But I said if you need me, you know to clean your dishes, I would be there. That's what I said. Because I know that as a new mom those are the things you don't want to do. I wasn't there to hold your baby," Hilda continued, attempting but failing to fog my memory.

"Mmhmm, but that's not what happened, Hilda," I said.

"I didn't..." Hilda started, but I cut her off.

"That's not what happened. You cooked dinner twice, so thank you for that, but you did not ever offer to do anything else."

Hilda was attempting to cut me off, but I kept talking.

"And I told Colt I wanted a day where you didn't visit and you still visited that day."

"I didn't want to come over at all!" Hilda exclaimed. "Colt called me every day and asked what I was doing. I said, 'I'm fine. I'm laying by the pool.' He asked when I was coming over. I asked, 'Did you need me for something?' I didn't want to come ever, for any days."

"Well, that's really weird. That's not the story I got from him. It was you texting him, but again, I'm not going to argue about what happened with you," I said.

"Okay," Hilda said.

"Well let's talk about your text a little bit," I said.

"Okay."

"Let's talk about the fact that you said that you were mad. Why are you mad in this text? You said..." I said, until Hilda cut me off.

"I said nobody is mad at you guys, except for me the other day, because Colt was very rude to me and hung up on me and basically said I was a mean person and that I've done all these wrong things that I haven't even done. So yeah, I was kind of upset with that phone call even though I didn't go share it with anybody or talk about it to anybody, so I don't understand why you say that I talk to everybody about you. I don't talk about you behind your back. I don't talk about you to everybody. I didn't even tell anybody about that conversation. Nobody knows about that conversation other than me, which is what I do most of the time: keep everything to myself," Hilda said.

"Hm. Okay," I said, not believing anything she was saying.

When Hilda spoke, it was difficult to keep my mind on course. I had to avoid getting disoriented with the manner in which she talked and twisted things.

"I keep trying to think how I was when I was your age, when I had my first child," Hilda blurted out. "Did I do any of that stuff to my mother-in-law? Like, you know, maybe she's not doing it on purpose. I keep trying to think about those kinds of things and giving you the benefit of the doubt."

"Uh-huh, it doesn't seem like you are doing that..." I said, starting to get confused. "Why was Clayton calling Colt and saying those things? Why are other people acting very strangely? Because nobody's treated me the same since you left Texas."

"Okay, well, Clayton is his own person. I have told him not to speak for me because he's completely wrong. I told him that and I told Colt that. When he complained, that was him on his own doing that. I have told him several times to stop doing that, we are not to come between Colt and his wife. You have no business in this at all, do not speak for me, because you're wrong. So that is completely wrong. I have never told him to say things to Colt. And I told that to Colt, too. I said, 'She needs a lot of space' and I've been trying to do that. I never once told people, Clayton, to tell you guys anything."

Hilda puffed air out of her nose and continued, "I have not done that at all. If people are treating you differently, I have no idea why people are treating you differently. You guys don't show up to any event, but I have not been telling them anything."

"Well, we haven't been coming to anything because of the way you've been acting toward us," I said.

"Everybody has invited you to places but you guys don't come," Hilda said.

"We have been invited to a fall party and we've been invited to Christmas and there was a storm, so..." I responded.

"Okay, and you were invited to Easter and birthday parties," Hilda said.

"I wasn't aware of anything else. So, I personally was not invited to those things," I said.

"You guys were invited to Mackenzi's senior nights, and you guys were invited to her dance competitions. I mean, you guys were invited to any of those things," Hilda argued.

"Okay so maybe you invited Colt..." I started, before Hilda cut me off.

"Dinners... Family dinners," Hilda continued.

"That's fine. Maybe you invited Colt, but he did not relay that information to me," I said.

"Okay," Hilda said, inhaling sharply.

"So that's, that's all. Every time we are having something people are like, 'Are Colt and the baby coming? Colt and Adison coming? Are they coming?' I'm like, 'No I don't think so.' So, I mean, I have not said 'No they are terrible people and they don't want to see us.' I've never said that. When Darla was going to see her mom I said, 'Hey, why don't you call Adison and see if you're able to stop and see the baby on the way up there. I know you need to give a little notice, but maybe if you call her since you're going that way.' I've told them, I mean before you guys didn't want anybody at your house. So, I said, 'Well no, you guys need to call.' They said, 'Well I thought they didn't like visitors.' I said, 'Well, I, I don't know,'" Hilda said, stuttering.

"Okay so first of all, Darla did come visit ..." I started, trying to keep my thoughts straight.

"I know she did," Hilda interrupted.

I blinked. My hands were sweaty. Luckily, I had the phone on speaker sitting on the counter in front of me so I wasn't trying to hold onto it with moist palms.

"I asked for two weeks when we first moved into the house. I told Colt I didn't want visitors for two weeks because I wanted to settle into the house, get moved in. We were moving across the country and it was very stressful for me when you guys came to Texas. I did not want another big moment overtaken by all the chaos. That's why I said two weeks. And two weeks isn't very much for someone that's going to be living here," I sputtered, slightly shaking.

"Okay, that has nothing to do with me. As far as people being upset, everybody, I didn't tell anybody you guys were moving there, but somehow everybody knew you were moving there and Colt lied to everybody when they were calling him on his birthday when you guys were literally driving there. So, people were asking me, 'What's the big secret?' I go, 'I don't know that there was a big secret. I don't know. I don't have their address. I don't know their specifics.' If people were upset about that, that was nothing of my doing. You guys chose not to tell people when you were coming or that you were even buying a house until you did it," Hilda said.

"Again, this is Colt's family like I'm married into it, but this is Colt's responsibility to talk to these people because I'm not going over top of him and saying things to people so..." I said before getting spoken over.

"Correct. But I'm saying I have not told people anything. I have not said, 'Be mean to Adison.' I have not done anything and to my knowledge nobody was being mean to you," Hilda said.

"Nobody is necessarily being mean, but nobody's been talking to me or being kind. Your mom and other family members used to text me, but it stopped pretty quick after you left Texas. So, I mean, that's fine, whatever, we can move on from that if you deny ever saying anything to them about not being around us or whatever, that's whatever," I shook my head and continued. "Um, I don't want to do this whole back and forth really. If you're interested in repair, I'll discuss with you my boundaries and what needs to happen going forward. I need time to heal. It's going to take work and time for me to trust you again. Are you interested in repair?" I asked.

Hilda was quiet for a second and then said with an attitude, "Um, I am interested in repair and I equally feel the same because I've felt very hurt this whole year. I get that you don't think you did anything, and I don't think I did anything so we're both feeling like we are in the same situation."

"Okay. Hilda, I just had a baby. I was in a very vulnerable place. And..." I said before Hilda cut me off.

"And I totally respect that," Hilda insisted.

"You are a middle-aged adult so you could've come to me at any point and tried to have a conversation. You could've said something. You don't need to be playing the victim right now. I just feel like a lot has happened and I'm trying to make an effort here with you. I really just need space, but here I am talking to you. So here are my boundaries. If we say no, that means no. No bringing up exes. No talking about us unkindly behind our backs. No arguing with our parenting choices. Everything needs to be discussed first, no surprises. Eventually, we can do a planned visit every other month for an hour or two, at a neutral location. This can begin after some healthy distance and healing. This can be adjusted in either direction. If things go well, we can expand and change the boundary, but if things go badly, we will have to be stricter with it," I said.

A heavy, thick silence followed.

After what felt long enough, I said, "Do you have anything you'd like to say?"

"I don't understand what you're saying. You're saying you don't want me at your house?" Hilda asked.

"No," I drug out the word.

"I'm saying that we need to have some healthy boundaries and that we can visit at a neutral location until I feel more comfortable."

There was another lengthy silence.

"Okay," Hilda finally said.

"Okay. Thank you for having the conversation. We do not need any help with Talli's party. We will see you then," I said.

Again, another long pause followed.

Finally, Hilda said with an attitude, "Okay."

"Bye," I said.

"Bye," Hilda barely spit out.
I hurried to hang up the phone.

29

⸙

Chapter Twenty-Nine

I sat there at the kitchen counter for a minute. The sun had set, and the windows were all painted black. I laughed in a scoff twice. What the actual heck was that? I felt confused. Hilda blamed her daughter for calling me a fucking bitch? Thinking back, it didn't sound like Mackenzi's voice and I felt like I would've heard Hilda tell Mackenzi to stop. No, that had to be a crazy excuse. Unless, I thought, Mackenzi did say that and I can't trust her now, either. Also, I still didn't feel like I had an explanation as to how she perceived me to be rude to her. She said I cut her off whenever she asked something. Besides that phone conversation, I had never cut her off before, to my knowledge. Every time she had been around the past year, I had been quiet. She made strange, uncomfortable comments and I would look away. I wasn't sure what she was referring to. It had to be made up. She was insane.

It sounded like she was literally calling herself out at times. She brought up how we moved to Ohio and hadn't told anyone. Except Colt told her. So, she is the only person that could have told the rest of her family. She also made that weird remark that she never told anyone to be mean to me. That kind of sounds as though she did exactly that. All in all, the conversation did not go well. There was no progress. All it was to me was validating that it was time to become stricter with our boundaries. She was incapable of truly listening. She had no empathy. I tried to address how her actions affected me, and instead she flipped it all on me. Instead of trying to work toward understanding, she just argued. She was so focused on "her story." That was another red flag. That means she did have something in her head and was more likely than not spreading that around to other people. I should've asked her what her story was, although I didn't really care. Her story was fabricated lies. Sure, there are two sides to every story, but facts are facts. She may have her own perception, but it is wildly skewed. I had tried to go down the rabbit hole and imagine what her story might be. It always made me feel crazy, because I truly couldn't fathom how any sane person would have stayed on the path that she did. If she was that offended that I went into my bedroom with my days-old newborn, you'd think she would have either said something or moved on. Instead of any kind, understanding or caring words, I got silence from her. With her silence, came Colt bringing up how his mom and I hate each other. That led to the unkind comments made in front of me as well as those that I would overhear or Colt would tell me about.

She was literally trying to confuse me and make me feel crazy.

"God, she is such a narcissist," I thought.

After all my research, everything that had happened and now this last phone call, I realized I was pretty much done. I didn't feel like there was any point in talking to her anymore. All she ever did was argue and try to confuse me. I ran into the bedroom to grab Talli and give her a giant hug. I was determined to never let this insane woman affect Talli the way that she had been trying to tear me apart. People that love you do not treat you like this. I would never in a million years talk to Talli the way Hilda spoke to me. I would never speak over her, argue with her about her experience and I would never cause our relationship to crumble. I would never treat anyone Talli loved like this, either.

I called my mom to tell her about the conversation.

"Oh my god, you recorded it? That's brilliant," she said after I gave her the background on what happened.

"Yeah, do you want me to send it to you?" I asked.

"Yes! Send it," she said, "I'll call you back after I listen to it."

Approximately fifteen minutes later, my phone lit up with an incoming call from my mom. I answered it.

"I am so proud of you. That was awesome. You did so well! She is insane. I couldn't believe what she was saying to you," my mom said, enthusiastically.

"Yeah, it was crazy," I said.

"Have you sent it to Daddy yet?" she asked.

"No, I was going to do that in a minute."

"I kind of want to be there when he listens to it so I can see the look on his face. It is such a crazy phone call," she said.

"It was tough at times for me, because I felt like I kept getting confused. I felt like she jumped around and also worded things in a strange way. A lot of it was also lies," I said, rubbing my eyes.

"Yeah, like that part about Mackenzi calling you an f'ing bitch? That is so weird that she said that. Even if it was Mackenzi, why would she throw her teenage daughter under the bus like that?" my mom said.

"That is so true. That is really weird," I agreed.

"I feel like if it were me, if you had said that, I would just take the blame for it. I would apologize and move on," my mom said.

We talked for a couple more minutes, changing the subject to what her schedule was like for the week, and then got off the phone. I pulled out my new DKNY pink suitcase that I had recently gotten at Marshall's and started packing. In all the chaos, I had almost forgotten Colt and I had at last decided to drive to Florida. I quickly packed my bags and then packed Talli's. I put Talli down for bed, but I was too electrified to sleep. I stayed up, watched *Ridiculousness* and ate an entire pint of Jeni's Darkest Chocolate ice cream. I needed to get my mind off of Hilda. *Ridiculousness* has always gotten me through my toughest times. It was my rock. Finally, when I felt my eyes starting to get heavy, I let myself go to sleep.

Only a few hours later, Colt arrived home. It was two in the morning. He slid into bed and went right to sleep. His entrance woke me up and I couldn't get back to sleep for an hour. I laid in bed and scrolled through my phone to read quotes about surviving narcissistic abuse.

The next morning, I woke up full of energy even with how little I had slept. I was so ready to get out of Ohio. Colt worked on packing while Talli and I went through our morning routine. Soon enough, the truck was loaded and I got Talli fastened into her car seat. I bounced on the seat next to her, overjoyed for the road trip. Colt started his truck and we sat in the garage while he pulled up the directions on his phone. I looked out the window at the neighbors feeding their chickens. Out of the corner of my eye, I noticed Colt had chosen the route that went directly past Barnesville, Ohio.

No.

"Uh, what are you doing? Why are we going that way? Going through Columbus is actually faster," I said, panicking.

"No, this way is faster. Why are you so stressed?" Colt asked.

"I don't want to go that way," I said.

"We aren't stopping there," Colt said.

"I know. I just don't want to go that way. It makes me feel really scared and anxious, just even being in that vicinity," I said. "Can we please go the other way?"

"No, we are going this way. If you want to go, then let it be," Colt answered with a firm finality in his voice.

I slumped back in the seat. I tried to distract myself, but as we got closer to Barnesville, I started to feel worse. My armpits were sweating, my face felt fiery red and I felt like I was breathing through a straw. My body felt heavy and my brain swirled.

"Will you listen to this phone call I had with your mom now?" I asked Colt.

Earlier, I had told him everything about why I felt like I needed to have this call, how I prepared and the basic summary of how it went.

"Uh, sure," Colt answered.

I leaned forward and held my old iPod up over the center console. I pressed play.

As Colt listened, he would say, "Huh," or make an exclamation like, "What?"

I told him to just listen and we could talk about it after.

"Well, that was crazy. First of all, that person my mom is talking about that my dad cheated on her with, she hated her being mentioned. My mom did not like her, so that's a lie. I also don't believe Mackenzi called you that. It was interesting how she kept denying it until finally she just blamed it on my sister," Colt said.

"I know, right?" I replied.

"Also, she was the only person we told that would tell anyone else we were moving to Ohio. She's the only one anyone would have found out from. So, it's interesting she lied about that," Colt said.

"She literally tried to throw blame on everyone except herself," I said. "She blamed you for not telling anyone about moving, Mackenzi for calling me a fucking bitch, Clayton for what he said... Which I mean, yeah, Clayton said it, but who do you think he got it from? No offense, but I don't think he is intelligent enough to do it all on his own. He listened to what Hilda was saying and then repeated it, or said it because of the lies she had told him. Also, did you hear the part where she said she told Clayton not to come between us? She literally called herself out there, because that is exactly what they were subtly trying to do. She was literally trying to drive a wedge between us by complaining about me behind my back to you so much. Ugh. It makes me so angry."

I needed to compose myself. We were only a couple exits away from the in-laws' town and it was making me feel foggy.

Colt had gotten quiet while my anxiety grew louder. I scrambled to find my AirPods that I packed in my blue book bag. When I found them, I quickly jammed them in my ears. Talli was sleeping in her car seat next to me. I turned on my hard rock music to try to get me through this part of the drive. I slumped further down in my seat and brought my knees up to my chest. I curled against the door, trying to comfort my trauma-filled self. The air escaped from my lungs as we passed the exit sign that would have led to their house. I held my breath. A year ago, before all this happened, we would've stopped to say hi. We would've gone down there for visits and holidays. Things are very different now. Now, I wanted to stay as far away from that little town as possible.

My breathing was shallow until we crossed the bridge over the Ohio River that led us into West Virginia. I finally was able to fully exhale. The rest of the day, driving was peaceful, other than when Talli had enough of the car seat and screamed. We stopped for the night in South Carolina. We continued driving the next day. In Georgia, I begged Colt to take a quick twenty-minute side trip to see the tree spirits as advertised at a rest stop.

"Can I just keep driving?" Colt asked me, groaning.

"Please. Please, I really want to see a tree spirit," I begged, pressing my palms together.

Colt obliged and I bounced in my seat, giddy. We got out in the cutest little Georgia beach town and walked around the side of a building to see an intricate life-size mermaid carved into the side of a tree. I felt the beachy, salty breeze blow through my hair and the sun kiss my cheeks. I breathed in and smiled on my exhale. I stared up at the mesmerizing mermaid. I ran my fingers over her scaly wooden tail. I felt at ease and happy. I hadn't felt like this in months. I felt free.

30

Chapter Thirty

Everything about our Florida trip to Miami was rejuvenating and revitalizing. We got to spend time with genuine, kind and fun friends. I felt myself returning back to me. I laughed, I had fun, I felt carefree. I forgot all about my stress and unhappiness in Ohio. I got to eat great food and jump in the crystal-clear waves at familiar beaches. We had lived in Miami a couple years ago, before I had gotten pregnant. I had an incredible job surrounded by remarkable people. Living there was a dream. The only downside was Colt was working in Texas and we rarely saw each other. It made things really tough for us. We made the decision for me to leave my job and move to be with him. It wasn't easy, but it led us to where we are now. We have Talli and she's my entire universe. I had moments of melancholy and bittersweetness as we walked into my old place of work and I saw my previous co-workers. I missed it. I was genuinely thinking about returning to work and moving back to Miami. Even Colt was into the idea, although, as I tried to make my decision and looked at daycares and homes in the area, I felt a deep, heavy feeling in my gut. It didn't feel like this was the right decision. How could I work five or six days a week and be away from Talli that much? Plus, the houses cost two-hundred-thousand dollars more than most places.

"We need to figure out what we are going to do," Colt said as we got settled back in at home after returning from our trip.

"Are we moving to Miami, Dallas or staying here?"

"Well, it doesn't seem like staying here is really an option. I am leaning toward Dallas. Your job would be more stable, it's more affordable there and the biggest factor is that I want to continue to be a stay-at-home mom. I don't want to be away from Talli," I said.

We had recently found out that Colt's company was going to be making some changes and he had an opportunity opening up in Dallas. We would have to live there. I was not opposed to that at all. I hadn't ever imagined moving from the house we bought less than a year ago, but things had changed drastically. I didn't want to live in Ohio anymore. I wanted to live as far away as possible from my in-laws. It was either I would work and we would live in Florida or Colt would work and we would live in Texas. We decided to sit on the decision.

I had my therapy session on Saturday and Sunday was Talli's birthday party. I had spent the past couple weeks before our trip making decorations. It was going to be outside at a local park and the theme was wildflowers. It was going to be pretty simple. Talli wouldn't remember it and due to everything that had been going on, I wasn't looking forward to it. Colt's family was larger than mine so it was likely I'd feel suffocated. I wasn't sure exactly who all was coming. More than half the people invited had not RSVP'd. I knew Nancy was not attending. I knew Didi was planning to be there because she texted me the other night.

Didi's text read, "Anxious and excited to meet little Talli Sunday! Was looking at the weather and it's going to be a little cool. Is the place enclosed?"

I texted back, "Yeah, it does look like it will be a little cool out. It is not enclosed."

I was annoyed she texted me that because it felt judgmental. I understood it was most likely harmless, but after everything I felt really on edge. My guard was up. I didn't trust anyone in that family. I was also annoyed the weather did show it would be potentially rainy and in the fifty-to-sixty-degree range. I was annoyed I paid to reserve this pavilion and had to have it at the park. If things felt safe, I would've actually been excited about my sweet baby's first birthday party, but also would've had the party at our house. With how uncomfortable I felt with Hilda and everyone else who cast me off, I didn't want them in my home. If they came over, I would potentially have a tough time getting them to leave. I just wasn't sure how this was going to go at all so I felt certain it must be at a neutral location.

The day of the party I fought to push down the sick feeling in my stomach. I buzzed with anxiety. I tried to keep myself busy. It was a cloudy, rainy day. Calli flew in from Colorado to go to Talli's party. She was a big part of why I was even having this event. Months ago, Calli had been asking if I was going to have a party so that she could arrange to be there. Her, our mom, our dad and our grandparents helped me put everything together. Calli and my mom picked up the cake and cupcakes to bring to the pavilion. They arrived there first, an hour and a half before the party was set to start. When we pulled into the parking lot, we saw Colt's grandpa on his mom's side, Will, there. I was surprised to see him over an hour early. I got Talli out of her car seat and put her winter coat over her pink onesie she wore that said "one" on it with a flower in the place of the "o." I walked with Talli in my arms over to the pavilion.

"Hey, when did he get here?" I asked my mom and sister.

"Just a little bit ago," my mom answered.

"Wow, that cake is beautiful! Thank you so much for getting that," I said as I took in the round white cake with colorful wildflowers covering the sides.

"Of course," my mom said.

I set up my decorations and then walked up to Colt's grandpa.

"Hi, how are you?" I asked him, uneasy.

"I'm good. Moreen is in the car. She isn't feeling well. She still wanted to come," Will said.

"Oh, okay, well I'll go say hi to her," I said.

I walked back to the truck to get more things I had brought. I tried to swallow the annoyed feeling that bubbled inside my throat. Why would someone who didn't feel well come to a baby's birthday party? As I walked toward the parking lot, Moreen waved at me from inside her car.

"Hi," I said to her.

"Hi, I can't get out. I'm sick, but I still wanted to come," Moreen said.

"I hope you feel better! It's good to see you," I said back.

I was trying my hardest to be myself and be kind, although I felt so guarded. I felt so uncomfortable talking to people I hadn't talked to in so long, people who were around Hilda and were hearing whatever she was saying to them about me. Moreen and Will were acting normal, though. I felt guilty for feeling annoyed and guarded. When we were all set up, Calli took a picture of Colt, Talli and I. Then my mom took a picture of our little family with Will. Colt talked to his grandpa as I welcomed my grandparents and dad. As time ticked closer to everyone's arrival, my nerves felt wired. Darla arrived with two of her teenage sons, my uncle arrived with his wife and two of my cousins. Didi arrived and got right in my face. She acted fine, but there was a look in her eyes that I could see through her clear glasses that made me feel uncomfortable. It was as if she was eyeing a sitting tiger, watching to see if it would attack, almost daring it to.

"We brought the sunshine," chirped Hilda as she sashayed up the sidewalk with Clayton and Mackenzi by her side.

I stood alone with Talli, surrounded by Colt's family. They all were talking amongst themselves, just eyeing me. I stood frozen for a minute before shaking out of it and scuttled over to Calli.

"I feel so uncomfortable," I whispered to Calli.

Just then, Cynthia arrived with Mary. Cynthia was bundled up so that you couldn't see anything but her tight frown. She had on a navy winter coat, black pants and her hood pulled tight over her head. She wore dark sunglasses. Mary stood next to her. They both looked like they were attending a funeral.

"We've got to get this started," my mom said quietly to me, before announcing, "Hey everyone, we are going to start opening gifts."

A couple people glanced her way before going back to their conversations. I sat with Talli on a picnic bench in the center of the pavilion. There were at least four picnic tables with no one seated at them inside of the pavilion around the one we sat at. Everyone in my family came inside, got food and sat down. Everyone in Colt's family stayed outside the pavilion. They peered inside while Colt, Talli and I uncomfortably opened Talli's gifts. When we opened the gift Hilda brought, Colt pulled out tissue paper after tissue paper.

"Well, the whole point was for Talli to have fun with it, but okay," Hilda muttered.

We ignored her. It was cold. Talli was wrapped in a blanket in my arms, watching us open her gifts. She still wasn't opening things on her own yet. Twenty pieces of tissue paper may have been fun for her if she was a half a year older. Hilda had gotten Talli clothes and an inflatable pool. It was the same inflatable pool that my mom had gotten. I could feel the tension radiating off Hilda as we opened the same pool from my mom.

"I can just return mine," my mom said to Hilda.

Hilda didn't respond. After we survived opening presents, it was time for cake. Since almost everyone was about ten feet outside the pavilion, my mom and sister moved a picnic table outside toward where everyone was hovering. Talli, Colt and I moved over to the table outside. Talli's beautiful wildflower cake came with us, along with the healthy cake I made for Talli. We were trying to avoid giving her any added sugar until after she was two. One day, she would enjoy a nice decorative, sugary cake, but while she was still so little it didn't hurt to wait. I had made her cake with oat flour, bananas, Greek yogurt, eggs, cinnamon and strawberries. I made the pink icing that topped it with dehydrated strawberries and Greek yogurt. I added a large pink candle in the shape of the number one on top.

Talli sat in my lap still wrapped in the blanket as the cool wind made me shiver. Talli's little pink cake sat in front of us. Colt's family moved even further back. They stood about fifteen feet away from where we sat at the new table. Everyone sang happy birthday to Talli. Talli was skeptical of her cake, but soon dug in. I helped her and scooped out little bites for her to eat. My mom sliced up the large sugary cake for the guests as I tried to keep myself from blacking out. I felt so uncomfortable and was trying so hard to simply survive this. I held on snuggly to Talli and reminded myself why I was doing this. For her.

"Adison! Hey!" I heard my best friend Ellie shout.

I looked up and saw her walking through the crowd of people into the open space. She looked around and made a "what the heck" face at the scene of everyone standing so far away from us, as if we had the plague.

"Hey, I'm so sorry I'm late! Traffic was so bad," Ellie said.

"No, don't be sorry, I am just so happy to see you! Thank you so much for coming!" I said and hugged Ellie with my free arm.

"How's it going?" Ellie whispered to me.

"Um. You know. Like this," I said, and looked out of the side of my eyes at the people standing back like we were dangerous animals at a zoo.

"So weird. Just remember, this has nothing to do with you and everything to do with them. You haven't done anything to deserve this," Ellie said, looking intently into my eyes.

I smiled. She was such a genuine, caring friend. I felt so grateful to have her there. Mackenzi came up to the table and sat down diagonally from Talli and I. She stared at us with uneasy, big eyes.

"Hey, how are you?" I asked her as she stared at me.

"Good," Mackenzi said with a shortness in her voice.

She continued to stare. Calli looked at me out of the side of her eyes. My mom started asking Mackenzi about school. Mackenzi continued to stare at me as she answered my mom's questions. After a few uncomfortable minutes, Mackenzi got up and went back to where her mom stood. Hilda stood with Paul, Jan and Clayton. Colt's aunt and uncle on his dad's side also stood near Hilda. His family on his late father's side had all been treating us normally. Whenever I saw them, I felt as though I could see deep in their eyes that they had heard things from Hilda, but they didn't change their kindness toward us. I suddenly noticed Hilda was waving her arms, smiling like she was on a talk show and putting on her best act. She didn't seem to care about anything else other than entertaining those around her and desiring to pull more people into her performance.

Ellie and I stood up as my mom started to clean the pavilion. Cynthia appeared in front of us.

"Hi, how are you doing?" I kindly asked her as she glared at me.

"I just want to see the baby," Cynthia harshly snapped.

She glared daggers into my eyes then looked at Talli for a second before turning and walking away. I noticed Mary had been standing back, watching, and had waited for Cynthia to reach her before they walked together to the parking lot.

"What the fuck?" Ellie said, staring at their backs as they got in their car.

"That was really weird," I said, taken aback.

"They are so fucking insane. That was so uncalled for. God, why are people like that?" Ellie said angrily. "I wanted to say something, but I was just in shock."

"I feel the same way. I'm just glad you heard that, too. I feel like I'm going crazy with these people," I said.

Next, Darla came up to where we stood by the picnic table.

"So, high school graduation is coming up. It's on a Tuesday. The date is May sixteenth, I believe. Will you guys be there?" Darla asked me intently.

"Oh, uh, I don't know. It's up to Colt," I stammered, looking around for my husband, caught off guard and uncomfortable.

"We are meeting for pictures at Aunt Mary's before, and then after will go back there for a family dinner," Hilda spoke up from a distance, talking out loud rather than to me specifically.

"I hope you guys will be there. It would be good for you guys to visit back home," Darla said, still looking directly at me.

"Okay," I said, trying to half smile at Darla.

Everyone left in their little groups until it was just my dad, grandparents, mom, Calli, Ellie, Colt, Hilda, Clayton, Mackenzi and me left. My family had been working on cleaning up the pavilion and loading up their cars. Hilda, Clayton and Mackenzi stood back in their own little circle. It was awkward as we waited for them to leave. I didn't feel the need to go near them. They hadn't come toward me and I was happy to not have to talk to Hilda. They said goodbye to Colt and slowly walked to their van. When they left, Ellie and I walked to our cars.

"Seriously, they are crazy. You do not deserve the way they are treating you at all," Ellie said.

"Thank you, I really appreciate you being so supportive and here for me today. I know it was a long drive. Thank you so much for coming," I said.

I was starting to zone in and out of consciousness. I felt really exhausted and overwhelmed. I felt like I was coming off my adrenaline rush. I needed to lay down. I hugged Ellie goodbye.

"Hey, you did a really great job today. You got through it. I'm proud of you," my mom said as she hugged Talli and me.

"Thank you. Thank you so much for the cake and everything you did today. I wouldn't have been able to do this if it weren't for you. Thank you for helping make Talli's day so nice," I said.

I got in Colt's truck and put Talli in her car seat. I leaned my head back against the seat and closed my heavy eyes.

31

✤

Chapter Thirty-One

Colt got in the truck and started it. He was quiet. As he pulled out of the park and onto a main road, he cleared his throat.

"So, something weird happened," he said. "I went up to my grandma and tried to give her a hug. She just stood there, arms at her sides. I said I love you to her and all she said back was 'Yeah.' She was really cold toward me."

"What? Are you serious?" I said as my eyes shot open and I leaned forward. "No, she did not. That breaks my heart. Colt, I am so sorry."

"It's fine. It was just weird," Colt said.

I felt my heart sinking. It sucked that they treated me weird and unkindly, but it was just plain heartbreaking that they were treating Colt badly. This was so insane.

"I really just want to move away and not tell anyone," Colt said.

"I mean, I would be fine with that," I said. "I just wish there was an end in sight to having to be around Hilda. I don't think I can go to that graduation. Everyone was so strange today. I can't do that again. I might go crazy. I definitely am not going to the graduation party that your exes were invited to. Then, your grandpa from Florida comes into town next month and we will probably have to see her then. It just is so overwhelming. I need a break so bad."

"You'll get a break," Colt said.

The day after the party was Talli's first birthday. We tried to enjoy it the best we could. I tried to stay in the moment and soak in Talli's excitement as she opened the gifts we got her. I tried to enjoy every second with her. It was difficult when my thoughts were buzzing around, threatening to drag me down into darkness. I couldn't get my mind off Colt's family, the way they were acting and how hopeless it felt to be tied to them. This is the rest of my life, I kept thinking. I questioned how Talli would grow up healthy around this toxicity. I was trying my best not to lose my shit, but I was losing it. I was barely holding myself together. The only thread keeping me from cutting all ties and moving out of the country was Talli. It all felt like a sick contradiction.

That same week, Colt went back to work and Talli had her twelve-month pediatrician appointment. Colt had been trying to decide whether or not he would attempt to come back to Ohio for Mackenzi's high school graduation ceremony. Things were changing rapidly with his job. He ended up interviewing for the same title with the new company and got offered the position. He would now have to be in Texas every other week instead of every third week. We were also expected to move as soon as possible. I was not upset about that. I was anxious. I felt like life was changing too quickly for me to process, although I knew it needed to happen. We needed to get out of here for our relationship's health, for our family's health and for my own health. Colt ended up staying in Texas and, luckily, I didn't have to stress about not attending the graduation. It felt bittersweet, though. I was glad to not have to be around his family, but I did feel sad to miss Mackenzi's graduation. Before Hilda had turned everything upside down, Mackenzi and I had been close. We talked, laughed and had fun together. Now, it felt like she was a stranger. I wanted to do something to change it, but I felt like I couldn't trust her anymore. Hilda and Clayton were her parents. She was young. She also didn't need to be put in the middle of this chaos. Even though she sort of was forced into it by Hilda, I didn't want to add to it.

The days all molded together. I started to pack up the items in the house that had taken me months to unpack and set up. I started to go through things and get rid of what wasn't needed or wanted. Whenever Colt was home, we were busy cleaning and finishing up projects we had started on the house. I ended my therapy, since it was an Ohio practice and I couldn't continue out of state. I felt chaotic, but better than I had been with moving so close to coming to fruition. Moving was the light at the end of the tunnel. I tried to enjoy every last sunset with our wide-open view. I soaked in our couple acres of grass, the trees in the distance and the quiet of living in the country. I got together with my mom, dad and grandparents. They were all sad we were moving, but understood it was for the best.

On Mother's Day, I spent the day with my parents. Colt was out of state for work. After my grandparents and dad left my mom's home, I noticed I had received a text message from Hilda. It was sent to both my mom and me in a group Hilda started. It was a generic Mother's Day gif.

"Did you see this?" I asked my mom, who was sitting on the couch above me. I was sitting on her rug doing puzzles with Talli.

"Yeah, I was hoping you wouldn't. It is strange that she sent it in a group to both of us. Like she is just putting on a show. She could've texted us separately," my mom said.

"Yeah, or she could've just not texted me at all. I'm not texting her back. She's no mother," I said.

My stomach felt like I had eaten gravel. I felt anxious and miserable just seeing Hilda's name appear on my phone.

"Oh, I'm not either. There is no reason to," my mom said. "Also, it is just some dumb gif."

"I feel like she does stuff like this to make me think about her. She doesn't mean it. If she was trying to be nice, she would actually try to change how things are. She would simply be nice. This generic gif that says, 'Happy Mother's Day' with a flower, is not nice. It is just another slap in the face to me."

I was getting worked up. I hated that I couldn't ever seem to rid Hilda from my head. She was in there lighting fires and beating my brain up with a bat. Why couldn't I get her out of there? Why did I care? Why did I let her get to me?

I left my mom's house shortly after. I stopped to get a milkshake and then took Talli to the park to try to save the rest of our day. I needed to keep myself and my head busy.

* * *

Before I could even process it, Colt was home from Texas and it was the week his grandpa on his dad's side would arrive in Ohio from Florida. His uncle had rented a house at Piedmont Lake. His aunt had started a group text with the address, dates and plans explained. They wanted everyone to come visit on Sunday and wanted to take a group picture. I wasn't ready. I actually felt worse rather than better, since Talli's party. I felt like I was caught in a giant's hand being squeezed. It was like my lungs were exploding and unable to take in any air. My brain had been getting fuzzier and less able to withstand any difficult situations. It felt like my lips were quivering, barely holding back my scream. My whole body was harder to control. I felt like I was close to a 2007 Britney meltdown. I felt like this twenty-four/seven, although it was greatly exacerbated by texts, Facebook posts or any mention of Colt's family. So, the imminent gathering was bringing me closer than ever to losing it.

On top of that, Mackenzi's graduation party, which Colt's exes were invited to, was Friday night. We didn't go, as we had said we wouldn't. On Saturday, my anxiety was worse since Sunday was the next day.

"You should just go. Talli and I can stay home," I said to Colt as we sat in our bedroom.

The morning sun was shining through the windows, making the room look dreamy.

"I don't want to go by myself. Also, I want my grandpa to meet Talli," Colt said.

"Yeah, that's true. I want him to meet Talli, too. This sucks. I am just so anxious and feel sick about this. I can't run into your mother right now. I really need a break. I seriously feel like I am crazy. I feel like I have barely any mental sanity left. To be the best mom I can be, I need to protect my mental health."

I curled up into a ball on the bed. Talli was hobbling around on the floor with her toys. She had been working on perfecting her walking skills lately.

"What if we go while your mom is busy? That way your grandpa can meet Talli and I won't lose my shit," I thought out loud.

"Yeah, we could probably do that," Colt agreed.

"Could we go when your mom is at Mackenzi's dance recital?"

"Yeah, that would give us a couple hours," Colt said.

"I mean, I still feel like this is going to be difficult for me mentally and emotionally, but I will try to do this for you and Talli. Just know that I am really close to my breaking point. I don't know what that necessarily looks like and I don't want to. I feel like I'm becoming very hopeless and miserable. I don't like how I feel or what it's making me turn into," I said, sighing. "I'm sorry I keep talking about it so much, but I just need you to know where I'm at. It's not a good place."

"Okay. Well, after this, you'll get your break. Not saying that we'll see my mom tomorrow, just that I won't ask you to do anything that puts you in that situation again for a while. Until you feel better," Colt said.

"Thanks, honey. I appreciate it. I really want to get better. I wish it was easier for me."

We had agreed we would go down to southern Ohio to visit Colt's grandpa, Bill, tomorrow, on Sunday during Mackenzi's dance recital. It was the safest time to go, when we knew we could avoid running into Hilda. If things hadn't gotten so miserable with Hilda and Clayton, we normally would have gone when they went. We would've gone to Mackenzi's dance recital, even though that probably wouldn't be the best place to take a baby. Before Hilda pushed things too far, we did what she wanted. It made me kind of sick to think about, how we did everything she wanted and it still wasn't enough, how one thing that wasn't in line with pleasing her made her make me out to be a monster. This all went back to me being days postpartum with my newborn and going in my bedroom to lay down with her. Hilda saw that as me being rude toward her. She didn't think she was being over-whelming or overbearing. She didn't think a young woman who had just pushed out her first baby and was still bleeding, swollen and in pain, needed rest. It was all about her. Me giving birth was about her becoming a grandma. It sickened me. I was tired of everything always being about her, having to think about her feelings before my own, having to cater to her in my moments.

I was also so exhausted thinking about everything that had happened, thinking about what could happen next and thinking about how to keep this from becoming a problem for Talli. All this dumb drama with Hilda was making it hard for me to function normally and fully experience Talli growing up. I couldn't continue this for me mentally, but also for Talli. When would it ever end? I thought about how Hilda could possibly start saying unkind and untrue things about me to Talli one day. I thought about how she could turn on Talli if Talli didn't follow her exact expectations. I didn't want this controlling our lives. My mind started to switch from trying to resolve this issue with Hilda to cutting Hilda out of our lives. Colt could make his own decision, but I was really starting to feel like Talli and I needed to be done with her. She had so many chances to make things right or to at least stop her emotional abuse. She wasn't changing. She continued to play the victim. I no longer cared what she thought of me. I no longer cared what anyone else thought of me. In a sick, twisted way, this had helped me kill off the people pleasing in me. I used to care so much about what Colt's family thought of me. Now, I realized that it truly didn't matter. People would think what they wanted and it wasn't my problem. If anyone cared about me, they would have talked to me or at least continued to treat me kindly. Instead, most people shut me out, ignored me or treated me like a three-headed beast.

Colt's dad's side of the family had been treating me normally, although I still felt uncomfortable around them. I was certain Hilda was saying something to them about me, too. It made me feel weird to be around anyone Hilda could be talking poorly about me to. I wondered if anyone was sticking up for me, or if they were just ignoring her. I wanted someone to stick up for me. Even though I didn't care what people thought about me, it still would have felt nice to have someone care.

When I woke up on Sunday, I again did all I could to keep the anxiety at bay. I got ready and even did my makeup. I needed some kind of mask or sense of protection. I didn't want to feel exposed. I got Talli ready. Colt wanted to leave early, so before I knew it, we were all in the truck. As we drove down, my throat closed. My heart was beating fast and my blood felt like tar, barely moving through my veins. I felt dizzy, like I was going to pass out at any moment. The closer we got, the worse I felt.

"Colt, can you please stop at the next gas station? I really have to go to the bathroom," I said.

"Sure. Didn't you go to the bathroom like five times before we left?" Colt asked, eyes on the road.

"Yeah, but I have to pee again," I answered.

I looked out the window. Another uncomfortable aspect of my intense anxiety was I had to pee like twenty times before any triggering event. Colt pulled into the parking lot of a random gas station. There was nothing else around the small building besides the road and trees. There were three people standing by the door, talking. I hurried inside to the bathroom. It was tiny and filthy. I peed and then stood at the sink with the cold water running in my hands for five minutes. I breathed in and out. I looked up and into my dark, wide eyes in the mirror. I looked terrified. I let myself have a moment alone in that grungy, stinky, gross gas station bathroom. It felt safer there than in the truck headed to see Colt's family. I composed myself, rolled my shoulders back and slowly made my way back to the car. We drove the last half-hour to the house they had rented on Piedmont Lake.

When we pulled into the driveway, another car pulled in beside us. I watched Bill get out of the car. I got Talli out of her car seat slowly, giving Colt a minute to say hello to Bill and me a moment to breathe. Bill's wife, Susan, also got out. It was my first time ever meeting her. I got out of the truck holding Talli. Bill came over and gave us a hug hello.

"And this is Talli, hi Talli," Bill said, waving at her in my arms. "She's so cute!"

"Thank you," I said and smiled.

"Oh, how sweet!" Susan said, looking at Talli.

"Hi, I'm Adison, I don't think we've met yet," I said with a smile.

"Oh hi, yes. I'm Susan," she said, still looking at Talli.

"Well, please come inside. Everyone else was still asleep when we left, but I imagine they will be up now," Bill said as he led us inside the rental house.

We said hello to Colt's aunts, uncle and cousins. Half the group left shortly after greetings to go out on the boat they had rented for the week. Colt's aunt, grandpa and grandma stayed behind in the house with us. We spent the time talking. Eventually, we moved outside and I held Talli's hands while she walked around the yard. It was all normal and fine. My head, on the other hand, was not. I felt panicky, scared, anxious and stressed. I was so scared we wouldn't leave before Hilda arrived. I was also so scared of anyone saying anything to make me feel uncomfortable. Luckily, that hadn't happened. Talli was making me so nervous by walking too close to the road and by preferring to walk on the rocky sidewalk. I tried to stay involved in the conversation, although it felt impossible with my fearful thoughts on top of trying to focus on Talli. At one point, Talli fell on her knees and scraped them on the rocky walkway. She cried and I held her close. She thankfully wasn't bleeding, it was only a red spot, but it made tears hover behind my eyelids. I hated when she got hurt.

The more time went on, the more chaotic I felt. I had to walk to the side of the house or go inside with Talli a couple times to try to get some deep breaths in. I was sitting inside on the floor helping Talli eat an applesauce pouch when Colt walked in.

"I hate to rush you, but can we leave soon, please? I am feeling really anxious and stressed. You can come back here on your own another day this week. Just please, I need to get home," I whispered to him.

"Yeah, we'll leave soon. Everything is fine, though. Nothing is happening," Colt said.

"I know, but I can't help how bad I feel. I feel like I'm going to explode," I said and then got quiet when everyone else walked back inside.

The others had returned from their boat outing. We had a couple group pictures taken before we started saying our goodbyes. Colt's sweet aunt, Milly, hugged me goodbye.

While she hugged me, she said into my ear, "You keep doing what you're doing." Milly pulled back, but kept her hands on my shoulders. She looked at me with concerned, kind eyes. "You guys are doing a great job. You're great parents. Don't listen to anyone who tells you otherwise."

I felt tears hot and heavy behind my eyes. I didn't know what to say.

"Thank you," I managed to get out. "That really means a lot."

I meant it. It meant so much to hear that from her. I felt warmth and care splash through the ice in my chest. The goodbyes were heartfelt and genuine. I got into the car feeling different. I put Talli in her car seat and waited for Colt to pull out of the driveway before I released my pent-up tears.

"Why are you crying?" Colt asked me.

"Because I had these tears pent up in me for a little while. Just from stress. But also, your aunt said something really nice to me. I almost started crying in front of her," I said through my tears. "Damn, it feels good to cry and let these feelings out."

"What did she say?" Colt asked, turning the car onto the main road.

"She said something about how we are doing a great job, we are great parents and not to listen to people. I forget exactly how she worded it. It meant a lot to me, though. It was really nice to hear."

I let my tears fall until there were none left. Colt wanted to stop to grab a pizza for the drive back. He pulled into a small pizza shop in Barnesville. I slunk down in my seat, focusing on my breathing, while he went in to get it. I felt better to be leaving, but the anxiety still felt in charge. Being in Barnesville fueled it more. Once we finally were back on the road and getting further away, I felt my body starting to relax a little bit. I felt exhausted.

32

Chapter Thirty-Two

At last, we made it home, surviving the lengthy two-hour drive. Colt and I both had to pee. Colt went into the bathroom off the living room and I brought Talli with me into the master bathroom. God, it felt good to be home. I was glad we went and were able to see Colt's family on his dad's side. I smiled, feeling accomplished. I was proud of myself for getting through it. I did my very best today, under the circumstances. When I walked out of the bathroom with Talli, I saw Colt laying on the couch. He had his knee crossed in the air with his foot resting on top of his other bent knee. His hands covered his face.

"What is it babe? What's wrong?" I asked him, worried.

"My mom must've called me while I was in the bathroom. I left my phone out in the kitchen. Anyway, she left me a voicemail," he said, lifting his hands to look at me solemnly. "It's not good."

He grabbed his phone and hit play.

"Hi, this is Mom," Hilda's voice blared aggressively. "I didn't figure you'd answer. You're kind of a coward that way. I'm very upset with you guys and I think it's wrong and I'm kind of pissed actually. Hurt in every way, shape and form. And your sister will never ever understand that and I just can't even believe, I can't even believe the things you've done."

Hilda sounded dark and accusatory.

"And Adison, I'm very upset with you because as a wife, you'd think you would care about your husband and his family. How you can allow this to happen... I don't understand this at all. At all. You're supposed to be Mackenzi's sister and you've been nothing but rude to her for an entire year and she is heartbroken."

My jaw dropped as I listened to Hilda rant on with tar in her voice.

"And we're all heartbroken. This is you. This isn't me. This is you. This is you," she repeated, pausing after each accusation.

"We're doing nothing but being here, being present, wanting to be with you guys and you're purposefully being selfish," Hilda yelled.

"Don't tell me I can't be the victim. You are being selfish and not sharing your lives with us on purpose. You're purposefully being mean. We are not being mean at all," she yelled viciously in the voicemail. "If you think I'm mean, it's definitely not on purpose. You are purposefully being mean and I, I just don't think I can ever forgive you guys. You're so rude. So rude! I can't even believe this is happening. So. Rude. I am very upset. And your sister's going to be very upset."

My jaw hung open. Colt locked his phone and put it on top of the couch. We just stared at each other.

"What the hell," I finally said. I was in shock. I set Talli down to play with her toys and slowly sat down next to her.

"I don't even know what to do," Colt said, pressing his hands over his eyes.

"Well, don't answer if she calls again. Don't call her back, obviously. She is a lunatic. There is nothing to say back to that," I said. "I need some wine."

I got up and went into the kitchen to open the bottle of wine I got from the store a couple weeks ago just in case I needed it. I had decided months ago I was never going to drink alcohol again, but after that voicemail, I needed it. It was my first glass of wine, my first drink, since before I got pregnant. I opened the bottle of Roadhouse Red. I poured it into a wine glass.

"So can we be done?" I asked Colt.

"What?" Colt asked, confused.

"Can we be done? Is this enough? I literally went to visit your dad's side of the family today so your grandpa, who we haven't seen in years, could meet Talli. I was terrified to do it. This is why. We can't do anything without some kind of repercussion. We can't win. And even better, this is now my fault," I scoffed, taking a long sip of wine.

Wow, that tasted good.

"She literally called me out in that voicemail. I did this for you and your grandpa. Why is everything always my fault? Also, this had nothing to do with Mackenzi. I don't want Mackenzi to feel bad, but I feel like your mom is using her to make us feel bad. If Mackenzi is upset, she can talk to us and we can explain why we didn't go. It's not because we don't want to support her, but because her mom is a psychopath. This is exactly why I need space from her."

I was pacing around the room tightly clutching my glass of wine.

"Yeah, I know," Colt said. "It isn't your fault. And you're right, Mackenzi can tell us if she's upset and we will talk to her."

I set my glass down on the table next to the couch and gave Talli a hug. I kept thinking about how this environment was no way to raise a child. This was no way for a child to grow up. Talli shouldn't be hearing these things said to her parents. I sat with Talli, occasionally taking sips of wine. Colt had turned on the TV and was watching a baseball game. The sun set, and as I drank my glass of wine, I started to feel numb in a great way. I felt almost invincible. Like Hilda's words and deadly voice couldn't touch me. Colt's work phone rang and he went into his office. I put my wine glass away and got Talli ready for bed. I came back out into the kitchen and my phone lit up. My screen showed a missed call and a voicemail from Hilda.

"Oh my god," I said, my jaw dropping again.

My hands shook as I unlocked my phone. I felt like I was dreaming. This didn't feel real. Colt walked into the kitchen.

"What?" he asked, looking at me.

"I got one," I said, holding up my phone so he could see.

I clicked on the voicemail and pressed play.

"Hi this is Hilda. I want to make sure you get the message I left for Colt," Hilda's voice came over the speaker. Her voice was even and dark. She sounded evil. She continued, pausing dramatically after each short sentence.

"I am very pissed off. I am very disappointed in both of you. You have hurt your entire family. You are very rude. You have hurt my daughter. I know she is crushed right now to have not seen you guys today. To have missed all her events her entire senior year. Being mad at me is one thing, being hurtful to me is one thing. You hurt my daughter all year and you really, really hurt her today. I am very pissed off at you. You are disrespectful. You are a horrible, horrible person," Hilda said with sureness in her voice.

As she spoke, I had a tipsy smirk on my face.

"Oh, yes, try and make me feel bad, Hilda," I thought.

Colt stared at the ground as he listened to his mom degrade his wife.

"You're not a good friend. You're definitely not a good sister to her. And you're not a good mom to your daughter. To let her miss her family, not take her around her family and be so rude and vindictive, you're just a mean person. You're a mean person," Hilda repeated, spitting.

I paused the voicemail. When she said I was not a good mom, my mouth drew into a straight line.

"Alright, this isn't funny anymore. I'm fucking done. She's cut out," I said, angrily but firmly. I couldn't believe she just went there. I pressed play again.

"I don't even like you right now. I am very pissed. I just wanted to make sure you got the message. Not even hurt anymore, just pissed. Very pissed," Hilda hissed through the speaker.

"Cool, I don't care," I said nonchalantly, and my fingers flew across my screen. I forwarded the voicemail to my mom, dad, sisters and two of my closest friends.

"So, we are done now, right?" I asked in more of a statement, my face blank, looking up at Colt.

"Yeah," he said. "We are done."

He silently turned and went back into his office. My phone rang. The caller ID showed my dad. I answered it.

"Are you okay?" my dad asked when I answered the phone.

"Yeah, luckily I had some wine so I'm pretty numb to it all right now," I answered.

"Okay, good," he said. "Do not respond to that."

"I wasn't going to," I answered while pacing in the kitchen.

"Good. There is nothing to say to that woman. She's insane. She's mentally not okay. None of what she said is true. You know that, right? She is crazy. Do not listen to anything she says. You're a great mother," my dad said firmly.

"Thank you," I said.

When I got off the phone with my dad, I looked at the texts that my sisters had sent me.

"Adison, holy shit. Bro WHAT!" Daisy's text read.

"Holy shit," Calli's text read.

My phone started ringing again, this time with a call from my mom.

"Hello?" I said, as I clicked the answer button.

"I am so sorry you and Colt are dealing with that. Poor Colt. That is so awful for his mom to be saying those things," my mom said.

"I know, I feel really bad for him."

"I feel bad for you, too. She really came at you. She really sounds unwell. That is not something normal people do. Also, why does she keep bringing up Mackenzi?" my mom asked.

"She is crazy. I think she keeps bringing up Mackenzi because we didn't go to her dance recital. We went to visit Colt's grandpa during the recital because it was guaranteed we wouldn't run into Hilda. With everything that has been going on, I need space from her. My anxiety has been really difficult for me to deal with. Honestly, I didn't want to go at all. I don't feel good socializing, I don't like being anywhere near southern Ohio, and I was scared someone would say something to make me feel more anxious. It went really well. They were really nice, but now I have to deal with this. I just never want to see Hilda ever again," I sighed.

"I don't blame you. That is so crazy. Well, I am sure you won't have to deal with her anymore, right? At least for a long time. You guys are moving and I honestly don't know how Colt goes forward from here. I don't know what you say after that," my mom said.

"I don't know, either," I said. "I think I'm going to go to bed. I'm really exhausted. It's been a long day."

"That's a good idea. I love you so much. I hope you are able to sleep well," my mom said, before getting off the phone.

"Are you coming to bed?" I asked Colt when I walked into his office.

"Yeah, I'll be in there in a little bit," Colt said, looking up from his work phone.

I carefully picked up Talli and brought her into my bed. I cuddled her as I tried to turn my brain off and go to sleep.

33

Chapter Thirty-Three

The next morning, I felt nauseous and it wasn't from the glass of wine. The day went by in a blur. Colt was working from home. In the early afternoon, Talli and I were spending our lazy, recovery day in our bedroom. Colt walked in and sat next to us on the floor.

"I just got a call from Clayton," Colt said.

"You didn't answer that, did you?" I asked, looking up at him.

Talli and I were rolling a ball back and forth.

"I did," Colt said calmly. "I shouldn't have. It was pretty bad."

"What did he say?" I asked, trying not to shake. It wasn't working. My body was betraying me.

"I don't remember all of it exactly. He just kept ranting. He said that same thing about me only having one mom and he said she's about done with me. He said everyone in the family is about done with us. He said he would have beaten me if he saw me the other day when we were visiting my grandpa," Colt told me.

"What? Are you kidding me? Colt, that is so bad. Thank God we didn't see them. I am so angry. If he would've touched you, I would've lost my shit."

I fumed. I got up and started pacing. My face felt like I just stuck it in a four-hundred-and-fifty-degree oven. I could literally feel the redness.

"Yeah. I am done with it all," Colt said.

"Me too. Please don't answer if he calls again. You do not need to listen to that crap. He literally threatened you. They are all so freaking crazy," I said.

"I'm not going to answer anymore. It's okay, you don't need to get so worked up," Colt said softly.

"I know, I'm sorry. I am just so angry. All of this is so insane. This is over going to visit your grandpa on your dad's side so he could meet Talli for the first time. This is so outrageous," I sighed, trying to calm down the best I could.

"I agree, it's not fair. You know, growing up we didn't go around the Witley side much. It was always about the Corrigons. We always did everything with my mom's side. I barely even know my cousins on the Witley side. It is messed up the more I think about it," Colt said, looking out the window.

The grass was especially green and the sky was a soft blue mixed with a fluffy pink and orange as the sun began to set.

"I'm sorry honey. It sounds like besides being a lunatic, your mom is also acting very hypocritical," I said.

"Yeah, she is. Oh well, I'm really done with all of this. I don't care about them anymore. We've tried. I am tired of wasting our time with it," Colt said, looking at me.

"Cool, me too," I said.

We hugged and picked Talli up to bring her into the hug.

"Family cuddles!" Colt said, smiling.

Talli laughed. We both kissed her on opposite sides of her cheeks.

A couple hours later, only minutes before eight at night, Colt's phone pinged with a new text message. He looked down at it for a minute and then sighed.

"Look at this," he said, sliding his phone over to me. We were sitting at the kitchen counter. I read the text. It was from his Aunt Nancy.

It read, "I want you to know that I love you and always will no matter what, but I'm very disappointed in how you have been treating your family. Your mom and sister love you unconditionally and you have hurt them by not showing up for her milestones this year. You should remember how important it is for people to show up and show support during the important times in your life. I don't know your reason but in our family we show up. I hope you can evaluate your situation objectively to determine your path moving forward. I love you."

"What the fuck!" I gasped, my jaw dropping. "I guess here come the flying monkeys." I rolled my eyes.

"Flying monkeys?" Colt asked.

"They are the people who go after the victim of a narcissist to try to corral them back in. I don't know, I read about it online. It's like how the wicked witch had her flying monkeys do dirty work for her," I said, shaking my head.

"I hope you can evaluate your situation objectively to determine your path moving forward," I repeated in a high-pitched voice. "What the hell? She's implying that you leave me. I am the situation and she's telling you to look at facts and then do something about it," I said, making air quotes around the word facts.

Her facts were Hilda's lies. I knew this aunt was being a snake. It sickened me that so many people who witnessed us get married and say our vows were working tirelessly to try to undo what we had built. Not only that, but trying to break apart a new family. Even worse, these people were supposed to be family! Shouldn't family be there to support and help bring a family back together rather than try to tear it apart?

"What do I say back to her?" Colt asked me.

"I wouldn't even respond," I said, disgusted.

"Yeah, but she just is hearing what my mom has been telling her. Maybe she would be acting differently if she knew our side," Colt said.

"She never asked for our side. She has just sent you these strange texts here and there. You can do what you want, but I don't think she is going to listen anymore. It seems that she is a pawn of your mom," I said.

"Well, what do I say?" Colt asked again.

"I don't know. I'd have to think about it," I said.

I got up to get Talli ready for bed. Colt went back to his office to finish his work for the night. Twenty minutes later, he came into the bedroom to show me another text on his phone. This one was from Clayton.

It read, "Going to Texas, I heard."

Another text immediately followed that read, "You gonna be broke or you already broke?"

My mouth was open again in shock.

"How did he find out about that?" I asked, looking at Colt. "Also, that second part took me a second, it's hard-to-decipher hillbilly."

"I don't know. Paul must have told him. I don't know how else he would have heard," Colt said.

"So, he called Paul? That is really freaking weird," I said, scrunching my face as if I had just eaten something sour.

"It is really weird. I'm not responding to him anymore. He is stupid," Colt said.

"That's probably a good idea," I said.

I had a sick, twisted feeling in my stomach. It made me feel really backed into a corner that they had found out we were moving. I suddenly couldn't wait to be out of here.

"I wish we could leave tonight," I said. "I don't feel safe here anymore."

"I know. We are leaving soon enough. I'm not telling anyone we are moving. I just want to leave," Colt said assuredly.

"Me too. I'm scared with how irrational they are acting that they'll do something even crazier and come up here," I said, shaking.

"If they do, you just stay in the bedroom," Colt said.

"I would probably call the cops."

"That's fine," Colt said, hugging me.

"Thank you for getting us out of here. I love you so much. I don't know what I would do without you," I said, hugging him tighter.

We watched TV in our room until we were able to fall asleep. I felt like my anxiety was eating me alive. I tried to cuddle with Talli, who was sleeping in the middle of the bed, but I still struggled to feel calm. I was tired, but my bloodshot eyes were wide open. I felt like I hadn't eaten in a week. My stomach growled. At some point after one in the morning, I lost consciousness, but regained it without much rest. I looked at my phone. It was three-thirty in the morning. I sighed, slowly and quietly getting out of bed. I went into the kitchen. My stomach was howling. I felt like if I didn't eat, I would end up dry heaving. I quickly made scrambled eggs and toast. I brought it back into the room. I turned on *Ridiculousness* and ate. Talli and Colt slept peacefully in bed beside me. Once I was done, I felt enough heaviness behind my eyes to lay down and try to sleep again.

Colt woke up at five in the morning to go work in his home office and I woke up shortly after. I sat in bed, thinking. I looked at the picture I had taken of the message Nancy had sent him. I started typing in my notes. When I was done, I read it over. I sent it to Colt.

It read, "I do show up for my family every day. I have tried over and over with my mom. I'd prefer my sister be left out of this since the reason I have not physically shown up is due to working in another state as well as my mother's behavior for the past year. It feels like everyone has forgotten I have a wife and baby, let alone a job and my own life in general. I don't understand why I have been made to feel as though I have to pick between my family I started (my wife and daughter) and the family I grew up with. This has been the narrative for a year with you guys. I understand you are my mother's sister, which is why I'm sure you trust what she says. She has been lying, manipulative, gaslighting, unkind, difficult and argumentative for a year. We have tried to fix things multiple times. I am no longer accepting her behavior. I hope you can also look at things objectively and determine how you will make an effort to be a positive part of my life moving forward. I love you, too."

I put up a blockade of pillows around Talli, who was still sound asleep. I tiptoed into Colt's office.

"Good morning, babe. I just sent you what I wrote up. You don't have to say that or you can edit it. I was just thinking and wrote what I would say if I were you," I said, standing in the doorway.

"Okay, thank you honey. Why are you up?" Colt asked, getting up from his desk to give me a hug.

"I couldn't sleep," I said.

"Where's Talli? Is she still sleeping? Why don't you go lay down with her?"

"She's sleeping. She's surrounded by pillows. I'll go lay with her, but I don't think I will be able to sleep," I answered.

I went back into the bedroom and laid back down in the bed. I stared at Talli's innocent, sweet face.

"I love her so much," I thought.

I felt tears stream down my cheeks. I curled up next to her, silently crying. I hated how profoundly weak and broken I felt.

After surviving the day, Colt and I headed into town to get dinner. With all the craziness, we had yet to go to the grocery store and felt too exhausted to cook. The sun was setting as we drove down the curvy back roads.

"I'm thinking we call the pizza place when we get to Handel's," Colt was saying as he drove. "They usually make the pizza really fast."

"Okay," I said before Colt's phone rang over the truck speakers.

Paul's name popped up on the truck's iPad-sized screen. Colt looked at me from the rearview mirror with questioning, narrowed eyes. I was sitting in the backseat beside Talli as I always did. He clicked the answer button.

"Hello?" he said, still looking up at me between looking at the road.

"Hey, what are you doing?" Paul asked.

"Driving to get something to eat. What are you doing?"

"Nothing. Where are you going? To that town close to you?" Paul asked.

"Yeah, why?" Colt asked, confused.

"Just wondering. Are you alone? Or is Adison with you?" Paul questioned.

"I'm with Adison," Colt said, looking up at me again.

"What the heck," he mouthed to me.

I shrugged.

"Well, call me back when you get home," Paul said in a strange tone. He hung up.

"Okay, that was super weird," Colt said to me.

"Yeah, it was. Do you think Clayton called him? It would explain how Clayton knew we were moving. What do you think he said to Paul to make him act so strange?" I asked, shaking as if I were standing underdressed in the arctic.

"I don't know. Oh, wait, he just texted me. He said to call him when you're not around," Colt said, scrunching his face. "This is really weird."

I shook as we got our milkshakes and pizza. The drive home felt more like hours than twenty minutes. We went into the living room and sat on the couch with our pizza boxes. Talli sat on the couch between us.

"I'm going to call Paul back, just be quiet so he doesn't hear you," Colt said.

He put the phone on speaker as it rang.

"Hey," Paul said. "Can you talk now?"

"Yeah. I'm home," Colt said, looking at me.

"Okay, so what the fuck is going on?" Paul asked.

"What do you mean?" Colt said, tilting his head.

"You know what I mean," Paul said.

"Not really," Colt replied.

"Yes, you do. I'm talking about whatever is going on with your wife," Paul said in an annoyed voice.

"Oh, so Clayton has called you?" Colt asked him.

"Yes, Clayton has called me!" Paul exclaimed. "He's called me every day so far this week. He's talked for over forty-five minutes, at least. I don't know, man, it doesn't sound good."

"I don't know what he's telling you, but my parents are crazy," Colt responded.

"He has gone on and on about how Adison is keeping your baby from them. And some other stuff. It just doesn't sound good," Paul said.

"Don't answer him when he calls. He's crazy. You don't understand what's been going on," Colt said.

"I don't know, man," Paul said.

"Seriously, don't answer him," Colt said. "I have to go, but I'll talk to you later."

Colt hung up the phone.

"I knew it," I said, shaking my head. "I knew Clayton said something to Paul. That is so messed up. Like, leave your friends out of it. Why do they have to keep isolating us from people?"

I groaned.

"It's really bad," Colt said. "I'm annoyed Paul is even talking to him about it. It's none of anyone else's business. I'm annoyed Clayton is talking to him about it, too, but I'm not surprised."

We ate our pizza, trying to enjoy it and the rest of our night. I tried to ignore the sour taste in my mouth and the sick feeling in my stomach. I should've been used to all these uncomfortable feelings by now. They had been almost a constant for an entire year. I wasn't sure how long I could last feeling so unwell. I hung tight onto the thought of moving and cutting them out of our lives. Those thoughts gave me a sweet, peaceful sense of hope. If only I could survive just a little bit longer.

34

Chapter Thirty-Four

It was Thursday, June fifteenth, four-thirty in the afternoon. I was sitting on the toilet in our master bathroom, peeing. I held toilet paper in one hand and Talli in the other. She was a little extra clingy due to her teeth coming in. I didn't mind, but it made it hard to do typical things like use the bathroom. Suddenly, Colt walked in.

"I want to show you something, but I'm worried you'll get upset. If I show you, can you promise not to freak out?" he asked, looking at me and then turning to the mirror over the sink to inspect his beard. "Um, I don't know if I can promise I won't feel upset, but I can try not to react as much," I said, unsure.

"Okay. Just know it is absolutely insane. It's so insane you shouldn't be upset, because it's more funny than anything," Colt said, holding his phone with both hands, the screen facing his chest.

I just looked at him expectantly and nervously. He turned his phone around to show me the screen. My vision blurred and then zoned back in. The contact at the top read, "Mom." Below that was a screenshot of some article followed by a message. I first read the message Hilda had typed.

It read, "Please seek professional help, I fear you are in a very toxic and abusive relationship, I'm scared for you."

There was another text directly below it that read, "This behavior is not normal."

I clicked on the image she sent.

The screenshot read, "They check on you all the time to see where you are, what you're doing and who you're with. They try to control where you go and who you see, and get angry if you don't do what they say. They accuse you of being unfaithful or of flirting. They isolate you from family and friends, often by behaving rudely to them."

I stared at the screen. Colt shifted in front of me.

"I honestly thought she was talking about herself when I first read it. It took me a minute to realize she was saying this about you," Colt said, laughing nervously. "Obviously it is insane."

I grabbed my phone that sat on the toilet paper stand and took a quick picture of Colt's screen. I handed his phone back to him.

"Who are you sending that to?" Colt asked.

"My sisters, my parents and probably Ellie. I need someone else to see this," I said, fingers flying across my screen.

Colt was quiet as I texted.

"I am trying not to be upset," I said, breathing in and out. "It's fine. It is really crazy, but if this is what she's telling everyone, then that really sucks. I guess it makes sense. It makes sense why Paul was being so weird. I guess I'm just kind of sad that anyone could believe this. Am I toxic? I don't want to be toxic to you," I said sadly.

I got off the toilet. My butt felt numb from sitting that long and I felt a red ring on my thighs. I went to the sink and splashed water on my face.

"Stop! This is why I didn't want to show you," Colt said, frustrated. "You are not toxic. You're normal. You're a great wife and mom. We are so lucky to have you."

He came over to me and hugged me.

"Okay, I hope you would tell me if I was being toxic. I think I try to be mindful about what I do and say. I think I am fairly self-aware. I try to be. I don't know. I just don't want to be toxic."

I splashed more cold water on my face.

"Honey, please stop. She's trying to get in your head. You're letting her win," Colt said, rubbing my back. "I think it's absolutely insane she texted me that. She's gone way too far."

"Okay," I said, patting my face dry.

I took a couple long, deep inhales and exhales.

"I really don't care about these people anymore. I am just ready to move and get far away from them," Colt said.

* * *

The next night, Paul called Colt again.

"Dude, seriously, what is going on?" Paul droned.

"What are you talking about now?" Colt asked.

"Clayton has called me every single day this week. Five days straight. At least forty minutes every single time. He just goes on and on about you guys," Paul said, annoyed.

"Dude, I told you not to answer him."

"He just calls again! He calls until I answer. And then when I try to get off the phone, he just keeps talking. I've put it on speaker, left the room and when I get back, he's still talking," Paul said.

"Okay, don't answer then," Colt said.

"You have to do something. Talk to him or something. I don't know, but something needs to happen. I'm tired of him calling me," Paul said.

"I don't know what to tell you, man. I'm not talking to him. He'll stop calling if you don't answer. Or just block him," Colt shrugged.

"Why is Adison keeping your kid away from them?" Paul asked.

"We haven't kept Talli away from anyone. Well, maybe now we are because of how psychotic they are acting," Colt said. "I'm telling you, stop answering him. He is delusional."

"I don't know, man. It just doesn't sound good," Paul said solemnly.

Colt wrapped up the conversation and hung up the phone.

"This is so annoying," Colt said, looking over at me.

We were on the couch again. We both had little energy to do much else the past week.

"I don't understand why they have to involve your friend. Paul seems to believe what they are telling him. It sucks because now it feels like we can't trust him. I don't know why they couldn't just leave your friends out of it," I said, shaking my head. "It feels incredibly isolating. I feel so bad for you. Who can you talk to about all this? Can you talk to your friends at work? Of course, you can talk to me and my family, but I'm sure you'd like to have a friend or someone to talk to."

"I'm fine. I've talked to Rowland a little bit about it," Colt said, staring at the TV.

"That's good. What did he say?" I asked.

"He said my parents sound like assholes and he feels bad for us."

"I'm glad you have him to talk to. I just wish you had more people you felt like you could trust. It sucks that Hilda has isolated us from your entire family. And now Paul," I said.

"Oh well, that's their problem," Colt shrugged.

It was their problem, yes, but for me, it felt like my problem too until I was rid of them. I felt like I was constantly watching my back. I jumped every time the phone rang or dinged. I started putting my phone on silent, still cringing whenever I'd tap the home screen to see whatever notifications I may have. I didn't feel like a person. I felt like I was clinging on by white knuckles to survival.

As we struggled through another day and neared Colt leaving for Texas, another phone call happened. Colt had been outside on his riding lawn mower. I was in the living room with Talli. I heard the lawn mower shut off, then Colt's voice and wondered what was going on. I couldn't hear much, but I heard something that made my stomach drop.

"Adison is family, too," Colt said firmly. "Adison is family, too."

He had repeated it again. I started to sweat. I didn't like this. Did Hilda call and did he answer? Who was he talking to? It had to be someone in his family. I couldn't make out much else, but I was aware that whoever he was talking to, he was in some kind of argument. Panic coursed through me. I left Talli within my vision playing with her blocks while I went into the kitchen to clean. I needed to keep myself busy so I wouldn't lose my head. I kept feeling like I was on the verge of screaming or breaking things. It was a chaotic feeling and I hated it. I looked at Talli. I maintained calm for her. As I had kept telling myself, she did not deserve this. I needed to be strong and protect her. If I was to lose my shit, I would be damaging her myself. I would be damned if I let that happen.

I focused on deep breaths and brought Talli into our bedroom so I could wash my face. The splash of cold water and cleansing soap being rubbed into my sensitive skin always made me feel centered. In the midst of frothing the suds on my cheeks, Colt walked in. He gave Talli a kiss and then looked at me.

"So, I don't know if you noticed or not, but I was on the phone for a while," he said.

"Yeah, I noticed. Who was it?" I asked, staring at my reflection in the mirror.

"Mackenzi. She called to ask some questions, which was fine. I'm glad she did. She asked why we hadn't come to her events. She just sounded confused. It seems my mom has been telling her lies, as we figured. I told her it had nothing to do with her, that we were trying to distance ourselves from my mom because of the way she had been acting. She argued a bit. My mom has been in her head. I think overall it went well, though. We talked about school and stuff she's doing. She said she couldn't wait to get out of that house. So, I think she'll come around, eventually. She just needs to go to college and experience real life," Colt explained.

"Okay, that's good. I'm glad she called you. I did hear something that made me feel weird. I heard you saying I am family, too. What was that about?" I asked.

"I don't know, I don't remember. I think I was just saying it," he said, looking away.

"Oh, okay," I said, feeling uneasy.

I finished washing and drying my face.

"I am going to run back outside and finish the yard really quick," Colt said, giving me a kiss before he went back out.

I opened up the Snapchat app on my phone. It was the only real communication line between Mackenzi and I anymore. She would send me a picture of the top corner of her face or the wall. It wasn't genuine communication, but it wasn't like we weren't in contact at all. I would send her a picture back most days, too, although I started sending nugatory pictures as well. I didn't feel very comfortable sharing pictures of Talli anymore. Or really of myself, either.

After talking to Colt, I took a selfie of me and Talli.

I typed and retyped until finally settling on a message that read: "I love you and I'm sorry we haven't been at your events this past year. It isn't you, it is because of the way your mom has been treating us. I have been trying my best to keep myself and Talli safe."

I hit send and then felt a rush of anxiety. Should I have done that? I didn't know. I would like to be in communication with Mackenzi. None of this had anything to do with her. She was young, those were her parents and she was hearing everything they were saying. It seemed so unfair that her relationship appeared to dissolve with the erosion of her parents' relationship with us. I checked a couple times throughout the evening, but she had yet to open my snap.

35

Chapter Thirty-Five

"Wow. Adison, you are very brave. I know you are well aware, but you were being emotionally abused by your mother-in-law. I want you to remember this isn't your fault. You are not crazy," my specialist said, looking into my eyes. "You were being emotionally abused by someone you had thought you could trust during your post-partum stage and while learning as a new mom. That is difficult. Anyone else in your position would likely be feeling the same way you are. Everything you have told me about sounds traumatic."

"Thank you for saying that. It was traumatic. At times, I still can't believe everything that happened. I don't understand how a person can be so unkind to a new mom, let alone someone in their family," I said.

"It doesn't make sense. People can be awfully cruel. It's hard to wrap your head around things you would never do. It is hard to wrap your head around the actions of a narcissist. It sounds like you guys visiting Colt's dad's side of the family caused her narcissistic injury. That is not your fault. You are allowed to make your own decisions. You are allowed to visit people or not visit people. No one is entitled to tell you what to do with your time or your life. If anyone is upset with a choice you make that they believe impacts them, they can communicate that kindly. Although, in this specific case, the only appropriate thing for Hilda to do is nothing. Either say something kind about how she is glad Talli got to meet Bill or say nothing at all. If she was to say that, it should be to Colt at this point. Did you see any way for Hilda to make amends at this point? Why or why not?" my specialist asked.

"No. I didn't see any way she could make things better. I think I was past the point of no return with her. So, the voicemails were my final straw. The texts were just extra nails in the casket, further evidence there was no chance for reconciliation or change. She told Colt he was in a toxic and abusive relationship," I said.

"It sounds like she was clawing to regain some sense of control and power over you. Why did she say you were jealous and controlling, do you think?" my specialist asked.

"Probably because I don't like to hear about Colt's exes. I'm not sure where the controlling thing came from. Colt does what he wants. I mean maybe in the beginning of our relationship when I said I didn't want him going to strip clubs. There was that time before our wedding that Hilda came over to tell me about how he liked to do that. I think I told you about that already. That just reminded me of another instance where Hilda brought up Colt having nude magazines hidden in the ceiling of his old bedroom. She was laughing while talking about it and I vividly remember her looking me in the eye. She had an intentional, yet feigning harmless sparkle in her eye. She was acting as if she was being playful, when in reality she was trying to upset me. She has been doing this to me for years. I never truly saw it. I was getting upset and triggered like she wanted. I was so oblivious to her true intentions. I feel dumb, looking back," I said.

"You shouldn't feel dumb. Narcissistic abusers are usually expert at subtle abuse. It is common for it to occur over time without a victim being fully conscious of it. You are a genuine, caring person who has wanted to see the best in your mother-in-law," my specialist said, "Do you want to unpack more or keep going? It's completely up to you."

"I should just keep going. I don't even know how to unpack this anymore. I feel like it's swirling down a rabbit hole of crazy and there's just too much to be said about it. At this point, I was messed up. I was feeling absolutely crazy. I got through it by watching too much TV, eating too much sugar, simply going through the motions and being around people who actually cared. My family did help a lot by coming over with food or meeting at a park. That was huge for me. Anyway..."

36

Chapter Thirty-Six

It was Sunday, June eighteenth, and Colt had left to go back to Texas for work. He was at his new job now and was headed to Dallas. Mackenzi had snapped me back sometime after he left.

Her reply was a picture of her forehead with the words, "It's okay," typed in the middle of the screen.

I didn't reply because it didn't feel right. I listened to the uneasiness in my gut. I needed to focus on my healing and Talli. I got out my journal and wrote to try to release some of the morose emotions eating me alive.

My pen glided across the paper as I wrote, "Colt's family has been making life really hard for the past year. I feel really messed up from it all. Hilda left me a voicemail telling me how horrible I am, his aunt is insinuating that he leaves Talli and me, Clayton just said a lot of fucked up things and has been calling Paul and saying who knows what. Hilda texted him saying I'm toxic and abusive. I'm really drained. I don't even feel like a person anymore. I am so unhappy and feel gross. I'm pretty sure this evil MIL is also talking to Colt's psycho ex. I'm really trying not to let it all bother me. I really want to become like a rock and not care. The biggest struggle is how do I protect Talli. This shit is hell. I cannot let her be exposed to it. It's scary because it's really all in Colt's hands. If he doesn't cut them out completely, this could go on for the rest of our lives."

I wiped away my tears.

"We are moving," I repeated over and over in my head.

Everything will be okay.

That week, I kept myself and Talli busy. We went for enjoyable, relaxing lunches with my parents or grandparents. We spent quality time with people we could let our guard down around. We went for walks at parks. I treated myself to milkshakes and lattes. I played music and danced with Talli while we packed up our life in our sweet house, which had turned into more of a prison. I soaked in that beautiful house, land and view of the sky. It was wonderful. Colt and I loved it so much. For me, it had been tainted with every visit. Each time his family left I scrubbed tirelessly, trying to rid every last particle of dust from them out of my home. With each visit, I had grown more uncomfortable. I saw their shadows around the corners. I heard Hilda's voice in each room she'd spoken unkindness in. The only room that felt very safe was my own. Whenever my fears overtook me, I would bring Talli's things in our room and close the blinds. I feared that when I was least expecting it, they would just show up, walk around the perimeter of our home, look in windows, and bang on the front door. I felt crazy thinking that, but I couldn't stop it. I jumped whenever I heard the sound of tires on gravel. I'd check the cameras, hands shaking. It was always only our neighbors pulling into their gravel drive. Whenever Talli and I went outside to play, I'd hide us in the backyard behind the house. If we walked around, I would freeze whenever a car drove by, ready to sprint back inside and lock the doors.

I had been working achingly to cure my messy mind. It was proving to be arduous. I was still trying to get out of the house and go live life. I was still making an effort to focus on positives. The days all felt molded together. I will admit, there were a lot of bright, happy moments in the murky, dark swamp that felt like my life. Thank God for those moments. They were probably the string holding together my fragile sanity. I kept trying to remind myself that my life, who I am, is more than this situation or these people causing the stress. After that week with Colt gone, I got out my notebook again.

I wrote, "I need to remember who I am and never forget it again. I am a kind, caring, intelligent, empathetic, adventurous and loving woman. I deserve peace and happiness. I think my mental health is super fragile right now because simply going on Facebook or talking about certain things makes me feel so anxious and sick feeling, I get a headache. Then my thoughts take off and I worry about everything."

Time had been working in my favor at last. We were nearing our moving day. My mom had been our realtor and had sold our house in record time. She was speeding through what was typically a long, tedious process. We were elated. Our realtor in Texas was also moving things along rapidly. It finally felt like things were falling into place. Colt got back from Texas and we stayed busy trying to de-clutter as we finished packing. Boxes flooded the space between the kitchen and dining area.

After this week, I wrote, "It is a busy week. My panic attacks have been getting worse. I keep trying to focus on the good and enjoy the days. It is also hard with big changes like moving because I am so excited, but also nervous. What if it doesn't help solve the problems? I will also miss certain things here and there is some guilt, but I have to remind myself that it will be okay. The existential dread has been heavy."

I closed my notebook for the last time in Ohio. On Monday, July third, my family and the movers my mom hired for us helped us load the truck. We said bittersweet goodbyes and I watched as we drove out of our driveway for the last time. My spirits soared while my heart ached.

"We did it," I said to Colt.

He was driving his truck with my car on a trailer hitched behind us. Talli was asleep in her car seat next to me. She had foregone her typical daily nap to stay alert to all the chaos that moving day entailed.

"Almost," he said. "We still have to get there."

"You're right, but this still feels really good," I said, smiling as I looked out the window at the passing trees.

My dad followed behind us driving the moving truck. We were headed to Columbus to pick up Daisy so she could ride halfway across the country with our dad.

Once we scooped up Daisy, our caravan busted out of Ohio. I felt another wave of relief as we drove over the wide river, leading us into Kentucky. We stopped overnight about halfway through Kentucky. The next day, we made it to Memphis for another break to sleep. Finally, we arrived back in the beautiful, expansive state of Texas.

Things had changed for us drastically, especially me. For the first time in months, I could breathe again.

Colt's birthday fell on the same day that we had our final walk-through at our new house. It had been an eventful day. Hilda had posted an old picture of her and him on Facebook, acting as if everything was normal and as though they were on speaking terms. Clayton had called Colt during the day while we were at a gas station, but he let it go to voicemail. Hilda called him while we were eating dinner at a western restaurant, but Colt again set his phone down after looking at the caller ID. Later that night, as we got into bed in our hotel room in Dallas, I looked over at Colt.

"Did they leave you voicemails?" I asked.

"Yeah, but I'm not going to listen to them," Colt said calmly.

"Okay, that makes sense."

I figured he didn't want to hear anything potentially upsetting on his birthday. I didn't ask anything further or bring it up again.

Two days later, after we had gotten our keys and moved into our new house, it was Hilda's birthday. I ignored it. I was scared Colt would say something to his mom on her birthday. I felt insanely guilty for feeling this way. I was so afraid he would break going no contact. I felt crazy wondering if he had said something to her or not.

While walking across the parking lot into a small taco restaurant that morning, I tripped over a curb and crashed down onto the concrete. As I fell, I twisted my body around to keep Talli protected from any impact. I successfully kept her from getting hurt and a group of bystanders rushed over to see if I was okay.

"You protected your baby from getting injured. That was amazing. Are you alright?" asked a kind woman as she and a man helped lift me off the ground.

"Thank you for helping me," I said as tears rushed down my face.

Colt was still at his truck, gathering trash to throw away. When I fell, he left the trash and made his way over to us.

"How did that happen?" he asked, looking over Talli.

"I don't know. I suddenly just fell. Somehow, I didn't see that curb, I guess," I stuttered, lightheaded.

"Are you okay?" Colt asked me.

"Yeah, I just feel really embarrassed, stupid and scared that I almost hurt Talli," I said.

I couldn't stop crying until we got our tacos to go and got back in the truck. Once Colt was driving back to our new house, I started to breathe deeply and clear my head. I noticed blood was streaming down my left arm from a deep scrape on my elbow. My leg and knee on the same side of my body were painted with road rash.

"Is Hilda a freaking witch?" I wondered in my head.

I never fall, and I just fell so hard on her birthday, of all days. It was as if she had put a curse on me or made some kind of cruel wish. I decided to rest and avoid any chance of further injury for the rest of the day. My fears were irrational and I was thinking like a crazy person.

"Colt, I am scared of what happens next," I said a few days after I survived his mom's birthday.

"What do you mean?" he asked me.

We were in our new living room sitting on the floor with Talli. She was reading a board book.

"I mean, like, I don't know how you talk to your mom again. I don't know how our relationship gets past all this and how it will continue if the issues with your mom don't end. I feel crazy. I don't want you to think I'm keeping you from them, but I also don't know how to feel safe if you do talk to them. Like, they'd have to genuinely apologize and you'd have to have a long, serious talk with them, specifically your mom. I wouldn't feel comfortable with you talking about me or Talli. After everything, I will not re-involve myself with them and, for Talli's safety, she won't be involved, either. It is my job to protect her and I don't trust them at all. She doesn't deserve to be treated the way they treat people they claim to love."

I was shaking, picking at the skin on the edge of my fingernails.

"I am not talking to her. It was her birthday a couple days ago and I didn't even say anything to her. You don't need to think about this anymore. It's over. We are done with them," Colt said. He scooted closer to me and hugged me.

"I just feel messed up," I said. "I still feel so scared. I feel crazy. I don't want to be toxic to you. I just don't know how we go forward."

"Adison. I don't care about them. I care about you and Talli. I don't want Talli around that or dealing with them. I am done with them. You don't need to be scared," Colt said, looking into my eyes. "I dealt with them for years. This wasn't new to me. I grew up without emotions. I don't feel anything by removing them from our lives. It isn't that surprising to me this has happened. I stopped talking to them for a period of time back when I was in high school. I can't remember now what caused it, but I do remember not being at home for a while. So, this isn't a shock to me, I guess. It sucks that it all happened the way it did, I didn't want it to be this way, but it is what it is. Now we know and can move on."

"Okay," I said, meeting his gaze. "I am really sorry you grew up with this and your family is like this. I wish it wasn't this way. You didn't and don't deserve to be treated like this. It's hard for me to say much else because I don't really have the right words. I feel for you a ton, but I am also in a really bad place mentally. All I know is I am going to keep working on healing and bettering myself. I love you so much. Thank you for protecting Talli and me."

"Honey, it's okay. I am sorry we put up with them for as long as we did. I know it was really hard on you. We are done dealing with them. I just want you to enjoy your life and forget about it. I love you more," Colt said, pulling me closer to him.

I let my worried thoughts wash off me. I would be okay. It would be okay.

37

Chapter Thirty-Seven

Summer flew by. Our lives improved immensely. Our new house kept us from missing our old one with its beauty and space. We unpacked in record time and settled in easily. I spun around in my closet which felt like it came out of a dream. Our whole house felt like a dream. Every day since moving, I had become more consistent with exercising. Talli and I loved to take walks together in the neighborhood. I was eating healthier and more regularly. I still struggled with sugar, eating way too much of it. I'd been reading self-help books, listening to music and watching *The Office*. I focused on everything I had to be grateful for, which was so much. From Talli and Colt to the clean water I drank, I was blessed.

Mixed in with all the wholesome was still the lingering darkness inside me. I still struggled with nightmares of my in-laws tormenting me. I would wake up multiple times throughout the night. I battled my brain to push out the unwanted thoughts that forced their way in throughout the day. I lived with persisting anxiety hanging out in my chest. I was always looking over my shoulder. I stayed off social media as much as possible to avoid feeling the overwhelming tsunami of nausea whenever I saw one of the names that triggered me.

I was clawing at normalcy. I was doing everything I could to incorporate positive habits and thoughts into my life.

"God, do I want to be rid of the hell inside of my head," I thought.

I was damned if I would let this evil win. I would get myself and my life back. Every thirty-minute walk in the fresh air with Talli, every kale smoothie and every uplifting thought brought me one inch closer. I just kept going with that. Achingly slow and not always steady, I was healing.

At the end of July, I made sure to enjoy my birthday this year. I filled my day with love and enjoyable activities.

Even Hilda's basic, "Happy Birthday!!!" text didn't faze me.

Neither did Nancy's bland happy birthday gif she texted me. I ignored them both effortlessly. Kind people don't simultaneously attempt to tear your life apart and reach out on holidays or birthdays. Kind people don't use holidays or birthdays as a means for manipulation.

I still noticed most of Colt's family didn't say happy birthday to me this year. That was okay. At this point, I was better off without it. It was weirder for someone such as Nancy to text me a happy birthday gif than to say nothing at all.

Hilda had tried to reach out, or should I say Hoover us back in at times other than just on our birthdays. She sent Colt random text messages about nothing pertinent. She sent me a text message out of nowhere one day with a link to an article called, "Five Reasons to be Nice to Your Mother-In-Law." That day I did lose my shit a little. I paced around, feeling hot and sick. I ended up going for a run in the one-hundred- and six-degree August heat, coming back only when I was numb emotionally due to the physical pain.

At the end of August, Colt, Talli and I went on a long, rejuvenating weekend trip to Colorado to visit Calli. My parents, grandparents and Daisy met us there. It was so good to see them. The mountain air was refreshing and it was cleansing to explore somewhere new.

One day in early September, my mom and I were talking on the phone about my trauma and how I still struggled with unwanted thoughts I couldn't seem to shake.

"Does it hurt you or help you to know when something happens?" my mom asked me.

"I want to know when something happens. I feel like I need to know about it," I said.

"Okay. Well, Hilda's mom commented something on that picture I had shared of Talli and me in Colorado. I thought I was private and people I am not friends with couldn't see my stuff. I guess somehow this was posted publicly," she said.

"Cynthia commented something? Did you screenshot it?" I asked.

"Yeah, she did and no, I'm sorry. It made me feel sick so I instantly deleted it. I didn't even really think about it," she said.

"It's okay, I understand. I just like to have proof of what they've done. Anyway, what did she say?" I asked.

"I don't remember her exact wording, but the first part was something about how at least one grandma gets to hold Talli," my mom said. "The second part was her saying I guess we weren't worried about Talli getting sick anymore. It ended with her saying Talli was never smiling in any of her pictures, she never looked happy. It was pretty awful. I felt sick reading it."

"Oh my god. That is so messed up. That is really crazy of her to comment and say that stuff. What did she think would come of that? What would all your friends think if they saw it? I mean, I feel like people would say something to her," I said.

"I know, right. My friends definitely would have said something to her and would have thought she was insane. I blocked her after I deleted the comment. I don't even know how she found me," my mom said.

"Yeah, that is super weird."

We finished our conversation and got off the phone. I still felt a little shaky and some of the sick feeling in my stomach, although it wasn't nearly as bad as it had been. It wasn't earth-shattering anymore whenever someone made a comment. The more they did it, the number I became to it.

After my mom told me about Cynthia's comment, I felt motivated to get on with my next step in recovering. I reported the pictures Cynthia, Hilda and Nancy had posted on their Facebook pages of Talli. It felt wrong for them to be there. I had never liked the fact that people I didn't know could see my baby, especially Colt's crazy ex. I also felt like it was all a facade that I didn't want Talli to play into for them.

Less than twenty-four hours after I reported the pictures to Facebook, I received individual emails per picture saying each one had been removed due to violation of privacy. Once they had been removed, I sat on my next move for a couple hours. I had been planning on blocking them. I was nervous to do it simply because I felt like I needed to watch over what they were doing to protect myself and Talli. I was aware that by doing that I was hindering my recovery and healing. I was also keeping them relevant, and I was ready to move on completely so Talli would grow up without even hearing their names. I looked at Talli. She didn't deserve to hear about the next thing they would do. It wasn't fair to her. I went on my phone, pulled up Facebook and did what was necessary. I blocked Cynthia, Gina, Hilda and Clayton.

I didn't care to see Gina all over Colt's family members' pages. She had been liking all their posts, wishing them happy birthday and they had been doing that back. I had clicked on Gina's page to see what exactly was going on. Gina was mostly private, but I did see on a few of her profile pictures that Cynthia and Hilda had been liking them. Cynthia complimented all of Gina's pictures.

It was stuff like, "She makes my heart happy," on a picture of Gina holding her baby and "You are beautiful," on a selfie.

It was so perplexing. I wasn't accustomed to people staying in contact with an old college ex of a family member, specifically their son or grandson's ex, specifically an ex that lied and cheated on their son or grandson, even more specifically, one that was unkind to the family member's new partner. If Hilda and Cynthia wanted to prioritize and tend to their association to Gina, cool.

"Have fun with all that. I'll be removing myself from the unspoken competition for Hilda and Cynthia's manipulative attention," I thought. "Enjoy each other's crazy."

My mind started twisting and turning.

"Damn, maybe I'm the one that's crazy," I thought.

I am the one in therapy trying to fix a multitude of mental issues. I'm the one overthinking and caring too much about people who don't show any care for me. Yet I didn't feel crazy removing these people from my life. It felt like emptying a clogged drain. Everything started to flow easily once the blockage was removed.

Anyway, I blocked Gina because I was simply tired of seeing her name pop up. There was no reason I had to have any sort of tie to her. She was not relevant to my life. I blocked Hilda, Cynthia and Clayton because of all their comments. Cynthia wasn't as emotionally abusive as Hilda and Clayton, although her comment on my mom's picture was enough reason to remove her completely. I left everyone else. I had already made my Facebook page super private. I had gone back and changed everything so that anyone who had any link to Hilda was unable to see it. That included posts and pictures from the past year.

I also had previously noticed that Didi had blocked me on Facebook at some point. I was looking at old pictures of Talli on my page and she had commented on one of them. There was no "like" or "comment" button next to her comment anymore. I thought that was weird so I clicked on her name. It led to a blank page that read that the page I was trying to visit was unavailable. Looking at Talli's old pictures was also how I noticed Brittany, Didi's daughter, had unfriended me, too. I was sure the bad apples would continue to fall by themselves.

It felt freeing to take that next step and continue to build a sturdy brick wall where a swaying, frayed rope bridge once was. My hands were wiped clean of maintaining that complicated bridge on my own.

It was no longer my place to be concerned with what Hilda was saying about me or what she was doing. We had escaped. We were a thousand beautiful miles away from that mess. It was my time to take back my power and my life. I was determined to live happily, peacefully, and be the healthiest mom for Talli. One day, if Talli asked about her dad's mom, we would tell her what we could in an age-appropriate manner. Maybe she would ask, maybe she never would. Someday, when she is old enough, Colt and I can tell her this story, the reason being it's important she knows that no one is entitled to treat her poorly, not a single soul on this planet, and if they do, she is allowed to let them go. Until then, ultimately it is our job to protect her and raise her in the healthiest way possible. The generational trauma ends with us.

Now, onto the rest of our lives.

Final

"I warned you it was long, I'm sorry," I said, blushing as I spoke to my specialist.

"You do not need to apologize. Thank you for telling me. How did it feel to talk about it?"

"Hard throughout parts of it. Other parts felt eye-opening since throughout actually living it I had felt pretty confused and crazy at times. It also felt like I was shedding it from me, though," I said.

I paused for a minute before continuing, "I have to be honest. My mom did tell me about something Hilda posted on Facebook after I blocked her. Can I tell you about it?"

"You can tell me anything."

"Hilda shared a video of a mom and daughter talking about the differences between moms in the eighties and millennial moms. She wrote something above the video. It said, "So funny... get over it, new moms, enjoy life with family and friends, they have all the advice you need, stay off social media." Jan reacted to it with the care emoji, which made me realize she was probably the one who told Hilda about the monster-in-law group. Anyway, I didn't feel much about Hilda's post. I feel pretty numb at this point. I found the video and watched it, too. It wasn't bad. It was a young mom talking about common day parenting things such as baby monitors, baby led weaning, etcetera and the older mom laughing while saying she just did whatever. The older mom talked about how she let her kids eat McDonald's fries off the floor of the car and didn't stress about her baby's safety, to put it frankly. To me, I took away that the new generation of moms has a lot more pressure compared to older moms. I'm sure Hilda saw the video differently. She probably saw it as the old mom laughing at the silly new mom's worries and how the older mom was much wiser. Later, when I talked to Colt about it, I got upset. I felt unable to control how chaotic I felt. Sometimes, I feel sort of unsafe in a way. How can

Colt see that kind of thing and ignore it? At what point does Colt say enough and take further steps to distance himself from her? I know it's his mom and I'm sure it's hard for him. I just wonder how our relationship is able to stay strong with so many people who tried to break us apart still within reach, especially his mom, who clearly has no intentions of changing. How do I feel safe with Colt when, in a way, it feels like he isn't protecting me, when I feel like he could put us back in the situation at any moment?" I said in wonder.

"It's hard to get our brains to shut off once we've been in survival mode for so long. I understand why you feel like you need to watch your back. It sounds to me like you are experiencing PTSD from the lengthy trauma you endured. It takes time and work to overcome post-traumatic stress. We will get you there," my specialist said. "In the meantime, it's okay for you to let go now, you're safe. You deserve to live your life peacefully and happily. No matter what happens, you are going to be okay. Trust in yourself. You are so strong. You got through everything, so there is nothing you can't get through. You are protecting your daughter. It also seems to me that Colt loves you and Talli so much. Let him do what he needs to do. Trust him. He will get where he needs to be, but you don't need to be in control of everything. I know it feels scary after all you endured, but you can live your life now. You know you have control over your own life because you've shown yourself that. You did what you needed to do to protect yourself and Talli from Hilda. No matter what Colt does or decides to do, you've set your boundaries. You never have to see her again if you don't want to. As you shouldn't."

I took a moment to let her words sink in.

I breathed out and said, "Yeah. I don't like feeling like it's not over, though."

"I know you have that feeling, but remember, it is over. You guys did it. You got out, you moved far away. You blocked her. You're focusing on yourself. You're reading self-help books, you're exercising, you're eating well, you're in therapy. You are doing the work. We can't simply snap our fingers and return back to the person we were before the trauma. I'll tell you what, that's a good thing. You won't tolerate the same mistreatment again from her or anyone else. You're going to recover and you're going to be happy again. Just keep going."

"You're right," I said.

I looked down at the floor before looking back up into my specialist's eyes. "Thank you."

That night, I was on the couch, leaning back against Colt with Talli sleeping cuddled up against my side. I had a giant bag of M&M's Minis on my other side. *The Office* was on TV. I had a newfound appreciation for *The Office*. It got me through some dark times. I laughed at something Erin said. The Texas sun was setting, casting a golden glow throughout our cozy home. Our house was clean and smelled like the autumn candle I was burning. Everything around me was aesthetically pleasing and made me feel happy, from our farmhouse-style kitchen table, to the dark hardwood floors, to the wine rack slowly filling up, to our fluffy white rug, to our various decorations. I tossed a handful of M&M's into my mouth and let them slowly melt on my tongue. The chocolate exploded out of the crunchy little shells as I bit down. Colt kissed my forehead. I leaned my head back against him, letting peace cover me. Our relationship had only grown stronger through it all. I brushed my hand over Talli's soft hair. I listened to the sweet sounds of her inhaling and exhaling. I was truly present in this magical moment. I was going to be fine. Actually, I was going to be more than fine, I was going to thrive. I smiled.

As I soaked in this moment I thought, "I love my life."

Acknowledgements

This book would not have been possible without so many people. First of all, thank you to my husband for being my best friend, biggest supporter and life partner. I am so thankful for you every day. Thank you to my daughter for just being. My daughter is my reason to keep going, growing, healing and to be the best version of myself that I can be. Thank you for keeping me sane through the insanity. I love you both forever.

Thank you to Rick Noland for editing. I am so appreciative of your time, skills, dedication and willingness to assist me. This book would not be what it is without you. I, also, would not be who I am without you. Thank you for also being a second dad to me and for continuing to impact my life in such positive ways.

Thank you to my family, Mom, Dad, Katy, Hannah, Grandma, Grandpa, Lisa and Nate, for all of the love and support. Thank you for reading my rough drafts and for all of your kindness. Thank you for being there through the worst.

Thank you to my friends for also showing so much love and support. Thank you for your excitement for my book, for asking for updates, and for being there for me. Thank you for being lights in the darkness.

Thank you to all of you who have read my book. I hope that you enjoyed it and that it has been able to help you in some way.

Resources

If you or someone you know is struggling with trauma, self-harm, anxiety, depression or another mental health challenge, please visit: www.helpguide.org.

If you or someone you know may be experiencing abuse, please visit: www.thehotline.org.

If you or someone you know are in crisis and need support, please visit: www.crisistextline.org.

For more self-harm prevention resources, please visit: twloha.com.

About the Author

Allyson Bennett is a mom and wife living in Texas. She grew up in Ohio and graduated from Muskingum University with a bachelor's degree. Allyson enjoys writing, reading, traveling and being in nature with her family.

Website: allysonnbennettt.com
Instagram: @allysonnbennettt